I0831811

The Sanctum of Souls

R.K. Pavia

The Sanctum of Souls

Published by Mage Guild Publishing in 2015
First Edition

mageguildpublishing@outlook.com

A CIP catalogue record for this book is available from the British Library.

ISBN 978-0-9927516-5-4

For Shadow ~ a dog with more soul than most people.
Miss you, little lady.

Uncharted Lands
Mountains of Nor
Whitestone
Eldenvale
Vaharia
Geryndor
The Blackthorn
Dragon's Pass
Sa'hahlenfell
DragonCrest Mountains
The Cabreecian Sea
Torwick
Maervell
Pitmen Lake
SOS
The Deadwood
Uncharted Lands
N
W
E
S

PROLOGUE

The night was hot and smelled of incense and alcohol. The stars seemed to sway in time to the spirited song of strings and pipes, with laughter echoing around the Ivory City and far beyond. It was the night before a battle, one that would inevitably cost a warrior his life, and everyone had gathered for the chance to honour them for the last time. Such farewell celebrations were held on the eve of every arena battle, and all who attended seized the opportunity for levity, as there might be little on offer the following day.

Every table in the plaza was overflowing with fruit, bread, and meats. Comely serving girls poured red wine into goblets, which were swept up by the eager hands of those already giddy with the effects of the alcohol. Even the flickering light from the countless fiery torches appeared to delight in the atmosphere. All of life's simple pleasures were displayed within the setting of this enchanting revelry, there for the night sky to witness as the moon watched on without judgement.

Rhyssian gripped his silver chalice, wine sloshing over the brim, as he wound his way in and out of the dancing couples. The dark-haired, muscular man had set his course when he'd seen a young woman enter from one of the beautifully sculpted arches on the far side of the plaza. She'd caught his eye as she'd crossed his line of sight while he'd been staring into the distance, his thoughts beginning to drift to preparation for the battle the following day.

All thoughts of blade sharpening and fighting techniques left Rhyssian's head. He smiled, straightened his white velvet tunic, and made his way towards the woman he'd been waiting for since the evening had begun.

She noticed his approach and smiled coyly back at him, coiling a loose strand of her raven hair around her finger. Going to meet him, she took the goblet from his grasp as if it had been meant for her, sipped the wine, and gazed up at him from beneath her long black lashes. Rhyssian reclaimed the goblet as she took it away from her lips, then leant forwards to wrap his other muscular arm around her waist, pulling her in towards him with no opposition. The sweet scent wafting from her silky black hair was more intoxicating than the wine, and pleasantly familiar. He bent his head down to hers and their lips met. As they kissed, they became oblivious to the surrounding merriment – and to the boy stealing the goblet from Rhyssian's loosened grasp. Both were lost in the moment, as the lively frivolity drew them in and engulfed them.

The hours passed swiftly. Having spent most of the night entwined in each other's arms, Dessema whispered something in Rhyssian's ear before taking his hand and leading him from the crowd, out into one of the white stone streets that converged on the plaza. The music and merriment drifted on the warm summer breeze, as the party showed no signs of abating, and the young lovers walked arm in arm towards the shadows of an unlit section of the street. Softly pushing Rhyssian against the white stone wall of a magnificent building, Dessema leant into him, her warm breath brushing against his mouth as she moved tantalisingly close.

"You aren't going to fight tomorrow, are you?" She considered her question already answered as she pressed her lips against his before he had a chance to respond. Placing his hands firmly on her hips, Rhyssian shifted her around to swap places, her slender figure now held fast against the wall beneath his well-built frame. Dessema smiled up at him, her eyes sparkling in the moonlight and her expression and touch telling him all he ever needed was with him at that very moment.

Until that night, everything they shared had been but a distraction – albeit a pleasurable one. However, feelings he'd never expected had developed and changed his perspective and, in that moment, Rhyssian knew he was no longer ready to die. Cupping her cheeks in his big hands, he kissed her passionately once more. She giggled as he swept her up into his arms and carried her through the large wooden double-doors of the magnificent building, kicking them shut behind him.

After they'd made love, they talked about a future that, until that night, Rhyssian didn't think he had. Plans were made to marry as soon as it could be arranged, a sense of urgency seeming appropriate given the circumstances. As crown prince of the realm, Rhyssian was obligated to have a long engagement, but he felt sure his father, King Niron, would make an exception. He'd be so pleased to know his heir no longer fought in the arena that he'd almost certainly forgo tradition.

As Dessema fell asleep in Rhyssian's arms, he pictured the king's reaction as he gave him the good news. Drifting off to sleep, his last thoughts were full of promise, as well as hope his father's shame could be easily undone.

It was as black as pitch when Rhyssian was awoken by what sounded like a distant scream. Two slips of sheer fabric billowed softly on the breeze coming in through the open window. Turning over to look at the naked beauty still fast asleep next to him, he was about to curve his body around hers and go back to sleep, when he heard the sound again; it was definitely a scream, and yet, not the same voice.

Sitting up, he instinctively glanced around the room for his sword, before remembering, as his eyes adjusted to the dark, that he wasn't in his own home. Then came another scream, only this time followed in quick succession by two more, which sounded like children. Something was clearly very wrong. He had to decide quickly whether to rouse Dessema, but his mind was spinning. He couldn't quite think straight, almost as if he was intoxicated, yet he'd drunk little alcohol at the celebration.

As more and more screams rose up from the buildings in the city, he stumbled from the bed and over to the window. Parting the voiles, he leant out into the night air, an unsettling feeling of vertigo causing his stomach to lurch and his legs to buckle beneath him. His vision was clouding over but through the haze he could just make out lights flickering to life in windows all over the city, most likely candles lit by others rudely stirred from their slumber.

He scrambled about the floor, searching for his tunic, stumbling in the dim light. His arm caught a lantern on a side table, sending the metal crashing to the wooden boards beneath. Dessema jumped awake and sat bolt upright at the noise, her long, black hair tumbling around her bare shoulders and breasts.

"What is it? What's going on?" she asked as she heard the dreadful cries coming in through the window.

"I don't know. I… I can barely support myself, and the sounds – the screams – they've been getting closer. My love, I need you to run, hide, find somewhere safe and don't look back."

"No, Rhyssian. I won't leave you."

Rhyssian's expression became one of determination and, without pause, he forced his way through his dizziness and towards Dessema. Clumsily gathering the sheets around her exposed torso, he tried to drag her from the bed. Fighting against him, her strength overpowering him in his weakened state, she gripped his shoulders and forced him to look at her.

"Whatever is happening, my love, we face it together. I will not hide like a coward while you fight to defend me. What kind of future queen would do such a thing? I… I…" Her voice trailed off and her skin paled.

"Dessema? Dessema?" he cried, but he couldn't reach her. As he looked into her eyes, it was as if her soul was no longer there. Life appeared to have drained from her body, yet she remained taught in his grasp. He shook her, but still she did not stir.

As the screams now pierced the night more clearly, it occurred to Rhyssian that after each new cry a silence followed, as if trailing after the wave of terrified sounds, dark and hungry in its wake.

Feeling the pressure building within, he attempted to get to his feet, letting go of Dessema to place his hands on the edge of the bed. He just managed to arch his back and was about to rise from his bent knee, when a terrible vibration started to fill the room, ringing in his ears and boring into his bones. He dropped back to his knees and slammed his hands over his ears. Looking back up at his beautiful bride-to-be, a single tear dropped from his eye as the pain became too much and he struggled to keep Dessema in focus. With one last desperate attempt to reach her, he stretched out a hand towards her face. As the intensity of the vibration reached a crescendo and his fingers shook violently, Rhyssian was thrown back to the floor – just as Dessema's head was sliced from her body, sending it crashing onto the bed and rolling down onto the floor beside him. He howled in both emotional and physical pain as the silence hovered outside the window, waiting impatiently to be let in.

Once Rhyssian's decapitated head had fallen to the floor to rest next to Dessema's, the silence burst through the open window. It moved swiftly through the magnificent building before continuing its journey throughout the city.

Finally, no more screams rang out, and no more shadows stumbled to their deaths. The hot summer night was left pillaged in the wake of the silence, and the eerie flickering of candlelight was the only sign of life.

CHAPTER ONE

Marcus didn't much care for magic, nor for most of the mages he knew - and he certainly didn't care for the one that was now trying to humiliate him.

Lord Spindley had crossed his path on the way home and was attempting to show off in front of his female companion by making Marcus the butt of his joke. It wasn't working, of course. At twenty-six years of age, he'd long since learnt to disregard the jibes of his peers, and knew exactly how to handle them.

Smiling a crooked smile, he couldn't help but be amused at the funny little man – balding long before his time and sporting a lazy eye, and a beard that grew in patches. At exactly six-feet tall and with a strong, toned body, Marcus was never belittled for his looks, but often, as was currently the case, for his socially unacceptable decision to spurn magic.

"Oh look, it's Lord Ryan. Marcus, do entertain my good Lady Havelroy and I with one of your 'charming' displays of basic fire lighting. Here, I've two perfectly good sticks for you to rub together." The balding man guffawed at his own joke, readily joined by Lady Havelroy.

Marcus waited, allowing them a moment of amusement.

"Lord Spindley, how good of you to offer the use of your arms for such a practical undertaking. However, I find wood is far better suited to the task. Not as brittle, or as likely to break when exerted beyond anything more than a rhythmic up-and-down movement. Judging by the less-than-impressed look Lady Havelroy is aiming at you now, I believe at least one of your arms may be required for something of a more *personal nature* this evening." With that, Marcus feigned respect for the woman with a mockingly low bow and flashed a charming smile, before brushing past his tormentors and heading home.

He whistled to himself as he walked. Having endured such taunts throughout his life, he'd grown accustomed to treating them with the indifference they deserved. He took neither himself nor life too seriously, a personality trait that had served him well as a magicless mage growing up in Whitestone. He was of noble birth and, like all nobility, had been born with magic in his blood. Still, unlike his contemporaries, he'd defied what was expected of him and refused to study the craft, spending his years from six to sixteen outwitting both his parents and his tutor; anything to avoid being schooled in magic. He'd never been able to explain why, but even the thought of using it made him feel uneasy.

However, there was no sympathy to be found within the walls of the Ryan mansion. Magical ability was considered a birth right, a mark of honour, and his rejection of it brought great shame upon his parents. The outcome was that his family didn't like him very much – but the feeling was mutual, so he didn't care.

As a result, he spent as little time as possible at home, preferring instead to walk to the city's outer walls where he'd find a quiet spot to read or daydream. He would spend hours by himself, enjoying the solitude. It was only the journey there and back that threatened to ruin a generally pleasant day, and if he was lucky, he'd avoid anyone who might seek to put a dampener on his cheerful disposition.

Unfortunately, today was not one of his luckier days.

Marcus took his usual shortcut, a narrow alley between streets that limited the chances of interacting with anyone. However, as he entered the alley, he was stopped in his tracks by Lord Spindley and two other men, whose faces he knew but whose names he'd not cared enough to remember.

They walked towards him from the opposite end of the alley as his whistling slowed and quieted, a lopsided smile taking over from the pursed lips.

"Lord Spindley, good to see you again so soon. We really should stop meeting like this."

"You made me look like a fool!" Spindley's eyes narrowed beneath a clenched brow, anger clear in his tone.

"Ah, you give me too much credit. I think you did a fine job of that, without *any* assistance from me."

Marcus never did know when silence was best. No sooner had the words left his mouth than Lord Spindley's hands tightened into fists and became enveloped in rippling flames. One glance at the hands of the other two men, and Marcus could see they, too, were prepared for a magical assault. A voice inside his head said just one word – *run* – and if he'd learnt one thing from growing up in a city of magic, it was how to flee.

As the three men shot balls of fire in his direction, Marcus was already sprinting back the way he'd come, the fireballs narrowly missing his behind and fizzling out as they collided with the corner of a building. Through the familiar streets he ran. His long, muscular legs took him effortlessly up and down side streets, dodging people and hurdling over wooden crates and barrows, turning corners seconds ahead of fire and ice projectiles, and leaping up to catch an overhanging beam to take him safely over the top when he couldn't outrun them. Twice he managed to hide behind a corner at a junction as the men sped past, doubling back as soon as they were out of sight. Another time, he just made it past a window cleaner about to throw water from a bucket. However, Spindley and the others weren't so fortunate. He chuckled to himself as he looked back to see them soaked through, then sped off faster as they stepped up their chase with increased fury.

Past noble children playing with mini-whirlwinds, around noble teenage boys conjuring shiny things with which to woo noble teenage girls, ducking behind carts laden with magical paraphernalia, and evading magic tutors showing their students how to light torches with their fingers, Marcus continued to run. Nevertheless, despite his speed and cunning, he eventually found himself cornered in a dead end with Lord Spindley and the others blocking his exit. Approaching him slowly, malicious intent emblazoned across their faces, the men sneered. Spindley's hands crackled with an electrical charge, and the hands of the other two bubbled with small water spouts. Marcus seemed to be out of options; he could only brace himself for what was to come. Darting his eyes around in one last attempt to find an escape route, he caught site of a discarded mirror, gleaming in the late afternoon sun. In a single swift movement, he made a lunge for it and thrust it forwards just in time to reflect the combination of spells aimed at him from the mages. The electricity and water met the mirror, bounced back at the men, and hit them with the effect they'd intended for Marcus, throwing them to the ground with a debilitating electrical bolt. He stopped briefly to snigger at their singed clothes and spiked hair. *They'll live*, he thought to himself, *but Spindley may not be coming out in public for a while.*

He jumped to grab at the edge of an overhanging balcony, pulling himself up and continuing onto the roof of the building. Coming down into the street the other side, he calmly resumed his journey home – totally oblivious to the dark-haired man who'd watched him leave, then grabbed the mirror and walked straight through a solid wall.

As he approached the imposing iron gates that guarded the path to the front doors of the family property, something occurred to him; there was no rational explanation for a perfectly intact mirror to be on the ground down a back alley. There'd been nowhere it could've fallen from, and Whitestone's elite weren't in the habit of using back alleys for the storage of household items. *Peculiar*, he thought. Coming up with no sensible answer, he then wondered what mood he'd find his father in, or if he could avoid finding him at all. Then his stomach growled and he stopped wondering, and pushed open the gates. The chase had made him hungry, and neither the puzzle of convenient mirrors nor the wrath of the elder Lord Ryan would stand between him and food.

Two hours and one confrontation later and Marcus stood outside the mansion once more. He'd eaten a sizeable supper before the inevitable quarrel with his father. So, as he paused on the cobbled street, the cool evening air reminding him of the season, he was at least warm and satisfied from a good meal. Mostly, he was unbothered by people's actions towards him, but altercations with

Lord Ryan unsettled him more than he cared to admit. That was exactly why he had to vacate the premises; he could almost feel his strings about to snap whenever they argued. For his own sake, he needed to be as far away from his father as possible.

The sun was just starting its descent behind the Stone Highway and the Geryndor Mountains beyond. Marcus looked upon the fading, fiery aura and felt drawn to head to the east of Whitestone. His whimsical nature wondered how far he would get before its journey was complete and the cool blue light of the moon filled the vacancy in its wake.

The city was a remarkable sight at any time, but particularly at sunset, when the long, low reach of the sun's farewell glory touched the white structures, briefly staining them with a pearlescent pink hue. Lit with tall, evenly-placed oil lanterns, the streets were wide and paved in the same white stone as the buildings they cut between, every one converging at a large open plaza in the centre of the city. Marcus had loved his home ever since he'd been old enough to appreciate its magnificence. Every tower, every arch, every intricately-carved balustrade - the entire city seemed to rise organically from the ground.

Reaching the entrance to a tavern as the last of the sun's rays faded from view, he realised he'd arrived in a part of the city his father disdainfully called 'the common quarter'. Most buildings in this part of the city were built from wood, ramshackle and giving the impression of an architect's afterthought. The few stone shops and houses were in a far worse state of repair than those where Marcus lived, with cracks extending out like veins and shutters creaking as they hung from broken hinges. Weeds had started to spread tendrils into the slightly larger gaps and several of the street lanterns were not lit, causing dark recesses where the buildings overshadowed each other.

However, it was the inhabitants of the common quarter that really earned the district its label. This part of the city had been allocated to commoners; those from non-magical bloodlines who had decided a life living off the land wasn't for them. To them, it was far better to serve the mages of Whitestone in return for the relative comfort of residing within the city walls.

Like all nobility, Marcus had little interaction with the residents of this part of the city, but he was sure they were still decent people. He wasn't prone to the supercilious manner of his peers and had never treated anyone with contempt purely because they had been born into different circumstances. Besides, if the Ryan family cook, Julia, was a good example of a commoner, he was satisfied he'd like them a lot more than he did the nobility.

Despite his lack of prejudice, the chill night air made him shiver, and he realised how dark it was away from the brightly lit streets around his home. Perhaps it would have been wiser for him not to be in this part of the city as night fell. Whitestone had its fair share of crime, and the dark niches provided keen cover for anyone who spied a well-dressed nobleman, stood alone and looking lost. With this in mind, he briefly considered turning around and heading home. If not for the inviting sounds coming from behind the aged and fading wooden doors of the tavern, he may have done just that; but the cold and a movement in the shadows helped make the decision for him. Laughter, music, merry souls, and a roaring fire – what could be the harm? Besides, his father would hate it if he knew, and he'd make sure he found out, one way or another.

It would have been fair to say that his arrival in the Crooked Wing tavern was not looked upon without suspicion. In his intricately-embroidered tunic, well-polished leather boots, and silk sash, he stood out. Gazing around the crowded room, Marcus knew there wasn't a person present who could even comprehend the world he came from. From the looks on their faces, it was obvious the establishment's regulars rarely, if ever, included anyone of nobility.

As he paused in the middle of the room, the noisy banter became hushed whispers behind cupped hands, and the music faded to a gradual, premature end. However, such a situation didn't faze him. He reckoned a wide-eyed stare and toothy grin would suffice, and pasted them onto his face before heading in the direction of the bar.

His prediction of the drinkers' reactions was astute. Most of them just assumed he was mad – some not-so-well-kept secret, noble son afflicted with lunacy, perhaps. He'd probably just drool and giggle to himself quietly if they left him alone. Sure enough, after a few tense moments, the revellers resumed their merriment and the music played once more.

Chuckling to himself, partly to keep up the ruse, Marcus sidestepped between the haphazardly placed tables and chairs, careful to avoid standing on anyone's feet, and approached the bar. Perching himself on a rickety stool, he began his evening of liquid solace.

Hours later and Marcus sat hunched over the bar, his head groggy, and the room starting to spin. He'd always considered it curious just how attractive any female could look post-ale-consumption, yet he knew he'd definitely consumed too much on this occasion. The overweight, greasy-haired barkeep, called Nathan, was beginning to exude an enticing aura. It was clearly time to call it a night.

Reluctantly sliding the last of his coins across the bar, the one for the road already poured, his noble manners obligated him to empty the tankard. Staring down at the dark-brown liquid, Marcus realised he didn't even like the look of it. He inhaled the musty, ale-saturated air of the dimly-lit room, fighting the urge to recoil in disgust, and downed the beverage in one go.

Stumbling over his own feet as he made to leave the tavern, he questioned his decision to drown his sorrows, especially as he and ale didn't enjoy each other's company that often. Fine wine he could handle, but ale was a different matter. The last time he'd drunk it was when, as a teenager, he'd snuck into the kitchens and imbibed some that was kept for cooking. The result was a level of drunkenness his father had said put him in the category of plebeians. Of course, that made it the drink of choice for one keen to irritate their father.

He laughed and hiccoughed as the image of a furious Lord Ryan crossed his mind. Wobbling towards the doors, Marcus dismissed the scrutiny of his evening's entertainment as pointless. Forming cohesive thoughts was making his head hurt, and he was enjoying his pleasantly intoxicated state too much to bother with tedious interruptions. It was quite clear this self-induced brain-fog was the reason ale had been created. For now, at least, he could forget, and push all thoughts of his father to the far recesses of his mind. He could pretend he was just a simple man from the common quarter, out for an evening's inebriation – if only until the harsh light of day, when reality bit into his backside with a vengeance reserved for drunken fools.

As the tavern's tired, wooden doors slowly closed behind him, the sounds of merry drinkers gradually became no more than a muffled hum, punctuated by the occasional high-pitched laugh and rowdy shout. Standing in the street outside the tavern, it dawned on Marcus that he'd never experienced an atmosphere quite like the one still filling the building behind him. His life had been dull in comparison. Though he'd taken every opportunity for levity he could find, the rigid rules of noble society restricted fun to sanctioned areas at predetermined times. According to his mother, the 'honourable' Lady Ryan, "*one must never deviate from the noble path, not even for a second.*" He could hear her voice in his head, scolding him for running around, flapping his arms and making duck noises while visiting the large house of some other 'honourable' noblewoman. He guessed the children of the people in the tavern weren't confined in such a way. *Oh, to be able to flap ones arms and 'quack' freely*!

Smiling to himself – a wicked, boyish smile – Marcus began to waddle up and down the dusty street, arms rising and falling.

"Quack," he said, pausing to laugh, "quack, quack." His return to deviancy providing no small amount of entertainment and his mind de-shackled by the alcohol-induced removal of inhibitions, Marcus was oblivious to the approach of a mysterious male figure from an unlit section of the street.

The figure remained still, head tilted to one side. He watched for some time as Marcus continued his duck impersonation, still in a world of his own and quite unaware of his curious audience. The man sighed as he observed the eldest child of one of Whitestone's most esteemed houses quacking and flapping beneath the flickering light of a common quarter street lantern.

Finally, stepping out from the shadows, he boldly approached Marcus from behind. Slowly raising his right hand, he paused as if considering his next move. The decision made, Marcus nearly leapt into the air as a hand firmly gripped his shoulder. He spun around to confront the owner of the hand, prepared to defend himself.

Now face-to-face with his assailant – a man with a mop of black hair, and dark-brown eyes, his olive-skin darkened by a neatly trimmed beard – Marcus adjusted his posture to appear as intimidating as possible. He noticed he was a couple of inches taller than the stranger, so, with his extra height providing added confidence, he clenched his fists and prepared to strike. To his surprise, the man's demeanour remained passive. His arms loosely resting at his sides, he spoke with an unexpectedly soft and refined tone.

"Marcus Ryan." A statement rather than a question. "We need to talk."

CHAPTER TWO

Marcus wasn't sure if he'd dreamt the events of the previous night. As the midday sun attempted to force its way through the untidily drawn curtains, he felt the predictable throb of a hangover, pushing behind his eyeballs and reverberating across his skull. *Well*, he thought, *the drinking part obviously wasn't a dream*. As memories began filtering through the haze, a small smile tugged at the corner of his mouth, only to make him wince in pain as it did so.

"Quack!" If only his father could have been there.

Still fully clothed, he shifted himself to a semi-upright position on his bed. The smooth silk sheets wrinkled beneath him, but were still pulled up and tucked firmly around the mattress. Obviously he'd managed to make it to his room and then slept where he fell. Fortunately, that had been the bed.

As he was about to lift himself, slowly, to stand, he realised he was clutching something in his left hand. How he hadn't noticed until now was a mystery. Had he really been that drunk? Opening his palm and looking down, he saw a crumpled piece of parchment. He carefully straightened it out, revealing exceptionally elegant handwriting. His head hurt to bend down and his eyes ached as he attempted to read the words, but, his curiosity piqued, he made the effort. The note bore only a name – *Sathom*, an unusual name he'd not heard before – and an instruction to meet at a certain time and place. Marcus looked up again, now even more confused. He vaguely remembered the man he presumed owned the name. A hazy memory of black hair and a strangely calm manner came back to him. *What was he doing lurking there in the shadows of the common quarter?* Marcus pondered.

Then he turned his thoughts to the writing itself. Penmanship of such quality was usually the result of years of tedious education funded by the coffers of noble estates. Marcus knew this all too well. Though he'd successfully managed to evade the most 'important' of his two tutors, he'd never quite learnt how to avoid the clutches of Mistress Thorne. He remembered being dragged from his latest hiding place to the study, where he'd spend hours writing his own name, this only ending when Mistress Thorne was satisfied with the standard.

Shuddering at the memory, he finally moved on to consider the destination the note mentioned – Eldenvale. Beyond the city walls, many miles into the east; he'd heard of the small village, but he'd never been there. He hadn't even set foot outside of Whitestone. There'd been no cause to, as everything he needed was located within the city walls. As such, he wasn't even certain he'd know how to get there, let alone the sense in finding out. Whether he liked it or not, he was a noble gentleman. Any fool could see it, and not only in the way he dressed. It was clear in everything he did, from the way he walked to the manner in which he sneezed. These things had been drilled into him from a young age. Indeed, he knew no other way to be. How wise would it be for someone of his standing to venture into uncharted territory, alone, wearing his class and associated riches like a banner? He may as well shout out, "*Hey, noble here! Come rob me!*" The note also providing a time for the 'meeting', he nearly choked. *At night? The man must be insane. Either that, or he isn't aware of the risks inherent in such an act of madness.*

Screwing up the parchment and tossing it aside, Marcus rose from the bed, deciding it was way past time he found something to eat. His hangover dulling the edges of his consciousness, he wanted to feel like himself again, and he'd always found a good meal cured most ills. Fortunately, his latest dalliance with ale appeared not to have affected his now-grumbling stomach. Leaving his room may involve crossing paths with his father again but, never one to ignore the desire for food, Marcus set off into the silent corridors of the family mansion, hoping to reach the kitchens without incident. He decided to ignore the note, as well as the strangely quiet man that had thrust it into his hand. He acted the fool on a regular basis, but acting one and proving he really *was* one were two very different things.

Of course, wishing not to encounter his father, or any of his family for that matter, did not make it so. As Marcus was about to descend the first flight of stairs – with still another two to go before the relative safety of the servants' floor – a familiar and thoroughly unwelcome female voice called his name. The *call* was more of a demand; shrill and with an air of entitlement, it stopped him dead in his tracks. He raised his eyes and sighed before turning to face his younger sister. She stood with her hands on her hips and her head tilted forwards enough that she peered up at him, menacingly, beneath heavily made-up eyes. So greatly did she resemble their mother at that moment that Marcus chuckled as he imagined her with grey hairs, wrinkles, and a sagging bosom. He'd give anything for this vain creature to wake up one day and find she'd aged prematurely. That would wipe the condescending attitude from her skinny little body.

Remembering how she would run to their father with some twisted version of the truth should he say the wrong thing, Marcus pasted on a fake smile.

"Porcia, my dear, you're looking resplendent today, as always."

"And *you* are looking like a stray dog... *ugh*, and smell like one, too. Where did you go last night? I know it wasn't to visit a friend, as you don't have any!" She grinned at him mockingly. It was obvious she felt sure she'd achieved a mortal blow – but she was wrong. She wasn't very bright and she didn't know her brother very well. He had no desire for friendship within the ranks of Whitestone nobility. Most of them were as irritating and condescending as Porcia. Fortunately, he didn't have to live under the same roof as any of them.

"Actually sister, I visited the common quarter. I consumed much ale in the Crooked Wing tavern, fell flat on my face among the feet of the drunken locals, and rounded off the evening with a duck impersonation beneath the light of the full moon." Marcus smiled mischievously as his sister gaped at him. To his delight, her thin lips had gradually grown further apart throughout the recounting of his foray into depravity. Still open-mouthed, her eyes wide with shock,

Porcia stood before Marcus as he continued to smile at her. After a few seconds, she looked at her brother through squinted eyes, pursed her lips, and folded her arms across her flat chest. Marcus remained resolute in his delight at her response. It was anticipated and desired in equal measure and she was too simple to see it. He'd been able to elicit such a reaction since they were children and still she hadn't realised when she was being wound-up – or if she had, she rose to the bait nonetheless. Of course, the events he'd narrated for her were all true – well, mostly – but seeing the cogs turning as she concentrated all her efforts on trying to ascertain their validity had him desperately trying to contain laughter.

Finally concluding there may be truth in his statement, Porcia adopted the look of a woman with a purpose,

"I'm telling father!" She flicked her long, brunette hair over her shoulder and turned on her heels. Storming off to find their father, she was clearly eager to report his degenerate behaviour. But Marcus saw the positive in most situations. The direction in which she'd marched meant his father was in his study and not anywhere between that floor and the kitchens. Chuckling to himself, he resumed his journey towards sustenance with a fresh air of relief. He'd much rather avoid another confrontation.

Almost entirely obscured from view by a huge pile of assorted cold meats, a chunk of freshly baked, crusty bread, and the contents of a small orchard, Marcus' torso was semi-prostrate over the wooden kitchen table. As he devoured a chicken leg clutched tightly in his left hand, the right clasping the apple he'd already taken a large bite from, Julia stood beside him with her hands on her ample hips. She watched as he ravenously attempted to cram the feast into his ever-growling stomach, shaking her head in disbelief as he finished both the apple and the chicken leg in what seemed like one bite. Though her demeanour was disapproving, her features told a different story; a small smile and warmth behind her ageing hazel eyes suggested affection nurtured over many years.

Julia had been in the service of the Ryan household since before the children were born. At sixteen, she'd been taken under the wing of the former house cook after her parents had passed away. Being the eldest of six children, the task of keeping them all alive had fallen to her, so she'd thrown herself at the cook's mercy, offering herself for whatever tasks may be required for whatever small amount of money she could get. Fortunately, the old woman had need of a kitchen maid, and thus began her life within the staff of the nobility.

She'd always had a soft spot for Marcus, from the first day the two-year-old had toddled into the kitchen and presented her with his beaming smile. He'd then lost his footing on the hard stone floor and fallen into her arms as she'd rushed to catch him. She'd held him tight as he sobbed, gripping her finger in his tiny hand. The little boy with green eyes and a mop of blonde hair had clung to her so tightly; it was as if he'd never been embraced before. From then on, he'd sought her out, running to her to dry his tears as well as to share his smile at some new delight he'd discovered. Julia and her siblings had lost their mother, but, for all that loss, she still felt little Marcus had things worse. At least she'd enjoyed a mother's love – felt it every time she'd been woken from sleep, at every goodnight kiss and all the hours in between. Marcus, she'd soon discovered, had experienced none of that. To have a mother that didn't appear to love you; no, she'd cherish what she had known over his situation any day.

Now, as she looked upon his feasting with a maternal fondness, she had to smile. His mop of blonde hair now shoulder-length and dark-brown, this full-grown man at her table was far different from the frail infant she'd instantly warmed to all those years ago, his broad, well-toned stature perhaps testament to a lifetime of her cooking.

Sensing her gaze, Marcus raised his head from his food and grinned with the full smile he reserved just for her. He shrugged his shoulders, as if questioning her amusement, before directing his attention back to the treats she'd laid before him. Giggling, Julia turned to resume the preparations for dinner. She'd just sat down at the table to peal vegetables when an almighty crash reverberated around the kitchen, rattling the copper pans hanging from their racks and causing the cook and Marcus to drop what they were holding and sit bolt upright in unison. The heavy wooden door had been flung open, and both occupants knew all too well the source of the rage now invading the previously tranquil atmosphere.

A man almost as tall as Marcus strode into the room, his build, though diminished with age, still imposing. He was closely flanked by

Porcia, whose determined swagger and jutting chin intentionally betrayed her actions.

"There, I told you he'd be in the kitchens, father." With a disdainful glance at Julia, Porcia turned her attention to Marcus. Clearly revelling in her perceived moment of triumph, she pushed back her shoulders and lifted her chin, staring down her nose at her brother in the process. Julia rose from her seat, careful to avoid eye contact with the grey-haired Lord Ryan, and backed away to the furthest recess of the room. A servant with any sense would not remain in the vicinity of the inevitable confrontation. However much she wanted to intervene, she knew Marcus could take care of himself. He'd been doing just that since he'd embarked on a rapid growth spurt as a teenage lad. Noticing his confident posture, she knew that was true now more than ever. She'd witnessed an encounter between the two men a few months ago; that same confidence had been present then, and she remembered a rush of pride at realising her little boy had become a man. With a little more thought, the cook realised the shadowy alcoves of the kitchen might not be far enough away. Things had become quite intense last time. Keeping a respectful distance, Julia pushed herself up against the wall and made to leave past Porcia and out into the servants' corridors beyond. She watched as Marcus, still seated, locked eyes in stony silence with his father, who was now looming over him as the confrontation filled the room with an almost tangible prickle. Having reached the open door, Julia had nearly made her reluctant retreat when Porcia stepped swiftly towards her and grabbed her upper arm.

"Oh no you don't!" she spat, "father would like a word with you too, *woman*." Porcia sneered at the cook. Taller than Julia, she stared down at her with visible contempt. Using herself as a standard for 'womanliness', Porcia considered the older female, with her buxom, middle-aged figure and grey-streaked black hair, unworthy of the title.

"Leave her out of this, Porcia!" Marcus demanded, jumping from his chair. He'd heard his sister's spite directed at the person closest to him throughout his whole life and turned in time to see Julia cowering beneath Porcia's angular frame.

"Marcus!" The domineering voice of Lord Ryan bellowed at close quarters, bringing his attention sharply back to the mounting pressure brewing between father and son. "Is there truth to your sister's reports? Would you really attempt to shame this house further than you have already by exhibiting yourself, in the *'common quarter',* of all places?" Lord Ryan spat out the location for Marcus' exploits, as if the words may leave disease in their wake as they passed through his lips, should they linger there too long. Marcus remained resolute, determined to show no fear and to defend himself against any verbal assault the man cared to throw at him.

"Yes, father. There *is* truth to it. It's *all* true, in fact. I *did* go to the Crooked Wing tavern in the common quarter, where I drank cheap ale poured by an unwashed innkeeper called Nathan. I enjoyed the laughter, and the music, and the feeling of being a commoner, and I flirted with a comely lass who smelled of straw and damp. I writhed around, drunk, in pools of stagnant ale and unmentionable things, and I finished the evening pretending to be a duck in the street, all the time with a smile on my face and a song in my heart. And do you know what, father? I'd do it *all* again!" Throughout Marcus' account, Lord Ryan's face had grown redder and redder, the veins visibly bulging beneath his ageing, translucent skin. However, even he was left in stunned silence at the final revelation. Had these simply been the actions of an obstinate boy fleeing discipline, the elder noble may have settled with putting his son firmly back in his place with an ear boxing and a boot up his backside. Yet, he actively sought out this den of depravity. He deliberately made a show of himself with full knowledge of the likely effect on the long established and esteemed reputation of their noble lineage. To then add insult to injury by declaring both his actions and his intention to repeat this deplorable behaviour; Lord Ryan was dumbfounded, and not amused.

Lord Ryan stepped forwards until he was within an inch of Marcus' face and boomed into it.

"How dare you, boy!" Many altercations had passed in years gone by where such an intimidating act would have reduced Marcus to a crumpled, quivering heap at his father's feet. Not recently though, and secretly Lord Ryan didn't feel very self-assured. The boy had grown into a formidable-looking man in recent years and youth was not on the lord's side. However, the older man did still have one 'tool' at his disposal; one that his son would have had, too, had he not thwarted all the attempts of his tutor to instruct him in its use.

Marcus remained steadfast even with the close proximity of the lord's hot, musty-smelling breath. He pulled himself upright, in direct conflict with his father's obvious intent to pound him down, and stared fixedly into his eyes.

"What are you going to do now, father?" he taunted the elder man. Then he noticed the lord's barely concealed and hurried assessment of his options. "Ah, so you resort to magic. What a surprise."

"Foolish boy!" his father said. "Do you think yourself so invulnerable that if I chose to use magic against you, you would have any hope of standing against me?" He laughed at Marcus. "You avoided every lesson, evaded every attempt to teach you anything of the power that is your birth right. Perhaps now you can finally see the misguided nature of such pathetic and weak behaviour."

"I have no such concerns about my actions. I stand by the choices I made as a child, for that's what they were – *my* choices. If *choosing* not to spend every sunny day inside learning how to freeze things made me weak, then so be it. If *choosing* not to spend every rainy day in the atrium setting fire to rain drops made me weak then, I'll take that. If *choosing* not to become *you* made me look pathetic in your eyes, then all I can say is thank my lucky stars for whatever abnormality took hold during the creation of my soul." Marcus could see that his words were having an effect. A less impulsive young man may have left it at that. However, he was snowballing along with the adrenaline now pulsating through his body. Besides, he had no desire to let this opportunity pass him by without making the most of it. "If anyone were to be charged with weakness, I'd wager the almighty *Lord Ryan* would be a worthy candidate. Bowing to the whims of the nobility of this city, and refusing to make a decision without first requesting leave to do so from men with no more status than yourself. Avoiding an emotional attachment to your children for fear they may cause you to feel something other than magic coursing through your veins, and beating a young boy into submission in an attempt to avoid the vengeance of the grown man he would become. That one didn't work out so well for you, did it, *father*?"

Marcus barely stopped to take a breath, and was about to plunge the vocal blade in for the final kill, his target noticeably staggered by his vocal onslaught, when he noticed the blue aura of magic twisting and curling from Lord Ryan's fingertips.

From that moment, time seemed to pass in slow-motion. Marcus froze; he knew he was unable to move fast enough to avoid the bolt of blue power that shot forth from his father's hands, slicing through the air and heading straight for his chest. Bracing himself for the impact, he could only hope his attacker hadn't put an ounce of the full force of his power behind the projectile. Hearing its magic crackling as it grew closer, he was ready to feel himself pelted across the room. Instinctively covering his head with his arms, he closed his eyes and waited for the strike.

"Marcus!" Julia's voice rang out as soon as she'd seen the spell caster direct his ball of blue flame at her precious boy. Freeing herself from Porcia's vice like grip, all she could think of was the crackling, burning mass of energy meeting its target. Porcia snatched at thin air as she failed to re-grasp the cook's arm. As images of the little, green-eyed, smiling boy of yesteryear flashed across Julia's mind, she rushed forwards, straight into the trajectory of the magic orb, placing herself between it and Marcus at the very last second. Taking the full force of the spell, Julia's body reeled backwards, sending her and Marcus crashing against the stone wall behind.

Confused and dazed from the impact, Marcus rubbed the back of his head. His vision out of focus, all he could see was a large shape slumped in front of him. The shape didn't move and as his eyes gradually regained their clarity, he realised with horror that the woman he'd known as a mother since he'd been old enough to walk was lying lifeless on the cold tiles before him. Her eyes fixed open, they didn't blink. Even before he touched her to find a pulse, he knew she was gone, her life instantly snuffed out to save him. Guilt seeped into every fibre of his being. The tears flowed freely and his whole body began to tremble as the shock set in.

As he stared, grief-stricken, at Julia's body, a shadow moved across it. He looked up to see Porcia staring down at the corpse of the gentle, loving woman, wearing the same smug expression he'd seen so often before.

"Aw, has poor ickle Marcus lost his mummy?"

Feeling the blood within his veins start to boil, the guilt was forced to the back of his mind, there to be found at another time. Now, another emotion began to surge through his body as he remembered who'd been responsible for the callous waste of a good life. He rose slowly to his feet, then shoved Porcia aside so hard she stumbled backwards, her posterior meeting sharply with the corner of the table. With anger picking up speed like an approaching tidal wave,

Marcus marched straight towards Lord Ryan, grabbing him around the throat and almost raising him off the ground before he could cast another spell. Feeling the rasping in his father's throat as he gasped for breath, Marcus, consumed by an uncharacteristic rage, held him there, unwavering. A red mist had descended over him and self-control seemed a far distant memory.

Finally, as the lord's body became limp and his eyes rolled back in his skull, Marcus' senses returned to him, and he let go. The brutal tyrant he'd known as 'father' dropped to the floor with a thud. He looked down and felt... nothing.

Suddenly, a screeching Porcia lunged at his back, leaping on him and clawing at his exposed neck with her finely-manicured nails. Stumbling around the kitchen with his sister scratching and biting at him, Marcus eventually managed to throw her off. Pinning her up against the far wall, his face was so close to hers they were practically touching. His eyes burnt with rage and, for the first time in her life, she looked at him with fear. As a bead of sweat formed and trickled down her forehead, he glimpsed a vision of a man he did not wish to be. Loosening his grip on her arms, Marcus stared directly into her washed-out green eyes, tears now forming at the edges.

"You're not worth it," he said, barely above a whisper.

Stepping away from her, he turned to find the table top to steady himself. The exertion and maelstrom of emotions had left him physically and mentally exhausted. Porcia slid down the wall and, with her arms wrapped around her legs, leant her head forwards into them and began to sob softly, her fear as much of a shock to her as it had been to her brother.

Slowly regaining a modicum of composure, it started to dawn on Marcus that things would not go well for him once the events of the day were discovered. Noble sons got away with many and varied misdemeanours in Whitestone, but they usually had family to support them and friends in high places. Marcus had neither. His mother would never dream of entering the servants quarters, but soon enough Porcia would return to form and run to her. As if the situation didn't look bad enough for him, he knew his spiteful sister would put an even worse slant on things. This was exactly the kind of fodder over which she would have salivated. He couldn't bear to think it, but it was highly likely she'd say he murdered Julia. There was no way he'd be coming out of this incident unscathed.

Realising his time was up, Marcus ran from the kitchens. He ran through the corridors of the huge house, running without stopping until he reached his room. When he arrived, he scanned his belongings for anything he may need, or wish to take. Of all the richly decorated finery among his clothes, all the precious gem-adorned jewellery, elaborate tapestries and ornaments crafted from rare materials found in the dwarven mines of Geryndor, nothing in this house meant anything to him; the only thing that did now lay lifeless and beyond reach of his final farewell embrace. As a vision of Julia's compassionate face flitted before his mind's eye, he could almost hear her whisper to him. "*It's alright, Marcus. Dry those eyes. I'm here.*"

He closed his eyes and watched as the vision of Julia held his hand and placed something into it, closing his tiny fingers around the item before gently kissing his forehead. Then she was gone, faded from view. Opening his eyes once more, Marcus remembered something. Rushing to the small cabinet beside his bed, he yanked open the drawer and pulled out a folded piece of cream fabric. Carefully unwrapping it, tiny, intricate, embroidered flowers seemed to tumble into place. He raised it to his nose and inhaled the delicate, familiar scent.

"*Take this everywhere you go, little man. That way if you need to dry your tears and I'm not with you, you'll still feel loved.*"

Refolding the handkerchief and placing it in the pocket of his jerkin, there was only one other thing he had time to consider may prove useful. Scrambling onto his bed, he searched through the crumpled sheets until he found the parchment the dark-haired stranger had thrust at him the night before. His trepidation from earlier that day seemed ridiculous now. Things had changed so much in his life in just a few short hours. After all, he had very little left to lose. Adding the note to his pocket, Marcus turned towards the door and made his way out of the house. Running again, he finally reached the street outside. Dusk had set in and the air had grown cooler. He got his bearings and began to run once more. His chest felt tight as his breathing matched the pace of his legs, but self-preservation spurred him on. Through the streets he'd known all his life, he kept going, heading swiftly towards the east gate without so much as a backwards glance.

CHAPTER THREE

It took Marcus many hours to reach his destination, his awful sense of direction playing no small part. Three times he had to double back when he realised he'd gone full circle and was heading straight back to the city.

The countryside beyond the walls of Whitestone was very wild away from the farms and villages. It was mostly open landscape, but the scattering of untended shrubs and meandering hedgerows made taking a straight route almost impossible. The ground undulated before him, the inclines often far steeper than he predicted in the dim light. One particularly steep mound caused him to lose his footing and tumble helplessly into the boggy trench at the bottom.

For much of the way, it seemed no one had travelled in either direction for quite some time. Once or twice he thought he'd discovered a stony path, but when he followed its course he'd been led into a thorny thicket, or grass so long that it nearly caught in his day-old stubble. He'd considered persevering through the undergrowth but, with only the light from the half moon and no discernible landmarks ahead, he dismissed as futile the notion of reaching anywhere other than where he stood.

Every now and then, as he'd reached higher ground, he could vaguely make out what appeared to be woodland in the distance. From what he could recall of the songs of the travelling minstrels, the village he sought lay beyond those trees. Attempting to keep them in sight would hopefully ensure Marcus' journey end in success – eventually.

As he stumbled through the countryside, only his shadow for company, he had time for reflection. After he'd found the city gates on the eastern wall and, for good or ill, left his past behind, the grief had hit him hard. The urge to sit and weep verged on overpowering. Yet somehow he resisted and willed himself to push on. As far as he knew the whole city may be hunting him. After all, he was the *evil murderer* of the esteemed Lord Ryan and his lowly servant; at least, that's how Porcia would have put it. She was the heiress to the family estate, the new head of the house of Ryan – of course she'd be believed. Plus, she'd not only be her usual vindictive, spiteful self, but now fuelled by grief, she was likely to be more exhaustive in her attempts to bring her brother down than ever before.

She'd always hated him. Three years his junior and not initially set to take up the mantle as head of the estate, he'd assumed it to be simple jealousy. However, when it became clear he'd never engage in magic tuition, Marcus' succession had been considered forfeit – Porcia no longer had anything to be jealous of. Magic ability was inherited among Vaharians of noble birth. It was considered an honour and all the children of noble blood were assigned a magic tutor from the age of six. Only with this tuition could the young mage gain full use of his or her abilities. The magic was part of them all, as biological as the blood coursing through their veins, but instruction was required to control it. Without that, the most magical thing they could hope to achieve was to singe the hair on the legs of a fly. Even that would be unpredictable and prone to accidental misdirection; not good if the fly happened to have rested on the back of a sleeping cat. Marcus had seen many poor singed kitties as a child.

As he'd grown into a young adult, his blatant disregard for the reputation and standing of the Ryan name had been the cause of great embarrassment for his parents. His refusal to embrace his birth right brought shame upon them all, making the decision to let his younger sister pass him over all but inevitable. For the younger sibling to take the seat of power, especially a woman, was practically unheard of among Whitestone's elite. Yet, it was still preferable to the alternative. Now, with their father dead, her time had come. He'd never wanted the title she now owned, but the thought of Porcia lording it over him at some point in the future had always evoked a mild feeling of nausea in the pit of his stomach. She would be intolerable. Thank goodness he wasn't around to see it.

Some good has to come from this mess – even as he thought it, the memory of Julia's lifeless body jolted him forcefully from his attempt to put a positive spin on the evening's events. He missed her greatly. The only person to ever show him any kind of affection, she was more of a mother to him than Lady Ryan could ever have been. Porcia had mocked him for his lack of friends, but Julia had been a friend as well as a maternal influence. She shared his sense of humour, his interests, and his love of food. She cooked well and he ate well; it was a reciprocal commonality. She'd often joke about how she would be held responsible if Marcus cost the family a small fortune in tailoring due to his ever-expanding width.

Joking aside, she never needed to worry on that score. He'd always been a scrawny child. Small for his age from birth, he'd only started to grow noticeably after his thirteenth birthday. Virtually overnight, he seemed to shoot up and fill out. Before long he was taller than his father, and with a strong, toned frame, he looked every inch the man of the house. However, the amount he consumed never resulted in so much as an inch of fat.

"You have hollow legs, Master Ryan," Julia had affectionately mocked, as he wolfed down an extra serving of the roast hog she'd slaved over for the family's evening meal. After the others had retired to their respective corners of the mansion, Marcus would help her deal with the aftermath of the feast. Once the dishes had been washed and put away, he spent many happy evenings at the kitchen table, talking and laughing with the cook. For hours they'd set the world to rights and share their hopes and dreams. She'd watch him proudly as he took care of his own plate once his extra helpings were done. Then she'd remind him of the lateness of the hour and, with a wry smile, place a small cake, baked just for him, into the palm of his hand before ushering him out of her kitchen. She would have talked with the lad all night, but she knew they'd both suffer Lord Ryan's wrath the following morning, should they be too tired to complete their respective duties.

Marcus knew she'd always looked out for him. One night, as they were chuckling together about some earlier incident with Porcia, the lord had burst into the kitchen. One of the more sycophantic servants had reported their merriment to him and he'd marched down to the servant's floor to drag Marcus upstairs, where he belonged. As he'd been about to take the back of his hand to ten-year-old Marcus' head, Julia had quickly risen from her stool and, before he could utter a word of protest, taken the blame, claiming that she'd asked the boy to help and then engaged him in conversation "*...even though he wanted to go to his room, ma'lord*".

He remembered how she'd bowed her head before her master and knew, even then, it was more to brace herself for the blow that followed than to show her respect.

As Marcus continued his flight from the past through the unforgiving vegetation of the Vaharian countryside, he felt the anger surging at the memories flitting through his mind. He'd taken a life, there was no going back from that, but in that moment he'd avenged the death of someone he'd cared for. He let out a rumbling shout from deep within himself, as if to release the anger building up in his soul. The sound was sucked out into the dark wilderness as soon as it rang out. Perhaps, he'd just alerted the hunters to his whereabouts, but he didn't care. If they were to discover him now, at least he would meet his punishment knowing his friend's murderer would no longer enjoy another second of his luxurious life. He'd find peace in that, at least.

The exertion of his outburst causing him to stop still, he had a brief period to re-evaluate and made the conscious decision to leave his emotions for another time, when he was safely away from the reach of the guardsmen. Though he wasn't sure he'd ever be completely out of their reach. Surely they would extend their search beyond the city walls once it became obvious he was no longer within. It seemed the only action he could take would be to find this man, Sathom, and throw himself at his mercy. That may turn out to be a mistake, but short of leaving the kingdom altogether, he had no idea what else he could do. Maybe, in time, he would have no choice but to leave permanently. However, that thought unnerved him a great deal. The wilds of Vaharia were foreign to him, but the world outside was far from anything he could conceive. The tales he'd heard told of nothing but hostility and danger. The creatures, the people, even the land itself. If the stories were to be believed, everything after the relative safety of the stone highway that surrounded the kingdom was likely to kill any man stupid enough to leave his homeland.

Marcus shuddered at the images his mind had begun to conjure up. For now, his path was clear; meet with the dark-haired stranger and beg for his aid. The man knew his name and hadn't appeared threatening. If he wished him harm, he'd missed a grand opportunity. At the very least, he hoped Sathom may be too stupid to present a significant risk. Marcus was confident in his ability to outwit anyone attempting to lure him into a trap. Fighting wasn't in his nature, but with a quick mind and fertile imagination, he'd gotten out of the odd scrape or two over the years. Most of the time things worked in his favour. If only his quick mind wasn't so prone to being over-ruled by his impulsive actions.

He was starting to wonder if he'd accidentally changed course again, until he scrambled up a particularly high mound and found the first copse of trees of what appeared to be substantial woodland, just a stone's throw away. With a sigh of relief, he dusted off the mixture of damp leaves and dirt and took the screwed up note from his pocket. The moonlight was bright enough to just make out the words.

'I shall await you from dusk at the entrance to Eldenvale.'

Presumably an entrance won't be too difficult to find, he pondered, staring deep into the trees as if he'd be able to see it from where he stood.

With one final glance over his shoulder to check he was still alone, Marcus headed towards the copse, hoping the minor details in the minstrel's tales had not been grossly exaggerated. For all he knew, he may arrive on the opposite side of this wood only to discover further treacherous terrain stretching out for miles before any village came into view.

Without incident, Marcus soon reached the edge of the crop of trees. The night air was still, and, except for the crunching of twigs and dry leaves under foot, it was eerily quiet. He'd been used to the sound of the city for so long, this hush was unfamiliar, and more than a little disconcerting. Even at night, there always seemed to be something going on within the high city walls; dogs barking, open gates clanking against posts as they swung in the wind, cats yowling as they fought over territory, the odd noble gentleman stumbling home from a chamber of commerce meeting, rather the worse for wear having over-indulged in fine wine. The environment in which he'd found himself as he fled was an altogether very different creature. Without the orange glow of lanterns, shadows were deeper and moved with the moonlight, giving the impression they had a life of their own. Any sound Marcus made was free to drift over the landscape, unrestricted by white stone walls. The soft, bumpy ground felt uncertain and he found himself yearning for the secure feel of solid paving beneath his feet.

Now, with the next leg of his journey straight ahead, Marcus scanned the line of trees for the cleanest access point. He was already dishevelled and grazed from his various encounters with spiny things and holes, and would rather avoid an unfair fight with a bramble bush or eye-level pointy branch.

At first, like the rest of the countryside, this area appeared unbeaten. However, upon closer inspection, he discovered a small gap between two of the mighty pine trees. Where once there'd been a lethal twist of low stems and thorn-armoured thicket, a clear break had been created. Bending down to examine the way through, even his unaccustomed eye could see it had been made quite recently. The gashes in the wood still exposed green, moist-looking flesh, and he could just make out the scattered remnants on the ground beneath. Instinctively, Marcus began to look around for any sign the path cutter may still be around. Discovering no one, he silently hoped Sathom had been responsible, and without further thought squeezed his way through the gap and into the shelter of the trees beyond.

It was so dark within the copse, the scant moonlight unable to permeate the dense mass above, that Marcus had to keep his arms out in front of him, feeling his way as he trudged through the blanket of pine needles on the ground. There were more sounds than before, every sudden scampering causing him to dart his eyes about, frenetically attempting to see the source. The woodland floor seemed to be alive with creatures, all rushing for the safety of whatever holes they'd emerged from. As a city boy, he had no idea what manner of creatures they were, and no desire to stick around long enough to find out. The only wildlife he'd ever encountered were huge rats that would scurry through the city as darkness fell. He liked animals – always stopping to pet a passing cat or tied-up dog – but, there in the darkness, he felt at a distinct disadvantage. Happy dogs and purring cats were the least likely creature he'd come across.

Moving as swiftly as his inhibited vision would allow, he pushed on through the trees until, eventually, a shaft of light heralded the way through another recently cut break on the far side. Side-stepping through, his eyes adjusting to the extra light, he glanced down at his clothes to see that they were torn in many places, revealing jagged scratches edged with dried blood. *Well*, he thought, *at least I don't look quite so wealthy anymore*. There was always a bright side.

Half expecting to see yet more wilderness, Marcus nearly cheered with delight as he took in the setting ahead. He stood at the top of a gradual incline leading down to a sizeable valley surrounded on all sides by more scattered pine copses. Nestled at the foot of the Geryndor mountain range, the valley was perhaps only one quarter the size of Whitestone, but to his relief it was glowing faintly orange from countless flickering torches dotted around numerous, randomly spaced, low wooden buildings. The settlement appeared warm and inviting, but he knew this could simply be wishful thinking, and, until he found Sathom, he still had to be careful. His trusting nature urged him to believe there was no reason the inhabitants of the village would wish him harm. However, the small, insistent voice that had taken him this far reminded him he was a fugitive, perhaps with a hefty bounty on his head. Even if the villagers weren't aware of that yet, he was still, no matter how dishevelled, adorned in the finest attire his family wealth could buy. He had no way of knowing if any strangers he may encounter would see him as a coin purse with legs.

Nevertheless, he had little choice but to venture forwards, down into the shallow valley. So he did; the aristocrat, whose life had changed drastically in the blink of an eye, now placed his immediate future in the hands of a mysterious man who'd merely known his name. At any other time, the whole scenario would seem outrageously reckless, but presence of mind was not a luxury Marcus could afford. Self-preservation had engulfed every action and every thought. What he intended to do made no sense in the world he came from. People like him didn't take such irrational forks in the road, but they didn't murder people either. That was it, he'd murdered someone. No, not just someone, but his own father. One minute he'd been alive and breathing, the next he'd become a cold, still corpse – by Marcus' own hand. As he made his way down the slope into the valley, that realisation truly started to take root.

By the time he'd gotten within sight of what appeared to be the village entrance, his face was pallid and his expression fixed and uncomfortable-looking. His head was beginning to throb, and there was an unsettled feeling in the pit of his stomach. His limbs were starting to ache, and every muscle in his body felt tired and strained. With a thousand-yard stare, he approached the roofed stone and wood gateway, taking in the slow, deliberate movement of a person rising from one of the benches within as he got closer. He recognised the man as Sathom, his black hair pushed aside to reveal the intense brown eyes he remembered from outside the tavern.

Though he nodded in acknowledgement of Marcus' arrival, the man's face bore no hint of greeting. No smile graced his lips and nothing but moonlight reflected in his eyes. Marcus might have considered this a warning sign, but something about Sathom's gaze seemed reassuring, almost comforting. Finally close enough to converse without raised voices, the two men stood in silence. By now Marcus's stomach was feeling tugged in multiple directions and his skin stuck to his clothes as clamminess seeped from his body. At last the young noble broke the silence.

"I killed my father!" he blurted out, without thinking. As the words had barely left his lips his stomach completed a full somersault and, only just managing to turn his head away from Sathom in time, he lunged forwards and vomited, his insides retching repeatedly until there was little more than fluid coming up. Sathom stared down at Marcus, who had slumped to the ground with the effort of being sick and was now sweating profusely.

"Well, that adds an extra complication," he remarked taciturnly, before offering Marcus his hand to help him stand. Wiping the beads of sweat from his forehead, Marcus accepted the assistance gladly. Without another word, Sathom turned and began to walk slowly through the gate in the direction of the village. Marcus was confused by this man's impassive reaction and minimalist use of speech, but he followed regardless.

Thus the two men took the winding, cobbled path together, total silence hanging tentatively between them, though it was obvious the uncertainty was one-sided. Sathom's demeanour was purposeful and deliberate, whereas Marcus trailed his course with the look of an obedient but perplexed dog following its master.

The village of Eldenvale consisted of numerous buildings, mainly constructed from the same wood and stone as the gateway. Grey, irregular-shaped rocks filled the spaces between dark timber frames, and the crevices had been daubed with some kind of clay substance to make the structures weather-proof. Most of the buildings were clearly homes, but located prominently at the edge of a central clearing, one, significantly larger than the others, gave the impression of importance to the community. Intricate engravings depicting hunts and gatherings were chiselled into the thicker timbers, and roughly sewn flags displaying crude symbols were hung from twin poles at either side of a set of large, ornately carved, wooden double-doors. The pathway that led from them eventually re-joined the cobbled grey stone path as it wound its way through the village, branching off at intervals to take villagers back to their respective homes.

The land on which the village was situated was obviously fertile. Even as autumn grew to a close, the grass still covered most of the soil; late flowering plants splashed their colour amidst the dense sea of green, and smaller, fruit-bearing trees held onto their foliage a little longer than the norm. The whole village was bathed in the subtle, orange glow of countless well-spaced torches staked into the earth, their flames flickering warmly just a few feet above the ground.

It was well past midnight when Marcus and Sathom entered the central part of the village. No one stirred inside or out, and every shutter on every window was closed, with not a single light emerging from within. Marcus looked about, trying to guess which cottage belonged to Sathom. He continued to follow the man without question and all the time still in silence. Though, by now, he was glad of the lack of conversation. Unable to stop yawning, he longed for sleep and wasn't sure how much more his body would give before succumbing to the increasing lack of mental or physical stamina.

They finally turned off the main path onto a particularly long offshoot that took them past other buildings and led to a modest looking cottage set apart from the rest. Unlike the others there was a faint light emanating from between the thin gaps in the shuttered windows. As Sathom reached the front door of the cottage, Marcus expected him to produce a key from his pocket and place it in the lock. However, he paused briefly before rapping lightly three times. With such little delay that Marcus doubted the occupant had not been expecting their arrival, the door swung open, the light revealing an elder man, who quickly ushered them both inside.

The warm air from the building hit Marcus as soon as he stepped over the threshold, causing him to shiver as his body realised just how cold it had been outside. The new stranger closed and bolted the door and turned to look at his late-night visitors. His head was hairless save for the odd patch of grey stubble and similarly coloured closely-shorn beard around his mouth and chin. The lines on his face indicated his years may have advanced into the fifth or sixth decade of his life. However, there was something about his eyes that hinted at a youth out of sync with his overall appearance. It was unnerving. As was the way those eyes now roamed up and down Marcus' body, appraising him with a distinct look of disapproval. With a 'humph', the man turned his attention to Sathom. Glaring at him, he spoke in a hoarse, low-toned voice.

"This is he?"

"Yes, Benedict. This is he," Sathom replied, unaffected by the old man's disdainful tone.

Benedict bore a stooped posture, and seemed to rely quite heavily on the cane that he grasped tightly in his right hand. Favouring it as he walked past them, he grunted something that Marcus didn't quite catch and slumped himself down into a wooden rocking chair set in front of a wide, open fireplace. Leaning his cane against a small table at his side, he raised his age-spot-covered hands before the glowing embers, staring deep into the fire that Marcus now realised was the only source of light in the room. He had been willing to forgo questions for the time being, given his personal circumstances, but with a palpable tension in the air and no explanation forthcoming from either man, his curiosity couldn't wait.

"I don't mean to be rude – I'm grateful for… well, I mean, you haven't actually done anything but… erm, what did you wish to talk to me about, Sathom?" His eyelids heavy and his shoulders hunched, arms hanging weekly at his sides, his tiredness was apparent. Therefore, it was not entirely unwelcome when Sathom suggested he sleep first, promising the answers to his questions once his mind was better able to digest them. Sathom glanced at Benedict who, without returning the look, waved his hand in the direction of a room leading off from the one they now occupied. Marcus was confused beyond measure, but with no energy to protest and an intense desire to be horizontal, he allowed himself to be directed into the smaller room.

A sparsely covered bed and a single chest were the only items of furniture, but as Sathom bade him goodnight, in the same monotone voice he was becoming characterised by, Marcus found no more enthusiasm for answers that night. Barely able to remove his boots before he could hold himself upright no longer, he let his weary body fall to the blanket-covered mattress. Closing his eyes with blessed relief, sleep took him more easily than it ever had before, though nightmares ensured even his rest was filled with pain.

Soon after Marcus had fallen asleep, Sathom took his leave and left the village to return to Whitestone. Needing to ascertain the threat to his charge from the city guards, he'd traversed the ether, appearing from a screen of blue light outside the Ryan house. As with most of the buildings in the city, the mansion was in darkness. The dark-haired man moved towards the front of the house and, with a singular step, he continued through the wall as if it were made of nothing but air.

Appearing without pause on the inside, he wasted no time in checking almost every room in the house. Moving swiftly through wall after wall, nothing stood in his way; everything solid he came across was as insignificant to his path as a curtain of water. When he entered the private quarters of the lord and Lady, he found the couple sleeping soundly in their four-poster bed. He approached the lord and proceeded to hover one hand over his head, barely an inch away. A faintly glowing blue light began to fill the small distance between Sathom's hand and the lord's skin. Closing his eyes, he stood motionless for a minute or two, watching the sleeping man's memories play out in his own mind. He witnessed the confrontation, the death of the family's cook, the actions that led Marcus to believe he'd murdered his own father, and the aftermath that showed Lord Ryan coming to with the aid of his daughter's magic. From that moment until he and his wife retired for the night, there was no sign of a report being made to the guard. From what Sathom saw, Marcus had merely rendered the man unconscious, but it was odd that none of the household had reported Marcus' act of violence. Perhaps his father cared more for him than the young mage thought, or perhaps he was simply glad to be rid of him. Either way, it seemed he wasn't a wanted criminal. But he had to make sure it stayed that way. Opening his eyes he kept his hand where it was as the blue light increased in intensity. Within seconds he'd insured the man's memories included nothing that would bring Marcus any trouble. Then, he subjected Lady Ryan to the same procedure, before travelling to Porcia's room and repeating the process. With his goal achieved, he left the mansion in the same manner he'd entered, materialising just outside Benedict's cottage moments after fading from view in Whitestone.

As the embers died down in Benedict's hearth, he and Sathom sat together, both facing the source of heat as two old friends warming their ageing bones. A look of concern was etched upon Benedict's face, while Sathom's features remained inexpressive, as always.

"You're absolutely sure he's ready for this?" Benedict questioned his friend in a low voice, the doubt lingering around his words.

"I am," Sathom replied before elaborating, "he is of age now and more than capable of understanding what will be required of him."

"Yes, but he knows *nothing* of magic. Are you honestly expecting me to guide that dandy-headed rich boy? He was barely able to make it from one area to the next without collapsing. Come on, Sathom, he was a wreck."

Sathom paused, choosing his words.

"The boy is strong, my friend, stronger than even he knows. As far as he is concerned, he killed his father this night, without magic. What will he be capable of once he is able to use the power he was born with?"

"You're not going to tell him, are you?"

"No."

Benedict twisted round to face his companion.

"Sathom, you can't do that to the boy. Besides, what happens when he discovers the truth? You don't think he'll pack up and return home?"

"Then we make sure the truth remains untold – at least for now."

Benedict grunted and turned back to the fire.

"You'll do what you need to – you always have. But I still don't see how 'nearly' killing his father makes him up to our task."

"Because he took on the strongest force in his life and brought that force down with only the passion to avenge the death of his friend. Imagine how driven he could be when he takes on the plight of a much greater victim of evil." Sathom sighed as Benedict raised an eyebrow. "I have watched him grow, as I did you."

Benedict interrupted.

"And look how well *that* turned out."

"That was different, you know that. The point is, I know the man he has become. When he discovers what happened and knows who he truly is, I promise you, Benedict, he will be more than ready."

Benedict remained unconvinced.

"Hmm, we may have to agree to disagree there, friend. He hasn't had my years to come to terms with the truth. On your head be it if he bolts the second you try to explain. This could be our last chance, you know that."

Sathom was used to his friend's pessimism. He'd endured it often over the time they'd known each other. However, this time he had little doubt Benedict may be forced to re-evaluate the situation.

"You carry out your duties as we have discussed and all will be well, I assure you."

Benedict grunted as if the assurance of his friend meant very little.

"Just know this – I'm not going to molly-coddle the lad. If you expect me to teach him, you have to let me do things my way. He won't thank me for it!"

Sathom bowed his head, visualising the memories he'd drawn from the lord's mind.

"I wouldn't expect it any other way. Trust me, it will work… this time."

CHAPTER FOUR

Marcus had no idea how long he'd slept. He woke to feel the warm autumn sunlight on his face as it streamed in through an uncovered window. As he yawned and stretched, he suddenly remembered he wasn't in his bed at home, and everything came back with a vengeance. Once again, the image of Julia's dead body flashed before his eyes. Everything else seemed so surreal he could almost tell himself it didn't matter, or hadn't happened, but with a reoccurring visual, the loss of his friend would not be so easily dismissed. He twisted his aching body into a more comfortable position, wincing as he caught one of his many scratches on the torn fabric of his jerkin. The bed on which he'd slept was a poor substitute for his duck-feather-stuffed mattress at home. It was as uncomfortable as it looked, if not more so, and he knew, had he not been exhausted, it would have taken him hours to fall asleep on it.

There hadn't been a lot of time to take in the events since arriving at the sparsely-furnished dwelling. So, with no great urge to see if his legs remembered how to work, Marcus remained where he was and took a moment or two to consider the situation. He'd spent some time with Sathom, albeit with scant conversation, but enough to feel he may be able to trust the man. He wasn't particularly adept at reading people, probably because he spent as little time with others as possible, but something about Sathom put him at ease. Unsure if it was his tranquil manner or the faraway look in his eyes, he decided to accept his instinct and focus instead on the other man. Benedict had visibly stiffened when he'd looked at him. They'd never met, so Marcus was irritatingly perplexed at what could have evoked such a reaction. Was it an issue with his class? Benedict was clearly not a member of the aristocracy and it was no secret that people of lesser means often bore little fondness for nobility. Indeed, many were deeply resentful of the wealth and power held by men of his standing in Vaharian society. Somehow, though, that explanation seemed a little flippant.

Not wishing to dwell on it any longer, he told himself to be content with that answer. He'd be careful to tone down any obviously noble behaviour when he and Benedict next met. He had no desire to flaunt his status in the face of anyone, least of all someone who'd been good enough to give him a bed for the night – even if it was damned uncomfortable.

The larger of the two rooms in Benedict's cottage contained only slightly more furniture than the bedroom. It was obviously a multi-purpose room; just beside the door was a narrow wooden table, providing for a basin, a set of knives, and various other utensils used for preparing food. A recently cut loaf of bread surrounded by scattered crumbs sat on a roughly hewn board balancing precariously over the edge of the surface. The large, open fireplace took up most of the opposite wall, a pile of logs sitting within easy reach of the wrought-iron grate at its centre. A long metal poker leant casually against the stone surround and a heavy copper pan containing the remnants of some kind of stew sat on the hearth, within easy reach of Benedict's battered old rocking chair.

The room had two windows. A small one was positioned over the basin on the counter, though too low for an adult to gain any worthwhile view of the village outside. The other was much larger, but, facing other buildings and trees as it did, allowed only a little dappled light to enter. Beneath this window sat a chest, similar to the one in the bedroom. On top of the chest lay an open, leather-bound book, an ornately cut silver-tone amulet on a thick leather cord, and a yellow wax candle, almost spent in its crude iron holder. A heavy lock hung from the metal clasp, like a proud guard boldly defending its charge. In the centre of the room stood another table, square and well-worn with two equally-shabby chairs set on adjacent sides.

It was at this table that Benedict and Sathom sat, as Marcus warily emerged from the bedroom. The chairs positioned as they were, he could only see Benedict's face and it was twisted into a sort of grimace. The man's eyes narrow and his top lip approaching a snarl, Marcus considered backing away quietly in the hope he hadn't been noticed. Perhaps he could slip out of the window in the other room. With any luck, they wouldn't detect his absence until he was miles away. It might have been a fine idea but, as Benedict caught sight of Marcus and gave him yet another disapproving glare, he realised executing that plan was no longer an option.

"So, you're alive? What time of day do you call this? I thought you'd passed away in your sleep, as *broken* as you were last night." Benedict didn't bother to try to hide his taunt.

Sathom watched Marcus as he walked further into the main room. Feeling awkward under their scrutiny, his eyes began to drift towards the slices of bread and butter half eaten on the table in front of the two seated men. He felt like he hadn't had anything to eat in days, though in reality it had only been hours. Still, that was a long time for Marcus to go without food, and the crumbly, pale bread with its golden coating looked like a meal fit for a king. Without thinking, he licked his lips as his stomach began to remember it had been neglected for much longer than it was accustomed.

"What time *is* it?" Marcus asked, rubbing sleep from his eyes and stifling another yawn.

"More than an hour since noon, but do not fret – you needed the rest. You must be hungry." Sathom stated the obvious without any hint of sarcasm and, rising from his chair, motioned for Marcus to take his place at the table. Marcus didn't need telling twice. He sat down and lunged at the bread in front of him, clutching the thick slices with one hand while breaking off large chunks and cramming them into his mouth with the other. He almost forgot he had company and practically choked when Benedict let out a deliberate, loud cough. With his mouth full, he looked up at the man opposite him at the table.

"Damn, boy! Don't they feed you where you come from?" Benedict's seemingly-permanent furrowed brow was now accompanied by a quizzical curled lip, which Marcus thought made him resemble a stone gargoyle. Restraining himself from laughing at the likeness, he gulped down the half-chewed mouthful and was about to consider explaining his excessive appetite, but it brought back too many painful memories of Julia. Instead he simply smiled inanely, and shrugged his shoulders.

"What can I say? This is good bread!"

"Marcus, we need to talk," Sathom interjected before Benedict could utter another caustic remark. The young man put down the bread and looked at Sathom, gulping down a mouthful before speaking.

"Yes, you've said that already. I'm sorry, Sathom, but, do I know you from somewhere? I think I'd remember if we'd met, but you seem to know me. Are you perhaps an acquaintance of my parents? I mean, I find that unlikely as you'd probably rather run naked through the city than talk to me, but..."

"No, Marcus. I do not know your parents. However, I do know you – just not in the way you think."

Marcus was more confused than ever.

"Really? Because I have no idea what I think. It seems you know better than I, friend."

He was sincerely grateful to his new acquaintance for, at the very least, not handing him over to the authorities. But, though he was safe from the city guards for the time being, he was beginning to think he'd jumped straight out of the frying pan and into the fire. He had no idea how Benedict was involved, and he was beginning to get mildly annoyed at the judgemental look in the old man's eyes. Marcus was an easy-going man, not usually one to fret over anything much at all, but burdened as he was with the weight of recent events, he found his tolerance for being kept in the dark wearing a little thin.

A silence hung in the air as if an almighty hammer was about to pound into the floor at any moment. Benedict and Sathom exchanged looks before Benedict got up, swapping his seat at the table for his rocking chair in front of the fireplace. Sathom turned back to Marcus and began to speak.

"Over one-thousand years ago, a great calamity occurred. This catastrophic event took place in your homeland, Marcus, within the walls of Whitestone, though it was known as the Ivory City in those days."

"Wait. Is this a story? Should I be getting comfortable?" Marcus said, humour turning up the corner of his eyes.

"Please, if you will just listen, you might learn something," Sathom responded.

Marcus nodded for him to continue, leaning back in the chair with his arms and legs crossed.

"The people of the time were of a race known as the Meranells. They were a good people, kind and wise, compassionate, and trusting… some would say *too* trusting." Sathom faltered for a moment, his mind seemingly taken from that room in Benedict's cottage. Still, his face remained unnaturally composed, even as his body betrayed a vague hint of something else. Pulling out Benedict's vacant chair, he sat down in front of Marcus and continued.

"Many thousands of years ago, the Meranells came to this world from another, far away and reachable only by a mystical portal they inadvertently discovered. In their world, known as Meran, their forms were incorporeal. They had no physical shape as you know it. Their souls moved freely and their world, very different to this one, suited them that way.

However, when a group of Meranell adventurers stumbled upon the portal that brought them here, they found themselves transformed. They were no longer intangible. Instead they had arrived contained within human-like bodies, or 'vessels' as they called them.

Of course, they were distressed, afraid, and, keen to return to their natural state, they attempted to go back to Meran via the portal; but to no avail. It seemed the doorway into this world worked in just one direction.

Trapped here, they made the best of their situation. Such an adjustment took time, of course, but eventually they settled here, developed a community, built a city. They soon realised their new vessels were, in theory, strong enough to carry them indefinitely. In Meran, their lives were long, but paired with a body they were able to live through numerous lifetimes. In other words, they were immortal.

However, even with this new-found longevity, some never gave up hope of finding a way home. They devoted their lives to that cause, but always it proved fruitless – until the elementals arrived.

When the council of Meran decreed the lost adventurers were to be found at all costs, the elementals eagerly took on the task. As friends and guardians to the Meranells, the welfare of those missing was paramount. It did not take long for them to discover the trail that led them to the portal and without a second thought they travelled through.

Now, time works very differently in Meran. When the elementals arrived here, many decades had passed even though it had been just weeks since the group had become lost. Obviously they wanted to return with the adventurers, most of whom now had descendants. So despite the new-world Meranell's assurances that return was impossible, they tried anyway. The first elemental attempting to go back with a willing volunteer managed to pass easily through the portal; it seemed elementals were able to return, but he found himself on the other side, without the Meranell. He travelled through again only to find that same Meranell had aged twenty years and had no further interest in going home. Taking someone back through the portal was only tried once more. The result was so horrible that it was agreed taking the adventurers home did indeed have its limitations. Apparently it wasn't totally impossible – but, there was a price"

Marcus was intrigued.

"Why was it horrible? What happened? What was the price?"

"As the elemental tried to go through with his Meranell volunteer, holding him tightly by the head—"

"By the head! Are you serious?" Marcus interrupted.

"You have to understand, Marcus, bodies weren't something either race was accustomed to."

"Ah, I see… I think."

"May I continue?"

Marcus nodded.

"Anyway, holding him tightly by the head, he walked through the portal. But as he passed through, he felt something strange. When he arrived in Meran, the soul was by his side, back in incorporeal form and unharmed. Going back to let the others know it had worked, he immediately discovered a skull on the ground. When he asked what had happened he was told the head had been dramatically ripped from the body, which had died instantly.

From then on it was known that Meranells could indeed return, but only in their original form. It was also deemed that though vessels were certainly strong, decapitation would be their end, and thus would free the soul. After that, a handful of those wishing to return took the lives of their own vessels. Sadly, this did not end the way they hoped. Though their souls were once again free and, in theory, able to pass through the portal, in Vaharia they were blind without the eyes of their vessels. To a free soul in this world, there was naught but blackness. They couldn't find their way to the portal, or to anywhere else. Thankfully, once the elementals realised this, they were able to harness the unanchored ones with a rite used in Meran for seeking lost souls. They could then guide them through the portal.

A party of elementals travelled home to inform the council of their findings, but the reaction of the Meran council was not what they expected. After relatively little deliberation, the council announced there were concerns over the possible repercussions of large numbers of their own kin coming back all at once. Many more existed than the small group that had left – multiple generations by this point. Meran, it was thought, could not sustain such an influx of new souls.

Fortunately, as the elemental ambassadors told the council, very few wished to return at all, happy as they were in their new world. Alas, the council remained unconvinced and made a new decree. From that moment on, no expatriate was to be granted passage unless they had earned their permit in an arena. Those wishing to return must fight and fight well. The elementals were to remain in Vaharia and act as judges in these bouts. They were to see to it that no gladiator took the easy way out. With elemental ability to see the true nature of a Meranell soul, the pass could not be achieved through cheating. Only when one warrior was judged to have lost his vessel's life, by fighting to the best of his ability, would the elementals be allowed to use the rite and guide the soul back to Meran. In this way, the council believed they could ensure numbers returning were kept to a minimum."

Marcus looked shocked.

"That's terrible."

"Yes. The elementals thought so, too. But, as servants of the Meranells, they were powerless to go against the council's ruling."

"So – and I'm sorry for going back to the beginning – these people, these Meranells, if they were immortal, where are they now? I mean, I'm sure I've heard nothing about such a race." Marcus had enjoyed the tale, but gathering Sathom was telling it as fact and not fiction, he was now entirely confused.

"The answers you seek will come in time, but for now, allow me to provide you with the information your history books omitted.

As I said, the people of this race consisted of the body, or vessel, and the soul. Now, generally speaking, all else being equal, the two would live on together, forever intertwined. Until the end of time, I suppose. However, upon the premature death of the vessel, the soul, still immortal, would continue to be. Unfortunately for a Meranell, this meant that his or her soul was in oblivion, set adrift in this world for all eternity, helpless… alone. At least with the elementals present, none had to accept that fate. The council were not completely heartless. Their decree did allow for accidental vessel death, or death caused by foul means. In those instances, they were permitted the rite the same as those who succeeded in the arena. When a vessel death took place, they were there to facilitate their journey home. The elementals would read the last rite as the soul was parted from the body, thus enabling the transition between worlds and saving one of their friends from a fate worse than death.

This way of life, harsh though it sometimes seemed, thrived for many, many years, and would have continued to thrive, were it not for the evil nature of those who coveted the immortality of the Meranells.

You remember I mentioned that some believed they trusted too easily? Well, it seems those that held that belief might have been more astute than they were given credit for at the time. Just over one-thousand years ago, some travellers came, entering Vaharia from the south. They claimed to be refugees, fleeing from an oppressive regime, and sought to find a new homeland, a place where they could be free and live their lives in peace. The good people of the Ivory City welcomed these newcomers wholeheartedly. But all was not as it seemed, as it so rarely is, and soon it became apparent that some – the ones that assumed the role of leaders – sought more than asylum.

There were seven of these men, and they were powerful in ways the Meranells had never known. They were mages, and it was they who brought about the end of a fine and peaceful civilisation. That night one-thousand years ago, as most Meranells were sleeping, the mages set about casting a spell. Now, understand, this was not a simple hex or a curse upon a single soul; this was a spell the likes of which had never been conjured before – a spell to do the unthinkable, to bring about the destruction of an entire race. Not only that, but from this devastation, the mages hoped to take from the Meranells the one thing they could not have offered them for all their benevolence; their immortality.

As the people of Vaharia slept in their beds, the spell was cast. Thousands of vessels decapitated, thousands of souls cut off from the world they knew and thrust into a nightmare. The screams could be heard on the winds from one side of the kingdom to the other; husbands calling for wives, brothers for sisters, mothers for their children. But with no substance and no eyes in this world, even if their calls were answered, they were unable to reach out and powerless to reassure. In that ineffectual state, when a mother finally heard the familiar cry of her child, she could not even hold them in her arms and kiss away the tears.

Then came the second part of the spell. Far away, beyond the Dragon Crest Mountains, the mages had constructed a tower. With one purpose in mind – to hold captive the Meranell souls – the structure had been designed and created with dark magic. To be capable of fulfilling its objective it had to have corruption running through every frame, every crack in the stone plastered with darkness itself. The tower was then further powered by the magical essence of one of their own, that of the seventh mage, Secronius. Unbeknownst to him, he was to be sacrificed. Betrayed by his own brethren, his magical energy was bound to the tower, finally sealing his fate by transforming him into a hideous beast, to act as the tower's eternal guardian. Then, the remaining six mages had nothing more to do but wait.

The mighty force of the magic within the tower began to gain strength. With increasing swiftness, each and every loose soul in Vaharia was drawn towards it, torn across the lands, ripped away again from those it had managed to find in the darkness, trapped forever once inside. Finally, when the last soul had been caught, the looming black tower crackled with magical energy before the mages sealed it shut forever, walking away with the prize of the ages – eternal life. And that is where they remain as prisoners to this day; confined in the dark tower I have come to call, for preservation of my own sanity, the Sanctum of Souls."

Now silent, Sathom closed his eyes, his hands making a steeple across the bridge of his nose. The telling of the story appeared to have affected him greatly. It was almost as if he'd expended all energy his body had to offer, the sheer weight of the words pressing down on him, with no relief provided from their utterance.

Marcus, who had been riveted throughout, now shifted uncomfortably in his chair, a puzzled look replacing his previous open-mouthed expression. Hesitation lingered once more, with only the sound of Benedict's raspy breathing permeating the silence. This continued until Marcus' mind finished absorbing the information and demanded his mouth get to work finding some answers, or a way out.

"Right, well… Sathom, er, thanks for the story. It was… erm, fascinating. Complete madness of course, but still, fascinating. Look, it was a good tale and I applaud your imagination, but as that is all it is, I find myself wondering just why it is that I'm here. And while I'm at it, how in Gadrionis do you know my name? Where have I met you before? You've promised me answers, twice now, yet here I am being told fairy tales. I appreciate you, and your friend, taking me in, I really do. But I have myself enough trouble. I can't say I'm reassured that staying here, with you, won't bring me a great deal more."

"What did I tell you Sathom?" Benedict said, a look of resigned satisfaction obvious in his smug smile. Both men stayed seated, neither showing any outward sign that they understood how close he was to leaving. Studying the faces of each of them, Marcus sighed and got up from his chair.

"Well, I believe there's nothing more to say then. Thank you, both, for your help and hospitality. I'll be on my way." Marcus had no intention of leaving; apart from anything else, he had nowhere to go. However, he'd put up with nonsense no longer. Someone needed to enlighten him with the truth rather than entertaining him with wild fantasy. Sathom had patently sought him out for a reason, surely he wasn't about to let him leave now?

"Wait!" Sathom's tone was hardly commanding, but it was enough to stop Marcus in his tracks. Managing to take just a step in the direction of the door before his assumption proved correct, he hid his smile as he turned back towards the room in anticipation of some words of a more sensible and revealing nature.

"Please, Marcus, if you will kindly offer me your attention for a little longer, you may discover the clarification you seek." Had Sathom's character been that of a normal man, his face might have conveyed a desperation that his voice did not, or vice-versa. But yet again, he displayed nothing of the emotions his words hinted at. It was getting increasingly disturbing.

"Fine, I'm listening." Sitting back down in the vacant chair, he waited for Sathom to begin again, though this time hopefully with less insanity.

"Marcus, everything I have spoken of is true, however much it sounds like a flight of fancy."

Insanity it is then, Marcus thought.

"Right, let's say I believe this… this story of yours. If the mages became immortal, where are they now? Why are they not men of power, of authority? Surely such men would have used their long lives to accrue wealth and status. Surely they would be ruling over us all?"

"They are!" Benedict interjected.

Marcus had almost forgotten the other man was there, he'd been so quiet.

"What do you mean, 'they are'?"

"Just what I said. You asked why they're not rulers and I told you, *they are*."

Marcus looked to Sathom for clarification as Benedict's contribution was obviously going to remain cryptic at best.

"The men you know as the governors of Vaharia – the six High Lords that preside over the populace – they are the original six mages that imprisoned the Meranell's souls, usurping their land and acquiring the key to unending life." Sathom let his words hang in the air, giving Marcus a moment to acclimatise himself to this revelation.

Though he could easily lose himself in a good book, Marcus was able to differentiate between fact and fiction – at least that was what he tried to tell himself. However, it was becoming difficult for him to disbelieve the claims Sathom was making. Aside from his matter-of-fact account of the alleged events, and the fact that he wasn't sure if a man such as Sathom was even capable of creating such an intricate fantasy, what little he knew of the governors caused him disquiet when paired with this new information. The governors were indeed mages, as was every noble in Whitestone, but that was about as much as he or anyone else knew of them. On the rare occasions they'd been witnessed in public, they were covered from head to toe in heavy robes, their faces hidden in the shadows of their hoods. Marcus' father was of great importance among the aristocracy, but even he'd never been granted an audience with them. They were certainly mysterious and perhaps the reason was to be found in such an account of Vaharia's past.

Now, as Marcus considered this, he began to see a fresh approach to Sathom' version of events might be necessary. It seemed what he thought he knew of the world might actually hold less significance than the vast amount that was unknown about the governors.

Taking in the enormity of the situation, his usually nonchalant attitude was nowhere to be found. If things had transpired as Sathom said, then a heinous crime had been committed. The people of the city needed to know about this. The governors may be powerful, but, with a city full of men and women with the ability to wield magic, something could be done. *Surely this terrible act could be avenged, at the very least,* he thought to himself.

"What would you have me do, Sathom? I want to help. I don't know how useful I'd be, especially after… well, after what happened. I will most likely be arrested on sight if I return to the city, though I'd gladly accept that if it means I can, I don't know, tell somebody. If this is the reason you wanted to meet with me. I will do what I can to… to put this right."

Benedict took one look at the earnest expression on Marcus' face and suddenly roared with laughter.

"Hah! Tell somebody? Who would you tell, lad, huh? The good people of Whitestone, the governors... *your father*?" Benedict spat out the words amidst his hysterical outburst. Sathom shot him a stern look and Benedict turned away, still sniggering to himself.

Crestfallen, Marcus hung his head. He'd endured his sister's mocking ridicule for years, yet somehow, this stranger had succeeded in beating him down where she'd always failed, and with only one attempt. Now, he wished to be far from this tiny room and the strange men he shared it with. He really did want to try to put things right. Such an evil act should not go unpunished. But Benedict was right, what could he do? Who would he tell? Even if he wasn't killed before he could speak, even if anyone would believe what he told them, there was no one within the city he could trust. No, what good could he do? He was pathetic and weak, just as his father had said.

"There is more I have not yet told you." Sathom interrupted Marcus' self-flagellating train of thought. Marcus raised his head to meet his gaze. There was nothing he could do but listen; he was still able to do that, at least.

"What I am about to tell you will undoubtedly be difficult to comprehend. It will certainly change your perception of yourself, Marcus, and you are unlikely to welcome this revelation."

"Right, now you're worrying me. Do I even want to hear this?"

"No, you probably won't want to hear it, but as you will soon come to realise, you need to understand who you are, especially if you wish to help as much as you claim."

A lingering doubt tugged insistently at his mind, urging him to rethink his decision to stay and listen. Curiosity had always been his undoing however, and – this time being no different – it hushed the doubt and compelled him to remain attentive.

"You will recall that I told you the Meranells of this world were immortal. Well, as I said, most were happy to live that way, with infinite centuries stretching ahead of them. Conversely, there were others who did not welcome their own longevity. For those people, few as they were, the promise of eternity in this world brought only despair. For their own reasons, they looked on forever here with dread. Keen to sever the connection with their solid form, they longed to go home."

"Why would they want to leave Gadrionis if they'd die sooner in Meran? Why would anyone strive for a shorter life?" Marcus was struggling with this particular part of the tale. Believing living was something to be embraced at every opportunity, the concept of not enjoying life was alien to him.

Sathom seemed about to answer his question until Benedict's familiar gruff voice cut in once again.

"They didn't want to stay here because this world had nothing left for them."

Benedict's expression was distant, his eyes staring out beyond the confines of the room. For a moment, Marcus thought he glimpsed sadness in them. He had difficulty reconciling such vulnerability with the acerbic manner he had experienced from the man so far. He stared at Benedict, waiting for him to elaborate, but instead he turned his head away from the scrutiny, pain filling the void that had been there when he spoke.

"Their reasons were their own, Marcus." Sathom continued. "Suffice to say they had the courage of their conviction and took steps to seek deliverance from their inner turmoil."

"They fought in the arena?"

"Yes. Dedicating what vigour was left within them to honing their skills in battle, they became great warriors. With their minds focused on one prize – Meran – they would face each other in the arena, each one hoping to be outmatched by their opponent. The rules were simple; fight with honour. Only by competing to the best of their abilities would the last rites be given upon their vessel's death. As I said before, the elementals were the arbitrators, as only they could look into the souls of the people and see their intent; such was the connection between them. When the final blow came and the vessel was no more, they would ensure the soul of the victor received safe passage to the peace they had earned."

"You mean… they fought to lose?"

"That was not how they saw it, but yes, the object was to be defeated. This was no simple deed. These were skilled warriors. Alas, such exceptional ability only comes from exceptional passion and when that passion is directed towards ending an eternity of misery, there is no other driving force like it. Besting a fellow warrior in the arena was challenging enough. Finding one that could best you when you were compelled to fight like someone who wanted to live… nearly impossible. It was what made the victory so well deserved and ensured the council's decree was upheld."

"It was cruel!"

"Yes… yes, you are right, it *was* cruel. Perhaps there could have been another way, perhaps the elementals could have protested more, perhaps…"

Sathom's words trailed off. He closed his eyes again before turning to look at Benedict. The two men shared a look and held it in uncomfortable silence.

"What does any of this have to do with me?" Marcus' question shattered the lingering quiet, breaking the men's connection and directing their attention back to his bemused face. Sathom paused before looking back and receiving a permissive nod from Benedict. Facing him once more, Sathom looked directly into Marcus's eyes, a look more intense than any he'd offered so far. Those dark, distant eyes bore into the young man as if searching for something hidden, probing him as if the words he needed would be discovered just beneath his skin. Finally, Sathom's eyes relinquished their search and he spoke.

"It has more to do with you than you have ever been aware, Marcus. Complicated explanation will do you no service so I will put it... simply. You are not who you think you are. You are not just a human mage from Whitestone. Your body – your vessel – carries the soul of another. Within you is one who fought in that very arena so long ago; the ancient soul of a Meranell."

CHAPTER FIVE

The chill north wind had taken its first brazen flight down from the Mountains of Nor, stretching out its reach until grasping, bitter fingers traced the footpaths that meandered around the village. Soon, every crack and crevice would feel its wrath as winter triumphed over autumn's defeat.

Erryn pulled her cloak tighter around her as the chill nipped at her exposed skin. Her auburn curls lashing at her face like tiny straps of leather, she inwardly cursed her father for sending her out with deliveries. She didn't begrudge him the help, but she'd spent the first half of the day on a hunt that had proved fruitless, and sprained her ankle when she'd taken out her frustration on an innocent rock. Erryn and her father, Haden, relied upon successful hunts for the meat to accompany the meagre crop of vegetables he managed to grow on their small plot of land. The plan had been to finish her chores before mixing up a healing poultice and elevating her leg for the evening; a painful, swollen ankle was not conducive to moving stealthily through the trees in pursuit of a rabbit that keenly wished to stay alive.

Now, hobbling along with the last of Haden's crafts tucked securely under her arm, she winced at every other step. Of course, she'd hidden her pain from her father. He would only fuss and let his compassion for his daughter compel him to deliver the items himself, and Erryn wasn't going to risk that. Haden had suffered a bout of ill health in recent months, and having been awake and working since before dawn, she knew a trip out into the cold damp air would not have been good for him.

No matter – just the one item to pass on and then she could rest up. With any luck, she'd still have time to recover enough for a less agile sortie early the following morning.

As she reached the well at the centre of the village, Erryn paused to rest her ankle, and unfolded the scrap of parchment given to her by her father. Mentally checking off the items already delivered, she read on to match up the last one to its destination, and sighed. Not only was the cottage the furthest away, up the steepest knoll, it was also home to the most reclusive man in the village. Erryn had set eyes on Benedict Cane no more than a handful of times, and spoken with him even less. The closest she'd come to conversing with him was exchanging polite greetings and farewells, along with goods for coin, through his narrowly opened front door. He'd been civil enough, but there was something odd about him. As he'd peered at her from behind his front door, she'd been notably taken aback by the distance in his eyes. She'd always been able to sense a person's soul with only a moment's face-to-face contact, an innate ability that had proved useful many times before. But if she hadn't known better, she would almost have sworn Benedict had no soul, such was the detachment she witnessed in those amber pools. It had disquieted her enough to avoid eye contact with the man the next time she'd been sent with a delivery from her father. Still, she retained her characteristic curiosity and resolved to hold his gaze as long as possible… someday. Not today, though.

What is it I'm delivering to him this time, anyway? She thought, taking the item in hand and unwrapping one end of the sackcloth that it was swaddled in. Confusion etched its way across her petite face. The item appeared to be a stick. A very long, thick stick, but a stick all the same. Of course, it was a beautifully crafted stick. Everything Haden made was of the finest quality, from a simple footstool to an ornate armoire. Not that he had much call to make the latter these days. Erryn vaguely remembered being a little girl and riding into Whitestone with her father. He'd sat up front driving their old pony, while she had been thrilled to ride atop various pieces of large furniture strapped into the back of the cart. Then the orders from the city started to dry up, and they could no longer afford to keep the pony. She'd never known why, and Haden didn't talk about it. These days, he just about managed to keep a roof over their heads and put food on the table from the sparse orders the villagers made. Erryn wasn't even sure they actually needed some of the items they commissioned. Haden was a popular man, well thought of and highly respected for both his skill as a carpenter and his good nature as a person. It wouldn't have been much of a stretch to assume at least some of his orders were expressions of pity. Not that she, or they, would ever let on. He was also known for being a proud man who'd never have accepted overt charity.

Carefully re-wrapping the cloth around the stick, Erryn turned in the direction of Benedict's cottage and, with a look of determination, hobbled slowly up the grassy mound that led to it. The afternoon sun beat down on her back, sending a pleasant warmth down her body. It was only a brief respite from the chill in the air, but was welcome all the same. At least she was now walking with the wind behind her; she tired of tugging strands of hair out of her mouth, and the extra push from behind helped ease the strain on her ankle.

Finally within arm's length of the door, Erryn was about to make a fist to rap on the wood when muted voices from within caught her attention. Were it the home of any other villager, this wouldn't have been cause for curiosity. However, Benedict didn't speak to people. She'd never seen the man at any of the village gatherings, never heard anyone else talk of him; she seriously doubted he interacted with anyone in Eldenvale but her and Haden, and it wasn't either of them talking with him in his cottage. Her interest piqued, Erryn carefully leant in closer to the door; her ear up against it, the voices were clearer, but still muffled. The door was too thick, made as it was from heavy oak. *This is no good*, she thought, with an air of frustration. Scanning the walls of the cottage, she noticed a small window had been left ajar. It was only a crack, but should be just enough to hear the voices more clearly. As she crept over towards her newly discovered vantage point, she felt no compunction for eavesdropping.

From her rather uncomfortable position, crouched on the ground beneath the window, she could make out three distinct voices. One of them she knew to be Benedict, though his were only scattered interjections – *quite fitting of the man*, she thought with a smile. The other two, both men, were unfamiliar to her. *No one from the village then*. She'd lived there all her life and knew every resident; it was definitely no one local. One voice was speaking in a low monotone, seemingly telling the others some kind of story; she recognised place names, but the events the man told of sounded like fairy tales. She was beginning to think the cramp spreading through her legs wasn't worth it, until she heard the mention of magic. Erryn knew plenty about magic, but now she was more intrigued than ever. Interested to learn what these men knew of the abilities she'd been born with, she listened on intently.

The monotone man finally reached the end of his tale, meeting with a moment's tense silence before the other unfamiliar voice spoke. From the tone and the phrasing, Erryn guessed that the owner of the voice was a young man, perhaps similar in age to her. At twenty-one and a bit of a loner, she'd had little experience of men her own age, so it really was just an assumption. But something about the way the man spoke hinted at youth. It also hinted at something else however; it was refined, eloquent, maybe even noble – she disliked nobles.

From the few times she'd travelled into the city with her father, she'd found them to be generally disagreeable. She'd never come across one outside the city though, and certainly none had ever visited the village. Which begged the question, what was this one doing here now?

As she listened on she heard an answer, but it threw up a plethora of extra questions. She was still huddled beneath the open window, her mouth hanging open, when the door to the cottage was flung wide open, and a tall, well-built man dashed out past Erryn and a little way down the slope. He was oblivious to her fixed stare as he leant forwards with one hand steadying himself against the trunk of a huge oak tree and proceeded to retch so violently she feared he may turn himself inside out.

Realising she would have to move quickly to avoid being seen by the vomiting man, or the other two still inside the cottage, she attempted to steal away, still crouched, towards the rear of the building. It was a fool's errand, and Erryn certainly felt like a fool as her tender ankle gave way beneath her, sending her tumbling sideways. Down the slope she rolled, arriving as a pile of arms and legs just in front of the tall man.

Suddenly distracted from his second bout of vomiting by a series of pained moans and groans, Marcus turned his head in time to see a ball of green fabric and red hair plummeting towards him. He was about to jump sideways to avoid impact when the ball came to an abrupt halt by his feet.

A small smile tugged at one corner of his mouth as he took in the appearance of the dishevelled young woman, now untangling herself and attempting to look like her tumble had been intentional. Briefly forgetting his newly acquired burden of information, he extended a hand out to the woman, expecting her to use it to help herself stand. However, he winced and shot his hand back as it was met with a sharp slap. The humour suddenly gone from the situation his face once again drained of colour and he turned quickly back towards the tree, his heaving now dry and unproductive.

With her tunic re-adjusted but her pride still in disarray, Erryn raised her eyes to heaven as she watched the man return to the tree. However, it was not long before her judgement of his actions softened. She'd immediately regretted the slap; only reacting that way to deflect from her own embarrassment. Now, as her eyes travelled up and down the well-dressed figure, she began to feel an overwhelming sense of concern. If she'd heard the words imparted from the monotone man correctly, it was no wonder this fellow was having difficulty retaining the contents of his stomach. After all, it wasn't every day you're told you contain the soul of an ancient, home-sick warrior.

Marcus had had quite enough of being sick. As he wiped his mouth with the back of his hand, he resolved to stop letting everything affect him in such a physical way. True enough he'd had a lot to contend with in the last twenty-four hours, but he was a grown man; '*it's about time you start acting like one*'. He could hear his father's derision as clear in his mind as if he'd been stood right next to him. The man had been a bully and he felt no pain at his passing, but each time he thought of his father his guilt increased. And each time, he had to remember Julia to remind himself there'd been a reason for what he'd done.

However, for now, the memory of Lord Ryan hanging lifeless in his grasp paled in comparison to what he had been told by Sathom back in the cottage. Struggling with the concept of not being who he thought he was, Marcus felt the urge to laugh. This was madness. He was Marcus Ryan, eldest child of one of Whitestone's most prominent houses. He'd never even felt a flicker of anything else; no flashbacks, no memories he couldn't explain, nothing. Perhaps this Sathom was simply a madman. Yes, that would be it. He mentally chastised himself for being taken in by the whole bizarre scenario. He would march back in there right away, set Sathom and his taciturn friend straight. He didn't know where he'd go from there, but he was certain this madness needed to stop, immediately. Turning quickly to storm back to the waiting men in the cottage, he stumbled backwards as he found the young woman standing in front of him, her hand reaching out about to tap him on the shoulder.

Erryn's heart missed a beat, but she didn't let on. Instead she smiled up at the tall stranger, doing her best to appear friendlier than she had before. She had to crane her neck slightly to meet his gaze. She was only just 5'5" and quite petite, so she felt remarkably small beneath his tall, broad shadow. Now that she was closer to him, she could see that he was, as she'd guessed, most certainly noble. His tunic was made from the kind of fine-quality material she wouldn't have been allowed to touch, let alone wear. She wanted to see if his trousers and boots were made to similar standards, but that would mean overtly ogling the man. Still, as he finally stopped looking stern and his features softened, the smile from earlier returning to his lips, she noted that he was worthy of ogling.

"Erm, my lady, if you plan to stare at me for any length of time, might I know your name?" Marcus teased the young woman that was blocking his path, gaping at him. He was still intent on being angry and forthright but he couldn't help but smile as the diminutive redhead snapped her mouth shut and folded her arms across her chest, obviously trying to convince him, or herself, that she hadn't really been staring.

"I would know yours first, *sir*." Erryn attempted to regain control of the situation. She should have given him the cold-shoulder for mocking her, but her mind was still in a spin from being called 'my lady'.

"Of course. My name is…" The man paused as if he couldn't quite remember. "Well, just Marcus, I suppose." For a split second Erryn saw something flash across Marcus' eyes; a kind of lost look that made her almost believe he really didn't know his own name, and gave her an almost uncontrollable urge to hug him – which she made sure to resist.

Quickly replacing his baffled gaping with an overly-cheerful smile, he seemed to realise how vulnerable he'd appeared, and Erryn was too much of a considerate person to draw attention to his discomfort.

"It's a pleasure to meet you… *just* Marcus. I'm *just* Erryniya – though you can call me *just* Erryn."

For a short time his expression was one of complete incomprehension, until he suddenly erupted with laughter. It felt so long since he had really laughed. Not the nervous chuckles or stress-induced giggles of the last two days, but true, mirthful laughter. It seemed his glee was infectious, as Erryn was soon laughing too. Finally, when they were both out of breath and holding their sides, their eyes rested upon each other once more, the tension alleviated.

Erryn sat down on the grass, beckoning Marcus to join her. *He probably thinks I'm being friendly*, she mused to herself. In truth her ankle was rudely reminding her of its injury; if she didn't *sit* down, she would likely *fall* down. Not wishing him to leave just yet, as his story had intrigued her curious mind, her neck ached from craning up to look at the tall man. Asking him to join her on the ground made sense, all things considered.

Marcus took a place on the slope beside Erryn. Stretching his long legs out in front of him, he was suddenly very aware of her proximity. She smelled like no smell he'd ever experienced; soft, feminine, fresh. The scent, he realised, was coming from her hair. As it blew about, the fragrance wafted past his nose on the autumn breeze. As they sat together, the silence between them grew in weight, until both attempted to break it at the same time. Marcus, ever the gentleman, nodded for Erryn to go first, her bonny smile sending unexpected shivers across his skin.

"So, Marcus, it seems there's more to you than meets the eye?" Her question hung in the air like a bubble of water, about to burst over his head. He really didn't know how he was meant to answer. *Did she know about him*? *Had Sathom or Benedict already discussed this with her too*? He felt a twist of annoyance that he should be the last to know about his… predicament.

"I'm not sure what you mean," he bluffed, attempting to discover how much Erryn knew without giving too much away. He wasn't sure it should be a secret exactly; it felt more important that he didn't sound like a complete madman in front of the attractive woman sat beside him.

"It's alright. I was listening at the window. I heard, well, everything, I assume." Erryn looked sheepishly up at Marcus, a small, mischievous smile curving her lips.

"Everything? Are you sure? "

"Well, I think so. I heard about an ancient race being wiped out by evil men. I heard about magic, a terrible spell and I heard about you and your… other… self." Erryn watched Marcus start to shift his position, obviously uneasy at the reminder of 'monotone man's' revelations.

The silence descended upon them once more, only this time with a vengeance, the chill in the air now attributed to more than just the elements.

Erryn was about to attempt some kind of consolatory remark when Marcus cursed under his breath and quickly stood up, nearly crashing into her in the process. She'd have to make a mental note to give this new acquaintance of hers some distance when he was on the move in future. There was simply far too much of the man to have spatial awareness problems.

"What are you doing?" She asked, honestly concerned that, in the state he was in, he may do himself an injury.

"I'm doing what I should have done hours ago; thanking Sathom for his help and bidding him, and his friend, farewell." He turned in the direction of the cottage and was all set to storm ahead when Erryn caught hold of his arm and tugged him around to face her.

"Marcus, look, I don't know anything about this Sathom, but I know of Benedict and I believe the very fact he's allowed you into his home must be an indication of… something."

"Yes, that he's as mad as his friend!" Marcus spat, his features twisted into angry lines.

"Why must you assume it to be madness? You're from the city, aren't you? Isn't magic commonplace among nobility there? Surely, your mind can't be closed off to other possibilities?"

She was firing questions at Marcus and it was making his head hurt. He didn't have the answers, and it was all too confusing. Of course he knew of magic, all too well. It had governed his life as long as he could remember. It had also taken the one precious person in his life away from him, and that alone made him desire no contact with it or anything else even remotely connected; this was ignoring the supposition that he may be some kind of otherworldly, miserable, immortal warrior… of whom he had absolutely no knowledge.

He stared down at the earnest face of Erryn. He wanted to agree to anything she had to say simply to make her smile again. She had such a beautiful smile. But it was all too much. Delightful as she was, however much she'd heard, Erryn didn't know it all. What he'd lost, what he'd done – things just weren't that simple. He had more pressing matters on his mind, without concerning himself with discerning the validity of tall-tales.

Sensing his position on the horns of a dilemma, Erryn persisted.

"I'm simply suggesting you perhaps go back in there and listen. Ask questions if you feel the need, but don't write it all off as fantasy until you are in possession of all the information."

There was something about this woman, something that was able to reach inside him and pull strings he didn't even know were there. In moments, she'd made sense of a situation he'd dismissed as beyond belief, and that was before he'd even considered doing as she suggested. His resolve beginning to break up and lie in shattered pieces around his feet, his posture became free of the rods of a man on a mission and he visibly sagged; his shoulders slumping and head bending forwards. Thinking about all this once again brought the memory of Julia carving its way through his mind's eye. The pain of her loss, though previously pushed to the back of his mind, now returned to claim its pound of flesh.

"Are you alright?" Erryn asked, the concern, evident in her voice.

"No! I'm not *alright!*" Seeing red, Marcus answered with slightly more vitriol than he'd intended. Meeting her gaze, he saw the confusion in her eyes and though part of him wished he could take back his reaction and start again, a bigger part was seething at the woman's insertion into his life and assumption she knew better than he did.

Erryn didn't do defeat. She'd only just met Marcus, but already she'd decided to help him. For all his bluster, she could feel that he needed her. Never one to be easily put off something she'd set her mind on, she'd be damned if she was going to let a little tantrum steer her off course. As he turned away from her once more, she walked around him, positioning herself in front of him again – repeating the action each time he turned away, until he finally snapped.

"What do you want, Erryn? Haven't I entertained you enough? Leave me be!" Marcus' face was contorted with anger but, as Erryn looked up into his green eyes, she almost staggered backwards. There it was, the same far away soul that she'd seen only once before in her life. Grabbing hold of his arms, she leant in as close to him as she could, her own eyes diving deep into his, searching, pushing her way in behind the glassy veneer. It was as if those eyes led her into the darkest of tunnels, winding through time until finally a flickering light, no bigger than the point of a pin, shone like the dying glow of a distant star. Had she been as tactile with Benedict, she was almost certain she'd have found the same in his eyes. However, as her mind retreated back through the shadowy depths, she realised there was something there that she doubted would be present in the eyes of the elder man; a warmth that caressed the edges of the tunnel, licking at the sides like flames up the inner walls of a fireplace. Looking towards the light, she realised she couldn't have reached it if she'd tried. She wasn't sure why she hadn't seen when she'd travelled further in, but now it was clearly visible; there was a barrier just in front of the light. It was magic, she knew that much. Not her kind of magic though. Not hexan. It felt… older, more unnatural. She shuddered as she pulled away, the aura emanating from it repelling her mind until she could stay there no longer. She wasn't sure of what she'd discovered in there, but her sense for picking up on such things told her it was something desperate to remain undisturbed.

As she once again merged with the world outside of Marcus' inner-self, an indescribable feeling overwhelmed her. It was unlike anything she'd ever known and it warned her to back off. She wanted to help him, but whatever magic it was she'd encountered urged her to reconsider. If her mother had taught her anything, it was to heed her own advice where magic was concerned. If it felt like she should stay away, then she probably should.

Releasing her hold on Marcus' arms and stepping back a little, Erryn took in his perplexed face and spoke softly.

"I really think you should hear what they have to say." With that, she turned from him and started to hobble her way back down the slope.

Marcus was left standing alone again, bemused by the strange actions of the young woman. Nothing he'd experienced in this village had been anything less than confusing. Sathom, Benedict, the weird tale of other worlds, other races – and now Erryn with her pretty face, alluring smell, and peculiar behaviour.

"Come with me?" he called out, impulsively, ignoring the voice that suggested he let her leave.

Erryn stopped in her tracks. Everything wise and sensible within told her to keep walking away. Everything she was, in spite of wisdom and sense, brought her back to him. Smiling up at his handsome face, she took his hand in hers and led him inside the cottage.

Hours later and the sun was beginning to set. The wind from earlier had died down and the cloudless sky promised the autumn's first frost.

There had been much to talk about in Benedict's cottage and the tension had become palpable many times. Marcus had eventually accepted the things he'd been told, though it was still a lot to take in. Erryn's arrival had caused much consternation, but when Marcus insisted she stay if they wanted him to listen, Sathom had nodded and Benedict had grunted and the rest was explained in her presence. They seemed more at ease with her once she'd recounted what she'd overheard, and informed them of her own magical abilities. As a commoner, she was bound by the oppressive laws governing the use of magic throughout the kingdom; it was outlawed among anyone other than nobility. Any commoner found to be using magic was put to death without trial. She was both commoner and practitioner of the hexan school of magic. Marcus, who'd never heard of hexans, had queried why her magical ability didn't simply make her a mage, as he was, to which Erryn had snorted her disgust at the comparison. *Hexans didn't play with or distort the laws of nature as mages did*, she explained. The magic she and her kind harnessed was natural and directly linked to the environment around them. If a spell could only be cast by bending things to ones will, then it was the domain of mages, and beneath a skilled hexan. Though Marcus had no desire to use magic at all, he couldn't help but feel ashamed as Erryn spoke derisively about mages.

That brought to the fore the subject of his refusal to use his inherited skills. He'd then attempted to put into words the way the very thought of using magic made him feel. However, having difficulty understanding it himself, the words just seemed to come out in a jumbled mess, and he felt his cheeks flush as the three people in the room stared at him blankly. He'd all but given it up as a lost cause, when Sathom rescued him from his distress, explaining that his unease around magic was likely the result of an unconscious connection with his Meranell passenger. The way in which dark magic had been used to destroy the Meranells was bound to have left a stain on their souls.

Benedict had become increasingly tense during this part of the discussion. Out of the corner of her eye, Erryn had noticed him starting to grow agitated as Sathom and Marcus conversed. Suddenly, the pieces started to fall into place. She walked over to the old man and before he could protest, knelt down before him and looked him straight in the eyes. As she suspected, she was confronted with the same long dark tunnel as the one she'd seen inside Marcus. But, as she was also unsurprised to note, there was no warmth; Benedict's connection to his soul was icy cold. However, as Erryn delved deeper, expecting to feel repelled by a magical barrier, she realised there was no such guard in place. In fact, the light at the end of Benedict's tunnel appeared much closer. It also seemed to grate against the tunnel walls, like it didn't quite fit. A desperation flowed from it and she could feel real, physical pain as it became more and more restless the longer she stayed.

"Get out of my head!" Benedict shouted, shoving Erryn away from him with such force that Marcus had to dash to catch her before she fell against the stone hearth in front of his chair.

"What was that all about?" Marcus demanded from the elder man. Erryn nodded to Marcus that she was unhurt, before once more directing her attention to Benedict.

"There's something you've yet to tell us, isn't there, old man?"

Sathom started to intervene but Benedict waved him aside.

"It's fine, Sathom, they had to know sooner or later. Though enough of the 'old man', young lady," he said, looking sternly at Erryn. "This body is almost three centuries older than you, and my soul is old enough to be your father. Whichever way you look at it, I deserve respect as your elder."

Erryn bent her head, embarrassment at being scolded in front of the others clear from the colour now spreading across her face. Marcus on the other hand, was about as alert as he could've been, his eyes squinting as he tried to makes sense of the confrontation between Erryn and Benedict. It quickly dawned on him what they were talking about.

"You're like me, then? You're a… Meranell?" He could barely conceal his enthusiasm. Could this miserable old man really be kin of his? Now he didn't feel quite so burdened. The pressure of this newly discovered 'condition' could be shared with another. Maybe not the kind of person he could imagine bonding with over a round or two of cheap tavern ale, while regaling each other with tales of the 'good old days', but nevertheless, he was not alone in this.

"Let me tell you about just where the similarity between you and I ends, shall I boy? Let us take a little trip down memory lane. My real name is Larris, and you and I…"

"Benedict! You have said enough." For the first time since they'd met, Marcus heard Sathom raise his voice as he interrupted Benedict's acerbic speech. Benedict did as he was ordered, an apologetic expression sitting uncomfortably across his wrinkled face. The remorse was only directed at Sathom, however; turning back to Marcus, his now familiar grimace returned. *Perhaps that theory about not being alone was a little premature,* Marcus thought.

"I think we've discussed this enough for one evening," Sathom pronounced. "Marcus, I suggest you eat and then retire for the night. You will need plenty of rest before we put our plan into action."

"Our plan?" Marcus had offered to help, but he'd heard nothing of a plan up until now.

"We'll talk more tomorrow." There was obviously nothing else to be gleaned from him that night, so Marcus reluctantly agreed. Besides, at the mention of food, his stomach had started to grumble, and he could never ignore that.

After her encounter with Benedict, Erryn had kept quiet. For the first time in her life, she felt like an outsider, as the connection between the three men had become apparent. But she'd listened intently the whole time she was there, every morsel of information absorbed and stored for cogitation later. Now she was certain Marcus would need her. He obviously wasn't the most worldly of people and something of this magnitude would require a certain degree of lateral thinking. She hadn't seen much to convince her he knew how to think *inside* the box, let alone *outside* of it.

She also knew that the other two men were suspicious of her, even though they'd agreed to let her stay. She'd noticed Benedict watching her, a look on his face that showed he'd been trying to figure her out. She supposed she couldn't really blame them for their concern; she was wise enough to know that, should this information get into the wrong hands, there would be trouble for all of them. Clearly the pair had a course of action in mind, something they required Marcus to be involved in, but they needn't have worried about her allegiance. If only she'd had time to tell them of her past and her personal experience of the governors of Whitestone. There was more to it than bitterness that she'd had to hide her true self away for fear of prosecution, but that would have to wait for another day. It was almost dark, and she could picture her father pacing the floors of their small home, getting more and more frantic the longer she stayed out.

"I'd best be leaving," Erryn announced, before anyone else could suggest it. "It's late, and my father will be worried." At the mention of Haden, she remembered the stick that she had been supposed to deliver to Benedict. It was leant against the wall just inside the front door. She was reluctant to approach the stern looking old man again, but she had to do what she'd come here for in the first place. Taking hold of the piece of wood and carefully unravelling the cloth wrap, she swallowed her trepidation and presented the item to Benedict. "Here, my father asked that I deliver this to you today. I, er… forgot, what with all the excitement."

The old man took the stick and without acknowledgement thrust it in Sathom' direction, who duly stepped forwards and took it.

"Ah, it is here. Good, good. I can get to work on this immediately." Sathom seemed pleased as he ran his hands up and down the full length of the well-turned and smoothly-polished wood. "Thank you, Erryn. Please, take this. Your father has more than earned his payment for this piece." Erryn took the bag of coin Sathom handed to her and nearly dropped it as its unexpected weight hung heavy from her fingers. Looking inside, she gasped. There was at least twice as much as Haden had charged for the work.

"No offence, sir, but, he won't take this. My father's a proud man and, as much as I appreciate your generosity, well, he will assume it as charity." Erryn started to tip out a large amount of the coin in to her hand, ready to hand back to Sathom, but he stepped closer to her and gently closed her hand around the purse.

"Then you pass on the amount he expected and deposit the remainder somewhere safe." He looked down at her, his almost-black eyes betraying a kindness that the rest of his face seemed incapable of expressing. She gazed up at the curiously mannered man and, for a moment, considered trying to read his soul, but something told her not to. Somehow it didn't seem right to intrude and for once, she resisted her own nature, nodding her thanks and turning towards the door to take her leave.

Marcus, who had been watching the exchange from a chair at the table, jumped from his seat and strode to the door ahead of Erryn. Pulling it open, a huge, self-satisfied grin spread across his face. Erryn just looked up at him, her auburn curls tumbling onto her shoulders as her head tilted back.

"I'm quite capable of opening a door, you know."

Marcus' smile was cut off in its pride, his shoulders dropped. At the sight of his dejected expression, Erryn inwardly chastised herself for once again reacting to the man in such a way. *Damn his noble manners!* She grumbled in her head. She simply couldn't get past her dislike of their presence, however much she found herself warming to him otherwise. Wanting to make amends, she smiled at him, and that seemed sufficient to return his features to their more handsome lines.

"Will you… come back?" he asked, his tone verging on pleading.

"Yes, Marcus. I believe I will." She smiled at him and, for a brief moment, their eyes locked, before she quickly looked away. "I'm not sure I have a choice. Benedict would likely hunt me down, after all I've been privy to this evening."

Benedict's grunting from his position by the fire indicated that he'd heard, though as that was intentional, Erryn simply chuckled. That was the second time Marcus had heard her laugh and it was fast becoming a sound he liked. An urge to take one of her small hands in his and bend low to kiss it almost overwhelmed him, but he was quickly learning she didn't take kindly to noble gestures. He forced the urge back whence it came and simply bade her farewell as she left, watching her hobble her way down the slope and along the winding path, until she was eventually out of sight.

"You're quite taken with her, aren't you, boy?" Benedict's gruff voice dragged him from his reverie. Closing the front door, he turned to flash a warning look at Benedict before heading towards the huge pot of stew that had been all the while simmering nicely over the fire. Bowls and spoons were already stacked on the hearth and Marcus was about to grasp the huge ladle resting at the edge of the pot when a sudden, puzzling thought threatened to upset the ordered information in his head. Directing his attention to Sathom, who was now sat at the table, still admiring the stick, he cocked his head to one side and vocalised his thoughts.

"How do you know all of this?"

Sathom raised his head to meet Marcus' scrutiny and replied, without hesitation.

"Few remain from that time. You and – as you are now aware – Benedict are the only souls not confined within the walls of the sanctum. Remember I spoke of the elementals. With great power at their disposal, they presented a grave threat to the plans of the governors and, as such, became the victims of a part of the spell reserved only for them. As the dark magic grew stronger, the tower channelling the force of the seventh mage's power, the portal was opened. With the first bolts of magical energy, the elementals were grasped by mighty, mystical hands and pushed through to the other side, back into Meran, the portal closing permanently behind them. At the casting of this spell, all of them were banished from Gadrionis. All, but one."

With that, Sathom hung his head.

"So you are that *one*, I presume," he asked rhetorically. Sathom nodded and, without speaking further, got up from his chair and left the room via the front door. For the first time in his life, Marcus ignored the aroma of food and went to bed still hungry. Sleep took him only when the last vestiges of mental turmoil had worn themselves out, but the disquiet persisted in his dreams. It was a long night.

CHAPTER SIX

Alone by the fire, his stomach now full, Benedict Cane absorbed the silence as if it had been absent far too long. As the heat radiated towards him, his skin welcomed its effects, but inside he still felt cold. The nights were chill now, that was true, but the old man knew the frost he felt came from no external source. He had very nearly jeopardised everything he and Sathom had worked towards this night, his bitterness leading him astray. He didn't let guilt take him down its treacherous path, however. Bitterness was his right, his domain, and if Sathom hadn't stopped him from reacquainting Marcus with their shared past, then perhaps the young up-start wouldn't seem quite so annoying to him any longer. Smirking to himself at the thought, Benedict lifted his feet to rest upon the nearby footstool and leant back in his rocking chair. It was damned uncomfortable, and if Sathom didn't return soon, Marcus may very well find himself relieved of his bed.

"My bed," he grumbled aloud, tugging a worn looking blanket tighter around his shoulders.

No sooner had he closed his eyes than the door to the cottage swung open and Sathom made a hasty entrance, a large cloth-wrapped object held close to his chest.

"I still don't know why you bother with doors when you can walk through walls," Benedict remarked without even opening his eyes.

"Because, my friend, it would not do to have one of your neighbours witness such an event, now would it?"

"Most of the villagers would assume they'd overdone it on the ale and think nothing of it."

"Yes, well that is not a risk we can afford to take." Sathom finished locking the door for the night and walked to the table, carefully placing the covered lump on the surface.

Benedict opened his eyes and turned his head to face his companion. He was about to consider apologising for his earlier outburst, but was struck dumb as Sathom unwrapped the item he'd been carrying, the cloth peeling away to reveal a large, perfectly formed crystal. As the last of the covering dropped from it, the cottage became visibly brighter as a white light pulsated from its core. As if it sensed that it was now exposed, the light from the crystal quickly dimmed, until barely a flicker could be seen.

"Is that what I think it is?" Benedict's voice bore a hint of awe.

"The Nexephia Crystal… yes, it is."

"But where – I mean – *how*? No one has laid eyes on it in centuries. Most had even begun to doubt its existence."

"And I am grateful for that. It may not have been as simple to retrieve had it been widely sought."

Sathom began to examine the now unimpressive-looking crystal, caressing its smooth, multifaceted surface, seemingly attempting to elicit a response. Yet, the inner layers remained passive, a dense mist filling the void left by the light. Finally abandoning his efforts, Sathom stepped back from the table, silently staring at the crystal.

"It's broken then?" Benedict asked nonchalantly.

"No. Not broken. I am unsure as to the cause of its inactivity. I will ponder on it more tomorrow." Sathom carefully replaced the cloth and, picking up one of the chairs by the table, joined Benedict by the fire.

"How fares our young friend?"

"I've heard nothing from him – not since I dragged him outside and left him snoring behind the woodshed." Benedict gave a sly grin, only prevented from laughing aloud at the mental image by Sathom's emotionless stare. "Well, tell me again why I have to give up my bed for him anyway?" he persisted. "I'm nearly three-hundred years old, you know. He's young and fit. Is he really that incapable of becoming closely acquainted with the floor for a few weeks?"

"Benedict, we have discussed this; it is only until he becomes comfortable with the situation he now finds himself in. He is not like you, he has not had to experience physical hardships, not until now. And with what he has been through in the last two days… can we really afford to have him crumble and be rendered useless from lack of a rested night?" Sathom's question was rhetorical, but Benedict still huffed in response, shifting his body to face away from his friend, signalling the end of the conversation by closing his eyes once more.

Sathom, unmoved by the old man's grumbling, closed his eyes too. Though, as an elemental, he didn't need to sleep, he felt an intense compulsion to shut out the world for a few hours. He had endured the last thousand years – and would continue to endure a thousand more if that's what it took to free those he counted as friends – but his shackled emotions were beginning to fray around the edges, and it was as if he could feel them trying to claw their way up from the pit he'd confined them to. Opening his eyes briefly to look at Benedict, who was already snoring loudly, Sathom wished that his kind could simply shut down for a few hours in a day.

For now, an enforced ocular darkness would have to suffice. He closed his eyes and leant back into the hard wooden chair, mimicking his companion.

Marcus cupped the bare shoulder of the attractive, golden haired girl that was fumbling with the chords on his tunic with one hand, while simultaneously attempting to lift it higher to expose his chest with the other. He bent down to kiss her heavily-rouged lips but flinched as she turned her face away, a strand of her hair whipping him across the eyes.

"You know, this would be so much easier if you used magic, Marcus." A barely concealed accusation present in her voice.

Not for the first time, he inwardly cursed at the mere mention of the word. Nevertheless, he was aroused, and the girl's intoxicating perfume quickly drew him from any thoughts other than his own desires. Pressing himself closer to her, moving one of his strong arms around her slender, corseted waist, he attempted the kiss again. Again, she moved away, only this time her blue eyes fizzled with irritation. The passion now all-consuming, he had no choice but to ignore the look and, resolving not to try kissing her again, he began his own fumble with the chords of her bodice. After several agonising moments of failing to remove even the top layer of the many draped expertly around the girl's enticing frame, he started to feel her body tense up beneath his touch and realised, with disappointment, it was all over.

Reluctantly moving his gaze from her chest back up to her piercing blue eyes he saw the familiar look of condemnation he knew all too well. The moment was gone, and in its place was a tense atmosphere. Marcus stepped back from the girl, his head bent down. Then, he looked up at her sheepishly from beneath his floppy brown hair. He was prepared for the tongue-lashing he was about to get; a torrent of derisive remarks about his unwillingness to use magic would not have been new to his ears. However, as a scornful smile began to twist at the corners of the girl's well-defined lips, his expression gave away his confusion.

He was still trying to figure things out when he suddenly found himself standing in the middle of the plaza. The fact the girl had used magic to transport him was confusing enough, but, as his senses started to recover from the effects of the spell, he could feel a chill across the surface of his skin… all of it.

Looking down he saw what he already knew – he was completely naked. To make matters worse, a crowd was gathering around him.

Quickly covering his modesty with both hands, Marcus managed to paste a thin smile on his lips, all the while feeling the heat rising up his neck and filling his cheeks. As the crowd began pointing and laughing, Marcus wished for the first time that he had chosen to learn magic as every other noble child did. If he had the ability, he'd have been far away by now.

The laughter grew louder and louder, the pointing fingers seemed to extend out on unnaturally long limbs until they were wagging mere inches from his nose. He wanted to run, to hide, but he remained firmly rooted to the spot, the cacophony becoming so loud that he couldn't even hear his own thoughts anymore. The faces in the crowd were now large and deformed, twisting in closer until they merged into one, the end result a mutated replica of so many faces he knew, but not one he could distinguish.

As the awful sound reverberated around his mind until he could take it no longer, he finally managed to turn and run, not caring for his exposed posterior but simply desperate to escape the din and the ridicule. With one final burst of energy, he made a dash for the nearest building, but came crashing down to the hard white stone as one foot tripped up the other. The laughter closed in around him, clawing at his senses until he would have rather died than take any more. With all hope of escape lost he closed his eyes and begged for an end until his world went black and the noise stopped with a jolt.

When Marcus woke, up he was dripping with sweat and he could hear his heartbeat pounding in his head. Sitting bolt upright, his breathing fast and shallow, he began to remember where he was and what had happened in the last two days. Unsure if reality was any better than the nightmare, he looked down, relieved to see he was wearing something, and laughed as his mind performed its usual trick of putting a positive slant on things. '*Not naked and not eighteen anymore. Thank goodness for small mercies*', he thought.

Casting his eyes about the room, he saw a small, jagged looking-glass wedged between the door frame and the wall. Marcus rose from the edge of the bed and wandered over to it. It was mottled with age but still captured a reflection adequately enough. He'd slept in just his small-clothes and, as his bare chest appeared in the glass, he sighed at the scattering of hair. He wondered if that had been the real reason the girl, and others like her, had spurned him in the past. Vaharian men weren't generally that hairy. Running his hand over his taught, muscle-rippled skin he considered shaving – then remembered the nicks he caused just shaving his face, and thought better of it. For a moment, he considered Erryn, and tried to decide if she preferred hairy men, but he quickly pushed the query from his mind. He had no room up there for such fanciful thoughts, especially when, with all likelihood, he would be rejected again anyway.

Well, he thought, *time to meet with Sathom and Benedict and find out exactly how we're going to put things right.* Presumably, it would involve returning to the city to expose the governors' monstrous crime – somehow. He didn't relish that idea. He wasn't even sure if he'd get a chance to open his mouth before an arrow was planted between his eyes. But he had to try; he owed it to his people. *His people.* That sounded so strange in his head. He'd taken a lot of what the elemental had told him on faith, for the thought of not being who he thought he was, of actually belonging to another race, another time… it was bizarre, to say the least. He didn't feel like anyone else, now he knew. Nothing had stirred in him at the mention of this ancient soul his body housed, other than the urge to be sick. Yet, something about Sathom oozed sincerity. He couldn't put his finger on why he believed him, he just did. Erryn had seemed to accept it all without question. He'd watched her from the corner of his eye throughout the tale. There was a confidence in her that reassured him and he'd found himself hoping against hope that she would stick around for whatever was to come. Her ease with the situation was almost tangible; like a big, soft blanket he could surround himself with as he walked into the belly of the beast. How he hoped his head was in control, and not somewhere lower down.

Erryn had arrived at Benedict's early. Finishing her morning hunt, she'd been in a good mood as, despite the tenderness still present in her ankle, she'd managed to catch enough small rabbits to heartily fill the stewing pot that night. A flicker of eagerness to see Marcus again had danced, briefly, through her mind – but she'd challenged it, tripped it up and locked it away in a cupboard before it started to get too enthusiastic. That was until he entered the main room while she and Sathom were discussing magical theory. She obviously wasn't as engrossed in the conversation as she thought as the sight of his broad, naked torso nearly caused her to choke on a mouthful of herbal tea. Noting her presence, he quickly apologised, muttering something about 'disrespecting the company of a lady', before pulling on the tunic that he'd had slung over his shoulder. Erryn had not intended to look but her eyes were compelled in that moment to trace the outline of his figure. Wearing just his trousers and boots, she could see he was well-toned, physically fit. Had he been anyone other than a Whitestone noble, she would have assumed he was some sort of hunter, lean and muscular to enable him to move stealthily through a forest on the trail of swift-moving prey. His shoulders were the broadest part of him, the rest of his torso tapering down to narrow hips, strong thighs and long calves evident beneath the supple, black leather of his well-made boots.

For the rest of the time they were in the room together, both Erryn and Marcus avoided eye contact, devoting far more attention than was necessary to Sathom, who seemed oblivious to it. Without further explanation, he led the discussion directly onto the reason they had convened – the plan.

When the elemental had finished speaking, even Erryn's mouth was hanging open. Marcus too was frozen in open-mouthed astonishment.

Firstly, it seemed his earlier assumptions had been way off the mark. He'd merely been concerned about how he'd get back into the city as a wanted murderer; now it was quite clear that was the least of his problems. The actual course of action proposed was beyond anything he'd ever have dreamt of doing three days ago.

Sathom, with the occasional grunt of agreement from Benedict, had outlined the plan as if he'd been directing someone to take a sip of water from a fountain right in front of them. The governors, it seemed, would pay for what they'd done – that much was certain – but apparently more could be achieved than simple retribution.

The goal, as far as Sathom and Benedict were concerned, was to actually release the imprisoned souls. It would mean leaving Vaharia and travelling south-east over a hundred miles, across kingdoms and terrain no Vaharian had traversed in living memory. The sting in that particular tale was that it would also mean entering the caves beneath the Dragon Crest Mountains. Little was known of the caves, save for the fact that it meant certain death to even step foot inside – or so the legends told. Stories of those that had been foolish enough to do so had become the stuff of nightmares, told in the dark by children playing with fear. What actually lurked within, what dangers lay in wait... such knowledge was not possessed. What was certain, in Sathom's opinion, was that Marcus had to venture into that place and make it out alive, as the tower holding the souls of the Meranells was located at the outer reaches of the charted lands, the Dragon Crest Mountains standing between him and his destination, with no way around.

As this information was conveyed to him, he thought he caught a compassionate look in Benedict's eyes, but he dismissed the notion as ridiculous – much as he had begun to consider doing with this foolhardy quest. He'd protested; he'd asked if there could possibly be another way. He'd even suggested Benedict would be far more suited to the task, but his request to know why it had to be him was met with a response that filled him with even more dread than the venture into the unknown and the dangerous. This was the second of the revelations that rendered Marcus speechless.

Apparently, only someone with magic in their blood would have the ability to break the seal on the sanctum – and it had to be a mage. Sathom had then stared at him pointedly and elaborated, in case Marcus hadn't quite understood, that it would take a person able to *use* magic, so now… he would have to learn.

The conversation had been more than a little one-sided after that. Marcus' face had become drained of colour and he didn't even respond when Benedict made a quip about him 'not being sick' again.

So it had come to this. He'd just discovered why it might be that he'd spent his entire life avoiding magic – that part at least, had even started to make sense – and now he had to go against everything that felt right and take up the power he was born with. Was that even possible? The mages of Whitestone were tutored from the age of six, and Marcus was about twenty years late for his first lesson. Just how was he ever going to learn enough to embark on such an important and dangerous mission?

"And who is going to teach me?" He startled everyone in the room with his first utterance in some time. For what seemed like the longest moment, the question hung in the air, Marcus and Erryn both looking expectantly at Sathom. Finally, Benedict spoke, so quietly as to be barely audible, even in the uncomfortable silence.

"That would be me."

Erryn couldn't help but laugh and Marcus cocked his head to one side and looked perplexed but Benedict simply snarled and turned away from them both.

"Excuse my incredulity but, and no offence is meant in this, you aren't exactly… qualified, Benedict." Erryn found it difficult to contain her amusement as she directed her remark at the crotchety old man, who was now doing his best to ignore everyone in the room. Sathom spoke out in his defence.

"Benedict has spent nearly a century researching the theory behind the ability that mages possess. I assure you, there is nothing he does not know of magic."

"Except how to use it!" Erryn's humour was suddenly conspicuous by its absence, a wrinkled nose and contemptuous scowl replacing the laughter lines of seconds ago. "If dusty old books and ancient manuscripts held the aptitude required to cast spells effectively then that would be all well and good, but they don't. You cannot 'read' magic Sathom; it is something you have to feel. You have to live it, breathe it. It's as much a part of the hexan… or the mage... as their own beating heart!"

Marcus looked on in awe. The girl he was having difficulty getting out of his head spoke with such passion, he almost felt a surge of pride at being a mage. Ironically, just a day ago, she'd succeeded in making him feel ashamed of his magical disposition. Something told him he was in for a bumpy ride in Erryn's company.

Returning his thoughts to the matter at hand, he listened intently as Sathom presented the details of how things would progress, from that day until such time he was deemed ready to leave the kingdom. Concerns that occasion may never arrive were instantly quashed by the pronouncement of a time limit.

For any ordinary mage to be able to have a hope of breaking the governors' seal, the attempt would need to be made when the spell was at its weakest. According to Sathom, that state only occurred every two-hundred-and-fifty years, when the governors returned to the tower to recharge their immortality. At that point, just before they began their ritual, the dark magic would be significantly easier to overcome. The next quarter-of-a-century confluence would be happening very soon.

"I have waited a thousand years to get this right, Marcus. We cannot miss our chance this time," Sathom had said, so caught up in his own determination he missed the burden of pressure taking its toll.

When all talk of training and dangerous journeys had been exhausted for the day, the thoughts of what was to come weighing heavy on the shoulders of everyone, Sathom walked over to a tall, fabric-covered object that had all the while been leaning unnoticed against the wall in the shadows at a corner of the room. For a moment, he stood in front of it, motionless, before picking it up with both hands, holding it with delicate fingers as if it might turn to dust at the slightest clench.

"Unfortunately, I cannot assist you on this quest in the way I would have once been able Marcus; the powers at my command are no longer… available to me. However, I have one thing I can offer you, one thing that, once you've mastered the magic within, I am certain will prove its worth."

Turning to face Marcus, Sathom walked over to where he sat and held the item aloft in front of him. Still lightly grasping it with one hand, he swiftly removed the cloth with the other. Erryn gasped as the stick her father had crafted came into view, though now it looked anything but a simple stick. One end was finished with a decoratively turned finial, expertly carved to form a tapered point. It was clearly Haden's work but Erryn wondered why she hadn't noticed it before. As her eyes followed the line of the dark, shiny wood, she was almost hypnotically drawn to look at the end that was uppermost – as was

Marcus, who was already transfixed by the large, clouded crystal resting proudly atop a gleaming, golden orb.

Both of them may have paused to consider the purpose of the golden spikes that jutted out evenly around the base of the orb, had they not been mesmerised by the crystal. As Sathom thrust the item further towards Marcus, he realised what it was. He had seen many magical staves throughout his life among mages, though none quite as impressive as the one that was being offered to him. Unsure as to whether he was impressed with the staff for its beauty or the magic that he could feel pulsating from it, he quickly dismissed the idea that anything connected with magic would incite such a reaction in him and ran his fingertips across the surface of the crystal. The moment his fingers touched the surprisingly cold object, the whole thing burst into life. It began to softly vibrate, causing an almost inaudible hum while the mistiness dissipated and the crystal cleared enough to see tiny lightning bolts radiating from its core to meet each surface. The crystal's glow much brighter than the last time it had been uncovered, everyone's astonished faces were illuminated with pure white light. Marcus had pulled his hand back as soon as the first lightning bolt had extended out towards it. However, within seconds of it being deprived of his touch, the crystal gradually became inactive once more.

"Touch it again!" Erryn urged, barely containing her excitement. Marcus glanced up at Sathom, who nodded. Standing up, he tentatively reached out to take the staff by the shaft. Once in his hands, the wood started to vibrate. No one could see it, but Marcus could feel ripples moving continuously up past his hands and towards the top. The crystal took on a life of its own; at its core, a mini-lightning storm churned and spiralled wildly, static bouncing off the sides before vanishing into the abundance of white light.

"I believe it reacts only to you, Marcus," Sathom surmised, stepping backwards and dropping his hands to his sides.

As the staff pulsated with magical energy, Marcus could not ignore the slight thrill he felt as the power coursed through him, into the staff, and back again. It was a heady feeling that made his legs feel unstable beneath him. Something must have hinted at his imminent loss of balance as Sathom, who had been watching him the whole time, was at his side in a heartbeat. He was surprisingly sturdy for a partially non-corporeal being, as he caught hold of Marcus by the shoulders and supported his weight with ease. Allowing the Elemental to guide him back to his chair, for the briefest of moments he felt a distinct sense of familiarity and… friendship. In that split second, it was as if he'd known Sathom all his life. This was beginning to be too much to take in, what with his head still spinning and strange feelings that he couldn't associate with anything he knew, or remembered knowing.

He let out a manic laugh as he passed the staff to Erryn, who in turn leant it against the wall. Benedict grunted and mumbled something about 'being glad he was coming around to things so easily', before storming off outside, slamming the door shut behind him.

With just the three of them left in the room and Marcus' head slowly returning to normal, the hysteria passed and the seriousness of the situation seemed to cloud over his green eyes, his mouth turning down at the corners. For a couple of minutes they all sat in silence while he bent his head, covering his face with his hands. Erryn fidgeted and played with her hair. Sathom simply stared, until the pregnant pause was ended by a determined-sounding Marcus.

"So, tell me, Sathom. Exactly what do I have to do?"

After producing a crudely drawn map and laying it out on the table, Sathom replied.

"As you know, the souls of your kin, the Meranells, are being held prisoner within the tower located at the southernmost boundary of the mapped lands."

Marcus and Erryn leant on the table and studied the drawing, watching as Sathom pointed out the relevant detail.

"I have named the tower The Sanctum of Souls purely for my benefit; it comforts me to think of my friends within a sanctuary, rather than the hell I know them to be suffering. What name you come to know it by is of your choosing, but one thing is beyond question; the souls *must* be freed and you *must* be the one to free them. I shall accompany you, as only an elemental can grant the souls their pass back to Meran."

Marcus inwardly breathed a sigh of relief at the fact someone would be with him throughout this madness. However, something required clarification.

"I thought you said the portal was permanently closed. How are the souls going to be able to return?"

"Once the seal has been broken and the souls released, everything the governors did will come undone. Secronius will return to his original form and the portal will be passable."

"What about the governors? What will happen to them?" Erryn asked, looking up at Sathom.

"They will die – quite horribly, I imagine."

Marcus and Erryn glanced at each other, then back at the map.

"Make no mistake, Marcus, this will not be a simple task. We will face many dangers along the way. Some, I have knowledge of; others, I undoubtedly do not. But know this – you are as much my friend as those we seek to save. I will make certain you are ready before we leave and I *will* remain at your side for as long as you need me, no matter the foe, no matter the end."

Erryn stood straight and folded her arms across her chest.

"And I'm coming with you, too."

Both men turned to look at Erryn, her face exuding sheer, stubborn will. Sathom made to protest, but Marcus held up his hand to stop him. He hadn't known her long, but he'd already gathered she'd not be easily dissuaded from things she set her mind on, and though a part of him knew he should try to convince her of the folly in such a venture, a bigger part welcomed the thought of her company. Not only was she another of magical persuasion, which would obviously be useful, but she appeared to have a beneficial effect on him. Somehow, she made him feel stronger, and he was in no doubt he would need that strength for whatever lay ahead.

Smiling at her and nodding his head, Marcus turned back to Sathom, searching his eyes for some kind of emotion, yet there was still none to be found. He resolved to discover why as soon as possible, though for now that would have to wait.

Glancing at the staff before straightening his shoulders and sucking in his stomach, he looked directly into Sathom's eyes.

"Let's do this!"

CHAPTER SEVEN

The next two months of Marcus' life were about as far away from anything he could've previously imagined as he could get. The days were long and filled with magical tutelage. Once he would have slept until noon, spent the day avoiding magic as much as possible, then been tucked up in his comfortable four-poster bed by nightfall. Now, he was getting used to watching the sun rise and would only sleep when his energy for spell-casting was spent and his body would carry him no further. In the small hours, when his eyes were barely able to stay open, he would stumble to a makeshift bed at Benedict's hearth, out for the count the second he rested his head. He'd insisted, from the night he'd spoken with Sathom about the quest, that Benedict be reunited with his own bed; with no complaint from the old man, of course. He might have regretted that decision had his body not ached for sleep so much at the end of every day. Benedict's bed was far from comfortable, but the cold stone of the cottage floor was not softened much by the folded blankets upon which he lay. Yet Benedict couldn't help but notice that his young student never once complained, nor appeared to hold any resentment against him, even though he'd more often than not given him cause. As he spent the days attempting to school him in the art of using magic, a reluctant friendship grew. They'd clearly known each other in their past lives, but Marcus' attempts to discover the connection bore no fruit. He'd guessed there was some kind of history between them from the old man's seemingly-unfounded dislike of him. It made sense once he knew of Benedict's true origin, and he was astute enough to figure out their shared history may not have been amicable, but, beyond that, he remained unaware. Marcus had finally ceased prodding Benedict for answers when Sathom had reminded him there were more important issues at stake, urging him to concentrate his mind on learning.

However, it didn't seem to matter how much he focused. After three weeks of training with Benedict, Marcus could cast no more than a weak fire spell; the tiny flame that he managed to bring to life at his fingertips fizzling out pathetically within moments, without a breeze in the air. Despite his determination and Benedict's frustrated chastisement, Marcus didn't appear to have it in him to make up for all those lost years. Nevertheless, much to his tutor's quiet admiration, he persevered, even though failure seemed inevitable.

This continued until one day, during one of her daily visits to the cottage, Erryn finally intervened. She'd watched from the side-lines since the beginning, screwing her face up at Benedict's methods and willing Marcus' efforts to amount to something, but she said nothing. Even as she'd seen Marcus' enthusiasm start to wane, still she'd said nothing. Finally, when, like a child, he'd grown excited as a flame had remained active for longer than usual, she could take it no longer, her heart reaching out to him as the disappointment etched its way across his face when the flame went out. Joining the two men in the secluded clearing tucked away behind the cottage, Erryn had respectfully suggested she be allowed to give it a try. Benedict hadn't needed any convincing and had seated himself beneath an oak tree to watch. He gave a wry smile as he observed the way Marcus' face lit up every time she touched his arm, how intense his gaze became as he listened to her speak. *If he learns anything now, it won't be down to better teaching,* he thought, chuckling to himself.

For obvious reasons, Marcus was more attentive towards Erryn, but there was more to it than mere attraction. Her manner when she spoke of magic was inspiring. It would have been hard for even the most indifferent person not to find her passion infectious. When he became despondent at the dissipation of yet another magical effect before it had a chance to thrive, she'd taken his a hand in hers and, stepping towards him, placed it against his chest above his heart. Looking into his eyes she'd urged him to search within himself, to try to listen for the magical hum that emanated from the blood coursing through his veins, to visualise its power as it surged beneath his skin. "Close your eyes," she whispered as she leant in closer. "*Feel* the magic."

Though he still struggled, the craft came a little easier after that. He had to try a lot harder than anyone else, but once he'd been shown how, he could indeed feel the way the magic travelled around his body. Once he knew what to look for, he wondered how he'd ever been unaware of its presence.

During his time learning from Erryn, Marcus attained more knowledge than he believed any tutor in the city could impart. Her magic came from the same place, but the principal was entirely different. Where mages used their minds to control magic, hexans used their hearts. "*A mage thinks too much.*" Erryn told him. "*A hexan's magic becomes second nature – like breathing.*" She taught him to channel the power, to open himself up to the possibilities within his reach. With her guidance, he came to realise - if he could imagine it, he could cast it, so long as he didn't *think* too hard.

But he still had a long way to go. He understood the theory, and he was achieving far more than when he was training with Benedict, yet where he needed to be seemed to always remain just beyond reach. If it weren't for Erryn's patience, he might even have thrown himself at the mercy of the city guard.

All the while Erryn watched him with her heart and mind divided. She delighted in seeing him try to learn, yet her own beliefs regarding mage magic caused her to go home each night with a weight on her shoulders. The memory of her mother, the only other hexan she'd ever known, tore at her dreams. Each morning she awoke feeling she'd betrayed her and everything she held close. It was mages that had taken her mother away from her at such a young age, and there she was helping another mage to reach his full potential.

She tried to reassure herself with the knowledge she was using hexan principals – but those principals were being used to teach a mage things no hexan would consider doing. It was all so confusing. Her mind told her to stay away from Marcus, but, in her heart she knew it was already too late for that.

With the days becoming weeks, Marcus's enthusiasm for learning grew, even if he'd reached a plateau as far as magic was concerned. Sometimes he even seemed to be going backwards, messing up spells he'd gotten right before. Now he could cast the magic, but a more advanced level of control eluded him.

Still, a firm friendship had grown between him and Erryn, despite the little voice that urged her to keep her distance. What he lacked in competence as a student, he made up for in making her laugh. Some days, they would spend more time giggling over some error he'd made than trying to make sure he didn't do it again.

As the sun went down on another long day of magic casting, teacher and pupil dropped to the floor in hysterics. Yet another of his attempts to magically move a rotten log had just ended badly. With anyone else, the mage would have allowed frustration to get the better of him. However, at Erryn's side, he felt anything was possible, no matter how much the techniques eluded him.

"You do know I'm useless at this? No amount of practice is ever going to make an ounce of difference," Marcus said, plucking a piece of bark from Erryn's hair as she lay on her back, looking at him sideways.

"It's true, you are just about the most hopeless mage I've ever met – but then, I've met very few, and I do believe all mages lack the hexan talent, anyway."

"Hey! Watch what you say about my fellow… no, say what you like. I can't stand any of them."

They laughed again, all anxiety about the forthcoming trip far from their minds. Before either of them knew it was happening, their gazes were locked and it was as if everything around them had ceased to be. Marcus shifted himself onto his side leaning up on one arm, head resting against his hand. He used his free hand to brush a stray hair from Erryn's lips, his finger lingering a little too long in the process. Her eyes flickered shut momentarily and her breath caught in her throat, a shiver passing swiftly down her entire body. Somehow, the air felt warmer despite the season, and an almost palpable sense of something-about-to-happen filled the space between them. Marcus slowly leant forwards, Erryn making no move to stop him, and, for the briefest of moments, a kiss felt inevitable.

"There you two are. Can't say I've seen that 'spell' before." The familiar voice of Benedict broke the moment.

The kiss interrupted, the pair jumped up, looking and feeling awkward.

Things between them could have been very different after that. However, both were too intent on making sure Marcus was competent enough to survive the journey and free the souls. Putting the moment to the back of their minds, they trained even harder.

After the third week of practice with his new tutor, Sathom suggested that Marcus may be ready to take up his staff. Hands were all well and good for minor spells, but real magic, the kind he would need to master before they embarked on their quest, could only come from channelling the magical energies through a conduit.

Marcus had visibly recoiled at the idea. The last time he'd touched the staff, he'd very nearly passed out. *Sathom* may have had faith he was ready to use it, but *he* certainly didn't, so he resisted – for one more week. The next time, the suggestion came more forcefully, Sathom's dark eyes boring into him until he yielded to the pressure. Cautiously taking the staff in both hands, Marcus stared in awe as the crystal sprang into action. Like a dog that had missed its master, the lights within whizzed around excitedly, bouncing from every internal surface until the mage feared they might actually crack the sides and break free. But this time, though the meeting of his skin upon the wood had roused the crystal, the effect on him was more tolerable. He could definitely sense the connection, but now he recognised the gentle hum. As the magic found its path between mage and staff, he could feel the power looping back and forth, an eternal flow of energy that he knew would only pause each time he put it down.

For the next week, Sathom watched with repressed satisfaction as Marcus and the Nexephia Crystal bonded. The light from fire, ice, and lightning spells bounced around the woodland behind Benedict's cottage, mimicking the young mage's new-found eagerness. Sathom kept a watchful eye, calling for an abrupt end to lessons should anyone approach a little too close. There was a limit to how much Marcus could practice his skills, thanks to magic being outlawed beyond the walls of the city. Should the governors discover someone was using magic in the village and send guards to investigate, their mission could be jeopardised.

When winter began to bite down hard on the village and the eerie, muted stillness that heralded the first snowfall of the season hung low in the air, Marcus was as ready as he'd ever be. Both Erryn and Sathom agreed there was little more he could learn in the time remaining. The journey was set for two weeks ahead and there was still much to prepare before they left.

Sathom spent most days diligently gathering supplies and hovering over his map, seemingly lost in thought, then gone for hours at a time; Marcus saw very little of him. He had offered to shoulder some of the burden more than once, but each time his offer had been politely, yet firmly, refused. There was still no deeper insight into his odd ways and Marcus had tired of attempting to dig deeper. Even Benedict remained tight-lipped, so he decided it best just to assume this was normal behaviour for an elemental – he'd never met another, after all.

Erryn came to the cottage less often once the training subsided, much to Marcus' disappointment. She'd said she needed to spend more time with her father, and it was obvious she felt guilty for having neglected him for so long. But Marcus knew she felt the same anxiety he did; the mission they were about to embark on promised no guarantee of their return. He missed her company, but he understood. However, still in the habit of waking early, he would often wander outside and sit on the slope in front of the cottage as the sun came up. His vantage point allowed him a view of the whole village, including Haden's humble dwelling, and he would wait until he caught site of Erryn returning from her morning hunt. That would set him up for the day ahead.

One particularly cold morning, he sat in his usual spot, waiting, oblivious to the biting wind against his exposed skin. His gaze was fixed on Haden's house, the tools of his trade just visible beneath a covered work area. The sun was only just above the horizon and Marcus shifted his position on the ground as he saw Erryn return home. He was considering walking down to meet her when he heard someone approach from behind. Turning to see Benedict, Marcus searched his face for a sign there may be something wrong; his fellow Meranell usually didn't surface much before mid-morning, not since Erryn had taken over the teaching.

"Ah, Marcus, I'm glad you're up." Benedict smiled, unnerving Marcus even more. Still trying to keep one eye on Erryn's home, he listened half-heartedly as his friend continued. "There's something we have to do today, and... it will mean returning to Whitestone." Now he had Marcus' full attention.

"What?"

"You heard me, boy."

"But I can't go back, you know I can't. I... I may not get out of there again. Everything we've been working towards will be for nothing."

"Look, do you seriously want to help, or are you going to quit when things get tough? We face far worse than a trip to the city, Marcus. If you can't handle that..." Benedict's voice trailed off as his characteristic frown returned and he glared intensely.

"But..." Marcus sighed, buckling under the weight of the old man's gaze. "Alright. Where's Sathom? Is he coming?"

"No, he's... busy. He wants us to complete this task."

"What task?"

"There's just something we must do, that's all. Look, boy, stop asking so many damned questions and put this on." He handed Marcus a full-length black cloak. "We need to leave straight away, it's a long way to travel and I don't think this weather will be kind to us if we don't return before nightfall."

With that, he pulled his own cloak tighter around his shoulders and, relying heavily on his walking stick, hobbled away down the slope and in the direction of the village gate, leaving Marcus to marvel at just how fast the old man could move.

Even the thick fabric of his cloak did little to stop the winter freeze burrowing deep into Marcus' bones as he and Benedict made their way towards the city. The wind was against them at every step and Marcus found himself longing for his blankets on the floor of the cottage. More than once, he had to stop and wait for Benedict, as it became apparent his surprising speed was strictly reserved for moving down frost covered, grassy banks. The landscape across which he'd fled over two months ago was as treacherous as ever; only, this time, with bright, unclouded sunlight to illuminate it, the ditches and boggy areas were at least easier to avoid. Of course, now it was a far more barren place. The last vestiges of autumn scattered under foot, mixing with the mud to create hazardous little slides of rotting vegetation.

As they got closer to the city walls, the tension became palpable. The thought of turning around crossed Marcus' mind as the early afternoon sun reflected from the white stone that surrounded the city, but he had not travelled so far to simply return without doing what they had set out to do – whatever that may be.

He readied himself for their approach to the main gateway, his mouth dry and his heart beating doubly fast, when Benedict veered off to the left and began to follow the wall in that direction, ignoring the entrance completely. Marcus had no choice but to follow once he realised he was stood, alone, in broad daylight, simply begging to be shot at. Catching up with Benedict, his cloak billowing out behind him, he grabbed his arm, bringing him to an abrupt halt.

"Where are you going? I thought we had to go into the city."

Benedict smirked at him, the hood of his cloak casting an ominous shadow over most of his face.

"If you'll recall, I said we had to return *to* the city. I don't believe I ever mentioned actually entering it."

"You mean, you lied to me? Why am I not surprised?" Marcus screwed his face up as the old man's grin widened to show an uneven line of yellowed and crumbling teeth. "So where *are* we going then?"

"There is a place, not far from here, beneath ground. However, there's somewhere else I want you to see before we arrive there."

Curiosity now wearing away at his anger with Benedict for winding him up, Marcus was intrigued enough to blindly follow as they started walking again, staying close to the white stone all the way around until, finally, they reached the other side of the city. He'd never set foot outside the boundary until that fateful night. He'd certainly never seen the area they came upon as Benedict finally stopped at the back wall. The grass there was overgrown, and, even though winter was well underway, every plant was still covered in lush green foliage. Tall birch trees dappled the sunlight, which glistened in pearls that skimmed across the surface of a lily-covered pond, and the breeze blew unseasonably warm. Amidst the vegetation, the same white stone that formed the city and the Stone Highway protruded in jagged, crumbling towers. As Marcus stepped closer to get a better view, he realised the towers were part of a larger structure, some kind of circular ruin, ravaged by the winds of time, yet the brilliant white still shone like a beacon, as clean and bright as the day it had been built.

"What *is* this place?" he asked in an awe-filled whisper. Benedict said nothing, but motioned for his companion to step forwards through what could once have been a magnificent entrance. It was now missing its roof and at least one half of a supporting pillar, the remaining pillar bound with winding tendrils of ivy.

Within the ruin, the full grandeur of what once must have been some kind of gathering place became apparent. Stone tiers rose up from the sides. Though broken like the rest of the place, it wasn't too hard to imagine crowds of people cheering and applauding from them.

"Wait! Is this the… arena? Is this where I fought?" Marcus asked, stopping abruptly and turning around to take it all in. He looked to Benedict for an answer when none was forthcoming. Benedict stood right at the centre of the arena, his eyes closed and his right arm outstretched, hand tightly gripping something that wasn't there. He seemed to be in some kind of trance, but it must have felt real to him, for his knuckles had turned white; such was the firmness of his grip on thin air.

"Benedict? Is everything…?"

"Shh! Can't you feel it?" Benedict interrupted without even turning in Marcus' direction.

The sound of steel against steel echoed around the arena, the roar of the crowd rising and falling at each near miss, each skilled sidestep away from an arcing blade arousing gasps of impressed approval. Benedict swung his sword arm from side to side, feeling the weight of his weapon as familiar and natural as one of his own limbs. Lost in his reverie, he was taken by surprise as Marcus' hand came down upon his shoulder. Turning around, ready to strike, his eyes still closed, he put everything he had into the thrust. *His blade piercing the side of his opponent, he let out a howl as his foe fell to the dust-covered cobbles. Blood spilling from the wound seeped beneath his feet. Yet it was not enough. As the warrior rose from the floor, the gaping wound in his abdomen, affecting him no more than a scratch, Benedict prepared to take the final blow as he had the advantage. With one mighty swing, he drew his arm back and sliced it swiftly forwards through the air, the edge of his sword making contact with his opponent's neck, and coming to rest on the other side. The head teetered for a second before relinquishing its connection with the severed neck and dropping to the ground, followed moments later by the decapitated body. The crowd went quiet and Benedict hung his head; though not the one defeated, he was not the victor. The silent crowd knew it and their pity for him was more than he could bear.* Finally opening his eyes, half expecting to witness the gore of the battle, Benedict blinked through the haze as he saw Marcus sitting on the ground in front of him, rubbing his side with one hand while holding his neck with the other.

"Care to explain why you just attacked me?" Marcus asked, a look of disgruntled confusion stretched across his angular features.

"Ha! Just be thankful I didn't truly have my sword" Benedict laughed.

"And *you* should just be thankful I didn't use magic," came Marcus' retort as he roughly accepted Benedict's outstretched hand to help him get up.

"What was going on there, Benedict? I'm not stupid, I know this is the arena I fought in, but it was as if you had a familiarity with this place, too." Even as he made the statement, the pieces were starting to fall into place; Benedict only confirmed what he'd already guessed.

"This was *our* territory, Marcus. This was where our hopes balanced on the edge of a blade. We fought here, you and I."

"We fought? You mean... each other?" *Then that was their connection. But then, why had they both lived?* "I thought the battles were to the death, wasn't that the idea?"

"We were both simply too good." Benedict chuckled at the irony. "We met on this ground many times. We fought to the best of our ability, as required of us. Once or twice you almost bested me, once or twice, I you. Alas, such battles were confined by the rules of the arena and time was restricted. Each timed bout ended in stalemate." The old man's look became wistful and distant, and for the first time since they'd met, Marcus felt sorry for him.

"Hold a moment. Why aren't you in the sanctum?" Marcus asked, wondering why he hadn't thought to ask before. Sathom had explained the answer regarding Marcus' own soul some weeks back. He'd told him that, just under a thousand years ago, almost immediately after the spell had been cast and he'd become aware of what had happened, he'd set about researching and planning for a way to aid the lost race.

With nought but time on his hands, he never gave up. Tirelessly working on perfecting the procedure he'd discovered, he eventually brought Marcus' soul away from the tower, harnessing it to a human vessel to prevent it from being dragged back. Thus, Marcus had been reborn, filling the void left by the soul of the Ryan's stillborn baby son.

Benedict now elaborated, filling the gaps in Sathom's narrative.

"*I* was the first attempt." The old man's tone was bitter, his eyes squeezed together, shooting daggers at Marcus. However, his expression relaxed as he directed his companion to the low wall that framed the arena. Together, they sat down, the implication in his words hanging between them like water droplets, frozen mid-fall.

When Benedict spoke again, all became clear.

"Yours was not the first soul Sathom released from the tower. A little over three centuries ago, I too was dragged from the blackness. I'd damn near gone mad. I remember voices, familiar voices, wishing me luck, telling me not to fear. And I remember laughing at them. *Me, fear?* They must have all gone as mad as I, to think me even capable of fear. But as those voices faded off into the distance, the last thing I remember was the fear I'd never hear them again.

Then, I was born. The light burnt my eyes and everything felt… wrong.

Now, Sathom – he'd spent so many years studying, planning, researching the arcane – he was thorough, I'll give him that. However, even elementals make mistakes. This body, my new vessel, it was… *incompatible*, you see. Weak and feeble, it started to split at the seams from the start. I had excruciating headaches from a young age. My joints were always stiff and painful. My skin never felt anything but tight, overstretched. And, throughout it all, even as a child, I knew, I remembered. Everything I'd been, all I'd known, what I'd suffered, what my kin *still* suffered, who I was and the way I felt about life; it all remained conscious knowledge, clawing at the inner walls of this pathetic human vessel. It was the memories, you see. Sathom hadn't considered the damage having them would do, the strain they would put on a body not made for housing a Meranell's soul. That's why yours were kept from you. Ha! I suffer, so that you may not – and here I was thinking you were the noble one.

Anyway, as if that reason for my failure wasn't enough, once Sathom had made himself known to me – when I was barely out of short trousers – he realised I should have been a mage. No, he didn't think that one through very well either, did he? Finally deciphering a particularly crucial element to whatever magic nonsense he'd studied, he discovered that only someone who possessed the same magical ability as the governors would be suitable to destroy them and save our brethren in doing so. There wasn't a magical bone in my useless body. And there you have it.

Sathom never gave up, he simply carried on as before. *Your 'birth' would be different, he wouldn't make the same mistakes he had with me, he couldn't afford to. This was the last chance.* Can you imagine how hard it was to find a noble child, a boy, whose life was destined to end before it had begun? I have no idea how he knew – never cared to know. Elementals were always a little mysterious, after all. Fortunately for all of us, this time it was a success. Sathom found a way to lock away your memories, creating a sort of inner-barrier around your soul, protecting your human flesh from deteriorating from the inside out, as mine had done. Your status as a Vaharian noble insured you had the necessary skills.

Of course, we knew there could be a flaw in even the most successful plan. Sathom had watched you since the day you were born. He grew concerned as you aged and it appeared you would never learn as your peers did. He'd expected you'd be ready when he came to you – but you weren't.

So, there was my purpose. After all those hundreds of years, I was to learn of magic so I could teach *you.* Unlike you, I don't have the luxury of only experiencing some unexplained dislike of it – I loathe it. I still remember, with terrible clarity, how it was used to destroy our lives."

And there it was; everything the man had been through, all those long years, all the horror played out over and over in his mind and then to discover he couldn't even save his people as Sathom had intended.

Marcus didn't remember his own Meranell past, but as they sat in silence, he believed he understood Benedict better. Perhaps some part of him, some ancient part, could empathise because of their shared history, or perhaps he simply recognised another soul in pain. Either way, he resolved to do what had to be done, if not for those held prisoner, for his friend.

After a while of silence, Benedict motioned for them to stand. He was about to make his way out of the ruin when Marcus stood in front of him, his face looking more serious than appeared natural for one who always smiled. He placed his hand firmly on the old man's shoulder and looked earnestly into his eyes.

"I *will* free them, my friend. I promise."

Benedict paused, a slightly bewildered look in his eyes, before resting his wizened hand over Marcus' and nodding.

"Come, we have work to do." And with that, the two men left the arena.

CHAPTER EIGHT

Beyond the city walls, to the far west of Vaharia, was more world than Marcus had ever imagined. The arena ruin, stone monuments to ancient leaders, untended but still glorious gardens surrounded by low stone walls, winding pathways that led to archway-covered stone benches; all of these built from the familiar white stone and wrapped in an abundance of green. Captivated by his surroundings, Marcus guessed that magic had to be involved, yet it was unlike any magic he'd ever experienced.

"How can all this exist this way?" he asked Benedict as they walked.

"It was a gift from the elementals to our people. They believed we should have a place, somewhere we could go, where everything around us would be as eternal and as full of life as we were. So they enchanted the ground, made it abundant with energies from the four elements. It was said that even the memories of our lost kin were stronger on this land. When a soul had moved on, we would cremate the vessels, bringing the ashes here. Look." Benedict pointed to an enclosed circular area with a raised stone platform at the centre. "It's a memorial garden. If a grieving Meranell took those ashes to the garden and placed them on that alter, they'd be able to close their eyes and see them as clearly as if they'd never left at all – but, just once. It would only work once."

Benedict's voice trailed off as he led Marcus along a cobbled pathway, meandering through long grasses that swayed in the warm breeze of the enchanted climate, until, eventually, they reached another building. Some distance lay between it and the last fascination. As Marcus set eyes on it, something looked – and indeed felt – very different to all they'd passed before.

It was a large building, compared with the others they'd seen. The walls were tall and imposing and the roof, supported at the front by two ornately carved pillars, rose proudly into the sky. Framed within the pillars was a pair of large stone doors almost the full height of the front wall. They bore detailed carvings the like of which Marcus had never seen before, though he got the impression they once had more significance than pure artistry.

Though made from the same stone as everything else on their walk, the building was not gleaming white but stained with a black slime that seemed to be visibly creeping across the surface. There was no plant life extending up the walls as there was on the rest of the architecture. In fact, as Marcus began to feel more and more unsettled, he noticed how the grasses and shrubs appeared to shrink back from the perimeter, any edges extending beyond a certain point curling up and turning brown.

"What *is* this place?" Marcus asked, his whole body bristling with tension.

"It was the crypt for the remains of our people, the few of them whose vessels found death." Benedict seemed unperturbed as he walked towards the building without hesitation.

"Wait! Benedict, I… I'm not sure we should get much closer. Can't you feel it?"

"Yes yes, it's drenched in dark magic, I know."

"Oh, is that all?" Marcus replied sarcastically.

Benedict turned to face him,

"It's why I needed you to come with me. And no, I can't *feel* it. It's magic, I don't *do* magic!" Benedict was about to continue towards the entrance when he was pulled around by Marcus' firm grip on his arm.

"I tire of blindly following you around, old man! Tell me what's going on, or I'm returning to the village right now!"

Benedict let out an exasperated sigh and forcefully freed his arm from Marcus' grasp.

"Inside that crypt lies an important ingredient for the continued immortal lives of the governors. We get inside and destroy them, we strike a massive blow to those bastards."

"*Them*? What do you mean *them*? What is this *ingredient* you speak of?" Marcus' unsettled feeling caused by the proximity of the dark magic was slowly being replaced by unease at Benedict's suspicious behaviour.

"Look, Marcus, all will become clear – once we're inside. And *that* is where you come in." Marcus cocked his head to one side and slanted his eyes.

"I'm listening."

"Come!" With that, Benedict turned and proceeded down the cracked grey path that led to the double-doors. Against his better judgement, Marcus followed, the disquiet of before returning as he moved closer to the source of his anxiety.

Once at the doors, he could clearly see the darkness oozing from the keyhole of a large, iron lock. It occurred to him that it wasn't so long ago he probably wouldn't have felt anything out-of-the-ordinary, had he been so close to such magic. However, with his magical senses heightened, it was as if he was automatically tuned in to the frequency, the connection between his own power and the echoes of the spells of others stronger than any force he'd ever known.

"The governors have barred this entrance with dark magic. I need you to 'unlock' it." Benedict looked up at Marcus, his voice giving no indication he understood the difficult nature of such a task.

"You want me to unlock it." Marcus repeated the statement.

"Yes!"

"And have you any suggestion as to how I am going to achieve this?"

"No. Like I said, you're the mage here. I've no advice to offer. Don't go expecting any girly 'feel the magic' crap from me." He saw the irritation on Marcus' face. "Look, you *are* feeling something, right? The best I can offer – use that, try to tap into it and, well, take it from there."

Why did the old man have to mention Erryn? The afternoon had been confusing enough as it was, now all he could think about was big, brown eyes and auburn curls.

But still, he had a point. Erryn would have urged him to do just what Benedict had suggested.

Tentatively extending his hand towards the lock, Marcus closed his eyes and concentrated on the energy, that within himself and that which emanated from the surface of the crypt. As the opposing magics connected, he could feel the governors' spell actively trying to repel his own power. The force pushed at his hand and his mind, sensing his will and trying to seek out a weakness. The audacity of it angered him and, with one final thrust, his eyes flashing open and glowing with pure white light, he overpowered the dark magic, sending it squealing back into the lock, where it bubbled within the ooze. Now in control, Marcus twisted his hand until it lay palm-upward and focused his gaze upon it. Within seconds, a shape began to form on his palm. The shape continued to extend lengthways, becoming more defined until it took on the recognisable appearance of a large, intricately-designed key. The key, clearly visible though made up of a swirling blue mist, began to rise until it was hovering just above Marcus' hand. Turning his attention to the magic-filled lock, he willed the key to move forwards, until, finally, like a hot knife slicing through butter, it moved through the blackness, finding a perfect fit inside the keyhole. As Benedict watched on, his mouth hanging open, Marcus, who had been acting as if in a trance, tilted his head downward, squeezed his brow and concentrated everything he had on keeping the key within the lock. With his eyes now glowing so brightly, the black slime seemed to shrink back away from its light. He slowly twisted his hand, fingers gripping thin air, as the mystical key turned within the lock, an audible click signalling the release as the last movement of his hand finished the task. His body slumping forwards, his eyes returned to their natural green hue, and he exhaled as if he'd been holding his breath, the key fizzling out of existence as the last of his magic returned whence it came.

Freed from their restraints, the doors moved slightly ajar.

"Well done, boy." Benedict gave Marcus a hearty slap on the shoulder and, with a satisfied smile plastered across his wrinkled face, pushed hard on both doors and stepped over the threshold, disappearing inside without a second glance.

Physically drained from the magical energy he'd expended and wondering how he'd managed to perform such a feat, Marcus shrugged, and, for the second time that day, ignored the warning voice in his head, shadowing Benedict's footsteps until he too was inside the darkened room of the crypt.

"Marcus, a little light wouldn't go amiss." Benedict's voice echoed in the darkness.

"Oh, yes of course." Marcus flicked his fingers and a small flame sparked to life at their tips. The orange glow gradually extended its reach around the room, allowing both men to see exactly where they were. It was clear the place hadn't seen that many visitors; Benedict's boots left shuffling marks through a layer of dust on the floor, and expansive cobwebs clung between ceiling and wall, their creators long departed. However, it didn't strike Marcus as a place that had been abandoned for as long as it would initially appear. Half melted candles still stood in arched alcoves, evenly spaced around the walls, and imprints of hands, possibly steadying someone's passage around the room, were covered in a much thinner layer of dust.

Benedict was heading towards another doorway at the top of a flight of steps, when Marcus noticed an ornate stone platform, pressed against the far wall, and surrounded by broken pottery and pools of hard, dry wax. Something drew him to it, coaxing him to take a closer look.

"What's this?" he asked his companion, who turned from his course and joined Marcus at the platform.

"It's… the altar, at which we'd kneel before our Gods and ask that the souls of our friends were granted safe passage back to Meran. Loved ones would come here, leave offerings, light a candle… pray."

This was the first time Marcus had heard of the Meranells having 'Gods'.

"Did you ever do that? Did you ever 'pray' here, Benedict?" Marcus asked, never taking his eyes away from the altar.

"No. Come now! We still have much to do and we've wasted enough time today." Benedict resumed his journey out through the door and down the narrow set of spiralling stone steps.

Upon reaching the lower floor which, to Marcus' surprise, was well lit by a number of fiercely burning torches, Benedict came to an abrupt halt. Almost colliding with him, Marcus stepped around him to get a better look at the room. The basement level of the crypt, though much larger, was similar to the entrance. Floor-to-ceiling alcoves with inbuilt shelves housed numerous clay urns of varying condition. Thick dust covered most surfaces, and cobwebs adorned the cracks and crevices. However, what seemed to have stopped Benedict in his tracks was a long line of sarcophagi, side by side, and each shrouded in a thin, smoky form of the dark magic that had barred their entry to the crypt.

"They *are* here!" Benedict whispered to himself.

"What? What's here?"

Benedict quickly turned round to face Marcus.

"Marcus, we have an opportunity here. An opportunity to strike the governors where it will hurt the most - their immortality."

"Excellent! Um, that's a good thing… right? What do we have to do?"

"Kill the men lying within those tombs."

"Firstly, if there are men in those, then aren't they already a bit, well, dead? Secondly – are you completely insane?"

Marcus' hands were becoming clammy, and he could feel the hairs on the back of his neck stand to attention. He had a bad feeling about the situation he'd been coaxed into. Noting the young mage's body language, Benedict realised he wasn't about to take anything on trust alone. He sighed and proceeded to explain.

"The governors aren't like us; they had to steal our immortality, and then they had to find an unnatural way of retaining it." The venomous resentment was clear in Benedict's voice. "Because their bodies, their vessels, were like mine; weak and crumbling from the inside out from birth, they could not sustain an immortal soul. The spell of which Sathom spoke would not be their only abomination. Once they had harnessed the power of our souls within the tower, they had to conjure a way to keep themselves from becoming fragile. Immortal souls are all well and good, but without a strong vessel to contain them, well, they'd be no better off than our kinsmen are now. So, each generation the governors lived, they would father two sons. These 'children' were not loved or brought up in the warm embrace of doting parents. Instead, they were entombed, cursed with dark magic so they 'slept', and nourished to adulthood until such time that they were needed."

"Needed? What do you mean needed?"

"I mean just that, boy! Do I really have to spell it out? When the body of a governor became too old and weak, or if its life were ended, their soul would jump into the elder of the two sons, awakening that vessel from slumber, where it would then continue life… as its own father. The youngest son, well, he was kept as a spare, eventually murdered if new sons were born before he could prove useful."

Finally understanding the meaning behind Benedict's cryptic words, Marcus recoiled as he thought on the horrific lengths the governors had gone to. His own father was practically parental love epitomised by comparison.

He was still thinking on what he had just learnt when Benedict made his way over to one of the sarcophagi, stopping at its side and unsheathing the dagger at his belt.

"Marcus, over here." Benedict beckoned. "I need you to use your… skills, again."

It took at moment for Marcus to realise what the old man was requesting of him. When the penny dropped, his eyes widened in shock.

"Now wait just a minute! Are you suggesting what I think you are?"

"I'm *suggesting* you get over here and dispel this dark magic for a start."

"What, so you can kill all these men? I will not help you murder innocent souls who are unable to defend themselves. No!"

"They aren't souls, just empty vessels."

"I said *no!*"

Benedict's face took on an expression that sent shivers up and down Marcus' spine. His face twisted in anger, he marched back to where Marcus stood, planting himself squarely in front of him and tilting his head to make up the few inches difference in height between their eyes.

"Listen to me, boy," he spat. "I've had about all I can stand of your childish whining. Sathom may think we should go easy on you, but he's not here, and as far as I'm concerned, you've had it too damn easy. You're facing the toughest time of your life, and it's about time you grow a backbone and do what must be done, because right now, I see nothing in you but a spoilt little boy, still cowering beneath the shadow of his father!"

The words hit home, as intended. At that moment, Marcus hated Benedict for his brutal honesty. But honest he was, at least in Marcus' mind. He was no longer a terrified little boy, quaking beneath the beatings of a tyrant. He wasn't even powerless anymore. It was time he grew up. If this was truly what must be done, then so be it.

Pushing past Benedict, a steely resolve on his face, he strode towards the first sarcophagus. The dark magic formed a constantly moving layer at the rim of the stone tomb. Beneath lay a young man, apparently asleep, and mostly naked save for a leather loin cloth. Smoky black tendrils were twisting and licking at his exposed skin.

Avoiding further thought, Marcus concentrated his mind and began to imagine a blade slicing through the blanket of miasma. As he did so, a split appeared across the haze, its edges curling back away from the white glow that pushed its way through, until, finally, nothing more than tattered cloth-like remnants clung to the rim, shrinking back as if in fear. Marcus expected to feel drained, as he had at the doors to the crypt. However, this time, the energy still flowed freely inside him, allowing him to progress to the next task. With surprising ease, he'd soon despatched the tendrils. Looking down at the muscular man, he tried hard to see him as an implement of evil and not as the vulnerable person whose life he would have helped end. For a split second, he thought he noticed a movement under the man's eyelids, but Benedict was already at his side, dagger in hand, before he could think any more of it.

"Here, we're not done yet." Benedict offered the dagger to Marcus, the intent clear in the action.

"What? You want me to do it? Oh, no! My part ended at clearing the magic. I can't… kill… I… I…"

"Oh, for pity's sake!" Benedict pulled the dagger back and shoved Marcus aside, causing him to stumble backwards. Without further hesitation, the old man grasped the pommel with both hands and with great effort, plunged the blade hard into the heart of the man, blood splattering widely.

"One down, eleven to go. The next is yours!" Benedict sent the dagger spinning across the floor towards Marcus' feet, turning away and using the sleeve of his tunic to clear the gore from his face.

Marcus couldn't find his voice; the shock at what he'd just witnessed was still holding his body in a vice like grip. He'd taken his own father's life, but that couldn't compare with the seemingly cold and calculated way in which Benedict had so easily acted. He felt nothing but numb as he quietly refused again.

"Do you know how hard it is to kill a man in this way Marcus? Do you understand how much strength is required to drive even the sharpest blade through flesh, muscle and bone? This decrepit vessel of mine barely found the strength for it. Do you think I could even attempt it again? Now do what has to be done so we can leave this place!"

Benedict walked to the stairs and sat down to catch his breath, bowing his head to rest in his hands.

Marcus slowly and reluctantly bent down to pick up the dagger, cringing as the skin of his hand met with the sticky wetness of fresh blood. With his emotions still dulled, he found himself by the side of the second sarcophagus, his path there taken as if in a dream.

Looking down through the black, magical haze, he saw another man, much like the first, though his features were somehow softer, less severe. The man was obviously slightly younger than his fellow sleeper. His uncovered state showed a highly muscular figure and, though probably as tall as Marcus, much stockier. His dark blond hair was shorn close to his head and there wasn't even a sign of stubble on his face. With forced determination, Marcus dispersed all dark magic from the sarcophagus and its inhabitant. Knowing what he had to do must be done fast, if for no other reason than he might change his mind if he thought on it at all, he raised the dagger with both hands, closing his eyes and gulping back bitter-tasting saliva. With one mighty thrust forwards, he mimicked Benedict's action, anticipating the meeting of blade against flesh, followed by the splash of warm blood.

But the dagger juddered to a dead halt. The resistance obviously not as he'd expected, Marcus opened his eyes, seeing a raised hand grasping the blade and a pair of ice blue eyes staring widely up at him from beneath.

Before Marcus could take anything in, the man let go of the dagger and leapt out of the sarcophagus, shoving him backwards, sending him skidding along the ground and crashing against the wall.

Benedict had looked up upon hearing the din and noticed Marcus' form curled up on the floor. He was about to go over to him to help him stand when the man from the sarcophagus yelled in a deep voice

"Stay where you are!" He was bent forwards in a fighting stance, muscular arms taught, hands rolled into tight fists. Marcus used Benedict's unintentional distraction to pull himself up from the floor. Thinking fast, he readied a fireball in his right hand and moved slowly to within the man's line of sight. Benedict, noticing the fiery glow emanating from Marcus palm, looked around for his dagger. At the same time, the man, cornered like hunted prey, darted his eyes about the room until they met with a large, dust-and-cobweb-covered sword leaning against one of the walls. Benedict saw it too, but hindered by his aged, stiff body and lack of youthful reflexes, cursed as the man made a lunge for it, brandishing the weapon with both hands like a seasoned warrior.

"Marcus, do it! Use it now!" Benedict's voice broke the tense silence as he kept his eyes fixed on the sword-wielding vessel.

Just then, the man's eyes flashed to the fire in Marcus' grasp. The realisation raced across his face and, with one swift movement, he dashed forwards and lifted the great-sword high and wide. Seeing his chance to gain the upper hand evaporating, Marcus seized the opportunity to avoid certain death and cast the fireball towards his assailant. In his haste his aim was off just enough to miss a direct strike, but instead the force it carried with it blasted into the man's shoulder, throwing him down and sending the sword flying from his hands. It may not have been the desired result, but it was just enough to buy some time. Marcus kicked the sword further away from the vessel, while Benedict retrieved his dagger and positioned himself above the scant-clad young man, holding the blade dangerously close to his throat.

Winded and dazed, he didn't struggle against the older man who held his life in his hands; he simply looked up at him with eyes that seemed to dare Benedict to take the cut.

"Benedict, wait!" Marcus ordered firmly.

Taken aback by his companion's tone, Benedict shot him a questioning look. But Marcus retained his resolve.

"You can't kill him now. He doesn't look very 'empty' to me. In fact, I'm beginning to wonder if there was truth in anything you said today, *friend*."

"I *may* have… altered things a little." Benedict stumbled over his words, looking uncharacteristically awkward.

"He *does* have a soul, doesn't he?"

"Yes, yes, he has soul. But you'd have been none the wiser if you'd not acted like a little girl, and killed him when you had the chance!"

"You would have had me murder this man…" Marcus eyes grew wider. "Wait! You murdered the other one. Did he *also* have a soul?"

"A soul that would never have been allowed to see the light of day… but yes, he too had a soul. Look, we haven't done anything the governors, their *father,* wouldn't have done himself. Only difference is, we're not parading about in their bodies. When their father was ready to 'move in', the souls they had from birth would have been extinguished via the same dark magic that sustained them all these years. We… I saved them from that. Well, one of them."

Both men had almost forgotten the vessel, who was now being pressed into the ground by Benedict's knee and starting to bleed slightly from the blade that was still grazing his throat.

"Get… off me!" The vessel's voice interrupted the discourse, redirecting both men's attention back to him.

With an icy glare from Marcus, Benedict reluctantly got up, stepping back but keeping the dagger clearly on show. Marcus stepped forwards and reached out to help the vessel stand – an offer that was accepted with a firm, forceful grip.

The nearly naked man darted his eyes wildly between his two assailants, his body remaining tense and ready to fight.

"Now, tell me what's going on, before I see if I'm really able to wield that blade."

CHAPTER NINE

The pallid orange light of the winter sun was slowly being replaced by the cool blue cast of a long-night moon, creating blended colours across thin clouds. High above the open Vaharian landscape, a black, winged shape presided over the skies. Taking advantage of the open space, the creature soared wide and circular before spiralling downward, only to ascend again when its shadow fell true.

From a vantage just beneath cloud level, it scanned the ground below. Through great reptilian eyes, it could easily see the three men walking, long before its thunderous, roaring call had alerted them to its presence. The creature knew they'd make a fine meal, but, though its cavernous stomach grumbled from the emptiness of a thousand years, the hunt would not be his that day. Calling once more, it took its last full circle and swooped back whence it came, over the Stone Highway and beyond.

"What was *that*?" Marcus asked, as he, Benedict, and the vessel emerged from beneath the branches of a gnarled, ancient oak, the only shelter available as the beast had passed over their heads.

"Dragon!" Benedict responded simply, yet the tone in his voice betrayed a concern his lack of words attempted to hide.

"You shouldn't have denied me a weapon!" The vessel grumbled. It was the first thing he'd said since they'd left the crypt. For most of the journey to the village he'd hung back, looking lost in deep thought; with good reason, considering his introduction to the world. Both men, who'd originally tried to kill him, had told him that which he'd not already summed up from being privy to their earlier exchange and, surprisingly, he hadn't taken a lot of convincing to leave with them. In fact, his fury was easily turned towards his so-called 'father'. Proclaiming a desire for revenge, he accepted the offer of Marcus' cloak and, after a brief altercation with Benedict concerning the great-sword, had followed his new acquaintances from the crypt.

"Dragon, huh? I've read about them. Big things that eat peop… I think it's time we got moving, fast." Marcus began walking more hastily than before, and the others followed.

"Wait! Seeing the dragon reminded me of something. Hold on!" Benedict walked back to the tree and then reached his hand inside a small hole in its twisted trunk. Marcus and the vessel watched on with confused faces as the old man scuffled about inside the hollow. Finally, he pulled out a small, metal box. Wincing as his shoulder creaked, Benedict straightened up, clutching the tarnished container tightly against his chest, and returned to stand with his companions.

"Well, don't keep us in suspense. What's in the box?" Marcus' insatiable curiosity showed itself once more.

Pulling the cloak tighter around his bare torso, the vessel tried to appear disinterested. However, when the thin creak of tiny, rusted hinges caught his attention, he was drawn to take a look. Inside, upon a cushion of faded blue velvet, lay what resembled a claw. Only, this claw was not made of flesh and bone, but of satin-sheened, dark grey metal. Benedict took the claw from the box and slipped his right index finger inside. It was not a perfect fit, sitting rather loosely around his bony digit, but the finely crafted metal scales doubled as junctions where a finger could still bend within. The old man brought the thing to life as he flexed his own arthritic joints, his movements seeming instinctive, if not altogether comfortable. A look of pride expanded over Benedict's face as he raised his hand to admire his adornment.

"I slew a dragon once. Sometime before… a bit over a thousand years ago. This was my reward, from the king, for saving a family it was about to eat."

"Why was it in the tree?" Now, it was the vessel's turn to be curious.

"I would always hide it there on the night before every arena battle. Should I survive, I would return for it the following day. Obviously, I didn't get a chance to fight my last battle, let alone retrieve this."

"So it's been in that trunk for a *thousand years*?" Marcus asked, fascinated. Benedict nodded, pausing as if he were about to speak, then abruptly closed the box and walked off in the direction of the village. Marcus and the vessel stared at each other, before hurrying to catch up with him.

"What was a damn dragon doing here anyway?" Benedict mumbled to himself as he hobbled up and down the wild terrain of the Vaharian countryside.

"Yes, I have to admit to being a little curious about that myself. I thought they'd died out." Marcus ignored the fact Benedict's question wasn't aimed at anyone in particular.

"The dragon I killed was one of a pair, the female. In our day, they were only seen in five-year cycles. When they were creating and raising a youngling, they would hunt; dwarves mainly, easier to eat in one bite I suppose." Benedict chuckled. "But we seven-foot Meranells were not unpalatable, and now and then one of the beasts would fly over the Stone Highway from the Dragonlands between here and Sa'hahlenfell. The female picked the wrong day to do just that. I'd 'won' yet another arena battle and came upon her – all claws and teeth – and some young family out for a stroll, cornered and about to become her next meal. It was my good fortune that I got to take out my frustration on her." Benedict gave a wry smile. "Anyway, I'd just killed her and wiped the blood from my sword when her mate arrived; heard her call, I imagine. To cut a long story short, we fought so long I started to wish I had an elemental nearby. Wouldn't want my soul out there with no one to give the last rites, after all. Finally, he simply gave up, stopped still at the point of my blade, then just… flew off. After that, dragons were not seen again, even after another five years."

Marcus had to admit, he was impressed by Benedict's tale. He truly must have been a great warrior in his day. He wondered if his own Meranell self had ever met a dragon, or anything else that would take such skill to defeat. He was about to ask, when he realised they'd reached the copse of trees that foreshowed the road to the village. The route ahead now only illuminated by moonlight, he was reminded of the first time he'd walked that way and decided to concentrate on more practical matters, like not getting covered in tiny scratches.

The night had grown bitter by the time they arrived back at Benedict's cottage. The inviting orange glow from the windows made them all eager to get inside, especially the vessel. Though his pride prevented him from admitting it, he was suffering for his lack of clothing in such cold weather. However, he was thankful for the chill cutting off feeling from his extremities; with no boots, his unhardened feet had taken a cruel thrashing.

Marcus was the last one through the front door. Turning to bolt it behind him, he froze as he heard Sathom's voice offer an unfriendly, though not unexpected, greeting.

"Where have you been?"

The question was aimed at Benedict and Marcus but Sathom's eyes were fixed firmly on the stranger in their midst. Away from the shadows of the crypt, the vessel's bulk was an arresting sight. Even beneath the loosely draped folds of Marcus' cloak, the swell of muscles was obvious. His pale blue eyes reflected the firelight as he returned Sathom's gaze, unwavering and brave; the same look Marcus had seen as he was about to take away his life.

After a moment's awkward silence, Benedict spoke up.

"I took Marcus on a little… errand."

"And who, may I ask, is this?"

Marcus felt he should be the one to introduce the vessel. After all, it was down to him that the man had returned from the crypt with them. He was about to step forwards when Benedict held up his hand and spoke first.

"Sathom, we went to the crypt."

"Then this is one of…?"

"Yes," Benedict interrupted. "Now, don't blame Marcus, he did as I asked. Well, almost. Actually, if he'd done exactly as I asked, we wouldn't be having this conversation."

Marcus glared at Benedict.

"You would risk bringing one of them, a vessel, here? Have you lost your mind?" Sathom's demeanour was tense, yet his voice, as always, remained monotonous. Benedict looked as if he wanted to say more, but he didn't answer.

"Just tell me then, is he a younger or an elder?"

"He's the younger brother."

"Then you must have… killed the first. Oh, my friend, what have you done? I asked that you cast all thoughts of vengeance from your mind. I thought you understood why."

Marcus, who'd been listening carefully, sighed and folded his arms across his chest. He knew the old man hadn't told him everything. Now Benedict's face looked fit to burst, something stirring within his aged eyes – something that a cautious man might have taken as a signal to say no more. But Sathom seemed to be about as good at recognising emotion as he was at showing it. "You knew the possible consequences of this action, Benedict, yet you took it upon yourself to ignore my warnings. Not only that, but you led our only hope into danger. What would have happened if you'd been caught in the act? Where would we be had Marcus been captured, or worse?"

"They took my son, so I damn-well took one of theirs! I'd have taken them all if I could!" Benedict's furious voice put an end to Sathom's lecture and, when he'd had his say, he stormed out the way they'd entered, leaving the other men in stunned silence.

Sathom wasted no time with concern over Benedict's outburst. An air of urgency now hung around him as he spoke to Marcus.

"It seems matters have been pushed ahead of us, and we must act much sooner than planned if we wish to maintain control of this situation. It may not be long before the governors discover what has happened, and we cannot risk them locating us now. We leave at first light."

Marcus considered protesting; it was too soon, he wasn't ready. He'd barely touched his staff and… *well, it was simply too soon.* The vessel, on the other hand, appeared to have no such qualms.

"I am eager to begin this quest. I am ready!"

"I take it my companions told you of our task?" The vessel nodded once and Sathom sighed. "You would join with us then, against your own father?" Sathom asked.

"I have no father! I think I'd like to make sure it stays that way!"

Sathom stared at the muscular man in silence before seemingly becoming resigned to the situation.

"Very well. Marcus, I take it you have no objection." Sathom's eyes once again bore deep into Marcus, who was now beginning to be able to read his body language in the absence of his emotional responses.

"I'm sorry Sathom, I didn't know. I…"

"No matter. Do not waste energy troubling yourself with things that cannot be undone. Time has always been of the essence; now, only more so. I shall visit Erryniya and tell her of our imminent departure. Vessel, you can come with me. If you insist on joining us, we must find you some attire more befitting travel. And perhaps a weapon – can you fight?"

"Oh, he can handle himself well enough," Marcus interjected. "He seems to have a fancy for large swords."

"Good! Then we must tarry no longer. Marcus, get some rest. We leave with the dawn."

With that, Sathom left the cottage, the vessel shadowing him, leaving Marcus alone once more.

Every fibre of his being tried to insist he collapse beneath the pressure, give up, and take no further part in this madness. However, for once in his life, he ignored his instincts. He knew their purpose was purely a selfish weakness, brought on by the deluge of out-of-the-ordinary circumstance, flooding into a soul that, until recently, had known of only one life. It may not have been an idyllic life, but it was familiar. His good humour had seen him through when he'd needed it, but he wasn't so sure he could joke his way out of the times ahead.

With a exhale of breath, his thoughts returned to Benedict, the man he'd learnt to call friend – even though he probably didn't deserve it.

That night he'd mentioned a son, where none had been spoken of before. Marcus couldn't recall ever seeing the old man as angry as he'd been a few minutes ago. Closeting his own anxiety, he decided to find Benedict. He *was* his friend, despite recent events, and he was certain he could use one of those right now.

Sitting on the trunk of a fallen tree next to the woodshed, Benedict looked upward, his eyes searching beyond the stars. Perhaps if he looked hard enough, he might catch a glimpse of the Gods. Perhaps they would feel his gaze and reach down to pluck him straight from that cold, dark world. Maybe his lost love, the one who took his heart when she left, would plead his case; ask that the council make an exception just for him. But what then? His people, his son, would still be trapped within the Sanctum of Souls. How could he find peace in Meran with that knowledge reverberating around his soul?

Lost in thought, Benedict didn't notice Marcus' approach, startling slightly when the mage's steps snapped a brittle twig close by. He laughed softly at his tall friend's lack of stealth, before shuffling along the trunk to make room. Marcus took the free space beside Benedict. For some time the two men sat beneath the cloudless black sky, the only sound coming from a light wind as it whispered through the branches of bare trees.

Eventually, Benedict broke the quietness, his voice soft and unusually calm.

"I didn't always wish to die. Before I became an arena warrior, I was married, had a young son. I was a blacksmith, a simple man. I wished for nothing more than eternity alongside my family. Then I met another woman. She awakened something within me, the like of which I'd never known could exist. Every moment of every day, she was all I could think of. Had my mind in knots, she did. But for all that, I knew nothing would ever come of it. When I met her, she'd already chosen her path. She was the first woman I'd known to enter the arena; that's how we met. For her I crafted the finest blade, the sword that would serve her as she sought her vessel's end. There was no hope of her ever returning my feelings for her, and I was honourable to the vows I'd made to my wife, in body at least... Until the day I discovered she'd been given the last rites. The wall I built around my feelings for her crumbled and I could live the lie no longer. I left my wife, and my son… and I trained with the other warriors of the arena. My true love was gone, and I could see nothing but an empty eternity stretching out before me. So, that's why I became a warrior. Of course my son grew up without me, and he hated me for that. I didn't blame him. I'd have felt the same. I spoke with him briefly, when he was seventeen, only days before the end. He told me he had no father, that he considered me dead already. Those words cut deeper than I could have anticipated, but in my selfish state of mind, they simply added to my desire to return to Meran."

Marcus placed his hand on Benedict's shoulder.

"I *will* save your son, my friend. This I swear to you."

Benedict turned to face Marcus. Sincerity was carved into the deep lines on his face and for once, his eyes were without their bitter, furrowed brow.

"I'm older than you, my boy. There were almost two decades between us as Meranells. Now with an added three centuries and a short passage of time spent in each other's company, I have come to… respect you, a great deal. You aren't the spoilt nobleman I first took you for; I was too quick to judge. I'm sorry."

"Benedict, I…"

"No, let me finish. You have it in you to do this, Marcus. There's a courage and a fortitude there that I don't think even you are aware of. Something of your old soul must have seeped into that vessel he walks around in, for I've only seen such strength of character once before – and that was at the point of my blade." Both men laughed. Benedict cupped his hand over Marcus', still resting on his shoulder. "I want you to know that I'm proud to have known you, to have helped you in some small way – though I think you'd have done just as well without me. I may not have been everything Sathom needed. My destiny was clearly never to free our kin, but you're all that I never could be and everything I could have wished for… in a son. I would have been proud to have been a father to a man as true as you, Marcus. Should anyone ever make you feel less than your worth, well, you just remember I said that."

"Come now, old man, you talk as if we'll never see each other again." Marcus responded to the sentiment with his usual joviality, giving Benedict a playful slap on the back as they both stood up. "You're not going soft on me now, are you? Because I'm not sure my constitution will take any more unexpected occurrences in this lifetime."

"Ha! Me, soft? Never! Now go, get some sleep. I'm guessing Sathom has you all leaving early tomorrow. You'll need all the rest you can get."

Marcus smiled a little more easily, his conversation with Benedict having allayed some of his disquiet.

"I'll see you tomorrow. Just make sure to have me a hearty luncheon ready to put in my pack. You can be equally proud to be my mother, if you like." Then he laughed and jumped aside as

Benedict aimed a piece of tree bark at him, the familiar stern look reappearing across his face.

As Marcus turned and walked away, disappearing around the wall of the cottage, Benedict sat back down on the tree and resumed his stargazing, suffering the cold until he heard the front door close behind the last of the temporary occupants of his home. There he stayed, at length, until he assumed the others had fallen asleep.

Finally going back inside and relighting a single candle, he gathered a piece of parchment and a quill and sat at the table, taking care not to wake Marcus, who was snoring beside the dying embers of the fire. His writing complete, he rose from the chair and took a brief look around the room, before collecting a pack and short-sword from the chest beneath the window. After slinging the pack over his shoulder and sheathing the sword at his hip, he cast a brief glance around the room before opening the front door, closing it carefully behind him as he vanished into the night.

Marcus awoke with a start. A quick glance towards the un-shuttered window told him it was still dark, yet his body-clock was aware of the hour. The sun would rise soon, and when it did, they needed to be on the road. Scrambling to his feet, he draped the woollen blanket from his bed around his bare shoulders and proceeded to set out some kindling upon the dead ashes of the previous night's fire. Holding his fingers against the wood, he flicked a tiny flame into life, keeping it in position until a good fire took hold, then leant back on his haunches to absorb the heat and ward off the morning chill.

It was a morning routine he'd grown accustomed to, but he knew today would be the last time he knew such comforts, for the foreseeable future at least. As he stared into the blaze, he didn't know if he'd return, and he didn't care to think on it. That way led to doubts, and he'd resolved the previous night to put those to one side. If someone like Benedict had faith in him, then he deserved no less from himself.

Leaving his thoughts in the fiery light, Marcus got up and retrieved his tunic from where it hung over the back of Benedict's chair. He'd laundered it the evening before and it was still damp, but for some reason it made him feel better to pull the clean linen onto his torso. Next, he took his black leather straps and began to expertly bind them around his arms. They were purely decorative, serving no useful purpose, but he'd always worn them, and habit seemed reassuring at that moment. Having slept in his trousers, only his boots remained. Tugging them onto each foot and straightening them out a few inches above his knees, he was thankful for his wealth. Good boots were a luxury, and, even among Vaharian nobility, he owned some of the best made boots in the city, purchased at great expense from the finest cobbler. Turning over the cuffs, he still marvelled at the perfect fit; he'd always been someone who took care to dress well, who took pride in his attire. However, he could never have predicted just how much comfort and durability would become so much more important than fashion. He knew nothing of the terrain they'd be covering in the coming days and weeks, but he felt certain the blackened leather uppers and solid wooden soles would serve him well. The thought of footwear reminded him of the state of the vessels feet. He'd caught site of them once they'd come into the light of the cottage the evening before. The poor man had said nothing of any pain, and Marcus had intuitively guessed that any concern he might express wouldn't have been welcomed by the proud bulk of a fellow that had accompanied them home.

Hopefully, Sathom had found him something appropriate to wear. He'd not been awake to see their return, and so far had seen neither hide nor hair of either man that morning. Sathom was often elsewhere at that time each day. He didn't sleep, so there was no bed to find him in. He assumed the vessel had slept on the floor in Benedict's room, as there was no sign of another makeshift sleeping area.

He was about to slice up some bread to toast over the fire when the man from the crypt appeared from Benedict's room, adorned in a rather fine suit of gold-toned armour with the pommel of a large sword visible behind his shoulder. Marcus was surprised to see it was possible for the man to look even bigger than he did barely-dressed. Beneath the well-fitted cuirass, he wore a simple black jerkin that extended down to cover loose black trousers. Bracers that looked as if they'd been made to measure protected his forearms and, as Marcus was pleased to note, he did have a sturdy pair of boots, made from gold-toned metal to match the other pieces of the suit. His shoulders were covered by extensions from the cuirass but the majority of his arms were bare, his huge muscles on show as he strode purposefully into the room.

"Sathom did well, I see." Marcus greeted the vessel with a cheery tone. "Though I'm not even going to ask how he came by such fine attire." After a moment's quizzical look, the vessel understood to what Marcus was referring and glanced down at his armour, before nodding in response. "I hope Benedict didn't keep you awake with his snoring. I'd have offered you my bed, had I been awake when you returned."

"I slept in the room alone. Your... *friend* was not there when I entered, and is not there now."

Confused, Marcus started to head towards the front door to check if the old man was still where he'd left him the night before. But, suddenly remembering their conversation, everything became sorely clear. Scanning the room, it didn't take long for Marcus to notice the folded parchment at the centre of the table. He hurriedly picked it up and opened it to read Benedict's words.

Marcus,

I've gone to re-acquaint the point of my sword with an old 'friend'. I believe he's waited long
enough to avenge her death.

There's one thing you should know before you set off. Your father's alive – you didn't kill him.

Now, don't hate Sathom for this. I know he should have told you – I said as much – but he was only doing what he felt he had to. Damn elementals! They don't think like us.

Whatever, my point is, just let it be, for now at least. You have bigger fish to fry. I just thought you deserved to know the truth.

Remember your promise to me. Save my son. Perhaps we will meet again, as once we were.

Farewell my friend. Good luck.
Benedict.

"He's gone!" Marcus stared at the note as if the words might change before his eyes. Oddly, he felt little anger at Benedict's revelation about his father. Perhaps it was as the old man had said, there were tougher things to deal with. Perhaps the anger would come later. Either way, he was content to push it to the back of his mind for the time being. He'd confront Sathom with what he'd learnt later – if he got the chance.

The vessel hadn't known anything of Benedict other than his intense desire to kill him, and thus, had little wish to see the man again. However, it was obvious the one who'd saved his life was taking his departure hard.

"Surely he'll return. You'll see him once our journey is done."

"No, I think not. He's gone to fight the dragon." Marcus spoke softly, more to himself than to the man now at his side.

"Then may he be victorious."

Marcus got up from the table, letting the note fall from his grasp.

"He won't be. Though he will fight to the best of his ability, of that I've no doubt… Ah, you don't understand – and I don't expect you to. Come, we have a quest to begin. The sun will have risen before we leave at this rate. I expect Sathom and Erryn will arrive shortly, and you look ready." Marcus walked over to a hook on the wall, next to the front door, and took down two heavy, woollen cloaks, handing one to the vessel. "Here, you'll need this." Both men draped the cloaks around their shoulders, fastening the ties at their necks, before collecting separate packs and heading out of the door.

"Wait, I've forgotten something. You go ahead, I'll be there in a moment." Marcus gestured for the vessel to go outside.

Once he'd left, Marcus picked up his staff from where it had languished too long against the far wall, in the shadows. As it sprang to life at his touch, the room was lit brighter than ever, allowing Marcus an unhindered view of the place he'd known as home for the past few months. What would happen to Benedict's cottage now he was gone? Would any of them ever set foot there again? Only time would tell – and time was a commodity dwindling by the second. Willing the crystal at the top of his staff to glow slightly less, Marcus bid the cottage farewell and left to join the vessel in the half-light of dawn outside.

Sathom and Erryn were stood with the new comrade when Marcus stepped outside. It seemed introductions had already been made, as all three were exchanging what passed for pleasantries in such an odd situation. Despite the crispness of the air, Marcus' heart warmed as Erryn greeted him with a smile.

"Are you ready?" she asked, the odd auburn curl escaping from beneath the hood of her cloak. She was dressed from head to toe in green; her usual clothing, *best for blending into the scenery on a hunt*, as she put it. Even the wool of her cloak was dyed to match the forest.

"As I'll ever be," Marcus replied with his familiar crooked smile.

"Good. Then let us depart. We need to leave Vaharia with haste." Sathom stood out among the party, the only one without an outer-garment of any kind. He was still dressed in the thin white shirt and light-weight brown trousers that he always wore; no cloak, and no pack either.

"Sathom, you appear to be a little… under-dressed. Won't you succumb to the cold?" Marcus' tone hinted at amusement, but he was worried for the elemental's well-being.

"Your concern is touching, my friend, but worry not. I am not vulnerable to the elements as corporeal beings are."

Marcus nodded acceptance and clenched the edges of his cloak together with one hand, his other gripping his staff tighter.

"Then let's be away. The sooner we get this over with, the sooner we can all be back here warming ourselves by the fire." His words were deliberately positive but, in his mind, he was no more certain than anyone else present that morning.

As the sun began to rise in the west, the group set off from the village, heading east towards the nearest set of steps that would lead them out of Vaharia and up onto the relative safety of the Stone Highway.

CHAPTER TEN

Leaving Vaharia had not been quite as simple as anyone in the party had hoped. Sathom's plan had been to exit the kingdom via the steps that led onto the Stone Highway and down the other side, straight into the dwarven kingdom of Geryndor. He'd meticulously planned the route firstly to cover the shortest distance, but also to ensure their passage didn't take them through the neighbouring forest-covered lands of Sa'hahlenfell. However, even the best-laid plans can change; as they discovered after almost two hours' journey, when they found the way down into Geryndor blocked.

Sathom loudly chastised himself, having not taken into account the lack of any trade with the dwarves for the last few decades, muttering about how he should have checked the stairway beforehand. With a huge, unmovable wall of rocks and boulders barring the way at the bottom, there was nothing they could do but turn back, taking the Stone Highway onward to Sa'hahlenfell. Sathom knew that way was clear, as he'd recently had cause to travel close by, but it was far from ideal.

The Stone Highway formed the south to south-eastern edge of the kingdom. Built long ago, of the same architecture and material as the city, it acted as both a barrier to threats from the outside world, and a safe trade route between kingdoms. With external walls higher than any building and a peaked roof running its entire length, it was a majestic sight. It curved organically; from the far-western edge of Vaharia, along the border with Geryndor, and passing between the crags of the Mountains of Nor. Small, arched openings perforated the thick walls at even intervals, providing light and a glimpse of the lands many feet below. Once the last of the group had ascended the stairs and set foot upon the smooth, white stone walkway, an air of relief settled over them all. Of course, there was still far to go and much danger ahead, but the simple change of scene was enough to raise their spirits.

Marcus seemed to revert to type once the pressure lifted. As they made their way along the highway, his long-legged strides put him a little ahead of the others and he whistled a cheerful tune. Holding his staff lightly and swinging it back and forth, now and then he would edge closer to the walls to look casually through one of the openings, before moving onward at a steady pace.

Sathom was next in line, deep in thought with his eyes glazed over in the grip of a thousand-yard stare. With no pack to carry and no cloak to encumber his movement, his arms moved freely at his sides, his gait loose and almost fluid; so much so that anyone watching him closely would have thought him gliding forwards rather than walking.

The vessel was behind Sathom, and had been keeping his suspicious eyes firmly focused on him for some time; there was something about the man's manner that made him uneasy. However, the intermittent questions and small talk from the auburn-haired woman at his side had kept him from concentrating enough to even notice how he walked, let alone figure out if he was to be trusted.

Erryn really wanted to catch up with Marcus, but her fear of becoming nothing more than a giggling girl in his presence kept her from doing so. She'd spent little time with him in the days before they left Vaharia, and it irritated her to realise she'd missed him. When he'd emerged from the cottage that morning, her heart had almost missed a beat, a lump forming in her throat as he'd acknowledged her with the smile she was already beginning to crave. So, she hung back with the vessel, attempting to convince herself the only reason was to make him feel welcome as the newcomer to their group.

"So, er… Vess. You don't mind if I call you Vess, do you? I mean, you haven't actually got a name, so I… well, a name would be nice. You'd like a name, yes?" Hoping that she hadn't offended him, Erryn looked up at the muscular man. He was gleaming from head to toe in golden armour and, for a moment, she was speechless. With his giant sword strapped to his back and the purposeful look in his piercing blue eyes, he resembled something otherworldly; proud and impressive like some sort of warrior deity. Realising that yet again she was staring at a man she'd only just met with her mouth hanging open, she quickly reformed her lips into a smile and returned to the business of placing one foot in front of the other, lest she repeat another of her embarrassing first impressions.

"A name… would be welcome, my lady." The vessel turned his head and looked down to meet her gaze as they continued walking, a small but warm smile softening his usually serious face. Erryn returned the smile and nodded.

"Then Vess it shall be." With that, the pair walked on in comfortable silence, following Marcus' lead and very nearly forgetting they were involved in anything more than a leisurely stroll.

After walking, uninterrupted, for many hours, Marcus brought the party to a standstill, a choice of direction laid before him. With Sathom being the only one who knew where they were going, and the mage having such a terrible sense of direction, Marcus waited for him to reach where he'd stopped, the highway forking off to his left.

"Which way now, Sathom? Onward, or do we take this road?" Marcus asked, motioning towards the turning with his eyes.

"Marcus, really?" Erryn said, trying hard not to laugh.

Marcus looked confused.

"I've not been awake long, but I think even *I* could direct us from here." Vess said, giving an exaggerated glance towards the Vaharian landscape below.

Marcus chose to ignore his human companions, and instead looked to Sathom to offer a serious response.

"Ah, yes, Dragon's Pass," Sathom said, staring down the new path.

"Well, that sounds ominous." Marcus echoed the thoughts of the others.

"This road will take us through dragon territory, but there have been no dragon sightings for well over a thousand years, and…"

"Er, I beg to differ," Marcus interrupted. "We saw one, only yesterday in fact. Isn't that right, vessel?"

"It's just Vess now," Erryn jumped in, proudly announcing her name-giving.

Vess nodded, looking awkward.

"My, you two have grown close. Should I be choosing a hat?" Marcus' sarcasm was rewarded with a sharp kick to the shin by Erryn, who then felt guilty as he winced in pain.

"If you three have quite finished..." Sathom regained their attention and continued where he'd left off. "As I was saying, regardless of the existence of dragons, we are quite safe on this road. It was constructed as it is to protect travellers from such beasts. I cannot guarantee safe passage once we leave the highway however; I had not considered danger from the skies. Still, we have no choice in the matter. Onward, then." Leaving his companions contemplating the possibility of being plucked from the ground by a huge flying monster with blades for teeth, Sathom turned left and resumed his smooth movement along Dragon's Pass. Now it was his turn to lead as Marcus no longer seemed quite so keen to reach the next leg of their journey.

They'd travelled but half way along the pass when they were all startled to a standstill by a deathly roar rumbling up from the landscape below the highway. The noise grew deafeningly loud as it ascended, passing so close to the wall that the stone vibrated with the resonance, and a black shadow momentarily eclipsed the shards of daylight breaking through the gaps. Though logic assured them the roof above their heads kept the creature at bay, all but Sathom remained frozen to the spot until the roar passed overhead and gradually faded off into the distance on the other side. When she was sure it had gone, Erryn dashed to peer out through one of the gaps. Unlike Marcus and Vess, she'd never seen or heard a dragon, and though her skin still tingled with fear, she was curious enough to want to see for herself the source of such a fearsome sound. To her disappointment, all that was visible was a dark shape on the horizon, which quickly dipped down behind the far off hills.

The remainder of their journey along the Stone Highway was mercifully uneventful. The roof and walls provided protection from the chilly air, but, every now and then, a stiff breeze managed to pass through the gaps, causing cloaks to be pulled tighter and hoods to be raised. After the dragon, Sathom had felt it pertinent to remind his relieved companions of the many and varied dangers that may await them. Thus a pensive silence had descended over the party, and every member of the group travelled on as if alone.

As the sun began its downward arch to the end of the day, they finally came to another set of steps. From the landing above, they could make out nothing beyond a dense wall of towering pine trees, the tips forming an undulating green line across the bleak greyness of the sky. Down the steps, the way lay forwards through a narrow opening. Edged with branches sculpted to resemble a doorframe, the knotty wood took on a twisted, yet beautiful appearance, gracefully creating an archway to rival anything man could design.

"Sa'hahlenfell lies before us, my friends. I advise caution. Keep your wits about you, as I fear the inhabitants of this land may not take too kindly to visitors." Sathom's words of warning were heeded as everyone made their way down the steps and on through the opening into the forest, three pairs of eyes now adjusting to the dim, green-hued light and scanning the surroundings. Erryn was the last to walk over the threshold. As she did so, an odd, yet familiar feeling tugged at her hexan senses; there was magic in this place, and they had just passed through some kind of barrier. However, it must have been an ineffective barrier if they'd been able to so easily pass through it. Her mind working quickly, it occurred to her that their arrival on the other side had been anticipated… and allowed. They were not alone.

Through the branch-framed doorway, a very different world spread out in front of them. The tallest trees they had ever seen created a web of winding passages, the thick, straight trunks marking the landscape with dark, sincere lines. Between the trees, a sea of green flowed seamlessly, the different shades of the grasses and wide-leafed shrubs moving together in the breeze, creating shifting shadows. The forest was so densely covered that none of the party could see much beyond the immediate environment, but as the day's fading light seemed unable to find a chink in the armour of vegetation, it seemed likely the land further in continued to lie beneath a thick canopy.

Moving slowly, the human members of the party huddled together, alert and poised to reach for their weapons. Sathom walked a few steps ahead, his dark eyes smoothly assessing the area around them.

With the steps to the highway now a fair way behind, Marcus began to feel more than the trepidation caused by the elemental's cautionary remark; a very real sense of another presence close by infiltrated his mind until he could ignore it no longer. Glancing at Vess, he noted his stance had altered, like a dog with his hackles up.

"You thinking what I'm thinking?" he spoke to the warrior, barely above a whisper.

"We're being watched," Vess replied quietly, confirming Marcus' thoughts.

No sooner had the words left Vess' mouth than, from high up in the trees, a figure landed directly in front of them. Instantly steadying his feet, the person straightened up to reveal a tall, sinewy man with his arms lifted from his sides, brandishing a dagger in each hand. Vess raised his arm to reach for the hilt of his sword, but a few feet above them, the movement of a shadow, until that point unnoticed, gave him pause. Marcus immediately became aware of more shadows, many of them, all clearly belonging to someone, or something concealed within the lower branches of the trees, and effectively surrounding the group.

"Elves," Sathom pronounced, taking a step back.

"We are the Fell, and these are our lands." The man's black eyes appeared threatening, his nostrils flared and his lips curled into a snarl. "At this moment, one-hundred arrows are aimed at your throats. I suggest the explanation for your presence is swift, lest the swiftness of those arrows is something you care to bet against."

Now, each and every member of the group was highly aware of the foe hidden in the trees. Her eyes darting around, Erryn could understand why she hadn't seen them before; without knowing, it was easy to miss the glints from the numerous pairs of eyes, the thin shadows of poised arrows or the sharp, angled lines of arrowheads just proud of the dense rows of pine needles.

Vess didn't lower his arm, continuing to take a grip on the hilt of his sword instead. As his fingers closed around the metal, the stretching creak of multiple bowstrings echoed in the trees above their heads.

"Vess, this is *not* the time." Marcus spoke with forced composure, both to talk down the warrior at his side and to attempt to appease the hostile-looking elf, who seemed to be in charge. Vess grimaced at

Marcus, before reluctantly releasing his weapon and dropping his arm back to his side.

"Your leader is wise, Vaharian." Perhaps it was the fading light, but everything about the stranger seemed dark. His long, black hair was tied back behind sharply-pointed ears and the exposed skin of his torso, arms, neck, and face was evenly tanned. "Now, I ask you again, what is your purpose in this forest?" Never taking his eyes from them, nor dropping his guard, the elf aimed his question at Marcus, having assumed him leader of the intruders in his lands.

Marcus was about to respond when Sathom positioned himself further forwards than him and addressed the question himself.

"We court no conflict with your people, your highness."

The elf crossed his arms, his eyes pinched.

"You speak as if you know me."

"I know *of* you, Prince Athalir of the Fell." The eyes of the others jumped to Sathom, as confused as the elf at the elemental's familiarity.

"Then you must also know that you have made a grave mistake coming here?" For a moment his almost rhetorical question hung in the air, before Sathom, his face a mask as always, spoke again.

"Your highness, we wish nothing more than safe passage through your lands. I assure you, once we reach our destination, you will see the last of us."

"Safe passage, you say?" The prince's smirk made him appear markedly more mocking than sinister. "Well then, it appears you will be disappointed… and *dead!*"

Marcus, Vess and Erryn looked to the prince for a sign he might be about to attack, or give the signal to do so to his fellows in the trees. Sathom, however, held the elf's gaze without flinching.

"Your highness?"

"There can be no 'safe passage' through Sa'hahlenfell; not for Fell, and certainly not for Vaharians. Or does your knowledge of me not extend to the 'situation' of my kingdom?"

If it was possible, Sathom actually looked confused; though he said nothing. Obviously interpreting his silence astutely, the prince elaborated. "My kingdom is at war. The Daelin'vahs – 'lost ones' – hold the forest to the east. Only fools would attempt to traverse those lands without a full company of Fell archers at their backs – though I'll readily believe any Vaharian a fool. So, *fools*, I suggest you turn back towards the highway and return whence you came… *now!*" The menacing look returned to the prince's face, the dark shadows across his eyes amplifying the effect.

Vess and Erryn exchanged a look and started to turn in the direction of the way they'd entered, but Sathom stood fast. Arrows and daggers were no threat to him, and he hadn't come this far to turn back at the first obstacle that stood in their way. Nevertheless, it appeared the elf was immune to the diplomatic approach and, once again, something had occurred for which he hadn't planned. His mortal companions, however competent, were no match for the skilled bowmen of the Fell; any attempt to get past Athalir and his men could only end one way. No, it was hopeless, what else could they do but turn back?

All the while, Marcus had been observing the impasse between his friend and the elf prince. He'd watched Vess and Erryn give up and turn back, and he'd grown irritated as it seemed Sathom was close to doing the same. He didn't doubt the ability of either the arrows in the trees or the daggers within the elf's hands to meet their target, but he was no coward. This quest was too important to simply abandon and return home. Whatever happened next, he had to try something.

Calmly moving out of the shadow that came over him as the light had dimmed, he stood next to Sathom, the sounds of numerous bowstrings tightening once more. Prince Athalir switched his line of sight to Marcus and raised his daggers higher in warning, glaring at him as he did so. Sathom began to urge the mage to follow his companions, but Marcus lifted his hand to hold back his words and proceeded to address the elf.

"Your highness, I'm afraid I can't do as you wish. You see, my companions and I are on a quest of great importance, one that stands beyond the boundary of your kingdom, and one that will, should we fail to succeed, mean the continued suffering of many innocent souls." Marcus' words were spoken softly and sincerely and, it seemed, had captured the attention of the prince, who tilted his head to listen with interest as he continued. "I would not presume that I or my friends could best you in combat, nor outrun you, but understand this; we have but one chance to defeat the governors and save those souls, and with all the power I have within me, until I am staring death in the face, I will push forwards… through you, if need be." Summoning the magic within him, Marcus was all set to conjure something suitably impressive, in the hope a display of his ability would turn the tide in their favour. However, before he'd even chosen a spell, the prince walked towards him, weapons lowered and a somehow less-threatening look in his dark eyes. Stopping within arm's reach, he stared curiously at Marcus.

"Did you say… 'governors'?"

"I, er, yes, I did."

"By which, am I to take it, you refer to the governors of Vaharia? And you seek to… destroy them?" The elf was pronouncing his words with precision, slowly requesting clarification on the meaning behind Marcus' speech.

"Well, I believe the word I used was 'defeat', but… yes, that's the general idea."

For a tense time, there was silence. Sathom stared at Marcus, blankly. Vess and Erryn had cautiously come back further into the forest as soon as they'd heard Marcus' words, and were now watching the proceedings avidly, though with the outcome of their friend's risk-taking not yet clear, keeping the choice of fight or flight in reserve.

Finally, Prince Athalir sheathed his daggers and raised his right hand above his head, palm open, one-hundred arrowheads disappearing back under cover of branches full of pine needles.

"Come!" And with that he turned and walked on, heading south-west and deeper into the dense forest of Sa'hahlenfell.

Marcus hesitated long enough to check everyone else had understood, then fell in line with the prince, with Sathom, Vess, and Erryn picking up pace behind.

With no one to see her face, as they walked on in the light of a full moon, Erryn smiled as she replayed Marcus' words in her head. It may not have been his threat of force or display of honour and courage that had changed the elf's mind – it was quite apparent that the intention of taking down the governors had appealed to him – but in that moment, she'd seen his soul and, regardless of who it really belonged to, she knew he was someone of true spirit.

CHAPTER ELEVEN

Sa'hahlenfell was a vast, tree-covered kingdom. The majesty of the forest was surpassed only by the grandeur of the mountains to the west, themselves covered from top to bottom by impossibly tall trees and lush vegetation. From between the highest peaks, a waterfall poured over the edge and divided the forest all the way down the slopes, powerfully tumbling into the crystal clear river below. The Returning River – or Raenfaren, as the Fell knew it – placidly wound its life-giving waters through the centre of the land, finally disappearing through the trees at the eastern border.

Following the lead of Prince Athalir as he'd crossed the landscape had been no easy task. His knowledge of the terrain meant that he physically anticipated the natural hazards, even in the evening light. However, Marcus and Vess stumbled often, Marcus laughing it off and Vess trying in vain to make it appear deliberate. Though Sathom and Erryn fared better, with Sathom walking through anything that got in his way and Erryn well used to negotiating woodland in less-than-ideal conditions, they still managed to lose sight of Athalir many times as he forged ahead, fast and oblivious. The warmer climate didn't help matters; with all but Sathom wrapped up in heavy woollen cloaks, it wasn't long before fatigue set in, as their clothing became damp with sweat.

The archers that had surrounded the group had been conspicuously absent, until Erryn had caught sight of a movement in the low branches alongside them. Grabbing Marcus' arm, she'd silently gestured to one side and they'd both squinted their eyes to make out the vague shapes of people moving swiftly through the heights of the trees. Even when they knew they were there, it had been hard to see them clearly. They were so adept that they became just shadowy outlines, leaping stealthily from branch to branch, tree to tree. It had been unnerving to know they were there, unseen, but it had also provided reassurance. No one in the party knew what the 'lost ones' from the east were capable of, yet, should they attack from behind, some comfort came from assuming the archers might see them first.

It was quite some time before the prince arrived at a large clearing, and stood on the periphery to wait for all of his followers to catch up. As everyone gathered with him, the rest of his company dropped from the surrounding trees, landing on their feet and rising in one fluid motion, much as Athalir himself had done back at the entrance. Their bows in hand and quivers full of arrows still strapped to their shirtless backs, they waited, proud and silent, looking towards their leader. The prince nodded once and every archer responded with a respectful but shallow bow of the head, before walking off into the clearing.

"Follow me, but stay close," the prince ordered the party. "Your presence here will be… unwelcome."

"And we were so warmly embraced before," Marcus muttered under his breath, smiling to himself. Athalir scowled at him, and the mage made a mental note to remember elves had excellent hearing.

The clearing spread over a considerable area, almost large enough to adequately contain half of Whitestone,. The buildings were entirely made from wood and supported upon short poles, small wooden staircases providing access to each doorway. Though well-spaced, there were innumerable buildings such as these, some with a flickering orange glow in the small, unglazed windows, others with the shutters closed and only thin shards of light visible through the cracks. The enticingly clear, narrow river flowed through the centre of the Fell settlement, the banks on either side connected by way of many arched wooden footbridges spread along its course.

Trailing in Athalir's wake, they passed only a few elves, their reactions to the foreigners ranging from guarded curiosity to open hostility. Yet with one direct look from their prince, they quickly went back to whatever they'd been doing before, though they could still be heard murmuring to each other in the background.

As they crossed one of the footbridges, the travellers paused for a moment to take in the environment. The Fell city, for it was large enough to be called a city, was obviously shutting up for the night, and yet all around it seemed alive. Brightly lit and with a residual heat in the air, it was like a great animal at rest, eyes aglow and breathing softly as it lay in the moonlight, preparing for sleep to come.

The magic of the place was not lost on either Erryn or Marcus. Erryn had experienced it as soon as they set foot on Sa'hahlenfell soil, but now they were at the very heart of the kingdom, it almost overwhelmed her. It was like no magic she'd ever experienced before, natural and more connected with the land than with people. It seemed to be all around her, floating on the warm breeze, flickering in the flames of torches, sparkling on the surface of the river. The effect was less intense for Marcus, but his mage blood seemed to move a little quicker through his veins as he took in the picture that surrounded him. Snapping them both from their reverie, Vess coughed and brought their attention to the prince, who was stood a little way off, looking impatient.

"Yes, I'm not sure keeping him waiting would be prudent." Sathom backed up Vess' unspoken urge to move on, he and the warrior resuming the course. Marcus glanced down at Erryn, their shared thoughts lingering between them, then gently took her hand in his. This time, she didn't object. Closing her fingers around his large hand, she smiled up at him before turning to face ahead. Marcus did the same and together they followed, a few strides behind the others.

Eventually, after Athalir had led the group towards the mountains, he brought them to a standstill in front of a much larger building at the foot of the slopes. Raised higher than the other structures, it overlooked the city, a wide stairway ascending from the ground up to a balcony that stretched around the exterior walls. Two Fell stood bolt upright either side of double-doors, their arms crossed over their dark-skinned bare chests, with an ornate dagger in each hand. As the prince approached the doors, the guards bowed as the archers had done, their faces stern and showing no sign they even saw the strangers at his back. Pulling open the doors, Athalir beckoned the others to follow, and they all entered the building.

Inside, the humans were taken by surprise. They had walked into a gloriously opulent hall, a room that seemed far larger than the exterior had indicated. The walls were adorned with giant, engraved wooden friezes, skilfully crafted and finely detailed. A long, ornately carved table surrounded by many equally decorative, high-backed chairs sat at the centre of the hall, lit from above by a gleaming silver-coloured chandelier, countless tiny flames dancing from within the reflective metal frame. However, most of the lavishness took the form of more natural decorations. Colour was in abundance, with various species of flowers arranged for the best affect against every wall. Broad-leaved plants created graceful archways and ivy twisted its way around supporting wooden beams and pillars. At the back of the hall, a wide dais held twin thrones. Framed by the foliage of tall fern-like plants, they were oversized and more extravagant than anything else in the room. The ends of the arms had been expertly shaped to resemble the head and neck of a majestic horse, and the back rests spiralled up in separate pieces of wood, finally connecting to each other high above via an upturned horseshoe.

The prince led everyone further in to the hall and, with an outstretched arm, directed his guests to take a seat at the table. Remaining standing at the end closest to where everyone was seated, for a time he looked as if he was deciding what to say, his angled jaw set firm and his gaze resting on each of his guests, one by one.

Everyone waited in complete silence, their eyes fixed on their Fell host. The protocol for such situations was unknown to any of them, even Sathom, and none wished to miss a vital signal that may allude to how they should behave.

Finally, the prince spoke, his demeanour pensive and his eyes locked onto Marcus, to whom he addressed his next question.

"First I must know this, Vaharian; what manner of man are you?" His voice carried a suspicious undertone, though he appeared calmer than at their initial encounter.

Marcus held the prince's gaze, and replied without delay.

"I'm a mage." He watched as Athalir's face showed no sign of surprise. "But I suspect that's a fact you're already aware of?"

"It is – though I admit your unashamedly-forthright answer has taken me by surprise."

"Do I have anything to be ashamed of?"

"If you have need to ask… then perhaps not. Tell me of your quest then. I am eager to learn why a Vaharian mage would seek the demise of the leaders of his land." Prince Athalir pulled the chair he'd been resting his hands on from beneath the table and sat down. Vess noticeably relaxed at the action, his guard having been up since they'd first met the elf. He'd internally questioned the sanity of his mage companion when it seemed he was about to talk his way into trouble, but a modicum of respect had crept in as he'd listened to Marcus' speech, and witnessed an impulsive audacity he felt admiration for. Even so, all the way from the outskirts of the forest to the moment the prince had become seated, he'd been prepared to strike, whatever the outcome.

Marcus deferred the question to Sathom, who, he pointed out, was much better at providing explanations, and who, for the next hour, retold the entire story, while adeptly fielding Athalir's intermittent demands for elaboration.

Given their first impression, none would have anticipated what had followed the meeting in the palace hall. The prince, having fully absorbed the information given to him, had offered lodging for the night to Marcus and his comrades. With a promise to guide them safely through Sa'hahlenfell the following morning, he'd called for servants to bring food to the table, and a welcome feast had been laid before the hungry travellers.

Athalir did not join them. Instead he bid them a goodnight, before leaving instruction to a rather anxious-looking elderly male elf to show his guests to their chambers once they were finished. He was unaware of Vess' icy stare at his back as he left the hall into the east wing of the palace.

With their stomachs full and their minds weary, those of the group that had the ability to sleep realised just how much they needed it, as they were led by the elderly elf through the west wing and into individual guest rooms located either side of a long, narrow corridor. The rooms were identically furnished and decorated, with similar lavishness to the main hall, a large, canopied bed at the centre of each. Marcus was the last to be designated a room, the one furthest from the hall. Closing the door as the elf left, he turned to face the comfortable-looking bed and was briefly reminded of his own room back in Whitestone. It had been so long since he'd spent the night on anything but a hard floor that he wondered if he'd even be able to sleep in a proper bed again. Sitting on the edge, he removed his tunic and boots and fell back onto the sumptuous bedspread, chuckling to himself as he bounced slightly before being almost absorbed by the softness. He was just thinking it wouldn't actually be that difficult to sleep in a bed again when a light rap sounded at the door. After the moment he'd shared with Erryn earlier that evening, a twinge of hope that it was her propelled him from the brink of sleep. Nearly tripping up over his discarded clothing, he composed himself in time, straightened his ruffled hair and opened the door, the disappointment clear on his face as an agitated looking Vess didn't wait to be invited in.

"Come in, Vess," Marcus mumbled sarcastically, closing the door behind his visitor.

"I don't trust him!" Vess turned to face Marcus upon hearing the door close, his features pulled tight with vexation.

"Is there anyone you *do* trust? I've noticed how you watch Sathom." Marcus was tired and it was too late for this conversation. Besides, he'd already come to a similar conclusion about this mysterious prince, deciding to keep him at arm's length until he'd fulfilled his promise.

"I don't trust someone whose face doesn't match their words." Vess remained resolute in his conviction as he spoke of the elemental.

Marcus had to see his point. Sathom's way was indeed difficult to get used to, even more so if your only experience of people was a joker who'd try to kill you and an old bitter man who'd ordered it done. The first faces he'd seen may not have been friendly, but at least there'd been no doubt about the owners' intentions. Though technically Sathom wasn't actually a person, it seemed wise to leave that discussion for another time.

Walking over to Vess, he placed a reassuring hand on his shoulder and smiled.

"I don't think he means us harm, though I agree we should be cautious." Marcus ushered Vess to the door. "Let him lead us to the border and we'll handle anything *else*, should it occur. Meanwhile, get some sleep, my friend. Who knows when we'll get this opportunity again?"

Vess glanced across Marcus' shoulder at the bed, and nodded, before heading back to his own room. Closing the door behind him,

Marcus resumed his horizontal position and, with a passing image of Erryn in his mind, fell asleep almost immediately.

With his guests oblivious to his departure from the palace, Prince Athalir took to the trees. Practically invisible from the ground, the elf expertly leapt from branch to branch, moving swiftly beneath the shadows. Only his eyes and twin blades could be seen, as every now and then a slither of moonlight broke through the spiny canopy.

After a much shorter time than it had taken to travel from Sa'hahlenfell's border, he arrived at the same spot in which he'd landed amidst the group of interlopers. Repeating his cat-like drop to the ground, he walked to the very edge of the forest, to where the light wasn't so restricted, and took a vial filled with a black, gelatinous liquid from inside one of his boots. Looking around to make certain he was alone, he hesitated, then pulled the stopper from the vial and carefully tipped it so that just one drop fell to the vegetation at his feet. He stood back and waited. For a short time there was nothing. Athalir began to wonder if he'd failed to do as he'd been instructed. He was about to try again when a swirling black ribbon of smoke rose up from the liquid. It rapidly grew wider and taller, a translucent figure forming within as the smoke expanded. When the figure was as tall as Athalir, it started to look more solid, until eventually the smoke dissipated and a black-haired man stepped towards the prince. The man looked pointedly past Athalir, then to either side, eventually moving a step closer until he looked directly into the elf's eyes.

"Surely you are not so stupid that you would summon me empty-handed?" The man's voice had a deep resonance that didn't seem to fit with his appearance, and, not for the first time, something about it sent shivers down the spine of the usually-fearless prince. His black eyes burnt into Athalir's until he could barely resist the urge to look away.

"I have news." It was all the elf could muster as the acrid breath of the other man assaulted his nostrils.

"What you should have is dead elf, Fell prince, or were the terms of our agreement not made clear to you at our last meeting?"

"No, I mean, yes, but… I don't believe the man you require dead is one of the Fell." Now Athalir had the dark-haired man's attention, a quizzical expression replacing the one of menace.

"This had better not be some kind of trick. There *are* no other elves but the Fell."

"No, and I'm not suggesting there are, but the one you seek is not an elf. He is human… and a mage." Athalir then went on to convey the information as Sathom had to him earlier that night, careful to omit the part about the mage currently sleeping in royal chambers at the heart of Sa'hahlenfell. He wanted this evil creature nowhere near his people or his family.

"So, the other race she spoke of was a Meranell. Well, well. I have to admit, I didn't see that one coming." The man spoke to himself and gave a low, dry laugh, before stopping abruptly to address Athalir once more. "You met with this man and you didn't think to, oh… *kill* him, perhaps?"

"I could have done, but as I said, he wasn't alone. Had I failed and been killed myself, there would have been no one to inform you of his existence."

"Hmm, good point. Wise move, prince. I originally questioned the governors' sense in choosing a pathetic elf to do their bidding – maybe I was… a little too hasty."

Athalir gritted his teeth at the man's insult, saying nothing.

"So, I'm assuming you know how to find this mage. Your side of the bargain has not yet been upheld."

"I do, but you will have to allow me some time. Killing him without alerting his companions will take some planning."

"Oh no, the situation has changed now, my pointy-eared prince. We need this one alive."

"Alive?"

"Yes, indeed." The man's tone was laced with a disturbing hint of cheerfulness. "It should be quite simple for one as… *cunning* as you. Get him on his own and then summon me again. I will take it from there. Oh, but first you must cut off his hands."

Athalir almost choked.

"What?"

"You heard me. He's a mage. They use their hands for spell-casting, you know. Cut… off… his… hands!"

Athalir opened his mouth to protest but the man held up a bony finger right in front of it. "Now now, you either accept the deal, or you don't. I'm sure your parents will understand your inability to save them, and curse the day you were birthed… *from their graves.*" The man moved back to his original position and gradually faded from view, surrounded in the same smoke that had accompanied his appearance, his malicious, unnaturally wide smile being the last visible part of him.

CHAPTER TWELVE

For the first time in weeks, Marcus was not the first one up. When, an hour or so after dawn, he emerged from the doors of the palace, bleary-eyed and still yawning, everyone else was assembled outside, a number of black horses and Prince Athalir added to the group.

The clearing now basking in sunlight, Marcus could see the full expanse of the Fell city. On each side of the sparkling river, there must have been enough raised, wooden buildings to house at least a thousand elves. However, other familiar components of a civilised community were also much easier to recognise in the bright light of day. There was a smithy, a food market, various workshops, and much more, all bustling with life in the oddly temperate environment.

Realising he wouldn't be needing his cloak, at least while still in Sa'hahlenfell, Marcus rolled it up and shoved it into his pack, striding down the stairway and towards the gathering.

"Ah, your leader graces us with his presence," Athalir mocked, as he finished adjusting a bridal.

"We're riding horses!" Erryn trilled out, her face positively radiant with delight. Vess grunted, and somehow Marcus could tell he'd already voiced his objection, to no avail.

Sathom was already seated in a saddle. The reins of his mount resting loosely in his hands, appearing to all the world the accomplished horseman.

Athalir approached Marcus, a small hide-wrapped parcel in his hands.

"Here, for the journey."

"What is it?" Marcus asked.

"Just some food. Never let it be said the Fell are ungracious. No visitor leaves the palace empty-handed. It is customary. I'm certain it will serve you better than a hand-crafted Meernavahn."

"Oh, I don't know, I've always wanted one of those." Marcus joked with smiling eyes, but stopped when he realised his humour was unreciprocated. "I'm sure it would be much more useful than a… er – Thank you." Marcus took the parcel and added it to his pack. Looking up at the prince as he walked back to the horses, he noticed a substantially-filled pack slung over his shoulder. *Looks a bit excessive for a relatively short trip*, he thought to himself. Perhaps it was another custom of the Fell to be well-prepared. After all, this elf knew the terrain, and knew what they might face along the way; who was Marcus to question what provisions may or may not be required? Nevertheless, with Vess' concerned words of the night before still in his thoughts, he couldn't help but wonder if they were about to be led into danger. It had all been a little too easy. One moment they had been seconds from having to fight for their lives, the next they were enjoying the hospitality of the formerly-hostile prince, who made no effort to hide his loathing of Vaharians. Why had he chosen to help them?

Questions that he should have perhaps addressed before following Athalir were now coming at him thick and fast; the city not the only thing to appear clearer in the morning sun.

"Marcus, we need to be on our way," Sathom called out, distracting him from his anxious contemplation. This was a situation they could no longer avoid, and Marcus realised the futility of devoting any more time to worrying. He walked towards one of only two horses left without a rider, and proficiently hoisted himself up into the saddle. Erryn's mount was next to his and she grinned at him as he appeared at her level. Her enthusiasm infectious, it was easy to put his disquiet behind him, at least for now. Laughing fondly at her childlike excitement, Marcus looked around to see if everyone was ready to leave. The last horse, the biggest one, had been reserved for Vess, who was stood at its side, staring warily up at its back.

"You need a hand there, Vess?" Marcus called back. Vess screwed up his face in response and took firm hold of the pommel of the saddle, heaving himself up and doing his best to keep his pride intact by not falling flat on his back in the process. Once seated, he flashed a false smile at Marcus, his expression returning to one of uneasiness the second the mage looked away.

With Athalir's mount at the front, they were just about to head out – when proceedings were brought to a halt by the arrival of a female elf on horseback, pulling up beside the prince. Like Athalir – in fact, like all the Fell they'd seen – her complexion was dark and her hair was black. Her elongated, sharply-pointed ears protruded outward through the thick ebony that surrounded her face, and a braid that reached down to the backs of her knees curved across her back and rested against the side of her saddle. Her features were tapered and elegant. High, well-defined cheekbones peaked below gently slanting eyes, and an elaborately-painted mask framed them and ran across the bridge of her long, slender nose. Marcus and Vess found themselves drawn to stare in her direction; she had the most striking looks either had ever seen, and a presence to match. The woman was well armed, a bow and quiver strapped to her back and two daggers, very similar to Athalir's, sheathed against her thighs. Though she was clearly on familiar terms with Athalir, he didn't seem particularly pleased to see her.

"Kahla, what are you doing here?"

"I'm coming with you, my prince," she replied, without any hint of doubt and her resolve clear in her eyes. Athalir shifted uncomfortably in the saddle, glancing awkwardly over his shoulder at the now intrigued audience at his back.

"That won't be necessary this time, Kahla. Stay here and watch over my parents for me until I return."

"And just what do you think your mother and father would say, were they to know I'd let you go to the east without escort?" The woman stared at Athalir, penetrating his steely determination to send her away. Sighing loudly, Athalir, slumped his shoulders with resignation, the normally-imposing character taking on a mildly defeated demeanour. Steering her horse in line at the front of the party, Kahla clicked her tongue, prompting the group to walk on.

It didn't take the riders long to reach forest thick enough that the city was barely visible. A short while later and it was as if it had never existed at all. The sounds of everyday life had gradually faded away, replaced with the various squawks and squeals of a menagerie of animals hidden among the trees. The sun's rays struggled to break through the canopy above, creating a green half-light that seemed to give the path ahead a mystical atmosphere.

Their route was clearly laid out before them in the form of the gently flowing river. Athalir had announced as they left the clearing that it would lead them directly to the far edge of the forest. As long as they followed its course, they wouldn't become lost. All agreed that it would be very easy to lose your way in such a place, and made sure to keep the winding waters in their sights at all times.

A bit further into the journey and a tentative calm had begun to settle over the group. The rhythmic plodding of the horses was almost relaxing, even for Vess, whose knuckles were no longer white from gripping the reins for dear life. Sathom had fallen back alongside Erryn and they were engaged in conversation. Marcus whistled quietly, lost in memories. The tune was one that Julia had sung to him when he was a child. It was a happy song, one that told of magical, faraway lands, and it felt appropriate for the time and place.

Only the Elves remained alert, bolt upright on their horses, both pairs of eyes scanning the trees as they passed by. Suddenly, Kahla's body became a little tenser. Sharing a knowing glance with Athalir, whose posture had also changed, she started to reach for her bow. However, without warning, an arrow shot out from somewhere amidst the trees and whooshed a hair's breadth from Athalir's shoulder, just grazing his skin on its way past. At the whistle of the arrow, the prince's horse had startled, rearing up on its hind legs before coming down again with a thump of hooves. There was no time for explanations. They were under attack. Kahla kicked her booted heals into the flanks of her horse, which immediately bolted forwards into a canter, the other horses naturally following suit.

The situation apparent the moment blood was drawn, everyone else braced themselves as their mounts took off at speed. Arrows now coming at them from all angles, Athalir and Kahla steered everyone adeptly through the barrage, each rider ducking as arrows came dangerously close to their targets. The horses now at full gallop, they continued to twist and turn through the forest, the wood-and-metal onslaught undiminished, no matter how far or fast they went. Trees appeared in their way as they were forced from the path the river had cut through the forest and low hanging branches dragged at clothing as they came too close.

Athalir took over the lead as Kahla let go of her reins and took her bow from her back, skilfully staying in her saddle while firing her own arrows into the trees each time she caught sight of an assailant. Erryn reached for her bow, sure she could help, but as she was about to do so, Marcus yelled in pain.

"Marcus!" she yelled as she saw the wooden shaft emerging from his upper arm. But there was no time to worry about wounds now. Turning sharply to avoid a wall of clustered trees, Athalir took his horse into a small clearing, and out again over a fallen trunk, the inexperience of those following irrelevant as it was the only way forwards. Making it safely across, he glanced over his shoulder to see Marcus' mount clear the obstacle, but as he faced forwards he heard the unmistakable whiny of a horse as it stumbled, followed by the cracking of branches and the rolling crash from an unseated rider.

"Athalir, wait!" Marcus shouted, the prince already having pulled sharply on the reins and turning his horse around. In the clearing, Erryn and Vess were still in their saddles, the three horses brought to a standstill and turning frantically as they looked for an escape. Sathom was on the ground, a few feet away from his mount. To Athalir's dismay there was no sign of Kahla or her horse. Marcus dismounted, running into a leap over the fallen tree and dashing to Sathom's aid as he entered the clearing. Against his better judgement, Prince Athalir did the same, though his mind was more concerned for Kahla's whereabouts than the well-being of the Vaharians. Strangely, the incoming projectiles had ceased. However, a second after Athalir had arrived with the group, thirty elves dropped from the trees, quickly forming a tight circle around the group, daggers and crude flint axes replacing the bows that were now secured at their backs.

Marcus, who hadn't had time to help Sathom stand, was now crouched on the ground, the elemental at his side, only a step away from the feet of one of the elves. The atmosphere tense, the heavy silence was only broken by the sharp and grating voice of another elf, who stepped out from the shadows of the trees and through the elven barrier.

"Well, well, if it isn't the mighty prince himself. I think we may have received a full lifetime of blessing from Isearia today. What do you say, men?" Raucous laughter rose up from the other elves as Athalir's mouth tightened into a stern frown.

"Fahlmaer!" Athalir spat the other man's name, venom burning in his eyes.

"Ah, I am honoured you remember me… *my prince.*" The leader of the attacking elves gave a low mocking bow, grinning as he straightened up.

"How could I *not* remember you? You were the leader of my father's forces, his friend… and the coward that fled into the forest rather than stay and fight."

"Ha, brave words for one cornered like the evening's meal." Again the elves laughed at their leaders taunt. "What I'm curious to know is just why the heir to the throne has ventured so far into my territory – without escort. Is the king so ill that he's lost all control of his brat, as well as his kingdom?"

"You *will* regret saying that, you…"

"Now, now, is that any way to speak to your elder? I can see I shall have my work cut out keeping you silenced while in my… *care.* Now, I asked you a question. What are you doing so far from the city? And what in Isearia's name are you doing travelling with Vaharians, of all things?" Fahlmaer looked over the group with disdain.

Athalir was bristling with rage. His muscles strained against his skin and his hands clenched, causing his knuckles to crack. However, in his mind, he was thinking over his next move. He knew he could unsheathe his daggers and be at Fahlmaer's throat in an instant. But Fahlmaer probably knew it too. Being the strategist he was, he'd no doubt guessed he wouldn't attempt it, given that he and his followers were outnumbered six to one.

"I owe you no answers, traitor!" Athalir snapped, deciding that antagonising his enemy may cause him to make a mistake, one that he, and hopefully the Vaharians, could take full advantage of. The judgement was wrong.

"Men, bind the prince. Kill the others!" Fahlmaer ordered.

Before anyone could do anything, Fahlmaer's next utterance was a howl of pain as an arrow burst forth from the trees behind, striking him perfectly in his left shoulder-blade. That had been all Athalir needed. As some of the elves dashed to their leader and other's switched their attention to scanning the trees for the hidden archer, the prince swept his daggers up into his hands and leapt through the air, arms outstretched, landing cleanly among the group gathered around Fahlmaer. Slashing the blades with rapid precision, he took out two men in one move, taking on the third immediately after the first two had fallen, throats cut.

Having seen the arrow before it had reached its target, Erryn was already poised to attack. Grabbing her bow, she channelled magical energy from her fingers and into the shaft of her first arrow. As she let go, the arrowhead began to crackle with white lightning, whizzing through the air and piercing the neck of an elf that was about to take a dagger to Athalir's back.

From her vantage on horseback, she could make out two other elves that had gone into the trees. Whoever had taken that first shot needed help. With nimble fingers, she took two arrows, imbuing them with more lightning and sending them over the heads of the skirmish, willing them to split apart as they came close to her intended targets. As the steel tips buried themselves into the exposed backs, the elves' bodies crackled and convulsed before dropping, still writhing, to the ground.

Vess had jumped from his horse barely a second after Erryn had loosed her first arrow. Grasping his great-sword in both hands, he'd rushed headlong into the fray, his bulk alone knocking one enemy to the ground, his sword slicing open the gullet of another without him even pausing to take stock. Careful to avoid the prince, he moved on, his huge blade swinging from side to side, splattering warm blood across him and anyone else within range. The remaining elves, who weren't engaged in battle with Athalir, turned their focus to Vess, one leaping onto his back attempting to bring the giant of a man down, others encircling him and taking short swipes at his arms with their weapons. Vess stumbled around, attempting to dislodge his assailant. His massive sword was virtually useless in such a small space, and with the elf on his back restricting his movement even more, he was in danger of becoming overwhelmed. Marcus had been desperately trying to see a way he could help since the skirmish began. He feared his virginal attempts at offensive spell-casting might harm the wrong side. Not only that, but most of the conjurations he felt confident using were fire based, and launching fireballs into a clearing surrounded by trees didn't seem wise. Suddenly, he caught sight of the surrounded Vess and saw his chance. Summoning extra strength from his magic, he envisaged a swirling ribbon of wind and directed the resulting effect to ensnare the elf clinging to the warrior's back; the wind pulled at the enemy's arms, loosening his hold around Vess' neck and throwing him off with a final gust. Vess glared across at Marcus, his pride wounded by the mage's intervention. But that was a matter for another time. The other attackers were only briefly stunned by the spell and were once again coming at him from all sides. Regaining control, Vess tightened his grip on his sword and spun round in a full circle, cleaving his blade through the elves.

With many of the elves down or dead, the ones left fought harder than before. Fahlmaer was back on his feet, shouting orders to his men, as he kept his right hand clasped over the wound on his shoulder-blade.

"Take out the archer on the horse!" he bellowed, and two elves skirted around Vess, heading straight for Erryn with their weapons drawn. In her concentration, Erryn didn't hear the instruction – but Marcus did. With a burst of fury, the mage stretched out his arms, using his hand as a sight, and thrust forwards a cannonball of air, pelting it into Erryn's attackers with a force that shocked even him. The move didn't go unnoticed by Fahlmaer, who reached his bloodied hand to grasp a dagger at his hip. Eyes locked on Marcus, he took aim and threw the dagger straight towards the unsuspecting mage's head. Athalir swooped down from the air, landing at Marcus' side just in time to deflect the dagger, causing it to spin harmlessly off into the undergrowth. The prince accepted Marcus' nod of thanks before dashing off to assist Vess as he dealt with the few elves left standing. Between them, they took out the final combatants with ease, stopping to survey the clearing for any they'd missed as the last man fell.

The battle over, everyone visibly slumped as the adrenaline flowed less fiercely. Vess dropped his sword to the ground, its weight suddenly more than he could bear. Erryn lowered her bow and dismounted her horse, dropping to her knees at its side. Letting out a breath he felt he'd been holding in the whole time, Marcus suddenly realised he'd not seen Sathom since he left his side to join the fight. Looking to where he'd left him, there was no sign. He was concerned for his friend, but, knowing he was unable to be hurt physically, he allowed his mind to attend to more pressing matters. Both Vess and the prince were injured. Many small gashes along Vess' arms were seeping blood, though he seemed oblivious to them. Athalir carried a small open wound across one side of his chest, a long, slowly replenishing trail of blood running down his torso and soaking into his trousers, the wetness visible even on the black fabric.

"Erryn. Can you help?" Marcus called out, directing her attention to the bloody wounds. Erryn nodded and got up, walking over to Vess to take a closer look at his arms. Running her hands an inch above his skin, a warming sensation emanated from her palms. As she swept her hands up and down over the wounds, the torn edges were gently brought closer together, a thin, oily film appearing over the surface, the blood drying up beneath. Marcus watched on in awe. Though the wounds were still visible, at Erryn's contact they had stopped bleeding, and looked half-healed. He'd never seen such magic from any of the mages in Whitestone; injuries were treated by an apothecary, using herb tinctures and balms. Erryn had mentioned healing magic during their lessons, but had scoffed at his request to be taught any. "I wouldn't teach you, even if you were capable of it," she'd said, before going on to grumble about the refusal of mages to abide by the laws of nature.

She was approaching Athalir, who'd started to hold up his hands in protest, when the sound of snapping wood heralded the arrival of someone from within the trees. Everyone tensed up, ready to fight again, however little energy they had left.

Their eyes all fixed on the direction of the sound, they waited, their breath shallow, their exhausted bodies primed for action. As an indistinct figure emerged, Athalir was set to leap before whoever it was had a chance to attack first.

"Your highness, is that any way to greet a friend?" Kahla's familiar voice brought sighs of relief, even before her face became free of the shadows.

"Kahla! What happened?" Athalir asked, his concern barely concealed.

Kahla walked further into the clearing, her face unmoved as she took in the gory aftermath of the battle.

"I lost you all as I tracked one of the archers. By the time I found my way back, you were surrounded. Thought I'd be of more use keeping out of sight."

"It was you who shot the arrow at their leader?" Erryn asked, a flicker of admiration in her tone.

"Yes. I knew a distraction was required. Didn't quite bank on some of them hunting for me, though. Still, I led them far enough away that the pleas for their lives were out of earshot… before I slit their throats. I just got back in time to miss all the action, I see."

Athalir laughed, a warmth in his eyes none of the Vaharians had seen before.

"Wait! Where's Fahlmaer?" Turning to look where he had last seen the enemy leader, he frowned as he realised he'd gone. "We need to be on our way, immediately. If he makes it back to their camp, more will come."

Quickly, they collected their packs from where they'd been dropped and mounted their respective horses, who'd amazingly stood fast throughout the frenzied battle.

Erryn gave Marcus a questioning glance as she noted Sathom's horse and the elemental's absence.

"I'm sure we'll see him again soon. He knows where we're going; it's his route, after all." Marcus tried his best to sound confident, though he had no idea why Sathom had disappeared, and, in truth, no real certainty they would see him again. But he let that be his concern alone.

Vess made it into the saddle with less trepidation this time. Once seated, he started to rub at his arms, a frustrated look on his face.

"Vess! Stop it, you'll open them up again," Erryn scolded.

"But they itch," Vess grumbled.

Athalir looked down at his own wound, which had finally stopped bleeding, a thin, moist scab forming over the hole.

"I should heal that for you," Erryn offered, but Athalir declined.

"It's fine, thank you. I heal fast. Perhaps you should tend to your leader though. I seem to remember a yelp coming from him some time ago."

Marcus looked uncomfortable at Athalir's deliberate use of a term that made him sound like a pathetic animal. Erryn suddenly looked horrified.

"Oh Marcus, I'm so sorry, I completely forgot! Let me see to it."

Marcus had seen how much using healing magic took out of Erryn and didn't want her to drain herself anymore for him.

"Ah, it was just a flesh wound. No need. As Athalir said, I made a lot of noise for nothing much."

"Don't be ridiculous. I saw it, Marcus. You had an arrow sticking out of your arm."

She pulled her horse alongside his and leant over in the saddle. Ripping his sleeve away from the wound, she gasped as the hole came into view.

"It's not as bad as it looks," The mage said, before wincing as Erryn caught his torn skin.

"Oops. I'm sorry." She looked up at him, meeting his eyes directly, then quickly returning her attention to the wound. "Come on, let's get this fixed."

It stung a lot, but in little time, the hexan had it taken care of.

"Thank you," Marcus mouthed as Erryn put her horse back in line.

Kahla explained that her own mount had been caught up in the fighting and had sustained too severe an injury, her eyes downcast as she recounted having to put him out of his misery. So, it made sense for her to take the one now without a rider. Everyone on their steeds and ready to go, they set off from the clearing, Athalir leading them in the general direction of the river, secretly hoping he could find it again.

With only a couple of wrong turns, they soon found their way back to the guiding waters. From that point they kept the horses at a steady trot to stay ahead of any further ambush, stopping just once to drink and let the horses do the same.

Thoughts were of death and bloodshed, having a sobering effect on the once pleasant mood. Marcus realised just how real everything had become. This was never going to be some cheerful adventure, but until that point, the seriousness of it all had been easily overlooked. They'd managed to survive that first encounter, but there was so much more that could happen. His own mortality, and that of his companions, was now omnipresent in his mind, and for once, he couldn't think of a funny side at all.

As promised, the river led the party all the way to the eastern edge of the forest. The trees thinning slightly, they could just see a small valley cutting through a steep hillside. The river continued on through the valley, and into the kingdom of Geryndor beyond.

The ride from the clearing had taken many hours, and the sun was low in the sky ahead, its rays peering through the gap in the hills. Erryn dismounted, her eyes wide as she walked to the invisible line between the two lands. Extending her hand over the border, she quickly pulled it back as the bitter winter air of the dwarven kingdom contrasted sharply with the comfortable warmth of Sa'hahlenfell.

"What kind of magic fills this place?" she asked, turning to face Athalir, who'd appeared at her side.

"It is the magic of our goddess, Isearia, the giver of life. My people, her children, steward these lands for her. In return, she protects us, keeps us warm where all else succumbs to the ravages of the cold. While in my kingdom, the only danger we face is from each other… as you saw."

Erryn was awestruck, giving her full attention to Athalir's words.

"I know of magic, but I've never in all my life felt such as that within this forest."

For a moment, the prince seemed to be lost in thought, before he looked directly into Erryn's brown eyes.

"I watched you, as we fought, back in the clearing. You aren't like your leader, you're no mage."

"No, I'm not a mage. I'm hexan. My kin were the guardians of the old ways, natural magics. We… I… work within the laws of nature, drawing my energy from the elements. I cast nothing that can't be accounted for naturally."

"Your people *were* the guardians?" Athalir queried the past tense.

"I am the last, as far as I know. My mother was one before me, but she died when I was a child. I know of no others. Or at least, I don't think so. The use of magic by any other than mages is outlawed in Vaharia. Many hexans were put to death before I was born, so says my father. I've spent my whole life hiding what I am for fear of meeting the same end. Perhaps there are others in my village who do as I do – though, I believe I'd feel it if it were so."

Athalir's features softened as he listened attentively to Erryn speak, a hint of something that may even have been compassion present in his eyes.

"You would do well in Sa'hahlenfell. I think Isearia would welcome you." He patted her gently on the arm and smiled, before they both walked back to the others. Both Vess and Marcus were also back on solid ground, adjusting their packs and weapons and welcoming the feel of earth beneath their feet. Marcus' staff had spent the entire journey secured to his back by a makeshift strap. He hadn't even considered using it during the skirmish. Now, above his shoulder, it glowed a little brighter, and he could feel a faint vibration connecting with his skin through his jerkin. His first instinct was to ask Sathom what it meant, but of course, he wasn't there. Marcus had hoped he'd be waiting for them at the border, yet he was nowhere in sight. Still, there was nothing to be gained from fretting even more. He knew they had to enter Geryndor; that much of the journey he'd memorised. Beyond that... '*well, let's hope, he returns before any further planning is required*', he thought to himself.

"Your highness, we had best be returning to the city soon. I'd like to try to get you back before daylight wakes the king and queen," Kahla suggested, still seated on her horse.

"I shall not be returning with you, my friend." Everyone's faces turned to stare at Athalir.

"I *knew* it!" Vess mumbled to Marcus.

"With all due respect, your highness... Athalir, what do you mean, 'not returning'?" Kahla glared, looking exactly like a mother about to scold her child.

The prince walked over to his friend and took one of her hands in his, gazing up at her with solemn eyes.

"When I discovered the quest these people embarked upon, I knew I had to join them. Kahla, if there's even a chance they can do as they intend, that they can bring an end to the governors, I *have* to be there, I have to help... it is my duty."

Kahla looked unconvinced and about to protest, but Athalir persisted.

"Think of it, mai fahlen; with them gone, we could heal our sick again. We could heal my parents." His face now pleading with her to understand, Kahla's resolve fell away, a look of sad resignation in its place.

"But you've never even left the kingdom before. What if we need you here? What if your parents...?"

"I place the kingdom in your hands while I'm away. I trust it will not falter on your watch. I *would* ask that you take care of the king and queen for me, but that would be an insult, as I know you would do no less. As for my leaving Sa'hahlenfell, one day I shall be king. What use shall I be to the Fell if I have to live with the knowledge that I could've done something to ease their suffering, yet did not for no more than fear of the unknown?" Smiling at the Fell woman as she finally nodded acceptance, Athalir, let go of her hand. "Lead the horses back to the city, and ride swiftly. Take care, mai fahlen. Ahlvaen shael mah." With that he proceeded to walk the other horses in line with Kahla's mount. He watched as she steered back the way they'd come. Kicking her heals lightly she set off at a fast pace, quickly vanishing into the lengthening shadows of the forest with the other four horses following on behind.

Marcus, Vess and Erryn had been taking everything in, questions flitting through their minds, yet none feeling the time was right to seek answers from the prince.

"Well." Marcus broke the silence. "If you're coming with us, you're going to need something a little more... practical to wear. You'll perish wearing so little; faster than any of us, I would imagine." The three Vaharians had already put on their cloaks in preparation for the return to winter.

"I'm sure you are right Vaharian. That's why I packed accordingly." Taking his pack from his back, he reached inside and pulled out a thick shirt, made from some kind of animal skin. Tugging it over his head and covering his naked torso, he then delved into the pack again and procured a heavy brown cloak, which he deftly slung around his shoulders and fastened at his neck.

Marcus laughed as he recalled his curiosity regarding Athalir's pack before they'd left the Fell city.

"Then if everyone is ready, may I suggest we move on?"

Vess muttered something under his breath, Erryn just smiled as Athalir stepped forwards in line at the forest edge, and Marcus gripped his cloak tighter over his chest.

But the freezing air was not the only concern in his head, as the four of them walked over the border and into the dwarven kingdom of Geryndor.

CHAPTER THIRTEEN

As the thin corona of the sun finally blinked out behind the Mountains of Nor, the group emerged from the gorge between the western hills. Before the daylight faded, they'd had a brief chance to get a look at the land that spread out ahead. The mighty, snow-covered mountain range provided the backdrop for a mainly open and uninteresting terrain. With few discernible landmarks or features, Gerryndor was a stark contrast to the forest-covered kingdom of Sa'hahlenfell, and Athalir had felt himself longing for the cover of trees.

The group had continued to follow the course of the river as it passed through the gorge, the ground alongside it a mixture of dark-brown earth and pale grey rocks. Though the clarity of the water had gradually lessened as it progressed into Gerryndor, the remaining sunlight had still caught on the surface and acted as a continuous beacon for the travellers to follow. However, now the sky was thick with cloud, and though it kept the chill from taking a firm hold, it also prevented any light from the moon reaching the land; with the sunlight gone, the thick blackness of a long, winter's night enveloped everything.

To save their torches, Marcus held his staff, causing the crystal to glow bright enough to guide them to a safe place to set camp for the night. With the aid of the cool white light, it wasn't long before the travellers came across some shelter in the form of a gaping recess in

the rock of the hillside. The space beneath the overhang of the hilltop was just large enough to comfortably accommodate the party, with room to spare for a small fire to be lit at the centre. A short while later and the flames crackled eagerly over some hastily-gathered kindling. Everyone huddled around as close as possible, the heat providing welcome relief from the cold that had penetrated through to their bones. Once they'd consumed the food that Athalir had provided back in Sa'hahlenfell, thoughts turned to sleep. There wasn't a soul present that night that had the mind to indulge in pleasant conversation, each burdened as they were with their own private concerns, and weary from a day of fighting and travelling.
"I'll stay on watch," Vess offered, before anyone considered the danger of leaving themselves off-guard.
"Are you sure, Vess? I don't mind doing so," Marcus said.
"I'm sure," Vess replied, before reaching for the hilt of his sword and keeping hold of it as he positioned himself squarely on a boulder at the front of the camp.
"Here, you'll need this." Erryn spoke softly as she took Vess' blanket from his pack and proceeded to drape it around his shoulders. Pulling the blanket further around himself, he stared out into the darkness all around them, and within minutes, all of his companions lay asleep under their own blankets.

Alone in the darkness, Vess' thoughts were uninterrupted, allowing him the freedom to reflect. He'd known nothing but what had happened over the last few days, a concept he'd struggled with since the moment he'd learnt how things were. He wasn't a great thinker – or at least, he didn't believe so – but that was just it; he didn't really know who, or what, he was. Indeed, considering how things had been meant to happen, he wasn't even truly anyone. His whole purpose had been to facilitate the continuation of his father's immortal life. He cringed as he thought of the word, *father*. Somehow, though he'd spent his whole life in suspended animation, knowledge of basic things was available to him. He knew of words, of how to walk and move, he knew of people and of a world beyond the walls of the crypt, and he knew of family and, strangely, of love. Somewhere within the jumble of a life known but not experienced, rolling around in his mind, he knew how fathers were meant to be. Looking out into the distance, Vess' eyelids felt heavy, a wide yawn reminding him further that he hadn't slept since waking in the crypt.

Resisting the urge once more, he straightened his posture, tightening his grip on his sword as if to anchor him to wakefulness. The others didn't know it, but he'd resisted sleep where they had welcomed it. Every night, with increasing insistence, his body had yearned for rest, only to have its needs denied. The first night, at the old man's cottage, he had lain down on the hard floor, the journey from the crypt taking its toll on his under-used muscles. As he'd closed his eyes and begun to drift to sleep, distorted figures had lunged at him from the blackness, talons clawing close to his face as if trying to rip their way inside. He'd flashed his eyes open, his body sweating profusely, every hair standing on end. Vess vowed that night never to sleep again. The fear had been there, even before the vision. Fear of never waking up had implanted itself and grown with the night-time shadows, but the nightmarish manifestation had convinced him. No matter how much his mind and body begged for sleep, he would never be that vulnerable again – never.

For the most part, the night remained uneventful. That was until an ear-splitting scream shattered the silence, sending Vess into a state of adrenaline fuelled readiness and Marcus and Athalir bolting from their makeshift beds, hastily searching for weapons among the belongings around the camp. It was Erryn's scream that had startled them all into a frenzy. As the three men prepared for an attack from the shadows, Erryn sat upright, her blanket tossed to one side and strands of her tousled hair sticking to her cheeks by the wet trails of tears. Marcus caught sight of her and motioned to Athalir and Vess to lower their blades, nodding his head in Erryn's direction. Both men looked confused, but gathered there was no imminent danger and returned, relieved, to their respective areas of the camp, Vess resuming his watch and Athalir shuffling down beneath his blanket.

Meanwhile, Marcus walked over to Erryn and sat down on the ground at her side. With the fire of the camp now little more than glowing ashes, he could only just make out her face and the nip in the air was coming back with a vengeance without the flames to keep it at bay. He noticed Erryn's body tremble as a gust of wind whipped around them. Holding his hand out flat in front of him, he looked at his palm and conjured a small ball of fire that, with a quick flick of his wrist, he tossed into the ash, reigniting the small amount of kindling that remained. It wouldn't burn for long, but maybe just long enough to allow them to put to rest whatever had so disturbed the young woman that night.

As the heat of the newly-lit fire reached them both, Erryn looked up at Marcus' concerned face and gave a small, grateful smile.

"Thank you," She said in a hushed, quivering voice. Marcus looked pleased with himself.

"For the fire? Oh, that was no trouble... even for me," he said, poking fun at his magical ineptitude, with a grin.

"No, not just the fire. For being here, with me. I... I wouldn't want to be alone after..." Her voice trailed off, tears once more beginning to well up in her eyes. Marcus shuffled closer and leant forwards. He paused with his face close to hers. For a moment, he wanted to kiss her, but instead, he reached to pick up her blanket and tenderly draped it around her shoulders, criss-crossing it over her chest before moving back a little, quickly looking away and into the fire.

Erryn had wanted him to kiss her. Disappointment almost made her chastise him for not doing so. But the moment had passed and memories of the nightmare quickly filled the gap.

Marcus had no idea what to say to a tearful young woman. Concerned his feeling of awkwardness may betray him and he'd say something inappropriate, he decided it was better to simply sit with Erryn until she felt able to go back to sleep. She seemed to want no more than his company, and that was something he could manage. Confident he couldn't cause a problem by just being there, he returned his gaze to her face. Her eyes were red and puffy, her face flushed by the heat from the fire. However, as the orange light flickered and danced, a scar that remained her natural colour against the pink of the cheek came into view. He hadn't noticed it before. Instinctively, he reached his fingertips to touch the scar, which was no more than a couple of inches long and sat diagonally below her cheekbone. He pulled his hand back quickly as she turned her face away.

"I'm sorry. I didn't mean to... How did you get that?" Immediately he regretted asking, and cursed his impulsive nature. To his relief, Erryn turned back to look at him, clearly not offended.

"I was six years old. My mother and I were having a picnic in the woods behind the village, next to a stream. It's gone now – dried up years ago." Erryn looked wistful, but carried on. "We would often go there. She called it our '*enchanted place'*. The trees were thick all around, but there was a patch of flat grass that was covered all summer long by masses of daisies. The sun always seemed to find its way to that grass and mother and I would lie on our backs in the warmth, counting clouds and creating our own magical ones above our heads, laughing as we made funny creatures. It was one of the few places we used our magic; she said the trees would protect us, so long as we didn't outstay our welcome. But that day, the trees could do nothing. When the men came, led by that… *thing*, I remember shouting at them to let her go, lunging at their boots as they sat atop their giant horses. One of them kicked me, right in the face, his metal boot-tip drawing blood as it ripped across my skin. I was thrown down onto the ground by the blow, my head coming down hard. The last thing I remember seeing before I blacked out was my mother, looking at me. Her face was red with anger, her long, black hair wild and damp. She started to cast a spell, but the leader of the men struck her before she could finish. As my vision went dark, I saw her head swing back so hard… the next I knew, she was gone. I woke hours later, evening drawing in, our enchanted place filled with nothing but blood and strands of my mother's hair."

Marcus took her hands in his and squeezed them gently.

"Who did this to you and your mother?" He had a good idea, but Erryn's vague description of the one in charge puzzled him.

"The governors' men, of course. Who else?" Erryn spat her answer, her eyes filled with hate as she glared up at Marcus.

"I'm sorry… but who, or what, led them? What did you mean by that '*thing*'?"

"I… I don't really know. I was just a child; to me, all those men were just thick-armoured legs and helmeted heads far above me. But him… there was something… *not right*, about him. He didn't ride, like the others; he walked ahead. Now I think about it, I remember '*feeling*' his presence, even before he entered the glade. I can't recall his face but…" Erryn paused, her eyes reflecting the flames of the fire.

"It's alright, I'm here." Marcus held her hands tighter; reassuring her it was okay to go on.

"I don't know what he was. A man, perhaps... But no, I think he was... something else, something dark, inhuman. If it's possible for one to *see* evil, then I believe *that* is what I saw!" Erryn shuddered and closed her eyes, pulling her hands free from Marcus' clasp. "We should try to get some more sleep," She said coolly, before lying down and wrapping herself up in her blanket, tighter than before.

Marcus was left in confused silence. After a moment's pause, he got up and, as the fire died down once more, went back to his own bed. Using his pack as a pillow, he lay on his back, staring up into the blackness overhead, Erryn's story echoing through his mind. Whoever – whatever – she and her mother had encountered in that memory it had left an ugly stain on her life. No matter the nature of the relationship he had with the hexan, he knew he cared for her, and it pained him to see her in such distress, but he could do no more than he'd done that night. Part of him felt rejected as she'd pushed him away, yet another part understood. With his mind more mixed up than before, Marcus irritably decided not to think any more on the complex issue of how she felt about him. His thoughts returned to the man – or thing – from Erryn's past. From her description and the mood that had come over her as she spoke of him, he couldn't help feeling unnerved. His vivid imagination conjured all manner of terrifying images every time he closed his eyes. Thus, he resolved to keep them wide open. With his brain refusing not to think, it didn't look like he'd be getting any more sleep that night.

Listening to his new companions as he tried to find sleep once more, Prince Athalir attempted to remain detached from his fellow travellers. A difficult task when, for the most part, they'd been nothing but friendly towards him. However, the one they called Vess clearly didn't like him. *And that*, Athalir thought, *could pose a problem.* The man always had at least one eye on him, suspicious concern evident in both the way he watched the prince and the cool way he interacted with him. Getting the mage alone long enough to remove his hands and summon the skaithen was looking more and more like an impossible task.

Yet, he had no choice. He'd have to make the impossible possible or his people would continue to die.

Pretending to sleep as Marcus returned to the bedroll next to him, he quashed the guilt that attempted to make itself known. Guilt could be dealt with when his parents were well, when the Fell were no longer vulnerable to the deadly illness that had already taken so many. Until then, his path was clear, and he couldn't allow it to become blocked by self-loathing.

CHAPTER FOURTEEN

The next morning, everyone was packed up and ready to move as soon as the first hazy rays of sunshine reached across the land. With nothing left of Athalir's rations, the walk would be on empty stomachs, but all were eager to get going. The overcast sky of the previous night had gone, but the biting wind, sweeping in from the north, had returned, tugging at hair and cloaks, and pushing the party sideways as they tried to forge ahead. In such conditions, walking took considerably longer than it should. However, as far as the eye could see, Geryndor was flat; the only exception being the mountains and hills that surrounded the kingdom.

One feature that did stand out, now it was distinguishable from the daytime sky, was the Dragon Crest mountain range on the southern border. Such was its size, the range could be seen towering over all things of height in all kingdoms, but only from Geryndor could its true magnitude be realised. The black rock jutted up into the sky, greatly resembling the spines along the back of a dragon, thus earning it the name.

As the group travelled, they couldn't keep their eyes from the ominous wall of stone. It, too, seemed to stare down at them, its obsidian-coloured surface not only shadowing the landscape, but so black as to look like the place in which shadows were made.

Its ever-present company along the way served as a relentless reminder of what was to come.

In the distance, they could make out what they assumed to be settlements, numerous collections of buildings scattered over the land. As they continued their travels, there were signs of a structured way of life all around. A dirt road appeared soon after they'd left the shelter of the hills, channelled along its length by the wheels of carts, and pitted from horse's hooves. It led them past open fields of heavily-fleeced, black sheep, lonely wooden huts with the trademark tools of woodcutters resting against their walls, and round, towering mills, with their sails spinning fiercely in the strong winds – though it wasn't until they drew close to a large lake that they saw the first dwarf.

The road followed the winding trail of the river until the waters finally filtered into the lake and the thoroughfare continued to run alongside the southernmost bank. It was Athalir that first noticed the shape on the ground ahead, his eyesight obviously as sharp as his hearing. Without warning, the prince sprinted towards the form, his companions exchanging puzzled looks, having seen nothing more in the distance than barren winter landscape.

They'd not walked much farther when Athalir called out to the group, demanding they hurry to where he now stood.

Marcus, Vess, and Erryn broke into a jog, the urgency in Athalir's voice succeeding in piquing their curiosity. Once at his side, the cause of the prince's concern was distressingly clear; a dwarf boy, barely more than a child, lay motionless on his back, eyes closed, skin and clothing splattered with blood. Erryn quickly dropped to the ground beside the boy. Carefully examining his body, she found no obvious wounds, yet the amount of blood told a contradicting tale.

"What do you think happened to him?" Vess' question gave a voice to what the others were thinking.

"Erryn, is he still alive?" Marcus asked. Erryn placed her hand on the boy's chest. Feeling a faint heartbeat, she nodded up at Marcus. "Then we should get him back to his people. What happened is a matter for his kin." Marcus' decisiveness left no room for further discussion. Without pause, Vess bent down and effortlessly scooped the boy's limp body up into his arms. Fitting comfortably in Vess' cradle-hold, the lad's diminutive stature gave the impression of someone a few years younger than his facial features indicated; the defined jaw line and first signs of beard growth suggesting he may have been around fourteen.

Without further ado, the group set off again, Vess marching ahead of the others with determination clear in his stride. At the absence of Sathom, Marcus had assumed leadership, but as they travelled towards the nearest settlement, pushing on into the wind, his mind was plagued by doubt. The second they'd entered Geryndor, his plan had diminished into one of wandering and silently hoping Sathom would show up soon. He'd never been the leader of anything and had been content to follow Sathom's direction, doing what was expected of him, but deferring to the elemental when it came to making the tough choices. Now, the eyes of his companions were on him. Even Athalir, for whom he had no doubt the role of follower was completely unnatural, looked to Marcus to take control.

For the moment he'd be satisfied with returning the unconscious boy to his people and getting closer to their destination.

It was late morning by the time the four travellers were spotted through the spyglass of a gate guard in Brinthorn. A commotion had begun when the guard had realised the lifeless body carried by the man in front was one of their own. At the sound of his horn, ten armed soldiers were despatched, the five chariots in which they rode pulled by the muscular bodies of ten large, grey wolves.

Within moments of bursting forth from the gates of the settlement, the company of dwarves and canines had formed a barrier in the way of Vess and the others. As the wolves leaned into the ropes that tethered them to the chariots, they snapped at the group with teeth bared and slobber flying. The dwarves hollered in a language neither the humans nor the Fell prince understood, raising giant battle-axes and glaring menacingly.

"Is *anyone* outside of Vaharia friendly?" Marcus muttered under his breath, fending off the frosty scowl from Athalir with a hastily-formed smile.

Vess glanced back, his expression questioning, though Marcus could make out the tell-tale signs the warrior was itching to reach for his sword. Knowing he had to do something before Vess dropped the boy and ran headlong into a wall of deadly teeth and blades,

Marcus inhaled deeply and tentatively walked forwards. Making his way past Vess and on until he was only a few feet away from the mouths of the snarling wolves, an inner voice suggested he might be pushing his luck. As usual, he ignored it.

The shouts subsided as he approached, bewildered looks passing across the faces of the dwarven men. Ten pairs of eyes beneath lowered brows were now focused intently on Marcus, who shifted from foot to foot as he felt the weight of their stare.

"We found this boy on the road. He's unconscious, but alive. I hope we've brought him to you in good time." Marcus raised his voice to be heard over the low growls emanating from the wolves and ushered Vess forwards. "Please, take him, and we'll be on our way."

"Nonsense!" A deep, gravelly voice bellowed from one of the chariots. Now it was Marcus' turn to look confused. Exchanging a quick glance with Vess, who was still cradling the boy, the mage was once more mentally preparing to fight another foreign welcoming committee, when a movement from the same chariot from which the voice had come drew his attention. From within the dwarven barrier, one of the soldiers appeared on the ground. Obviously in charge, he made a downward motion with his right hand, a signal that resulted in axes being lowered and the wolves brought to heel at the tug of their ropes. The dwarf marched purposefully to stand before Marcus. Though rugged, he had a commanding presence, with sturdy legs supporting a square, heavy-set body. At no more than five feet tall, he was forced to crane back his neck to meet the six foot mage's eyes. Yet, when he did, there was no hint of the threatening glares of before. Instead, the warmth from a friendly smile extended across the rest of his rough, weather-worn features.

"I will hear nothing of your departure without you, and your fellows, first tasting some fine dwarven ale – in thanks for your service. Glin, Rekk, take the boy to the healer. And when you are done, tell his mother he yet lives; my ears will welcome an end to the woman's whining." Laughing loudly, the dwarf went on to introduce himself as Rannan, son of Rann, while two more dwarves jumped down from separate chariots and proceeded to relieve Vess of his charge. "Come, I will take you to the great hall to meet with the larn. There will be food, drink, and women at his behest, I'm sure of it. It has been far too long since Brinthorn welcomed strangers."

Before anyone could speak, he barked an order for the remaining dwarves to return, and led the group into the settlement, bombarding Marcus with questions every step of the way. Everyone in the group was aware of the need to press on – they would certainly have to allow extra time for navigation without the aid of Sathom's map – yet none wished to incur the wrath of the previously angry-sounding dwarf by rejecting his offer of hospitality. Besides, having eaten nothing since the evening before, the offer of food was, without doubt, an attractive one.

Beyond the entrance lay a sprawling settlement consisting of long, low, wooden buildings haphazardly sited but spaced well-apart. Perforated by pot-holes, the ground was, beaten by the elements and worn by footfall, so that mud and grit were more abundant than anything green. The group's arrival in Brinthorn was apparently cause for great excitement. Dwarves young and old, who'd been going about their daily lives, paused to stare as the strangers walked by. No dwarf stood taller than Rannan, but what they lacked in height, many made up for in width. However, most of the younger men's girths were made up of muscle, only the elders having a comfortable layer of fat. The females, on the other hand, were generally more curvaceous than rotund, with ample hips and bosoms either side of slim waists. Seemingly unhindered by social graces, they came closer, their faces overtly curious as they followed the group's passage. Marcus had to stifle a laugh as Vess found himself trailed by a group of dwarven children of varying ages, all eager to touch his shiny armour, and all calling out one word, *horggen*, over and over again.

"The word would be '*giant*', in your tongue." Rannan explained as he took in Marcus' amused expression. "You humans are all too lofty for your own good, but that one – he's like a dwarf on stretched legs; as wide as he is tall. Did you give him the scrawny one's share of the rations?" The dwarf motioned to Athalir, who frowned back at their stout guide, the unflattering remark heard all too well by the elf's sharply-pointed ears.

"I am no human, *dwarf*," Athalir bit back, the contempt at the notion clear in his tone.

"Ha! Yet he doesn't protest at the physical description!" Rannan guffawed loudly, much to the chagrin of the Fell prince, as they arrived at a grander building at the heart of the settlement. Without pause, he used his muscular arms to push open two heavy wooden doors, barging through and onward into the building, announcing their arrival at the great hall as the party followed him inside.

Larn Ossern of Brinthorn was seated casually on a wooden throne; its raised position on a platform at one end of the elongated building, providing a sweeping view of the entire hall. To the outsiders that found themselves in his presence, he appeared to be asleep. His head was tipped backwards resting against the back of the throne, his eyes closed and his mouth gaping open. Though one foot was resting on the floor, the other was dangling limply in mid-air, the leg it was attached to hooked loosely over the armrest. Rannan approached without hesitation, making his arrival known with a hearty slap across the larn's dangling, leather-booted foot.

"Larnsman, has no one ever told you, you should show more respect for your larn?" The seated dwarf spoke without shifting his position or opening his eyes.

"*You* have, my larn, on many occasions. But on those same occasions, you also told me to do the dance of the seven kings at every meal, and to make sure I'm always wearing boots – even when I bathe. I assumed I needn't take any of your words from such times seriously."

At that, a loud rumbling laugh from the larn echoed through the building as he opened his eyes and sat upright in his throne. He was a slightly larger man than Rannan. Beneath light fabric garments, it was clear his girth was made up of more fat than muscle. His wiry hair was fair with thick streaks of grey, worn loose about his shoulders. A short beard, covering his chin and surrounding his mouth, betrayed his advancing years with even more grey, and matching bushy eyebrows shadowed his faded brown eyes.

"Ah, I see we have guests. I take it these humans were the cause of all that din earlier?"

"They were, my larn. Though one of them claims not to be human." Rannan motioned, again, towards the prince, who straightened up with his shoulders back as everyone focused on him.

"I'm certainly not human! I am Prince Athalir of Sa'hahlenfell, home of the true elves, the Fell, and I do not take kindly to the inference I may be anything less." Athalir spoke of his role and his kingdom with pride bolstering his words, staring directly at Larn Ossern, as if daring him to question his race further. There was a brief pause after Athalir spoke, the tension in the air palpable, with

Marcus wishing he'd kicked Athalir in the shin mid-sentence to shut him up, and Vess and Erryn unsure as to whether or not to reach for their weapons. Fortunately, the larn soon rumbled with more laughter, taking the bluster from Athalir's attitude and relaxing the others.

"Elf it is then. Rannan, did you hear the man? No more suggestions otherwise."

Rannan nodded, a wry smile just visible through the straggly hairs of his own, rather unkempt, light brown beard.

"My larn, these outlanders returned one of our sons to us. Bassa Widengirth's boy."

"I see. Excellent news! Tell me outlander, what state did you find him in? Were there signs of any others?" The larn addressed Marcus, his aged eyes looking intently at his face as he waited for answers.

Once again Marcus became the spokesman. He was starting to get used to stepping forwards to play the leader, and for some reason everyone they had met so far automatically assumed he was such.

"He was unconscious and bloody, but still alive. We saw nothing of any others, though the minor injuries he had couldn't account for the amount of blood…" Marcus purposefully left the statement unfinished, the implication clear enough without giving it words.

Larn Ossern closed his eyes, his mouth turning down at the corners as he listened to Marcus.

"My larn, it appears the others may be lost. Perhaps we should consider mounting a full offensive, before this beast takes any more of our clansmen." Rannan rested a leather gloved hand on the larn's shoulder, his voice imploring him to do as he suggested.

Another uncomfortable silence hung in the air as the larn continued to stare off into the distance. Suddenly he slammed his hands down on the arms of the throne and abruptly stood up.

"A matter for another time, larnsman. Tonight, we feast, in honour of our guests and the safe return of young… what's the boy's name again?"

"Stogg, my larn." Rannan prompted.

"Yes, yes that's it. In honour of the return of Stogg! Rannan, see the outlanders get the best seats at my table. We'll see them well fed and well drunk before they leave."

Rannan's face bore a look of resignation, and he made no further attempt to sway the favour of Larn Ossern towards his proposition.

Instead he guided Marcus and the rest of the group towards a massive table that ran almost the full length of the hall, two equally long benches on either side. The best seats were apparently closest to the larn's throne, meaning the group only had to walk four or five paces before Rannan prompted them to sit; Marcus and Erryn one side, Vess and Athalir the other.

Some hours later, long after Rannan and the larn had left the building, the group still sat at the table. Marcus had grown irritable as he felt the time slipping away from them, a feeling obviously shared by his companions. Within the first half hour, talk had turned to the time of day and losing valuable daylight hours for travel. Prince Athalir had even started to question Marcus' leadership, at which point Marcus would have happily agreed to step down and hand the reins to the elf, had Erryn not jumped to his defence. Vess too was quick to point out the fact this was the Fell prince's only excursion from his kingdom, and he, for one, would not be following someone who may as well be blind.

Everyone had fallen into a silence tainted with disquiet after that, Athalir and Vess purposefully avoiding eye contact, Erryn seemingly lost in thought, and Marcus fidgeting as he tried to achieve some level of comfort on the hard wooden bench. Once or twice, stirred by Erryn's passionate defence of his leadership, he'd attempted to engage her in conversation, even tried to hold her hand once more, but she spurned every advance. Confused, he finally gave up, and was just about to get up to stretch his legs when a sudden loud creak echoed through the building. As everyone turned their heads to look at the entrance – from whence the creak had emanated – the doors burst open and a rabble of very excitable-looking dwarves poured into the room. They were huddled so close together, pushing and shoving, that it was almost impossible to tell where one dwarf ended and another began. With determination written over the face of every one, the dwarves lunged towards the table, some splintering off from the main group to skirt around to the side furthest from the doors, others making extra effort to surge nearer to where Marcus and the others were seated. However, it seemed they'd not noticed the presence of the outlanders before; as they took in the sight of the best seats at the table, filled, they came to a stumbling stop mere inches from the now-anxious-looking travellers. After a moment or two of tense silence and indignant frowns, Rannan entered the hall from a door off to one side of the platform. As he approached the table, he glared sternly at the assembled dwarves. This was apparently an unspoken order to take any seat they could get, as each of them did just that, many of the elders huffing and grumbling at the injustice.

Rannan chuckled as he directed his attention to the larn's most honoured guests.

"Damn sycophantic fools! They would have likely hauled you all from your delicate human backsides just to get one place closer to the larn," he said, in a whisper deliberately loud enough to be heard by the nearby dwarves.

Athalir glared at the dwarf, and was about to register his annoyance at being referred to as human again, until a quick warning glance from Erryn compelled him to keep quiet.

"I assume that's why we've been '*kept*' here so long?" Athalir wouldn't keep *that* particular gripe muted.

"I believe what my friend is trying to say is, though we thank you for your hospitality, we really must be on our way, very soon." Marcus' noble manners spilled out as he attempted to appease Rannan, whose face was now screwed up in obvious consternation at the prospect of the group's departure before the food arrived. Rannan's expression remained serious just long enough for Marcus to believe he may have offended the fellow, until the now familiar wide grin spread across his face once more.

"Come now," Rannan spoke in a jovial tone. "The hour is late and the night's deathly cold this time of year. I don't know your destination, human, but surely it would be preferable to get there without the hindrance of amputated, frostbitten limbs, yes?"

Though the group had been aware of the hours passing them by, it hadn't occurred to any of them, as they sat in the artificial light of the torch-lit windowless hall, that they may have lost daylight altogether. It seemed then that they really had little choice but to take what the dwarves offered, and then find somewhere sheltered to set camp for the night.

Marcus inwardly sighed at the thought of a day's travel wasted, but the aching chasm that was his stomach had been reminding him for ages he'd skipped at least two meals, and it almost jumped for joy as trays of food started being brought in by dwarven serving girls. Reluctantly, he accepted Rannan's reasoning, telling him they would stay to eat and then must take their leave to find a safe place to rest for the night.

"Nonsense! You'll rest here. Bassa Widengirth's already petitioning for the outlanders that saved her son to take on the mantle of heroes of Brinthorn. The least we can offer you is a roof over your head for one night." Rannan cast his eyes down the length of the table, towards a plump middle-aged woman with blonde hair as grey-streaked as the larn's. The woman flashed a huge gap-toothed smile, aimed more at the travellers than Rannan, and waved her hand frantically.

"Ha ha! It's fortunate she isn't as fast as she once was. I wouldn't see much food get past your lips with her seated at your side." Rannan rumbled with laughter before looking back at Marcus, awaiting his decision.

Marcus glanced at his companions one at a time, each one signalling their approval of the plan to spend the night in Brinthorn. Satisfied it was the right choice, he smiled and graciously accepted Rannan's invitation.

"Excellent! I didn't relish the thought of being the one to inform the larn you'd gone. Now, enjoy the feasting, outlanders. It's in your honour, after all. Once the larn retires for the night, I'll clear the hall and you can bed down here, then…"

He was suddenly interrupted by an excited murmuring running from one end of the table to the other, up and down both sides.

"Ah, the larn has arrived." Rannan spoke without turning around.

True enough, Larn Ossern had just entered from the side door. However, as Marcus and the others noted as they looked up, he wasn't alone.

At his side was a female dwarf, only slightly shorter than Ossern but half as wide. She moved gracefully alongside the larn as they entered the hall. When he took his seat on the throne, the young woman elegantly lowered herself to a cushion on the floor next to it, demurely gazing out across the room as the gathering waited in hushed anticipation.

Suddenly, the larn clapped his hands together, triggering what could only be described as organised chaos. The table, now laden with food, became obscured by a sea of arms, all grabbing at things beyond comfortable reach. Rannan had urged the group not to wait, before taking his place at the larn's side, the meal of those on the platform served separately.

Even before everyone's plates were full, the serving girls started their journey around the table, pouring honey-coloured ale from large flagons into waiting wooden mugs. There were so many to be filled, and so often at the speed it was immediately drained by the dwarves, that accuracy was almost impossible as the girls were kept busily moving around the outside.

Marcus had tucked into the food with enthusiasm, but as his mug was filled, he viewed the liquid with suspicion. It looked more pleasant than the ale he'd had in the Crooked Wing; the colour, and smell, both significantly less off-putting. However, with an early start the following day, and without the luxury of his own bed to sleep in, it would seem sensible to avoid his body's reaction to alcohol.

In the mad entanglement to reach the fruits, meats, and pastries, the others had settled with less. They'd watched on in amusement as Marcus had readily attacked the feast with an appetite to match that of any dwarf. Now, as they each took sips of their ale, they noted Marcus' avoidance of his.

It seemed the mage's disinterest in the beverage had not gone unnoticed by some of the dwarves either.

"What's the matter, human? Can't take your ale?" A shout from further along the bench, followed by raucous laughter, alerted the other diners to Marcus and his still-full mug. Before long, a chorus of "drink, drink, drink!" had gathered momentum and a loud cheer broke out as Marcus finally bowed to the pressure, taking a large swig of the drink. Even his companions joined in, Athalir finding their leader's hesitance especially funny. It was the first time the atmosphere between them all had been relaxed since coming together as a group. After that, the evening became positively enjoyable. Erryn was even beginning to rethink her frostiness towards Marcus. She wasn't entirely sure why she'd pushed him away before. They'd grown closer almost without her knowledge up until they reached the dwarven settlement. Yet, when he'd openly shown any sign of affection, however subtle, she'd instinctively rejected him. She tried to catch his attention as they all spoke of trivial things, far removed from their quest, but he broke contact each time their eyes met.

Marcus was confused, and the ale he'd been coerced to imbibe wasn't making it any easier. His head was slightly fuzzy, his eyes not focusing as well as they should. Once or twice he thought Erryn had been trying to hold his gaze, but he'd dismissed it as more wishful thinking. The barrier she'd erected between them earlier couldn't have been clearer and, though disappointed, he'd been there before, too many times.

He'd turned away from her, concentrating on Athalir's rather graphic description of Fell alpha male sparring contests, when music began to play from a group of musicians that had gathered in the hall. The sound was like something from a dream, mysterious and slightly disorientating, and Marcus found himself distracted to the point of ignoring Athalir to look towards the tune. However, the instruments paled into insignificance as a female voice started to spiral above the pipes and strings, calling to him to face the platform. There, the dwarven woman, who'd accompanied the larn, was now stood next to the throne, her voice being the one that Marcus was now drowning in. Though she sang in a language he couldn't understand, he hung off every word, her voice the most beautiful he'd ever heard. The constant hum of chatter from the dwarves at the table had ceased and, as he watched the attractive woman, he began to feel like the only person in the room. As if to support the feeling, she looked straight into Marcus' eyes as she sang, her intense stare and slight smile seemingly intended for him alone. It may have been the ale, but each note that passed the woman's lips seemed to call to him, desire hovering around every word.

Vess frowned as he noticed the mage's mesmerised state, glaring too at Athalir, who seemed to also have noticed and was smiling in response. He didn't know much about his new friends, but he'd picked up on the fact there was definitely something between Erryn and Marcus.

Erryn was not unaware of Marcus' enthralment, but she'd also noted the subtle signals emanating from the singer. She followed the seduction in her eyes as it found its way to those of the man at her side, and she was angered at the sharp stab of pain that jabbed beneath her ribs.

When the song finished and the musicians continued on with a livelier tune, the woman smiled at Marcus, her eyes lingering on him a moment or two before turning away in feigned coyness.

"I do believe you have an admirer there, Marcus," Athalir mocked, his usually stern manner softened by atmosphere and ale.

Marcus simply blushed; a little embarrassed at realising his fellow travellers had all been witness to the musical flirtation.

"Who is she anyway?" Erryn blurted out, trying to sound as nonchalant as possible.

"*She* is the larn's daughter, Adrenna," Rannan answered, arriving at the table in time to hear the question. "Her singing pleased you?" he asked Marcus.

"Oh yes… er, I mean, it was… she has a beautiful voice." The mage stumbled over his words, desperately trying to regain some composure. He felt hot, his palms damp with sweat, and he feared his overt attraction to Adrenna may be inappropriate and cause offence. He needn't have worried. Rannan chuckled, and leaned to whisper in his ear.

"The lady wishes you to meet with her this night. She asks that I bring you to her once the feast is done."

No one else had heard the larnsman's words above the music and the chattering, but Erryn turned her back on Marcus and engaged Vess in conversation. She was young and inexperienced, but she wasn't blind. Guessing what Rannan had spoken to Marcus about, she made a vow to ignore it and to in no way let on that she was vexed – even though she most certainly was.

After another hour or so of music and merriment, the larn stood from his throne, a sign that his tiredness was bringing an end to the festivity.

Rannan bellowed a command to empty the hall, and before long, the humans and the Fell prince were left alone to settle down for the night; all but Marcus, who made a joke about the call of nature and followed Rannan out through the main doors.

Erryn watched them leave. As the doors closed behind the two men, she jumped to her feet, grabbed her cloak, quickly draping it loosely around her shoulders, and dashed out the doors before either Athalir or Vess could utter a word.

Once outside, she stuck to the shadows as she followed some distance behind Marcus and Rannan, her years of hunting training her movements to be almost noiseless. They walked some way before finally coming to a large building set back from the others, candlelight flickering in small windows, in one of which was a woman's silhouette. Erryn watched from around the corner of another building close by as Rannan knocked at the door and the silhouette moved from the window. Seconds later, the door opened and her heart sank as she saw Marcus enter, Adrenna taking him by the hand and leading him further in. Once Rannan closed the door and walked away, Erryn pulled her cloak tighter as the icy air bore into her, cruelly adding extra numbness to the horrible lack of warmth she now felt. Slowly, she walked with little care for stealth back to the great hall, ignoring the questions that met her as she walked back inside.

CHAPTER FIFTEEN

Vess had been staring at the high-vaulted ceiling for a couple of hours. He'd mastered the art of not sleeping to the point where he almost no longer felt the need. He'd thought on many things that night; his mistrust of Prince Athalir, the whereabouts of Sathom, Benedict's sudden departure. He'd listened to Erryn's tossing and turning for half an hour after she came back inside the hall, and then moved on to wonder what Marcus was doing. Well, he had a general idea of *what* he was doing, but the why eluded him. It was clear there was something between the mage and the hexan, but apparently he saw it better than either of them did, as they both seemed determined to do the complete opposite of admitting how they felt.

Midway through pondering some other distraction from sleep, a loud rumble penetrated the walls of the hall from outside, followed soon after by screams and shouts, seemingly coming from every direction. The floor juddered briefly as the noise had begun, jolting Vess from his thoughts. Scrambling up from his bedroll on the floor, he exchanged concerned looks with Athalir and Erryn, both also getting to their feet.

"Well, I don't think there are too many things that could have moved the building," Athalir said, confirming the suspicions of the others.

"Our dwarf-eating friend from the Stone Highway," Vess replied wryly.

"You could have just said 'dragon', Vess," Erryn quipped, flashing a mischievous smile at the warrior.

"We should assist," Athalir proposed, instantly receiving nods of agreement from Erryn and Vess.

They were just about to leave the building when the prince stopped suddenly, darting his eyes about the room. "Wait, where's the mage? Did he even come back inside?"

"I know where he is," Erryn responded, her voice now lacking the humour of a moment before, her face downcast. "I'll go get him."

Vess caught her eye, sympathy written all over his face.

"Do you want me to come with you?"

Erryn shook her head, and with no further comment disappeared through the doors into the still dark outside.

A short while later, and the company of four came to a skidding halt at the centre of the settlement. At its heart, illuminated by the flaming torches of those brave enough not to have fled, an enormous black creature was turning wildly, lashing its spiked tail and snapping its jaws at the small army of dwarves attacking from the periphery. Though axes were occasionally making contact with the dragon's body, they did little damage, barely drawing blood as the thick, scaly skin sufficiently armoured the beast.

With each attack, the dragon grew more determined. As one axe-wielding dwarf lunged forwards to attempt a blow across its flank, the dragon swiftly twisted its long neck around, its tail swiping half a dozen warriors off their feet as its giant body followed suit. The brave dwarf had no time to react. As a look of horror flashed in his eyes, the dragon's head shot forwards and closed its mouth around his muscular body, the crunching of bones a sickening reminder of mortality to the other fighters. However, the dwarves were a courageous people; those that had been thrown back by the tail were soon back to their feet, the cuts and bruises to be felt when the battle was done. Others, spurred on by the death of their comrade, launched a coordinated assault upon the dragon's bulk, charging forwards and bringing their battle-axes down upon the creature with mighty force. One dwarf even managed to draw blood from the underside of the creature's neck, but he was immediately crushed by a huge foot, and none had been able to attack that tender spot since.

For all their strength and valour, the dwarves were outmatched. Before long, more warriors fell, limbs and faces torn by teeth and claw, the centre of Brinthorn stained with more dwarven blood than that of the dragon.

Rannan stood with his men, leading the defence of the settlement and its people. His rugged features pulled into a tight expression of conviction, he bellowed to the fighters to stand firm. The dwarven stamina was renowned among the races, but even the battle-hardened larnsman was beginning to show the signs of fatigue. With each man down, a tiny piece of his resolve seemed to be chipped away.

"We have to help," Erryn insisted, readying her bow and taking an arrow from her quiver.

"Agreed, but you see how ineffective the dwarves' weapons are against this thing. We need a strategy," Marcus quickly replied, a plan already formulating in his mind.

"I have a strategy – we kill it!" Athalir's daggers were out before he'd even started speaking, and with no desire for a response, he sprung his lithe body forwards, sprinting towards one of the dragon's front shoulder blades, daggers poised for the plunge. The others could only watch as the Fell prince tore on, hurdling fallen dwarves and twisting around outstretched axes in a dramatic attempt to assault the dragon before it became aware of his presence. However, though impressive, his attack was ill-fated. Within a second of his final lunge for the target, the creature extended and opened up its vast, leathery, black wings. Athalir's body was struck head-on, lifting him clear off the ground and sending him hurtling through the air, back the way he'd come. Marcus, Vess, and Erryn followed the prince's trajectory with their eyes until he came crashing down on the ground beside them, bruised and scraped, but otherwise only his pride sustaining serious injury.

Vess looked up from Athalir's grounded body to face Marcus.

"So, let's hear this strategy of yours."

Minutes later and Marcus had managed to scramble onto the thatched roof of a single-story building, and Erryn was positioned in the nearest watch tower with her bow aimed towards the dragon. Meanwhile, Vess stood among the dwarven warriors, great-sword gripped with both hands, the defensive role he'd been assigned clear in his mind.

Having witnessed Athalir's agility during his failed assault, Marcus knew exactly how the prince's skills would be best used. With his eyes sharply focused on the dragon's hindquarters, Athalir bristled with mounting anticipation of the move he would need to make, should the rest of the mage's plan come to pass as intended. His job was to scale the dragon's back, get to its head and gouge out its eyes with his daggers – *easy*, he thought. Still smarting from his undignified failure, he was eager to prove himself. *Ha!* Prove himself to a Vaharian, and him a Fell prince. Were it not that he truly believed this temporary alliance would bring his people what they so desperately needed, even the idea of proving oneself to a human would have been considered ridiculous. For now, however, he and the mage shared a common goal. He couldn't risk Marcus deciding he'd be more hindrance than help, and he couldn't take on the governors alone. Casting away his pride, he returned to focus on the task at hand, just in time to see a tremendous spray of fire thrusting upwards ahead of the dragon.

Certain that everyone was in their positions, Marcus seized the moment to cast the harmless firework display the instant the dragon was facing the right way. As planned, the bright orange light caught the creature's attention. Craning its long neck exposed the softer area of flesh that one dwarf had been able to reach. Hopefully, it was soft enough for one of Erryn's expertly-aimed arrows to pierce. She'd suggested imbuing the arrow with a spell, but Marcus knew precise timing was imperative and it would take valuable extra seconds for the hexan's magic to be channelled into an arrow.

Up in the tower, Erryn watched from the corner of her eye as Marcus' spell shot into the night sky, a hair's breadth from the wooden supports at her side. Then, her eyes focused on the dragon, she took aim and let off the arrow without delay. The tip met its target with ease, burying itself into the throat of the beast. The dragon jerked its head downwards, as Marcus had predicted. It was instinctively covering the wound with its lower jaw, while raising one giant clawed foreleg in an attempt to dislodge the comparatively tiny piece of wood now jutting from its neck.

So far so good, Erryn thought. *If Athalir can manage to stay on his feet, this plan might just succeed.* No sooner had the thought left her mind than she caught sight of a movement from within the lines of dwarven soldiers. Darting out from behind Vess, one of the dwarves ran towards the dragon, axe-wielding and full of fury. "Damn it, that wasn't supposed to happen!" All she could do was hope Vess noticed and dealt with the problem in time.

Vess barely had time to register what was going on before the plan was already beginning to fall apart. With a lone dwarf now hacking at the air close to the dragon's front legs, the creature's attention was diverted from its injury, causing it to once again shift its immense bulk from side to side. The metal-clad warrior knew that Athalir's role would be nigh-on impossible if the dragon turned around anymore – not to mention that stupid dwarf was about to get himself eaten. Vess had conveyed a brief explanation of the plan to Rannan while Marcus and the others were still getting into place, but obviously it had not reached the ears of this particular soldier. Before any more harm could be done, Vess drove his body into the dwarf, knocking him back into the legs of his fellows. The dwarf was out of harm's reach, but the damage was already done. The dragon was now turning this way and that, its hindquarters getting further from where Athalir needed them to be with every move. There had only been a brief window of opportunity at this point in the plan, and it was closing fast. Seeing no other chance for salvage, Vess took a tighter grip of his sword and thrust himself in front of the dragon, taunting it into turning around again as soon as it knew he was there. Waving his blade and roaring as loudly as he could, he stayed firm once the creature's head was once again facing the watch tower. The dwarves at the periphery watched on in awe as the giant of a man mimicked the ferocity of the great beast. Then, with widened eyes, they let out a communal gasp as the dragon began to lunge its open mouth at Vess, who, for all his size, suddenly looked minuscule in the shadow of the gigantic dragon.

Marcus and Erryn, who'd both been watching events play out from their heightened vantage points, exchanged worried glances as their companion placed himself within reach of the dragon's jaws.

"Come on, Athalir," Marcus urged under his breath.

The prince didn't have the benefit of aerial vision. From his shadowed location, he'd been about to begin his sprint up the dragon's tail when it suddenly turned around, nearly swiping his legs out from underneath him in the process. Determined not to end up on the ground again, he'd jumped up just in time, the tail passing beneath without incident. Something must have gone wrong, because things weren't proceeding as they should. *Still, no matter*, he thought. *I'll just have to move where* it *moves.*

But it was no good; every time he was in the right place, the dragon shifted again. Athalir was beginning to lose faith, when he heard a commotion from somewhere beyond his line of vision. Beneath the thunderous roar of the dragon came another rumbling sound, a voice bellowing in competition. *Is that… Vess?* He thought, recognising the tone. Then the beast turned again, at last its tail exactly where the prince needed it to be. Immediately, he began racing forwards, pushing off from his heels and bolting ahead as fast as he was able. He was within inches of the tail when something hurtled into him from behind, throwing him to the ground with such a force that his daggers were cast from his hands. Dazed and confused, Athalir looked up to see a dual axe-wielding dwarf ascending the tail, long ash-blonde hair and woollen coat billowing out behind him as he reached the apex of the dragon's rump and continued onward.

Vess stood his ground beneath the dragon, his ice blue eyes fixed on those of the creature, as its huge head came lower for a closer look. The open jaws were soon so near, he could see nearly every razor-sharp tooth, each one the length of one of the warrior's arms, and just as thick. As he felt the dragon's hot breath reach his face he choked back the urge to run, silently praying the elf was about to strike at any second. Resolutely refusing to close his eyes as he faced death, he was about to raise his sword in an attempt to go out fighting, when a stocky figure appeared between the horns on the beast's head. Questions raced through Vess' mind, but there was no time left to answer them. With one final roar, splattering the warrior with saliva, the dragon pulled back and then struck out, ready to close its mouth around its meal. Instinctively, Vess finally closed his eyes, holding his great-sword aloft as he waited for the inevitable end.

From the rooftop, Marcus' hands heated up, a ball of fire beginning to form in each. He'd wanted to avoid using magic to directly attack the dragon as he doubted his ability to control it; one misjudged aim could spell death for many dwarves. However, with his companion about to be eaten, he no longer had a choice. The plan had failed and all he could do now was try to save Vess, and keep the dwarven casualties to a minimum. Erryn had no such qualms about using magic and was already imbuing arrows with fire and taking pot shots at the dragon as it threatened Vess' life. None were piercing its scaly skin, but she hoped they might at least act as a distraction as they bounced off around its eyes.

With no more time for doubts, Marcus raised his hands full of fire and started to cast the magical orbs, until he saw the dwarf appear over the peak of the dragon's hips, running fast and brandishing a mighty axe in each hand. Before he'd had a chance to release the fireballs, the dwarf reached the summit of the beast's neck. Without pause the stout man swung the axes outwards, slicing them back down again, retaining control as they curved inwards and collided with the base of the two scythe-like horns at the front of the massive head.

Surprised his death had not come as expected, Vess opened his eyes just in time to see the horns sliced from the dragon's skull, a fountain of dark scarlet blood erupting from the base of each one. As the horns crashed to the ground below, the blood continued to spurt skywards; the dragon's roar was now more of a pained shriek as it writhed about in obvious agony. All the while, the dwarf kept his balance atop the gigantic neck, moving with it until finally the creature succumbed to the blood loss. Its legs gave way beneath its body and the neck and head sunk to the ground where it crashed forwards, breathing its last breath.

A jubilant cheer rose up from the crowd of dwarven soldiers and onlookers as the victorious dwarf slung the axes into holders at his back before striding down the slope of the slain dragon's forehead, jumping off from the space between the nostrils. The drop must have been twice his height yet he landed firmly on his feet.

Amidst the chaotic celebration, where ale was already being passed around and the number of dwarves clambering up onto the body of the dead dragon was steadily growing, Marcus scrambled down from the roof, keen to do nothing more than find out what had happened to Athalir. He was aware that the Fell prince had never set foot outside his own kingdom, and though it had been the elf's decision to join this quest, he had resolved at the border between Sa'hahlenfell and Geryndor that he would make it a priority not to deprive the Fell of a much loved prince.

He didn't have to wait long for reassurance; as Erryn and Vess joined him, Athalir appeared from behind the huge corpse. Sheathing his daggers and straightening his clothing, his eyes bore a look of annoyance as he caught sight of his companions. Within moments, he was stood with the group, bristling with anger and demanding answers.

"So much for the plan. I thought this lump of muscle was supposed to be keeping the dwarves out of the way." Athalir looked at Vess with an accusatory glare.

"Hey, I almost got eaten for the sake of the plan!"

"Well perhaps if you had been almost eaten earlier, I might have been able to carry out my task before some *shortling* barrelled into me."

"Oh just carry on, elf. I'm in exactly the right mood to put you down."

"You honestly think you could…"

"Enough!" Marcus interjected, stepping forwards and parting the two men before they came to blows.

Vess and Athalir glared at each other, then glared at Marcus, who was about to come out with a witty remark to ease the tension, when Rannan arrived among the group, ale sloshing over the wooden tankard he gripped loosely in one hand.

"The men want the hero to join them," The larnsman announced, motioning towards the dwarven revellers atop the head of the dragon.

"Well I don't know about hero, I just…" Marcus began, but was quickly interrupted.

"No, not *you.* The *horggen*!" Rannan shouted his reply, causing a boisterous cheer to rise up from the celebrating dwarves at the mention of Vess' recently-acquired nickname.

"*Me*? *I* didn't kill the dragon. What do they want *me* for?" Vess' perplexed expression mirrored Athalir's.

Rannan didn't get a chance to answer before another dwarf strode over and slapped Vess firmly across the shoulder-blade, shoving Athalir out of the way as he inserted himself among them.

"Because you *heroically* offered yourself as a replacement meal, human!" The new dwarf grinned up at Vess before turning his attention to the rest of the group, his long, straw-coloured hair whipping around in the light wind. He folded his chunky arms, displaying two rough and scarred hands, the right one missing half of its smallest finger.

"You! You were the shortling that ruined the plan!" Though he'd only seen him from behind, Athalir recognised the two features that he remembered from his earlier prostrate position as they disappeared up the tail of the dragon. Indeed, even without the wild mane of hair and ground-scraping, black woollen coat, this dwarf would have stood out among the others. His features revealed a man of imperious nature, every rustic pore of his skin exuding arrogance, and the heavy fabric of his outer-garment doing little to disguise his stocky, muscular build. As Vess appraised the newcomer, the two blood-stained axes strapped to the dwarf's back sparked the memory of his brush with death.

"You're the one that slew the dragon!" Vess announced the true hero with palpable awe.

"That I am. And you might want to give your elf friend some instruction on how to address a mighty dragon-slayer, lest I put him on his back again." The new dwarf seemed to revel in the Fell prince's ire, a wicked glint in his eye as he watched Athalir anger.

Rannan's posture had instantly stiffened the second the 'dragon-slayer' had arrived, almost as if he were standing to attention. However, his expression held little respect as he spoke his name.

"Hessan."

"Rannan! Good to see you still know how to use that weapon in your advancing years. Your courage is waning though, larnsman. It must be all that bending over. Oh yes, I think I can just make out Larn Ossern's boot print on your backside." Hessan seemed pleased with himself as Rannan curled his hands into tight fists. "Now, now, we wouldn't want you exerting yourself, old man." The younger dwarf continued to taunt.

Erryn had never had the opportunity to see the soul of a dwarf before, but as she looked beyond the laughter in the eyes of the one having fun at another's expense, a maelstrom of emotions appeared shrouded in a thick grey fog. Assuming this wasn't how all the souls of dwarves looked, this man was bottling up some serious inner turmoil.

"What are you staring at, girl?" Hessan gruffly broke Erryn's inspection of his soul. In her concentration, she hadn't noticed that the dragon-slaying dwarf had become aware of her gaze. Now, she blushed as he eyeballed her, his good humour replaced with mild irritation.

Noting her awkward predicament, Marcus spoke out.

"Oh, she doesn't mean anything by it, sir… Hessan, er, sir. She's just looking for your soul. It's a hexan thing. Now, if you'll excuse us we really must be…"

"Hexan? But…" Hessan's eyes squeezed together, his thin lips curving down at the corners as his mind took in what Marcus had just said.

Rannan too was looking puzzled, and watching Erryn more intently than he had before. Marcus, Vess, and Athalir tensed up as their female companion came under closer scrutiny. Marcus decided he'd be wise to move things on diplomatically before one of the more volatile men she travelled with chose to play the gallant hero. Besides, though the winter sun wouldn't rise for another few hours, he could already sense it would be morning soon, and he knew they should be resuming their journey without further delay. Though they'd had little sleep that night, he didn't wish to waste any daylight by sleeping in. There was still the matter of the absent Sathom, and the mage's mind was desperately trying to quash the disquiet that was threatening to cloud his thinking.

"Yes, well, like I said, we need to be on our way. Thank you, Rannan, for your hospitality. Please pass on our gratitude to your larn. We've yet to return to the hall to collect our belongings, but we should be back on the road by dawn. Farewell." With that Marcus nodded to the group before striding away promptly so as to avoid any further conversation, the others hurriedly falling in line. Erryn glanced nervously back over her shoulder at the pair of dwarves, who were now engaged in heated discussion. She had no idea why, but it seemed the mere mention of the term 'hexan' was the cause of the sudden shift in the demeanour of both men. All her years of having to hide her true nature had taught her to be naturally cautious. Now, she couldn't quite shake the feeling that Marcus had inadvertently brought trouble she'd spent so long trying to avoid.

No more than an hour later and the party had found their way back to the track on which they'd discovered the dwarven boy. All except Vess dragged their heals as the lack of sleep caught up with them, making every step feel leaden and their packs unnaturally heavy. The metal-clad warrior, however, strode on, seemingly unhindered by tiredness. He hadn't slept for four days, but he felt good. Narrowly escaping death only bolstered his vigour, and it was all too easy to push his fears to the back of his mind. As he walked, his train of thought moved on to the one that had saved his life. He'd certainly made an impression on the young man, and his sharp retort to the elf had almost caused him to break out laughing. He still didn't trust Prince Athalir, and didn't like him much either. His haughty attitude irritated Vess, and he would have rejoiced to witness the dwarf knocking him to the ground.

He was chuckling to himself at the mental image of the Fell prince floored, again, when a low grinding sound from behind caught his attention, making him stop and turn around. The rest of the group had done the same and, in the dim first light of a cloudy sunrise, they could just make out a horse and cart trundling along the dirt track, the wheels carving through the grooves on either side. Vess walked back to stand with the others as they moved off to the side to allow enough room for the cart to pass. However, as it reached them, the heavy horse halted, pulled up by a soft '*whoa*' from the driver.

"Get in!" A familiar male voice called from the back. The travellers exchanged looks but remained where they were. After another moment's silence, a figure stood up in the cart. Even in the subdued dawn light, Hessan's outline was unmistakable.

"Come on! You all look like walking corpses… well, most of you. Still running on adrenaline, eh horggen?" The dwarf addressed Vess with a wry smile.

"We will manage well enough, shortling," Athalir called back, his voice dripping with scorn.

"Oh come now, even on a full night's rest it's another half day's walk to the next settlement. I'll wager you'll all be dead on the road when the sun sets. I'm heading home, to Hildthorn, and there's room up here for you all. You might even manage a couple of hours shut-eye – I'm not one for small talk."

Hessan had presented a convincing argument; even Athalir couldn't deny the appeal of travelling the rest of the way on wheels.

One nod of agreement from Marcus and everyone eagerly clambered up onto the cart, dumping their packs with relief on the wooden floor and settling onto the benches on either side. It wasn't long before the gentle rolling movement had lulled Erryn, Athalir, and Marcus into a light slumber. As usual, Vess stayed awake, though as he noticed his companions sleeping he decided it would be wise to close his eyes and pretend to do the same.

With most of his fellow passengers asleep, Hessan leant forwards to the driver. "Take it easy. There's no rush," he said in a hushed voice. He knew he'd glean more information from the outlanders if they were awake enough to talk, and many things had his curiosity piqued. There was the impressive golden-armoured man sat adjacent to him for a start. The dwarf knew his unconscious state was a deception, and he had a feeling it wasn't only for his benefit. Of greater interest still was the female human; a hexan, the mage had said. He and Rannan rarely saw eye to eye on anything, yet even they had both agreed something wasn't right… and Hessan knew of only one person who may be able to shed some light. Now, all he had to do was persuade them all to accompany him to the tavern in Hildthorn. *That shouldn't be too hard*, he thought. *Persuasion's my gift.*

As he leant back against the wooden rail of the cart, he smiled to himself, closed his eyes, and began to plan.

CHAPTER SIXTEEN

Sathom bent down over the remnants of something that could once have been a dwarf. All around the flattened landscape were more body parts and bits of clothing; things so hard and tasteless as to be undesirable, even to a dragon.

There would have been no doubt in his mind, as he surveyed the wasteland, that the creature he'd seen sleeping just months earlier was now awake. Yet, if more proof were needed, it came without warning, as an enormous shadow was quickly followed by the dragon coming in to land.

Sathom remained passive; an elemental had nothing to fear from fangs or claws, no matter how large or sharp. However, somewhere deep inside, buckling against the magical binds that kept his emotions in check, an uncomfortable feeling became rooted.

Watching silently as the dragon set aside its latest quarry to tend to a smooth, grey egg, the elemental pondered on the certainty his investigation had revealed. He briefly considered having the necessary discussion with Marcus as soon as he returned to his side - then instantly dismissed the notion. No, he had not spent a thousand years trying to achieve this, only to jeopardise everything with a subject that was bound to weigh heavily on the mind of the young mage. The souls must be saved - anything else could be confronted another time.

Sathom closed his eyes and imagined himself elsewhere, his form blinking out of existence and reappearing seconds later, many feet above on the Stone Highway. Visualising his companions fighting rebel elves in the forests of Sa'hahlenfell, he closed his eyes once again and was about to return to Marcus' side, when a very strong sense that he was being watched interrupted his thoughts. Calmly scanning the furthest reaches of the road, he couldn't see anyone, but the feeling was still present. Anyone else may have dismissed the sensation, but Sathom's condition didn't lend itself to the bouts of stress or nervousness that might otherwise cause a man to imagine things.

Then, with complete clarity, he knew where to look. He walked to the edge of the road, and looked downward to the open grassland of Vaharia. The light was not the best, the sun had already started to set, but Sathom's sharp eyes instantly recognised the figure staring up at him. He could also see the malevolent grin spread across the gaunt face, the accompanying dark eyes meeting the elemental's gaze with evil delight.

A tight sensation travelled through Sathom's body; in the absence of emotions, that was as close as he could get to terror. For almost ten centuries, he'd remained unknown to the governors and their familiars, hidden with the aid of their belief that every elemental had been sent back to Meran and sealed inside. Now, as the skaithen below made his move, Sathom's advantage disintegrated; there was nothing he could do but flee.

"So, you see, it was pure evil." Erryn slurred her words as her head rested heavy on both hands, her elbows framing a large tankard sat on the ale-stained wooden table. "Ha! *Pure* evil. Can evil *be* pure?" She giggled, a hiccough escaping as she did so, causing her to blush, and giggle again.

Vess sat next to the drunken redhead, a tankard in one hand, and the hilt of his sword in the other. He'd rested it against the tavern wall when the group had first sat down, grabbing hold of the hilt when the first effects of the dwarven ale had made themselves known. That had been over an hour ago, and he'd not loosened his grip since.

"My friend," Vess slurred. "If you say the drink was *pure* evil, who am I to challenge… Is it just me or is this place moving?"

On the opposite side of the table, Athalir grinned at his two companions. His own tankard had just been refilled for the fourth time and he was only just beginning to feel slightly light-headed – the humans would be lucky if they could still stand.

The prince had questioned the wisdom of yet another delay in their quest, but when the brash dwarf had forcefully suggested they rest a while in the tavern at Hildthorn, Marcus had been quick to agree. The mage was most probably trying not to offend their shortling host, especially after he'd so kindly offered them transportation. Much as he was now obviously trying not to offend his female admirer by suffering her slightly smelly attentions. *Too polite for his own good that one*, he mused. Athalir was intent on keeping his thoughts on their human leader ambiguous at best, but he was finding it increasingly difficult to dislike the man. The Fell prince's experience of human mages had confirmed the negativity spoken of in the tales of the elders. Yet Marcus Ryan was different – a fact that was beginning to make what he'd agreed to do substantially harder. Athalir turned his head to look at the tall man at his side.

Marcus hadn't indulged as much as Erryn and Vess, despite the insistence of the dwarf that he do so. In fact, the tankard sitting on the table in front of him was still half-full with the first pour, while he was busy attempting to keep the wandering hands of a middle-aged dwarven tavern wench from wandering too far.

"It seems dwarven women have a *thing* for you, mage," Athalir teased, turning his attention back to his own drink.

Marcus inwardly groaned at the elf's jibe, screwing up his face before having it roughly jerked back to be scrutinised by the determined woman.

The Miner's Rest Tavern and Inn was an inviting place. Little nooks with built-in seating adorned the side walls, while, from across the well-spaced sets of tables and chairs, a gaping open fireplace faced the bar from the back wall of the large room. Comfortable, high-backed armchairs were set nearest the fire, their fleece-filled cushions subject to the unwritten rule that they were to be reserved for the elders alone – even if no elder was present.

The bar ran almost from one side of the room to the other, a wooden framework long enough to accommodate several customers and their large orders. On either side was a heavy wooden door, one concealing the staircase that led to the first floor guest rooms and owner's quarters, the other being the main entrance into the tavern.

It was a dull, wet morning, and thus the light entering the building through the few small, arched windows wasn't enough to sufficiently light the room. When everyone had walked in a little over an hour ago, the warm orange glow provided by both the crackling fire and the flames in the numerous wall sconces had been a welcome sight to the damp travellers, and unlike that of the Crooked Wing back in Whitestone, the smell was rather pleasant. There were hints of bergamot and cinnamon blended with beeswax-polished pine, the smoke of the pine kindling on the fire, and, every so often, a trace of vanilla wafting past from some well-concealed source.

The dragon-slaying dwarf, who'd finally introduced himself to his stunned guests as Hessan Northwynd, High King of Geryndor, stood at the bar. Resting one arm on the wooden counter, one leg casually crossed over the other, he watched his guests with obvious interest as he gingerly stroked the short blonde beard that adorned his chin. He'd brought them to the tavern under the pretence of showing them some dwarven hospitality, and indeed, with the unplanned assistance of Gearda, and the very-much-planned free-flowing ale, the outlanders couldn't say they weren't being made welcome. However, Hessan's curiosity led him towards a more self-serving goal. These were the first people from beyond the borders to set foot on Geryndor soil in three decades – and an elf was among them. That alone sparked questions that, in Hessan's mind, demanded answers. The human that appeared to be in charge had unintentionally piqued the king's interest with his attempt at nonchalance. Of course, their presence was enough of a curious thing, but in Hessan's experience, when someone wants you to know little, they say much. Marcus' awkward babbling when asked about the reason for their arrival in Geryndor had been indicative of a secret, and Hessan wasn't about to let them leave without discovering exactly what that secret was.

Returning to the table, he pulled up a free chair, turning it backwards so that he could sit astride it as if riding a horse.

"Gearda, I think the boy's had enough of your wayward fingers for now. Old Seddan is at the bar. I believe he's had just enough to drink to ignore the stench and missing teeth." The high king raised his eyebrows at the lusty wench, who'd started to protest, before removing herself from Marcus' lap and flouncing off towards an aged dwarf seated on a stool at the bar, looking rather the worse for wear. Glancing back over her shoulder at Marcus, she winked and smiled, before frowning and slapping old Seddan across the back the head – an act he seemed to barely notice – and taking a telling off from the barkeep for neglecting her duties.

"Thank you." Marcus directed his gratitude at the newcomer to the table, relief pasted all over his face.

"Ha! Think nothing of it. Gearda's been known to leave men with a little more than a few love-bites. Wouldn't want you taking any uncomfortable itching along on your journey, now would we?"

Athalir grimaced at the dwarf.

"Is disrespecting your women a dwarven trait, or simply what passes for regal manners in this soulless land?"

"I think you'll find I'm representative of neither dwarf, nor royalty, elf. And as for calling my homeland *soulless*, I suggest you've been drinking with the wrong dwarves," Hessan replied with a sardonic smile.

Though the dwarf's words appeared light-hearted, his blue eyes locked with Athalir's, an unspoken warning present in his stare. Not one to back down, the Fell prince stared back, the atmosphere between the two men electrically charged and threatening to spark at any moment. However, starting a fight with the elf would not be conducive to gaining information and so Hessan laughed, low and deliberate, before resuming the task at hand.

"So, what brings a party of outlanders into dwarven lands? And this time, I'll hear no talk of 'just passing through'." It was the same question he'd asked before, but Hessan was losing patience fast, the silent altercation with the elf doing nothing for his inclination towards subtlety. Besides, this time he was banking on the ale having the desired effect, and information being more freely offered.

"Well, it's like this, see. We're on our way to rescue some old souls from a great big tower in the..."

"Erryniya!" Marcus jumped in with haste, as the inebriated hexan began to blurt everything out.

"Oops." Erryn giggled, hiccoughed, and then let her head thud onto her folded arms. "Oh, my head hurts. I think I'm going to be..." Before Vess' alcohol-dulled senses could react to Athalir and

Marcus' urgent prompting to move, Erryn leant towards him and threw up in his lap. The great warrior looked down, then instantly shot his head up as the smell of vomit assaulted his nostrils.

While Marcus fussed over the now-pitiful redhead, Vess got the attention of the wench, who took one look at his lap and tossed the ale-stained rag she had hooked into her belt in his direction, before sighing, raising her eyes, and flouncing off. Athalir couldn't contain his amusement and leaned back against the wall, sniggering as he watched the proceedings.

Meanwhile, the gears were hastily shifting within the mind of Hessan Northwynd. He'd discovered the purpose for the visitors travels – well, most of it; certainly enough to warrant further investigation – but something else now toyed with his intrigue. The girl's name was Erryniya – a dwarven name, and one with which he was very familiar.

A memory flashed through the man's sharp mind; a conversation held in whispers in the small hours, accompanied by an alcohol-filled jug, two tankards, and the subdued last hurrah of a dying fire. Hessan glanced over towards the fireplace and the silhouette of one of the high-backed armchairs, then back at his foreign guests, who were now returning to their respective places around the table, the commotion of before having settled down.

His eyes were narrowed, his mind swiftly unravelling the past and tying neat bows in the next five minutes. Before anyone had noticed his look of concentration, he pasted on a wide, toothy smile and addressed the group.

"May I suggest I procure you all some rooms for a few hours? Journeys aren't well-trodden on bellies full of ale – or so my great aunt Stregga used to say."

Though the elf protested, Marcus and the others saw the sense in sleeping off the worst of their intoxication. With their agreement secured, Hessan loudly paid the innkeeper double the cost of the four rooms, while covertly holding a kitchen knife to his abdomen, ensuring the current tenants were cast out until the next day.

After the outlanders had settled, the king returned downstairs and took a chair at the fire, next to one already occupied.

"I have some guests I think you might be interested in meeting, Erryniya. I'll bring them to you when they're rested."

A hand moved from the other seat's armrest and gently held Hessan's, acceptance in the gesture. The dwarven king's mind would not stay idle, and he spent the next few hours in silence by the fire, impatience nudging at him the whole time.

Many hours later, when he could wait no longer, Hessan beckoned over the innkeeper's young son and, handing him a shiny, golden coin, gave him instructions to rouse the outlanders and tell them to meet him at the bar.

Within a few minutes, the group emerged through the doorway, eyes half-closed and feet dragging across the stone-tiled floor.

"Ah, feeling better, I see!" Hessan bellowed, causing Vess and Erryn to flinch at the sound. "Come, there's someone I think you should meet." With that, he made his way towards the fireplace, the shuffling of four pairs of feet and rustle of clothing and packs assurance he was being followed.

As they approached the chair, a small, feminine looking hand rose from the armrest and made a beckoning motion, prompting the dwarf and his companions to proceed without delay. Hessan stepped back slightly, allowing Erryn, who was next in line behind him and looking very unsteady on her feet, to sit in the other armchair.

Slumping into the spacious seat, Erryn's eyes were drawn to the frail woman in front of the fire. In the warm light, her advancing years were easy to make out, as was the horribly scarred flesh where her eyes should have been. Gasping in shock, Erryn then mentally scolded herself for her impolite reaction, until the female dwarf leaned forwards and, without searching, gently placed her hand on the hexan's knee.

"Shh, my dear. There's no need for shame." The dwarven woman smiled warmly. There was something calming in the way she smiled. It was an almost familiar feeling that dispensed with any awkwardness, at least for Erryn; now gathered around the chair, her three male companions displayed varying amounts of discomfort across their faces.

Hessan had gone to the fireplace. Leaning against the mantle with one hand, he scrutinised the meeting as if waiting for something to happen.

Erryn was about to speak, her hung-over mind confused as to why their host had felt this meeting necessary, but as her lips parted, the dwarven woman spoke first.

"Boys, I'm well aware my face is not a pleasure to look upon, but if you would offer an old lady a few moments, I'm sure what I have to show you will prove to be an interesting distraction from my lack of eyes. Erryn, is it? Would you lend a fellow hexan your hand? My magic is not as strong as it used to be."

Her head spinning from the revelation the dwarven woman had just made about being a hexan, not to mention the fact that she knew her name, Erryn had no time for questions before the elder female clasped her left hand, entwining their fingers, and squeezing tightly. With her free hand, the dwarf made a vertical swiping motion in the space before her. Instantly, a blurred oval of light appeared, hovering above the floor and swirling internally with purple mist. Erryn could feel the magic bleeding from her hand, a painless yet distinct sensation similar to pins and needles, and one she hadn't felt since she last held hands with her mother. However, something felt different about this connection; she stared with curiosity at the face of the female dwarf, while everyone around her gaped at the image beginning to appear within the mist.

A blurred scene started to play out inside the magical window. First, silence, then voices joined the moving picture. Erryn turned to view the display at the sound of a voice she found vaguely familiar.

The image became clearer until those watching could easily recognise the woman who stood among them, holding Erryn's hand. The dwarf in the image was much younger, and still in possession of both eyes, but her dainty facial features were a definite match. Her long, flaxen hair was loose and unkempt, her clothing torn, and stained with what looked like blood. There were narrow cuts across her cheeks, and her eyes were red and puffy as if she'd been crying, but tenacity shone out from the large, brown irises.

The older dwarf woman waved her hand once more and the image zoomed out, revealing a poorly-lit and sparsely-furnished stone room, with the female dwarf tied to a wooden chair in the middle. A man dressed in a uniform, which Marcus immediately recognised as that of the city guard, stood with his back against a heavy wooden door, his arms folded over his chest. A shock of red hair stuck out from beneath his guardsman's helmet and a cruel smile played on his thin lips. But his wicked smirk was nothing compared to the voice that drew everyone's attention to the other man in the room.

That voice, the one Erryn thought she knew, had been audible, but its owner unseen. Now, it was clearly coming from a man with his back to the watchers. Even from behind, he exuded malice. His scarlet-coated shoulders were back, his head, with its black hair slicked flat like a slither of oil, was held high, and in each hand he gripped a wickedly sharp-looking dagger, dripping with blood.

Erryn stiffened, her hold on Marcus' hand tightening to the point where he abruptly turned away from the scene to cast a questioning look. With the colour almost completely washed from her skin, the hexan hoarsely whispered two words as the man in the image turned so that his dark-eyed, gaunt face became clear, his malevolent grin echoing the evil that seeped from his presence.

"That's him!"

With cruel comprehension of who she meant, Marcus was drawn back to the image, though now his heart rate had increased and his face was taut with constrained anger.

Athalir also recognised the man in the image. He shuffled nervously, feeling as if those around him knew his secret. Obviously, they didn't, but he had to try very hard to quash the urge to run from the building to hide his face.

In horror, everyone watched as heinous acts of torture were dealt to the younger dwarven woman. Every so often, the sickening voice of the black-haired man would ask the same question, "What did you see?" and each time, through her sobs, she would defiantly reply, "I will tell you nothing, skaithen!"

Finally, with her garments and hair soaked in blood, and a steady stream of crimson-tinged tears trailing over her cheekbones, it became apparent her will was broken, that she could take the pain no longer. When next the question came, she gave the skaithen the answer he sought.

"You wish to know what I've seen – then I will tell you, and may you and your cowardly masters choke on it."

"Hmm, choking – not a method I'd considered, but the idea intrigues me." The skaithen laughed at his own twist on the woman's insult, placing the daggers on a side table and making a throttling motion close to her throat. She leant as far away from him as she was able, powerless to suppress her own fear. "Oh, just spit it out, dwarf. Much as I revel in your pain, I tire of this… no, I don't. I never tire of inflicting pain, but I do need an answer, if you'd be so kind." He swooped in as he finished speaking so that his face was just a hair's breadth from hers, grinning so widely that his jaw threatened to split in two.

Taking a deep breath, the woman's face once more reflected inner strength, a bold last burst of courage as she spoke. "The reign of the governors is nearing its end. I've seen a man, one of another race, a tall race – though not human. He will bring about their downfall – and yours, *skaithen.* I saw a better Vaharia, one where the dark magic of those that falsely wield immortality is destroyed, once and for all."

"When? When will this '*tall man'* come?"

"But thirty years from this day. And how I hope I'm alive to see it come to pass!" The dwarven woman bravely stared into the skaithen's black eyes, and then spat bloody sputum at his face.

Unperturbed, the skaithen smirked and leaned in closer.

"You'll be alive, my lovely seer – but you won't be '*seeing*' anything."

Everyone watching could practically feel the sadism oozing from the words of the torturer, yet nothing could prepare them for what they witnessed next. Raising his hands, the evil creature curled all digits but his thumbs into fists, the smirk ever-present across his pale, black-veined skin. Both thumbs began to glow at the tips, with the skin beneath turning jet black until resembling red-hot pokers. Whether from premonition or just natural realisation, it was clear from her expression the dwarven seer was terrifyingly aware of her captor's next move. As his thumbs burnt into her eyes, her screams reverberated from the mystical image, out into the tavern, clawing at the spines of all present, while causing all but Hessan to instinctively turn away or squeeze shut their own eyes.

When everyone viewed the window again, the dwarf had been unseated and dumped onto the stone floor. Still crying in pain, she had curved her small, battered body into a tight ball, her bound hands brought up to cover where her eyes had once been.

"She's all yours." The skaithen coldly addressed the city guard as he approached the door. "Though I hope you don't expect pleasure from her watching your… *performance.*" With that, he laughed and, without looking back at the woman, left the room. The last anyone saw, as the image faded, was the red-haired guard moving towards the crumpled woman, leering at her as he began to hastily remove his leather armour.

With a flick of her free hand, the other still holding Erryn's, the female dwarf made the window rapidly shrink until it closed in on itself and disappeared altogether. For a few moments, everyone remained in stunned silence, an awkward tension inserting itself in the physical space between them all.

"Well, that was… unpleasant." Hessan filled the void, but received little reaction. The dwarf woman turned to face Erryn. Taking the young hexan's other hand in hers, she spoke with an extraordinary calm.

"My name is Erryniya, same as yours, and I knew your… your mother. We were good friends. She helped me once, and now I have the chance to repay her kindness." Letting go of Erryn's hands, Erryniya reached into a deep pocket at the front of her faded brown tunic, pulling out a leather cord from which a crudely-carved wooden star dangled freely. Once again, she took Erryn's hand, laying the necklace on the girl's palm before folding her fingers around it.

"Take this, wear it – please. You'd not welcome the reason, but trust me; this talisman will prove invaluable when you need it most."

"But…."

"Shh, there isn't time. I know you have questions, my dear girl, but fate is drawing the veil on our brief time together." Erryniya went on to speak to the men that had been patiently watching the exchange. "You all have questions, but the answers are within you already – just look to your instincts; they will guide you. I will say this, prince of the Fell; do not judge yourself too harshly. The path we travel is the right one… while we believe it is. Vessel, let not your fear keep you from sleep. The dreams will fade – as will your life-force, if you neglect its needs. Marcus, your royal highness, trust in those that have put their faith in you, for to mistrust yourself is insult to their judgement. It is within you to achieve what you fear you cannot."

While those she'd spoken to looked questioningly at one another, Erryniya walked towards the fireplace, reaching out to Hessan as she neared him. "My dear friend."

"Hah! My *only* friend." Hessan gently took the small hands in his own, a warm smile momentarily softening his hard features.

"That will change, son, I've told you this. One day your people will accept you as their true king. One day you will earn their respect – and their friendship."

"Erryniya, I respect you as I do my own mother, you know that, but there are times I believe your visions have skewed your wisdom somewhat."

The woman chuckled.

"If I were your mother, you'd have been bent over my knee for your insolence."

Stepping back to face the travellers, Erryniya addressed them all. "I have shown you all what you needed to see. Thirty years ago, I saw what fate had planned for the governors of Vaharia. Somehow, most likely through the evil magic of their skaithen, news of my vision reached the ears of those ancient men, obviously causing them enough concern that they sought me out. You all know how that went for me." Erryniya chuckled again, much to the discomfort of those who'd witnessed her torture.

Marcus had been quietly reflecting on what had been said. A number of things confused him, not least the way the elder dwarf had referred to him as 'your royal highness', but one thing was beyond questioning; this woman had had no choice but to tell that monster what she'd seen.

"My lady, please know we understand why you had to say what you knew."

"Oh, but I didn't." Confusion etched its way across Marcus' face. "I gave him nothing but a red-herring; I bought you some time. Had I told them exactly what I saw, you wouldn't be standing before me at this moment, Marcus."

Now it was Athalir's turn to look confused.

"But you told them everything. A man of tall race – the Meranells were tall, yes?" The Fell prince looked to Marcus for clarification. Marcus simply shrugged and passed along the look to Erryniya.

"I believe they were – seven feet, if the tales are true. But why would the governors, or their minions, think a Meranell would be their nemesis? As far as they were aware, the vessels of that race were long rotted; their souls imprisoned within their own evil construct. No, I gave them what they wanted – without giving them anything that would lead them to the truth. Their minds focused on what they knew; three known races, two distinct from humans, just one that could possibly have been classed as 'tall'. I gave them-"

Prince Athalir cut her off.

"You gave them an elf!" Now, with visibly stiffened stance, the Fell prince glowered at the elderly dwarf.

"I did."

"For Isearia's sake, why? Your red-herring has been the cause of my people's suffering these past thirty years. The governors closed the borders – because of you! I should cut you down where you stand!" Athalir took a step towards Erryniya, his hands poised above his sheathed daggers. Within a split second, Hessan had placed himself between them, his substantial bulk forming a wall in front of his friend. He glared at the elf, the threat of violence buckling against a thin barrier in his eyes.

"Marcus, I'd warn your '*pet*' to back off, unless he'd like to find himself put down… *again!*" The dwarf didn't take his eyes from Athalir the whole time he spoke.

"Athalir! What are you talking about?" This was the second time the prince had spoken of his people suffering, but Marcus was yet to understand the relevance to what the dwarven seer had done.

The prince's posture relaxed, slightly, as he turned to look at Marcus.

"When the borders were closed, three decades ago, trade between the kingdoms ended. The dwarves didn't lose much, everything they needed could be sourced in Geryndor. Not so for the Fell. We could still trade with the dwarves, had we wished to, but they didn't have the one thing we needed most – thiervan, though you know it as hembleweed."

"Ah, hembleweed. I use that as a hair tonic." Erryn piped up.

"Yes, well, it has a rather more essential use for us – it saves our lives!" With new clarity, Marcus began to understand his companion's anger.

"So, when you could no longer trade with Vaharia, you lost access to this thiervan. How, exactly, does it save elf lives?"

"There's a disease, a wasting, to which my people are uniquely prone to affliction. It dooms an elf to a prolonged, debilitating malaise, followed by immeasurable pain, and finally, death. A concoction of thiervan and a few other ingredients provides the only cure. Since it became unavailable to us, so many have succumbed… including my own parents." Athalir's gaze dropped to the floor.

Erryniya gently nudged Hessan, who reluctantly stepped aside. Placing her frail hands on the arms of Prince Athalir, the blind woman looked upon his features as though she could easily see his pain.

"I do not regret my words, your grace, but I *am* sorry they have burdened your lands with so much sorrow. It may not seem much consolation now, but the path I know you'll choose will bring the resolution you seek. Your pain, and that of your kin, will end."

The fight drained from Athalir at the recounting of his parent's condition, and he moved back, composing himself while Erryn linked her arm with his, her face expressing concern.

Vess had been watching the goings-on without word; much of it made scant sense to the man who'd only been conscious for a matter of days. However, mistrusting the elf as he did, Athalir's outburst had piqued his interest. He would have defended Erryniya had the dwarf not done so first, but as it was, he was able to stand back and listen. Something bothered him.

"My lady, if I may ask, what is this 'choice' you keep referring to each time you speak to Athalir?"

"Ah, that is not mine to reveal, Vessel," Erryniya replied.

Marcus hadn't thought about it before, but Vess' question made him realise its possible pertinence.

"But it *is* important – you've mentioned *choosing a path* twice."

"As I said, I am not the one to give you answers. I see things, yes, but it is unwise of any seer to reveal exact details of the future. So much can be altered upon even a few uttered words of the sight."

Erryniya's reply had only served to trouble Vess more, and Marcus' idle curiosity was turning to concern. He was vexed by a strange feeling that the choice the seer spoke of might affect him. And without Sathom there, he felt the weight of responsibility – of leadership – greater than ever.

"I'm sorry, but I *must* know if someone I'm travelling with is keeping something important from me. I've spent most of my life in the dark; I'll do so no longer!" Marcus was the one to speak, but the sentiment resonated with Vess' own thoughts.

Erryn let go of Athalir's arm and attempted to dispel the mounting tension.

"Is it really so bad for him to have secrets? Don't we all have things we'd prefer to keep to ourselves? I know I do. Leave him alone!"

"Erryn, I know you mean well, but the more I think on this the more it feels like something I should know is being deliberately withheld." Spurred on by the mage's determination, Vess approached Athalir, muscles visibly tensed.

"Tell us what you're hiding, 'prince'!"

"No! Stop this, you two."

Athalir had to do something or he'd never manage to get Marcus alone. The only thing that came to mind was to tell the truth – or at least, a version that would sound plausible to Vess. The hope was he could throw himself at Marcus' mercy by swearing to be a changed man. If he'd judged him right, it may just work. He put his hand into his pocket and fingered the vial of skaithen blood, before taking a deep breath and carefully choosing his words.

"Erryn, don't. Please don't defend me; I'm not worthy of it. I will tell them." Athalir smiled weakly at Erryn, nodding as she stepped back to let him face Vess and Marcus.

"Marcus, the choice she speaks of is the one I made when I saw no other way – the choice to take your life."

CHAPTER SEVENTEEN

Hessan stepped away from the mantle where he'd gone back to leaning.

"Well, well. Now things get interesting," the dwarf said, watching with a keen eye for conflict.

"Oh. I see. Any particular reason why you were going to… Hold on – the choice you *had* made? Past tense? Am I to take it you've – what – gone off the idea?" Marcus retained his usual air of nonchalance, his casual smile hinting he didn't feel particularly threatened.

Erryn stared at the prince, a look of disbelief in her eyes, and her mouth agape. Vess was prickling with pent-up rage. He'd known Athalir was not to be trusted from the moment they met.

"Why you…" The warrior reached for his sword, a murderous intent clear in his eyes. Athalir reacted immediately by whipping his daggers from their sheaths.

"Stop!" Everyone turned at once to see Sathom, emotionless as ever, standing just a step away from the wall at the far side of the tavern. Attention gained, the elemental marched swiftly across the room.

"*Sathom*! Where have you been?" Marcus couldn't quite contain his relief at the return of his impassive companion, or at the abrupt halt to the two other companions killing each other.

"There is no time for explanation, my friend. We must leave – *now*!"

"Did he just walk through that wall – or have I had more to drink than I thought?" Hessan asked.

"Yes, he does that," Marcus replied. "Sathom, if it's possible, you sound troubled. Is something wrong?"

Sathom sighed. There were often times he felt his lack of ability to express emotion was a hindrance, but never more so than since he'd met Marcus Ryan.

"Marcus, please, stop asking questions and take heed. While away, I was seen by someone – some*thing* – I've spent most of the last thousand years trying to avoid being seen by. That 'thing' is a skaithen. It is evil, it is dangerous… and, it is heading this way."

"You *saw* a skaithen?" Marcus asked.

"Yes."

"And you led it *here*?" Erryn probed further.

"I attempted not to, but, yes, I fear I might have."

"Then, my friends, there is no time to lose. You *must* leave immediately," Erryniya urged, before walking towards Hessan. "My king, lead them safely out of Geryndor. They have to reach the caves, and they'll need your help to do so."

Hessan briefly remained silent, a thoughtful look narrowing his eyes – and then it was gone.

"Fair enough," he agreed, clasping his elderly friend's hands for a moment before nodding and heading for the door. "Well, come on. What are you all waiting for?" With that, Hessan left the tavern. A few fleeting farewells, and the outlanders followed.

The tavern restored to its usual daytime quiet, Erryniya wearily lowered herself into the armchair in front of the fire. Her knees creaked as she bent them, and she sighed as she found relief from the façade of good health, put on for the benefit of the foreigners. She turned her aged face to absorb the heat of the crackling flames, her scarred eyes seemingly delving deep into the orange glow, and spoke softly to herself. "Farewell, my child. Farewell."

"How do we get to the caves from here?" Vess scanned his surroundings.

"And where did the dwarf go?" Athalir looked all around for Hessan, who was nowhere to be seen when they all arrived outside. Unresolved tension lingered in the minds of almost everyone present.

There were questions to be asked and probably confrontations to be had, but they would keep. Sathom had his eyes firmly fixed westward and kept muttering that they needed to depart. The skaithen couldn't be far behind. Over the last two days, he'd attempted to lose him by transporting himself to various locations around Gadrionis, anywhere but where he knew Marcus and the others to be. However, each time Sathom emerged, the skaithen emerged too, just moments later. As a dog follows a trail with its nose, the creature was able to pick up some kind of essence that followed Sathom each time he traversed the ether. There seemed to be no escaping him. Finally, knowing he had to get back to the group, he used all his energy to travel faster. At a speed beyond which he'd ever travelled before, he whizzed from place to place, looping and doubling back, not stopping anywhere for more than a second. Eventually, he materialised just outside the tavern wall and walked through without pause. The plan appeared to have worked, for now, but it seemed likely the elemental's trail was still accessible to the skaithen; it was only a matter of time before he caught up.

Erryn started to pace.

"Sathom, show me the map. The dwarf is obviously not a man of his word. Let's just get going, shall we?" Anxiety seeped from every pore of the hexan girl's skin. Marcus stepped in front of her, mid-pace, holding her still with a gentle grip on her arms.

"Erryn, I won't let him get to you, I promise." The mage offered a reassuring smile, but Erryn pushed him away.

"I don't need your '*protection*'!" She craned her neck back to look angrily into his eyes, ignoring his saddened face, then barged around him and snatched the map from Sathom. "I simply want to get moving."

"Yes. You are right. We cannot wait for Hessan. We need to head east, find the cavern entrance. I am certain I can…"

"Er, anyone know what that is?" Vess interrupted Sathom, who had started to walk away while still talking. Everyone turned to look in the direction the warrior was pointing. Some distance away to the west, just ahead of the Stone Highway, something dark and expansive was hanging in the air. The humans all squinted their eyes to try to get a better focus.

"Is it… storm clouds?" Erryn suggested.

"No, no. Too low, I think. What *is* that?" Marcus walked a few steps closer, using his hand as a shade above his eyes.

Prince Athalir needed to neither squint nor walk closer. His keen, elven eyesight had never had the chance to be tested in such an open environment before but, as he made out detail not yet visible to the others, it was clear he could see just as well over flat landscapes as through the dense forests of home.

"*Run!*" The urgency in Athalir's voice was all anyone needed. With only brief glances back, now they could all see that the cloud was moving towards them, fast.

Packs and weapons slung over shoulders, everyone did as Athalir ordered. Over the frost-stiffened ground they sprinted, the feeling that their lives depended on it swelling over them all.

"Where are we going?" Marcus called back to Sathom as he ran at the front of the group just behind Athalir.

"Just head east!" came Sathom's shouted reply.

Faster and faster, the cloud closed the distance between it and the party. As though it could sense its prey was close, it accelerated. Erryn looked over her shoulder. Her eyes were met with the cloud now no more than a hundred feet away. Something black was threading in and out of the billowing greyness. With horror, Erryn realised it wasn't a something, but a someone; in fact it was many someones. Pitch black bodies, caught up in an entanglement of limbs, writhed amidst the cloud. Every so often a faceless head would appear, followed by a mighty outstretched arm lunging downward in an attempt to grab at any poor soul in its path. When one unsuspecting dwarf out for a stroll was plucked from the ground, he was absorbed into the mass, only to be propelled from it at great speed seconds later. Erryn was mesmerised at the sight and returned her gaze forwards too late to see the rock in her path. Her boot tips caught it, hurling her forwards and crashing to the ground. She let out a yelp of pain as her ankle twisted unnaturally. Vess had been just ahead, and halted when he heard her cry. With the swirling mass almost upon the hexan, he rushed back to her, wasting no time in scooping her up in his arms just seconds before a monstrous black hand grabbed at the space where she'd been.

The cloud was getting faster and it looked like there was no way they'd be able to outrun it. Then, as the group pushed forwards, a cart pulled by two giant wolves swerved in towards the track from the land alongside. With their eyes ahead, no one had seen it coming, but as Hessan came into view at the front, his hands tightly grasping a set of reins, they were certainly pleased to see it now.

"Get in!" the king yelled as he got close enough and slowed down.

"We are not going to escape that thing on a cart pulled by dogs!" Athalir sneered with disdain as the others quickly climbed onto the back of the vehicle.

"Those *dogs* are two of the finest steed-wolves in the royal kennels! You'll find no swifter beast. Now, get in!"

Athalir turned to see the cloud on their heels, and hoisted himself up.

"Go!" he shouted, and Hessan immediately whipped the wolves into action.

"Yargh!"

As the cart flew over the uneven ground, the passengers gripped the sides with white knuckles. They all worried silently that the wooden vehicle wasn't made to withstand such speeds, but with only a few extra feet being put between them and their foe, they had greater concerns.

"We're not going to make it," Erryn said, echoing the fears of her companions.

"What happens if we *do* reach the cavern entrance, if we get inside? What then? Won't the cloud or this *skaithen* just follow us in?" Vess finally voiced what he'd been thinking since they'd fled.

"The cloud is dark magic, as is the skaithen that created it," Sathom explained. Everyone looked back at him blankly. "Magic is impossible in the caves beneath the mountains. Neither it nor he can follow us in there."

"And you thought it best to leave this bit of pertinent information until now?" Marcus' alert mind quickly thought beyond escaping the cloud, as the realisation hit that he'd be defenceless in the most hostile area of all Gadrionis.

"It won't matter if we don't get there!" Athalir snapped, mumbling something about carts and dogs under his breath.

"The prince is right, Marcus. Hessan's wolves have bought us time, but we cannot make it without… a diversion." Sathom looked expectantly at Marcus.

"What can *I* do? I have trouble aiming a fireball at a stationary target!"

"Now is not the time for doubts, Marcus." As if to illustrate Sathom's point, an ominous screeching drew their attention back to the cloud, which was almost within reach of the back of the cart.

"Marcus, you can do this – I believe in you!" Erryn shouted above the din of the rattling wooden wheels.

The mage looked into the hexan's brown eyes to see the warmth he'd been missing, and with a small smile and curt nod, turned to face the open rear. "Alright, I'll give it a go. Hold onto me!" he hollered, letting go of the side. Vess switched places with Sathom to be closer, and together he and Athalir wrapped an arm around one of Marcus' thighs, as he stood up.

Meanwhile, with a final push, Hessan's steed-wolves managed to gain a little more speed, once again taking the cart and its passengers just out of the cloud's reach, but making it a rougher ride in the process.

Marcus stood, legs apart, with the points of his boots teetering on the wooden ledge. Forcing himself to have confidence in the strength of the two men at his back, he closed his eyes and spread his arms outward and above his head. The cart bounced off the ground with nearly every complete turn of the wheels, forcing Vess and Athalir to tighten their hold on their companion, anchoring themselves to the cart with their free hands.

Sathom and Erryn watched as Marcus began to vibrate, a feint white glow outlining his entire body.

"What's happening back there?" Hessan called.

"Just keep going!" Erryn shouted back, not taking her eyes off Marcus for a moment.

The cloud was picking up speed and, for all their swiftness, the wolves had nothing more to give. Marcus was in a trance, no longer aware of the danger as he concentrated on summoning the magic required to save them all, and oblivious to the black hands that stretched out towards him.

The cart jumped as one of the wheels ran over a large rock. Athalir lost his grip on the side and fell forwards off the bench, pulling Marcus back and halting the flow of his magic. Fortunately, Vess managed to retain his position and took the strain, but the collision had clearly damaged the wheel, which was now wobbling erratically as it revolved.

"Whatever you intend to do, mage, now is the time!" After scrambling back to his seat, Athalir took a brief look over the edge at the wheel on his side; it didn't look good.

Marcus resumed his standing position and once more closed his eyes. Drawing on the magic within, he stretched his arms out in front, flicking his eyes open and focusing on a white glow forming on his upturned palms.

Time had run out. The wolves were flagging, the cart's uneven drive sapping their stamina. The wheel was gradually working its way loose and everyone on board held their breath as the cloud closed the gap.

Marcus had little confidence his casting would work. It was bigger than anything he'd attempted so far and could so easily go awry. Through a bright white haze he could see the cloud, rolling towards him. Monstrous hands, made up of the same dark magic ooze from the crypt, thrust at him, closer every time.

Ice, he thought to himself as ebony fingers brushed his clothing. A black head shot forth on a serpentine neck. It came so close to Marcus' face that he could smell the acrid stench of evil.

"Ah, so it's a kiss you want. Well, why didn't you just ask politely?" The mage grinned at the form, his glowing eyes looking up from beneath a tensed brow. A wicked gaping mouth melted across the front of the head, and grinned back. "Pucker up," Marcus said, as a swirling ball of ice appeared over his palms. He made a kissing sound and blew a gale force breath towards his hands. Immediately it shattered and spread out in the air, forming millions of tiny ice crystals that swarmed towards the cloud. As the swarm hit the hand, the arm, and then the head, each one froze solid. Without pause, the ice continued on until it reached the greyness, where it blasted across the entire surface. By the time its propulsion had ceased the cloud was completely covered and came to an abrupt stop, every black limb within halted in suspended animation. It hung in the air as Marcus collapsed to his knees, only prevented from falling from the cart by Vess and Athalir.

"Is it over?" said Athalir.

"I'm not taking any chances!" Erryn, bow at the ready, positioned an arrow and shot at the immobilised cloud, the arrow-tip blasting the icy mass to pieces on impact.

Within the hour, the group arrived at the point along the mountainside where Hessan knew there to be an accessible passage down into the caves.

Erryniya's words had been astute; Sathom knew the general direction, but the rock-face was densely covered with trees and brush, and only someone who'd seen the entrance would know how to find it.

"My father was one of the last people to come this way, when I was but a lad," the dwarf king said as he used one of his axes to thrash at the overgrown, knotted shrubbery. "A dwarf corpse was found here hundreds of years ago, having used his last ounce of strength to drag his battered body out from that place. My father was always a little… paranoid, but one day, something unsettled him more than usual. He rode out here with a contingent of his most trusted men – I was taken along for the ride." Hessan continued to clear the path until finally he stood before a dry-stone wall, some three or four feet above his head. "Ah, here it is. I was beginning to think this might have fallen."

The wall continued into the bush on either side, making it unclear what distance it spanned.

"What did he build it for?" Vess asked, running his hand along the stone.

"Are you joking? Didn't you hear the bit about the dead dwarf? Now, you look like you've got some strength in you – give me a hand here." Beckoning the warrior further forwards, Hessan kicked the wall, which didn't appear to move at all. Vess followed suit, putting his weight behind the kick. It took some time, but eventually their combined effort yielded a result and the wall began to feel less steady.

Meanwhile, the others watched and waited, the minds of each tense with their own private anxieties; only Erryn voiced hers.

"What of the skaithen, Sathom? Was he within that cloud?"

"Alas, he was not. I believe he set that thing after us, most likely returning to report my existence to his masters. I doubt very much that he is aware of Marcus or our plan, so he would have assumed the cloud would suffice in dealing with just one elemental. Even if I had been in possession of my own powers, I would not easily have defeated such a concentration of evil."

"You have powers?"

"I did – before I sacrificed them, along with my emotions."

Marcus looked up from his feet where he'd been lost in thought.

"So that's it. I *knew* there was something odd about your behaviour. Why didn't you say anything?"

"What would you have me say, Marcus?"

"Oh, I don't know. How about, 'by the way, don't expect me to cry at your wedding, or laugh at your jokes'. That might have been a good start."

"Marcus, no one laughs at your jokes," Erryn said, frowning.

"Good point."

"So, why did you 'sacrifice' your powers? Surely they'd have been useful, especially with this undertaking." Athalir placed his hands on his hips as he probed.

"It is a long story."

"We have time. That wall won't fall quickly, and if you're sure the danger has passed..."

Erryn and Marcus joined Athalir in looking expectantly at the elemental.

"For now, yes, though we would be wise to remain on our guard…" Sathom realised, as he took in the interested faces of his small audience, there was no avoiding giving them an explanation. "Very well. If you insist. Back when the Meranells were still free, I was… well, let us just say, I was a non-conformist. While my brothers spent their days in meditative states or pacing the halls of the scholars, tending to lost souls or counselling the king, I whiled away the hours imbibing sickleberry wine and… appreciating my corporeal state in the company of Meranell men and women."

Marcus gave a hearty laugh.

"So, you were a drunken philanderer. Sathom, I'm shocked!"

"As you should be. I was a disgrace to my people, a reprobate who lay comatose and in a state of undress as my brethren were banished, and my friends decapitated and cursed."

Sathom may have been unable to express emotion, but his self-loathing was still clear to the three listeners. "When I regained consciousness, my self-afflicted condition seemingly having 'saved' me from the spell that cast the rest of the elementals out, I awoke to a scene of horror, and a deafening silence. I walked the streets, entering homes, seemingly drawn to witness every corpse, every blood stain, as if forcing myself to endure it as… as penance.

I cried that day, but not tears of sadness for the suffering of those lost. Mine were tears born of selfishness, of guilt and shame. When that realisation came upon me, my woe turned to anger. Fiercely I raged, striking at walls, only angered more at my own lack of blood. My nature as it was, my elemental being intrinsically connected to the natural forces, my temper bore surges of electricity, a lightning storm developed over the city – as I heard the approach of men speaking to one another of celebration of their achievement. I listened from the shadows as it became clear who these men were and that it was they who had caused the devastation all around. A new focus for my wrath presented itself and the storm grew in intensity. I was but a moment away from revealing myself to the mages, when one of them, Alerick – the one I now know to be their leader – voiced a suspicion that the storm resembled power he had seen used by an elemental. In that instant I realised I needed to discover more before they became aware of my presence. Where were my brothers? Why had they done this? What had become of the souls of the Meranells? These questions would not be answered while in plain sight. I did not know the whereabouts of the other elementals, but I could not feel their energy, and that could only mean one thing – they were no longer in the same dimension as I. I knew they would not have left willingly, and so I concluded their departure had been the will of the mages. My very essence boiled with anger, but even through that haze I retained some good sense. To discover the truth, I would have to remain undetected, and to do that, I could not allow my emotions to take control. They needed to be bound."

"So, you somehow 'bound' your emotions. But what of your powers?" Athalir's curiosity was piqued.

"Yes, I am coming to that part. I left the city and made my way to a place few of my people visited since they had arrived in this world – the area to the north of Vaharia, where the portal that brought us here was secreted. The small woodland that concealed it was still there, the portal too. It was active, so far as I could tell, but when I attempted to go through, I found my way barred. A magical force field, acting as a lock of sorts, had been put in place; it was not much of a leap to conclude that the rest of my kind had been sent back and shut out. That notion answered the first of my questions at least. But

I digress. You asked about the binding. Surrounding the portal is a thin frame of something we call baranite. Baranite is a crystallised essence that, in large quantities, is the only substance known to incapacitate and ultimately, 'kill' an elemental. Exposure to tremendous amounts will result in the vanishing; the elemental version of death. Conversely, briefly passing through a baranite frame will temporarily halt the flow of elemental energy. As we first passed through the portal, we experienced a loss of our powers for a short time – but quickly recovered. The powers and emotions of elementals are interwoven; one will not work without the other. I had to restrict my emotions in order to keep focused, to keep control and not allow myself to make rash choices that would see me exposed. I cut away a small shard of the baranite and inserted it as close to my mind as I could, just here." Sathom turned his head to the side and parted the hair behind his left ear.

"I can't see anything." Erryn leant into look closely, along with Marcus and Athalir.

"We do not have the same 'physical state' as fully-corporeal beings – it is… difficult to explain. The shard began to release its toxin into my mind from the second it was placed – and has continued to do so ever since, disabling my powers and thus, my emotions. It was a roundabout method, but it had the desired effect."

No sooner had Sathom finished his tale than a victorious whoop came from the two men who had spent the entire time working at bringing down the stone structure.

"Ah, it appears we can move on." Sathom abruptly walked towards the now-exposed cavern entrance, leaving his audience to briefly reflect on his story before gathering up their belongings and following.

Erryn's ankle was still painful and even her stubborn pride didn't object to Marcus' offer of his arm to support her weight.

"Shouldn't we try to do something about that ankle of yours before we continue?" Marcus asked as they walked.

"It'll be fine. I have a herbal poultice made up in my pack. I'll apply it when we next stop to rest; it worked last time."

"We can stop now, Erryn. I'd…"

"Marcus, it's fine. I'd rather not stop here," the hexan interrupted, a look of determination barely masking the fear in her eyes. The mage understood her lack of desire to linger. He, too, would rather not come into contact with the skaithen or one of his conjurations again, at least not until he'd recovered from that last burst of magical activity. He'd surprised himself with the power that he'd successfully wielded, even more so with its accuracy, but he was a long way from certainty he could repeat it. He didn't know what they would face in the cavern, nor relish the thought of lacking the magical skills he'd so recently gained, but the skaithen couldn't touch them there, and for that, he was thankful.

The cavern entrance faced them just the other side of the rubble from the wall. It was wide enough for two people to walk in side by side, with a little extra space to spare. According to Hessan, the dwarves had intended to mine beneath the mountains, the unique rock tempting them to seek out whatever ore could be found within. However, once the miners had tunnelled many hundreds of feet inside, they'd discovered a gigantic cavity – and a hostility that had rendered them so fearful they evacuated straight away, never to return in such numbers again.

In complete silence, the group made their way towards the opening. Once there, they peered inside, but could see very little due to the black walls absorbing the exterior light.

"We'll definitely being needing torches," Marcus said, as he strained his eyes to see into the darkness.

"I would suggest the staff – but I presume that won't work in there either?" Erryn said, turning to Sathom for confirmation.

Sathom shook his head.

"Right. Then we'd best be on our way." Marcus stepped away and addressed Hessan. "Your majesty, thank you for getting us here. We couldn't have made it without you. It's been an honour."

Hessan laughed.

"My boy, with that magic-crafting of yours, I think you could've made it just about anywhere. Besides, this is no farewell – I'm going with you."

"What? Why?" Athalir jumped up from the ground where he'd been rummaging in his pack.

"My reasons are my own, elf. Anyway, are you telling me an extra pair of blades won't come in handy?"

Marcus looked to Sathom, who nodded.

"He is right. We are not so well armed that we would turn down such an offer."

"Very well, your majesty, I'll not question further. Your presence would be most welcome." Marcus extended a hand to seal the arrangement. Hessan reciprocated vigorously.

"Excellent! And Marcus, it's just Hessan. I very much doubt the cavern is any kind of place to stand on ceremony – we're all brothers in arms from here on in."

A few minutes later and, with Vess, the prince, Erryn, and Sathom all making their way into the cavern, Hessan and Marcus stood at the entrance.

"Are you ready?" The dwarf spoke without facing his companion.

"Yes, but I wish I knew what for," Marcus replied, with a hint of his usual humour.

"Well, let's start with stumbling down a dark tunnel into a dank, monster-infested cavern of horror and death, from which no mortal has ever escaped and lived to tell the tale – and coming out the other side alive – shall we?"

"I'm no mortal, Hessan."

"Hah! And I'm no storyteller! Let's get this done."

Hessan gave Marcus a jovial slap on the back and both men laughed before taking their first steps into the black hole that served as a doorway into the mountain.

The mood was temporarily lightened but, as Marcus set a first tentative foot inside the dark rock-face, he was about the furthest from finding the funny side as he'd ever been. He silently promised imaginary guardians that if he did make it through this place alive, he'd make every effort to take things more seriously from then on.

CHAPTER EIGHTEEN

Darkness beyond that of natural shadow trailed in the wake of the skaithen as he marched the corridors of the most important building in Whitestone. The palace was impressive by anyone's standards. Expansive, architecturally glorious, and the whitest building in all Vaharia, it stood behind high stone walls with enormous metal gates that remained barred to all – all but the skaithen, of course.

He'd traversed the ether as soon as his cloud of destruction had shattered under attack from the mage, as, much to his chagrin, the governors had willed him to return. He'd been about to get close enough to succeed where the cloud had failed but, as a construct of their dark magic, his service belonged to them. He'd had no choice but to allow the cart and its passengers to go free.

Now within the cold, gloomy halls of the once-lively palace, he took large, physical strides, constantly cursing the will that not only bade him there, but also restricted his means of travelling those halls to that of mortal beings. The governors disliked surprises, and insisted he cease his sudden arrivals. It was their will. He could not disobey, however much it vexed him.

Thus, he rapped loudly on the heavy wooden door that barred the way into governor Alerick's chambers.

governor Alerick stood in the middle of the large room with his back to the door. His tall, narrow form was draped from head to toe in heavy, charcoal-grey robes.

As with the chambers of the other five governors, the space provided all that was required for day-to-day living. A grandiose fireplace filled most of one wall, while a canopied bed had pride of place opposite. One corner was set out for lounging, with cushioned seating and low tables, while another provided a dining table long enough to accommodate the eight chairs evenly spaced around it. The room was lit by nothing more than the raging fire and a single candle on a cabinet beside the bed.

"What news?" The robed man spoke without turning around. Closing the door, the skaithen confidently strode over to stand at Alerick's side.

"The mage has more power than the elf led us to believe, your eminence."

"You mean to say, your own magic failed." The statement was said in a measured yet clipped tone.

"I mean to say what I *did* say. The mage is powerful. However, had *you* not dragged me back here, I have no doubt I would have bested him. As it is, the group now make their way into the cavern beneath the Dragon Crest Mountains, where we cannot reach them… your *eminence*." Alerick ignored the skaithen's contemptuous criticism.

"And the elf, he's still with them, I take it?"

"Yes, though I am unsure if he can be relied upon to fulfil his agreement. He appeared to be… helping, a little too well."

"He will do as he agreed – the lives of those he holds dear depends on it."

"That's if any of them survive the cavern. The elemental will be of no use to them, and the mage can no more use magic down there than you or I. I'll wager they'll be nothing more than torn flesh and bloodstains soon enough." The skaithen grinned, his black eyes reflecting malevolent delight.

The governor paused, raising and turning his cloaked head to face the skaithen.

"What of my son?"

"He lives."

Alerick sighed as if with relief.

"My lord, that's not… *fatherly love*, is it? Now, that would be most unbecoming – and very odd." The skaithen peered, still grinning, into the shadowy recess of the governor's hood.

"Of course not, you fool! It may have escaped your notice, but that boy has taken my last vessel into a place from which it may never return."

"Unscathed, at least."

"And what use would 'torn flesh and bloodstains' be to me, skaithen?" Alerick's voice bore the tone of one losing his patience.

"Your eminence, with dark magic at your disposal, if we could somehow retrieve the vessel, perhaps he could be… repaired? If not, well, if I might be so bold, I suggest you *take* another wife, produce another vessel. You're not getting any younger, after all."

Governor Alerick groaned and turned away, leaving the skaithen in no doubt the meeting was done.

"I will take my leave, then."

As the creature pulled at the door, his dark mind was already working on a plan should the company actually make it out of the magic-dampening cavern, when Alerick's voice interrupted his thoughts.

"Watch them. Be ready."

The skaithen's grin appeared, wider than before.

"Oh, I will, my lord. I will."

Governors Wymond, Hamon, Tolbert, Randal, and Ealdwin filed in through the door as the skaithen walked out. The five men, dressed in similar attire to that of Alerick, took their usual seats around the table and waited patiently for their leader to take his place.

But Alerick remained standing, his back to them as he stared into the fire.

Minutes passed in silence before Governor Hamon spoke in a gravelly voice.

"Is there a problem, Alerick?"

"A problem. Let me think. Is there a problem? Why yes, Hamon, I do believe there might be *a problem*." The head governor gave his reply still facing away, irritation dripping from his words.

"Then perhaps you should let us in on it, *dear* brother." Ealdwin spoke next, his thin, higher pitched tone grating on Alerick's nerves as it had for centuries.

He finally turned away from the fire and walked to the table, ignoring his chair and towering over his fellows.

Slowly, he removed his hood, letting it fall into folds about his neck and shoulders.

As his head became exposed, grey hairs that had been barely rooted loosened. He rubbed a wrinkled hand over his scalp and more hair came free. Looking at the strands stuck to his skin, he tutted and brushed his hands together a few times before addressing the gathering.

"Our *problem* is the coming to pass of the seer's vision, brothers. A human mage with the soul of those we hold prisoner – guided by, of all things, an elemental – is, as we speak, entering the cavern beneath the Dragon Crest Mountains"

"How can this be?" Wymond asked.

"We sent the elementals away," Hamon said, bewilderment clear in his voice.

"All but one, apparently." Alerick lifted his hood back over his head.

The five governors began to mumble between themselves as Alerick raised his eyes to heaven and questioned, not for the first time, the sanity of a spell that would see him forever in their company.

Randal the mute, as he was known for his consistent lack of input, looked up at Alerick, his vacant eyes staring straight through him.

"Why is this a problem? The cavern will stop them."

Everyone else stopped talking and stared at Alerick with wide eyes, all aghast at Randal's bold – and unprecedented – move.

But Alerick was in no mood for chastisement. Instead, he smiled briefly, then spoke directly to Randal, knowing full well how much that reaction would both surprise and vex the others. *They think they know me so well*, he thought to himself.

"Of course, brother, you are quite correct. It is unlikely this man and his guide will emerge from the cavern. Their threat to us *is* minimal. However, they have my vessel and I'd rather like it back – in one piece." His last words were sharply precise, his lips thin with the effort of remaining calm.

"So, we are to leave it to the cavern, then? Send commoners to retrieve the vessel later?" Wymond requested clarification, still reeling from Alerick's uncharacteristic reaction to insubordination.

"I have the skaithen standing ready to keep an eye on them, should they survive long enough to emerge. That should suffice, for now."

The chattering began again at the mention of the skaithen. The entity was an unpleasant side-effect of their dark magic, and none of the governors were prone to placing their trust in him, least of all Alerick. Confusion and concern were rife.

Alerick's tolerance for interaction had reached its peak; a headache was developing, and he wished to once more sit alone by the fire.

"Gentlemen!" The head governor raised his voice to be heard over the chuntering voices. Their indistinguishable mumblings came to a gradual end. "That will be all."

Hamon started to protest.

"But, brother, do you not think we should..."

"Get. Out!" Alerick shouted, grimacing as his head throbbed.

The five governors exchanged glances before rising and making a hasty departure.

As they left and the door closed, the head governor took a small bottle from a side table and took a large gulp of its contents. The bitter, red liquid almost made him retch as it reached his throat, but it was the only thing that took care of his headaches. They'd occurred more frequently since the discovery of the death of his elder vessel, worsening still when he found out the second vessel was conscious and travelling with his enemy.

He sat down in his armchair and allowed the flames to hypnotise his mind, gulping down the tincture and enjoying the diminishing lucidity.

CHAPTER NINETEEN

The hike through the dwarven tunnels took nearly an hour. The route was about as straight as chiselled rock could be, but their torches only provided a small circle of light, and everyone feared what may lie ahead in each further inch of the darkness.

All were silent, save for Marcus, who had started whistling after the first ten minutes. His cheery tune was out of place and grating in such a lifeless environment, yet no one asked him to stop. Without its distraction, the only other thing to hear would be whatever might be moving about further along the tunnel.

Athalir was the first to make an exit, his lithe body and elf senses giving him the confidence to move a little faster. Next was Sathom, closely followed by Vess, who waited to help Erryn as she stepped out of the black opening. Marcus and Hessan had started the journey together, and ended it the same way, sharing a knowing smile as they strode out to meet the others.

The air had been warm and notably thicker inside the tunnel, causing the lungs of the fully-corporeal members of the group to work harder to inhale. As they entered the openness of the cavern, they were all relieved to breathe slightly fresher air.

Though their torches were all still lit, the first thing they noticed was a strange green illumination that seemed to be coming from everywhere and nowhere specific. It was so bright that, if they hadn't had their own light source, they'd still have managed to see the way onward.

For a hundred-or-so feet, their path wound around mighty cones of solid, black rock that protruded up from the ground, so high they almost met similar protrusions hanging down from the ceiling. As they passed, their torches reflected in the sheen of moisture that coated the rocky surfaces, and, somewhere, water could be heard dripping rhythmically from different heights.

Huddled together, the group finally came around the last of the rock-cones, gasping in unison as the enormous space opened up ahead. With the green glow now substantially brighter, they were able to see the immensity, and the strangeness, of the terrain. Naturally-forming archways and bridges were everywhere. Ledges so far up as to be unreachable, as well as trenches filled with slow moving water – everywhere they looked there was something different to see. And most notable of all, the cavern stretched on for miles in every direction.

As they absorbed the vastness, the realisation of the task ahead hit them all.

"Did we bring enough supplies?" Erryn asked of no one in particular, as everyone else just stared vacantly ahead.

"We should set camp for the night." Sathom turned around, heading back towards the relative-seclusion of the rock towers. Nobody had any urgent desire to wander further just yet, and so the decision was made.

Using a torch and the kindling Hessan had made sure to collect before they entered, a small camp-fire was set alight. The other torches were extinguished so as to conserve the long-burning oil in which their binds had been soaked, and everyone gathered around the fire, more for safety than warmth.

An uncomfortable silence hung over the companions, though bizarre sounds could be heard from somewhere beyond their camp. No one thought sleep would come easily that night, even with the knowledge that two would remain on guard. However, after a meal of fire-roasted rabbit haunches washed down with a swig of dwarven ale provided by Hessan, the exhaustion from the trek, combined with full stomachs, finally enforced an almost universal light slumber.

Athalir and Marcus took the first shift, at the mage's insistence after Athalir had pulled the first short straw.

"Marcus, he admitted to wanting to kill you," Vess warned.

"I admitted that I intended to kill him – not that I wanted to," the Fell prince corrected.

Marcus smiled.

"It wouldn't be very wise to kill me now, would it, Vess? Either he kills me, and you kill him, or worse, ostracise him, or he kills me and, by some unnatural luck, manages to kill everyone else here. Either way, his death would be the likely outcome."

Vess took a moment to process the mage's words, then gave a low 'humph' and took to his bedroll with no further objection.

"So, I think it's time for an explanation," Marcus said, a few minutes into their vigil. He didn't want to exact revenge, as Vess did, but he had to admit to himself; the situation needed to be addressed, and some questions couldn't go unanswered. There was a brief silence before Athalir answered.

"Shortly before you arrived in Sa'hahlenfell, I was approached by a man I believed to be an emissary of the Vaharian governors."

"You 'believed'?"

"Yes. I now know him to be the skaithen from the dwarf woman's memory."

"Ah, I see."

"No, you do not 'see'. How could you?" The prince stood up and began to pace.

"It was a figure of speech, Athalir. Look, I'm making no judgement upon you until I've heard what you have to say. Just… explain." Marcus' attempt to calm the Fell prince seemed to work. Athalir sat back down on the ground at his side, though he kept his face turned away.

"I told you of the disease that has blighted the lives of my people – including my parents. Well, this… skaithen knew of this malady, and of its cure. We know he was also aware of the dwarven seer's vision – that is what led him to me."

"Did he think you were the tall man of whom she spoke?"

"No. But, as she intended, he did believe him to be an elf. He offered me a deal; discover the identity of the governors' future nemesis and kill him. In return, the governors would allow entry into Vaharia to gather as much thiervan as we required. When I heard of your quest and what you intended to do, I knew, or rather, I hoped the skaithen's information was not entirely accurate. I hoped your death in place of an elf's would suffice. Indeed, the weeks spent searching had born no results; I found no sign any of the Fell had such a plan." The two men said nothing for a few minutes, before Marcus broke the silence.

"What made you change your mind?"

"Change my mind?"

"Well, assuming you *have* decided not to kill me, your people will continue to suffer. Surely it is still in their best interest to do as the skaithen demanded."

"Their interests can be best served another way. If you can do what you set out to do, and I am trusting that you can, the governors will soon be nothing more than a dark passage in time – and death need come to no one but them. I come with you so that I may fulfil my duty to them. By assisting you, I feel I'm doing… something."

"Then I'm happy to have your assistance, and we'll speak of this no more."

"What?" Vess' voice boomed from behind them.

Marcus stood up with a start, turning to face the red-faced warrior.

"Vess, I thought you were asleep. What are you…?"

"I haven't slept since you woke me up in the crypt". Vess snarled, as he marched towards Athalir and the mage. "Are you mad? We can't trust him! Don't you see?"

By now, the whole camp was awake, their nervous slumber disturbed easily by Vess' raised words. Of course, Sathom hadn't been asleep, but his mind had taken to wandering of late, when the world was dark and others slept. His attention was jolted back at the warrior's admission.

"Vess, he's explained everything – I understand his reasons." Marcus didn't relish the idea of stepping between the two volatile men, but if someone didn't, bloodshed was inevitable.

"And you think he's just *decided* against it now, do you? Just like that?" Vess wore a look of disbelief as he questioned his companion.

Strangely, Athalir remained uncharacteristically calm, even as Marcus waded in in his defence.

"I think he was put in an impossible position by that monster and with time, and clarity, he's seen a way out of the deal."

"Then you are not as wise as I thought." Vess' tone was bitter and accusatory. He'd had a great deal of faith in Marcus. But the man's naïvety seemingly knew no bounds. Vess had lived in the world for such a short time, yet he'd never trusted the Fell prince, and he wasn't about to start now. *Twenty-six years of living have obviously not taught the mage anything*, Vess thought, as he turned his back on his friend and returned to his bedroll.

Marcus threw his hands in the air in frustration and went back to watching the periphery of the camp. He hadn't asked to be leader of this mission. He certainly hadn't wanted to spend so much time with so many strangers, and he was more than a little tired of trying to live up to expectations. For weeks, it seemed all he'd done was struggle to become someone other people wanted him to be. All his life, he'd disappointed those around him, one way or another, but at least being anyone other than himself hadn't been essential to some important quest. He wasn't even sure how to be himself anymore, let alone a person to lead, a person to cast magic, or a person to save souls. Who was he, anyway? When last the autumn sun had made the city of Whitestone glow, he'd been Marcus Ryan, young lord and social outcast with a sanity-saving sense of humour. Yet, one foolish loss of control, and he'd been set on the path of fugitive, with an ancient soul wearing his body as a suit of armour, using magic even though he detested it, and voyaging into dangerous lands.

With their leader's trust grating against the knowledge that he hadn't been entirely honest, Athalir said nothing more that night. As he sat beside Marcus for another hour, he looked into the green-hued distance, his second meeting with the skaithen weighing heavily on his mind, and doubts resurfacing once more. He'd told Marcus he had faith he could defeat the governors, but the words had felt shallow even as he uttered them. The mage was a better man than he'd wanted to believe, but he'd seen little to convince him, beyond doubt, that he'd have the power or will to even reach the tower, never mind succeed in opening it if he did. And with so much at stake, there was no room for doubt. Much as it turned his stomach to think on what he had to do, and though regret at betraying someone who'd done nothing but offer friendship would be felt, Athalir mentally prepared himself for it. At Sathom's revelation the skaithen could not enter the cavern, the deed would have to wait until they were elsewhere – and there was still the matter of getting Marcus alone.

With no visible moon or sun, they rose at Sathom's insistence they'd slept long enough. Despite the oppressive atmosphere, most of the group were in good spirits and eager to move on, though Vess spoke to neither Marcus nor Athalir, and Athalir spoke to no one. With the camp packed up after what had turned out to be an uneventful night, they set off further into the cavern.

An eerie silence accompanied the group as they walked. It was some time before Erryn realised why it felt so odd; there were no birds. Back in Eldenvale, her morning hunts were carried out to the calls of blackbirds and the excitable chatter of sparrows. In the evenings, the cry of a lone eagle soaring above would take her mind to faraway places, and when she sat on a bench outside her father's home at night, male and female owls finished each other's hoots before beginning their search for rodent prey. Night and day, whatever the season, there was always bird-song. The bird-less silence was unnatural, and she needed to take her mind off it.

"How did this place come to be?" Erryn asked Sathom as she arrived at his side. Sathom looked down at Erryn, having not heard her approach.

"Legend tells of a gigantic dragon that once fell asleep across the lands, its body so big as to span multiple kingdoms. The tales say that one particularly cold winter, the dragon simply froze solid, never to wake. When eventually the lands grew warm again, the beast' soul had carved its way out of its skin, leaving the hollowed-out dragon carcass as a reminder to other dragons never to sleep outside in the cold. From that day forth, all dragons slept in caves – or so the legend tells it. But no one knows for certain. It sounds rather fanciful to me." Sathom returned his attention to continuing onward, and Erryn wished she hadn't asked; now, with the lingering thought of walking around inside a dragon carcass, she felt even more uncomfortable.

The passing of time was immeasurable in a place where the sun's progress across the sky could not be tracked, so no one knew how long they'd been travelling, or the exact time of day. However, when someone finally spoke aloud about the unseen thing that had been trailing them, much distance had been covered.

"Something is just behind us – and I don't think it's nice, friendly Fell archers this time," Erryn said in a hushed voice, as she caught up with Marcus.

"Hmm, I thought so. I looked back but couldn't see anything, so I didn't mention it. But if you felt it too…"

"Yes, but it came quite close, and there's been nowhere for it to hide – why can't we see it?"

Marcus looked mystified before beckoning the others to him and Erryn. As they all continued to walk, though now grouped together, it became clear that everyone except Sathom had sensed the presence, and all had declined to mention it for the same reason; when they looked around, there was nothing there.

"Sathom, what's the matter with you lately? It's like you're somewhere else. Did you see anything?" Marcus' words snapped the elemental from the elsewhere he'd been visiting; apparently, it was the second time the mage had asked him the question.

"Sorry, Marcus. No, no I saw nothing, I… Wait. What was that?" Sathom's eyes darted across the land, ahead and to each side. "Ready your weapons."

The rest of the group jumped into action; all but Marcus armed themselves in an instant, five pairs of eyes scanning the surroundings for the threat.

"What are you talking about? There's nothing," Hessan said, confused.

"Don't you see them?" Everywhere Sathom looked his eyes found another creature. Tall but hunched over, they walked on two legs, their sinewy arms and clawed hands extending past their thighs, with one scythe-like claw practically scraping the ground as they moved. A large, bony, eyeless head sat atop their hairless bodies. Their pale grey skin appeared to be tinged green, but as he looked harder, Sathom realised he could see through them, and that the green tinge was simply the same glow that filled the cavern.

"Look, in front of you, to the sides… behind now, too," Sathom said as he spun round to face the way they'd come. Taking in the baffled expression of his companions, it became all too apparent – they couldn't see the beasts that were now edging forwards from all sides.

With horror he couldn't express, the elemental watched as a small rodent-like animal scuttled past the feet of one of the creatures, only to be stabbed in a flash by a heinous talon. The rodent's movement ceased immediately and it fell, frozen, to the ground. It made no attempt to flee and, as the creature skewered the animal on its sharpened appendage, bringing the motionless body up to a gaping, tooth-packed mouth, Sathom could see the rodent's eyes blinking rapidly. It was paralysed, yet still alive.

"They are all around us. Trust me." The words had barely left Sathom's lips when one creature made a lunge towards Erryn.

"Erryniya. Straight ahead."

Erryn loosed an arrow directly in front of her, though she still couldn't see anything. The familiar sound of arrow-point meeting flesh came next, followed by a figure coming into view as it fell to the ground, the arrow lodged in its now-visible head. There was no time for any reaction to the sight as Sathom started rattling off directions of incoming attacks. He could see the horde closing in as his friends looked wildly and hopelessly for anything they could see to aim their weapons at.

"Vess!" Sathom called out as another creature made a determined dive at the warrior, its long claw outstretched.

"Where?"

"To your left."

Without pause, Vess cleaved his sword through the air on his left side. The blade meeting with resistance, he pushed through until finally another of the creatures came into view clutching its side as blood spurted out from a gaping wound.

"At least we know we can kill them!" Hessan said, looking to Sathom for direction.

But with a few of their number down, the enemy seemed to forgo the single attack strategy. Now, with the creatures moving as one, Sathom could do no more than warn everyone to stand back-to-back, weapons poised, making sure to keep Marcus at the centre as he had no way to defend himself.

With the beasts closing in, the gap between them and the group diminishing, Sathom began to fear hope was lost. Taking out one or two, under his direction, worked well enough, but he couldn't give the exact location of every single creature; there had to be at least thirty still alive. With an able mage, they might have stood a chance. However, Marcus was without magic, and if anyone was caught by one of those long claws, it would all be over. However, it was pointless to warn them of the risk. They couldn't see to steer clear of the danger and causing extra anxiety would serve no useful purpose.

Staring at his companions, wishing there was something else he could do, Sathom thought he saw the Nexephia crystal at Marcus' back flicker to life. He looked again and gasped as he realised his eyes had not been mistaken. It was weak, but definitely there; a white glimmer, practically straining against the magic-dampening atmosphere. He called out to Marcus, mouthing 'look at the crystal' when he got his attention. Marcus turned his head to look up and behind him at the top of his staff. Seeing what the elemental had seen, he didn't have time to wonder what it meant; he couldn't see the incoming threat, but they were no longer practising stealth, and he could hear their shuffling footsteps, and some kind of scraping, getting closer. He had to think fast.

"Get down!" he shouted, silently hoping everyone would know what he meant. With only fleeting confusion, those surrounding the mage squatted down on the ground where they were, just in time to avoid the blast wave that emitted outwards. Numerous squawks, thuds, and crashes indicated Marcus' blast may have had the desired effect, but he couldn't see to be sure.

"Sathom, did it work?"

Sathom was confused, but also relieved. He nodded. But the effect was only temporary; the creatures were dazed, but starting to stagger to their feet, their eyeless, mouth-filled heads flicking back to face their prey.

"It is not done. They are regrouping. Everyone, be ready." Sathom felt useless, and that was compounded by the fact the things apparently had no desire to attack him.

Athalir, like everyone else, could now hear the invisible assailants. Whatever Marcus had done, it sounded like, though it had bought some time, it had also aggravated them.

"I thought magic was impossible in this region." The prince said as he stretched his dagger-wielding arms forwards.

"So did I," Marcus replied.

"Can you do it again?"

"I don't know. I don't think so; the crystal no longer glows, and I believe it enabled me to do what I did… sorry." Marcus offered a pathetic smile, which the elf brushed off with a guttural grunt. There was no time for idle chatter. As the first creature made its presence known with the sound of raspy breath close to Prince Athalir, he lashed out. It was a reflex action, but it clearly caught some part of his attacker, as hot blood splashed across his arms, accompanied by a squeal of pain. From then on, they came thick and fast. Sathom did his best to guide the group's defensive moves, but they were overwhelmed and disadvantaged.

Exhausted and infuriated, Athalir, Vess, Erryn, and Hessan closed around Marcus, swords, arrows, daggers, and axes aimed outward. Through some strange fortune, none of them had been injured thus far, but with hope and space dwindling, that was likely to change in no time.

"Arrrgh!" A new voice broke out from the route the party had trekked. Everyone turned to see an armoured figure charging towards them. Rushing past the group, the metal-clad warrior pushed into nothingness with a shield, a long-sword slicing madly through the air. Bodies of the creatures came into sudden view as they encountered the blade, the cuts so accurate as to completely sever several heads from necks.

"A little assistance, if you'd please!" A muffled voice came from within a fully enclosed silver-tone helmet, the person wearing it still barging and slashing with shield and sword.

Encouraged by the warrior's success, Hessan, Vess, and Athalir broke the tight formation surrounding Marcus and pressed forth into the unseen horde. Erryn remained at the mage's side, but quickly loosed arrows as Sathom shouted where to aim, picking off those that had managed to keep out of the melee.

"Keep your weapons at arm's length. The hollows have one claw that will paralyse you if it pierces your skin," the newcomer said, causing the men to abruptly alter how they fought.

With his comrades engaged in blind combat, Marcus could do nothing but stand and wait. He closed his eyes and concentrated, trying desperately to feel the familiar thrum of magic through his veins, but to no avail. *Just a one-off, then*, he thought to himself, feeling helpless as his friends were in danger.

"Athalir. Watch out." Sathom's voice rang out above the din. By the time Marcus had turned to face the prince, he was on the ground and backing away from a hidden foe.

"Marcus, the creature is right in front of him. It is preparing to attack with the claw." Without a second thought, Marcus skirted around Erryn, making a sprint towards the fallen elf. He jumped in front of Athalir, shifting his upper body to one side as a whoosh of something blade-like skimmed close to his neck. He had no weapon, and magic was out of play. A distant memory of punching his way out of a negative social encounter flashed through his mind and instinctively, he balled his hands into tight fists and started striking. Successfully hitting a body enough to push it away from Athalir, Marcus had briefly looked back to check on the prince when a sudden, stinging sensation ran across his chest. Everything played out in slow-motion after that. Marcus staggered backwards, his knees buckling beneath him. Every muscle started to constrict painfully as he dropped to the ground, until finally, he lay on his back, close to where Athalir had fallen, immobilised and terrified. His head facing upward, he could only listen as the skirmish ran its course all around him. He'd expected the thing that had brought him down to launch a final attack, but that had never come.

After many minutes of fighting had passed, Sathom reported, with relief, that the last of the creatures had fled, obviously intelligent enough to realise when they were outnumbered. Twenty-or-so slashed or decapitated bodies lay all around, as the blood-spattered group sheathed their weapons and dashed to where Marcus still lay flat on his back. Erryn was the first to reach him, dropping to her knees and staring down at his face, deep concern evident in her eyes.

"Marcus, can you speak?" The hexan moved a strand of hair from his mouth where it was stuck in drool. He could, but only weakly and when he tried, it hurt his chest.

"Not… much," was all he managed to say, feeling like a curiosity as everyone stood over him, looking down.

"We have to do something. Sathom?" Erryn pleaded with the elemental.

"I have… no idea. This is beyond my experience. I…"

"He'll recover." The voice from the helmet came again as the silver-armoured warrior joined the gathering.

All eyes turned to the person that now spoke. Their shield was hanging loosely on one side, their blood-smeared sword sheathed at the other.

"Who *are* you, and where did you come from?" Athalir asked, curious, but also determined to take his mind from the guilt that was threatening to cloud his thoughts.

The warrior stepped back a little, before lifting their hands up to their helmet and pulling it off. A mane of golden blonde hair tumbled free, falling to rest about the person's shoulders and down their back.

"My name is Rohesa – you can call me Roh – and I hail from the kingdom of Torwick. Now, *I* would like to know, what in Nexephia's name are *you* doing in Dragon's Belly Cavern?"

CHAPTER TWENTY

Marcus had stared up at the ceiling, far above, for what seemed like an age, before the paralysis wore off. During that period of enforced stillness, the woman who'd made such a timely arrival reluctantly explained her presence in the cavern, as a condition of Sathom doing the same in return.

With her voice hinting that she felt the whole experience to be beneath her, Roh told of her position in Torwick, a kingdom on the southern side of Gadrionis. She was a general of the highest order, in the direct employ of the priesthood of Nexephia. Only Sathom had heard that name before the woman had uttered it, and this woman's connection with it troubled him – though he said nothing of his unease. Instead, he'd pressed her to tell them why an important person such as herself would be wandering in the most hostile region of the known lands. Her answer had been blunt; she was bored. Apparently, Torwick's most honoured military officer often ventured into the cavern, looking for something to kill. Her excursions had been made all the more appealing by the fact that the priests forbade her from leaving the kingdom. Hessan had roared with laughter at that point, prompting the others to direct angry looks in his direction, chastising him for risking drawing the attention of any other thing that might wish to kill them.

"What?" he'd said, shrugging his shoulders. "That's my kind of woman – one after my own heart."

"Well, you could have been quieter in your admiration, dwarf," Athalir had said, still giving the king the evil eye.

"Is that why *you're* here, then?" Erryn had asked Hessan. "Because you were bored?"

"Pretty much. Add to that the fact most of my people despise me, including my wife, and you've got a persuasive argument for taking a little time away." No one had known quite what to say in response. Erryn tried to push him to elaborate but he'd simply replied, "Ah, lass, that's a tale for another time." There had been time enough for a somewhat slimmed-down explanation of the quest from Sathom, before Marcus had returned to full mobility and it was unanimously decided the group should move on immediately. Nobody was keen for a repeat performance against the creatures Roh had called hollows, and the warrior woman had said the group they'd fought was merely a scouting party, and more would pick up their scent – eventually.

"Well, since you're all safe, it's time for me to return home. Just… try to stay out of trouble. This place harbours more hazards than just the hollows." Roh habitually checked on her sword and adjusted her shield before lifting her helmet to her head.

"Wait! You're leaving?" Vess piped up. He'd spent the hour Marcus had been incapacitated watching the woman, then trying to pretend otherwise each time she noticed him staring. The only female human he'd ever met was Erryn, and though he'd easily grown fond of the little redhead, she didn't illicit the internal juddering that Roh had, the moment he'd seen her face. It was all he could do to keep his eyes averted, and he wasn't sure he enjoyed the attraction. Neither had she, it seemed, for she'd given him a look that could surely have frozen fire the last time she'd caught him watching her.

Realising his vocal reaction to the promise of her departure had been far too swift, and a little too high-pitched for such a burly man, Vess did his best to seem indifferent. Everyone stopped what they were doing to fix their companion with puzzled looks, while he shuffled about awkwardly and, rather too deliberately, crouched down to fumble with his pack, speaking without looking up.

"Er, yes, well, I, er, I simply meant that your assistance was, erm, appreciated and that… I, er, I mean, we, yes, *we* could…"

"Is he simple?" Roh asked the question of those around her, while keeping a suspicious eye on Vess.

Hessan started to laugh again, but was silenced by a shove to the shoulder from Athalir.

"Do that again, elf – I dare you!" Hessan said, making no attempt to be quiet, and drawing concerned looks from the others. Vess, however, welcomed the distraction, and managed to gather his pack together with no more awkward scrutiny from Roh, or anyone else.

"Come – we should move on," the warrior prompted, striding away without a backwards glance.

After a few hurried words of gratitude, the rest of the group made to catch up with Vess, who had covered some distance in his haste. Roh set off the way she'd come, but soon stopped to turn around and stare after the travellers. She knew she was duty-bound, but something tugged at her conscience – or was it her habitually concealed need for excitement? Either way, the thought of allowing the strangers to venture further into such a dangerous land without her did not sit well. She took one last hesitant look towards Torwick, a mental image of the priests' disapproving scowls flashing across her mind. That was all it took. A mischievous smile lifted the corners of her mouth and tweaked the curves of her dark-blue eyes. Checking her sword once more, she started walking after the group, keeping her distance and putting all thoughts of honour and duty to the back of her mind.

Oddly uneventful – that was how Sathom had started describing the next leg of their journey. After the company had walked far enough that their feet were beginning to feel every step, they stopped to take stock, the elemental cross-referencing his map with their approximate location and everyone else remaining on alert for attack. Not only had nothing crossed their path, let alone attempted an assault, but, for the last mile or so, the already unnatural atmosphere had grown increasingly silent and peculiar.

"Anyone else beginning to think Sathom isn't as prepared for this voyage as he led us to believe?" Erryn stood facing the others, casting a quick glance at Sathom, who was off to one side, mumbling to himself.

Vess made a noise that sounded like a snort mixed with a burst of laughter.

"I'm willing to believe just about anything when it comes to him."

"What is it with you and mistrust, human?" Hessan asked from the warrior's side, craning his neck to close the distance between their eyes.

"I have no issue with mistrust."

"Sure, you can tell yourself that. But I see different. The elf, the… strange, not-quite-of-this-world man…" He paused. "Fair enough. Forget I asked."

Vess had noted Athalir's evasive look away as the dwarf had mentioned him.

"Alright, yes, I mistrust. But I reserve it for those that appear to have something to hide. Athalir may have convinced Marcus and Erryn, but that's largely due to their strong desire to believe the best of people. I've seen the duplicity in his eyes from the first day we met." Now Vess had everyone's attention, his speech being the most he'd said in one go since being awoken at the crypt. "As for Sathom, I'm uncertain what to make of him – and *that* is why I cannot bring myself to part with caution in his presence. Perhaps it's his… odd manner; I've not long known emotion, and yet here I am presented with one for whom it is disturbingly absent. He… unnerves me… and..." Vess shrugged his shoulders. "Walks through walls."

Marcus chuckled.

"Yes well, there is that." The mage patted Vess across the back. "Come, there's more than enough tension in this place without creating more between ourselves." He looked down at Erryn, who'd been studying Athalir as he fidgeted in a manner unbefitting with what she knew of his character.

"What say you, fellow gullible soul?"

"I say Hessan made the question rhetorical, and I'm not altogether sure why we're even discussing it." Erryn gave Marcus an impish smile. "That is, if my judgement is to be trusted at all."

Marcus chuckled at her sarcasm before noticing Sathom's approach.

"Something wrong, Sathom?" he enquired of his friend. It would normally have been difficult to tell if something was indeed wrong with the elemental, but as the one among the group that knew him best, Marcus' had noticed subtle changes in Sathom's behaviour a while before the others.

"I… am uncertain." Sathom checked his map again, before looking back up at the surroundings. "Does any of this seem… familiar to any of you?"

"Every part of this damnable cave looks the same, if you ask me," Athalir answered, stress etched across his defined features.

"What troubles you, Sathom? Surely you weren't expecting variable scenery?" Erryn asked questions with an air of flippancy but, as her eyes scanned the immediate area, it did feel as if they'd come this way before.

"Yes, we have come this way before – I am sure of it." Sathom refolded the map and hastily returned it to the small leather pouch at his hip.

Hessan threw his hands up in exaggerated exasperation.

"You mean we've been going in circles? For Morsynia's sake!" The dwarf turned away and stood aside from the company.

"I don't know if 'going in circles' would be the right term. More like 'blindly retracing our own footsteps'," Erryn said as she squatted to examine some wet boot prints.

"I don't believe the manner of our folly is what's important here – and for once I find myself agreeing with the shortling. We've made barely any progress!" Athalir was already coiled tighter than a rusty spring, now the tension in his voice was brittle and threatening to snap at any moment.

Even Marcus could feel frustration sneaking in through his normally well-maintained wall of positivity. They'd walked for hours and somehow had covered no real distance. The oppressive air of the cavern didn't help. A headache had been pushing at the inside of his skull for some time. His mouth was dry, and his throat sore. Kicking at some loose stones with the nature of a petulant child, the mage let his pack drop to the floor and sat on a nearby boulder, head in hands. Vess looked at the glum faces around him and felt compelled to join them. Like everything else, he'd had little experience of travel, so had nothing useful to add to the conversation, nothing to neither lift spirits nor change the way things were. However, he wasn't about to simply stop moving. He'd done enough staying still for any man's lifetime.

"So we start again," the warrior said, sounding reassuringly certain.

"And from how far back do you suggest we start, pray tell?" Athalir turned on Vess, gritting his teeth as if to stop himself saying more.

"I'm not saying we go any further back, just that we take stock of where we are now and move on, with greater care."

Erryn sprung to her feet.

"Yes! We could leave some kind of mark, something to show we've already been here." Excitedly she thrust her hand into her pack, searching until she pulled out a length of twine.

"What are we supposed to do with *that*?" Hessan asked as both he and Marcus returned to stand with the group, cautiously encouraged by Vess and Erryn's infectious optimism.

"We tie it to something." Looking hopefully around, she could see nothing suitable. No trees or man-made structures. There simply wasn't anything the right shape for the short bit of string. Her eager smile fell away.

"We could leave the elf here and tie it to him," Hessan offered, receiving the prince's predictable glower with a wicked grin.

Throughout the discourse, Sathom had remained silent. The voices of his fellow travellers had blended into one seamless noise in the background while he stood apart, thinking. The Dragon's Belly Cavern was a disorientating place. With no roads, it was hard to stay on course. Wandering through a sea of stony towers that all looked alike could play tricks on the minds of any men. Yet he wasn't a man, and he'd normally need no route on a map, or indeed a road, to navigate anywhere. Alas, he couldn't use his preferred mode of transportation in that valley, travel through the ether being magic-based after all. And even if he could, the others couldn't travel that way. Feeling the frustration deep within but being unable to express it, he thought on how much easier this quest would have been had he simply been able to transport himself and Marcus directly to the sanctum. But what use was thinking such things doing him or the group now? He felt as if he'd already failed. So much hadn't gone according to plan, and his hope of getting the mage out of the cavern alive was dwindling faster than he'd like. Marcus had already come so close to death once, and now they couldn't even find their way out of the damned place.

"Sathom!" Marcus' call of his name snatched the elemental from his contemplation. He re-joined the group and spoke quickly, as much to distract himself as the others.

"Let us move on at once. Standing here debating the issue gets us nowhere."

"Agreed, but which way?" After his brush with death at the claw of a hollow, Marcus certainly felt staying on the move was better than standing still, awaiting another attack.

Sathom looked around, hoping for inspiration to appear around a tower of stone. Then he saw it. Still some distance away, a light that seemed more natural than the odd green luminescence. Its source apparently coming from the ceiling of the cavern, it beamed downwards. He couldn't see where it fell, hidden as it was beyond rock pillars and other such structures, but it hadn't been visible before and it might just be something they could use as a compass.

"There is a light over there." He pointed. "We have not seen it before, thus we must not have travelled that way. It can be used as a point of navigations to prevent us from getting lost again.

"What if it *does* take us back to the beginning?" Marcus asked.

"I truly do not think it will. I believe we would have noticed if we had passed beneath external light – would you not agree?"

Marcus thought about it, then nodded.

"Good, then we have a plan. But time is wasting, so let's get as far as we can before nightfall. If that is daylight, we can use it to tell the time, then look for the light again at dawn. All agreed?" Marcus amazed even himself at his commanding, decisive tone, and was relieved to see the others, even Athalir, accepting his leadership with nods of approval.

With a clearer direction and renewed positivity, they turned towards the beam of light and picked up speed, in an attempt to cover as much ground as possible before it faded. Marcus strode on ahead, his shoulders back and his head tall. To those that followed, he resembled a leader, and something about the way he moved gave them the impetus to walk faster and further than their aching legs would have allowed otherwise. To Marcus, the responsibility of his companions' lives weighed heavily on his mind. His trust in Sathom was fading, and he knew the others were now looking to him to reach their destination, where once they'd also trusted the elemental would get them there. That kind of pressure reminded him he'd lived a sheltered life. No, he'd not had it easy socially, and nobility came attached with daily pressures and duties, but at least he'd been financially secure, warm at night, and enjoyed the luxury to dream now and then. He'd never had anything more to concern him than avoiding his tutors, the wrath of his father, and the jests and japes of his peers. Now, not only did the fate of an ancient race depend on him, but that of the eclectic bunch of people behind him, too. He kept his head up while he walked, knowing they had to see him as strong, even if inwardly he felt anything but. "Come on, Marcus," he said quietly to himself. "You *can* do this."

CHAPTER TWENTY-ONE

No one else had seen the attack, or how many hollows there were, but the displaced air that swished all around them as the things closed in was terrifying.

"There are too many this time. Run!" Sathom shouted. Everyone, including Sathom, ran.

But the creatures were fast. Hessan, whose body and legs were built for stamina, not speed, felt his coat ripped as he brought up the rear. His instincts urged him to face his foe, but he wasn't stupid. A blind man was no match for an enemy with multiple eyes – and multiple blades.

The slashes came from every side. No matter how fast the group moved, it seemed the hollows' lethal claws were never more than a fraction of an inch away from bringing them down. It was a coordinated assault, designed to overwhelm, and it was working all too well.

Erryn let out a shriek as another talon tore at her clothing, barely avoiding breaking her skin. The close call spiked her adrenaline and lent an extra push to her waning energy.

It seemed there was no escape, and each of them knew it. Survival instinct was the only thing that kept them going, when common sense and reason insisted they would all die.

Marcus' stamina was flagging. He remembered how close he'd come to being a meal for the creatures but, as he put every ounce of his strength into driving his weakening muscles to keep moving, he didn't know how much further he could go.

The landscape ahead of them had been wide open, but was narrowing significantly as their escape route passed through hundreds of black, stony columns. Connected floor-to-ceiling and tapering in towards the middle, the stony spikes were spaced densely either side of what had become a darkened corridor. At the front of the group, Marcus' quick mind took in the sight and formulated a hasty plan.

"In there, quickly!" the mage hollered back, pointing towards the columns before veering off into the labyrinth. He could only hope the others had understood – as much as he hoped his idea would work. Once he'd squeezed into the tight space, he managed to catch his breath. As he'd guessed, it was difficult to move within the rock field; the columns were so closely-formed. Pushing his way deeper in, he was startled as his hands came into contact with a body. But his shock was short-lived as Athalir's face peered out at him from between two spikes.

"Athalir! Did everyone else follow inside?" Marcus whispered.

"I believe so. I heard you, and called out to Erryn. I heard her pass it on." Marcus had heard that too, but it was little proof they'd made it. Still, at this stage, it would have to be enough.

"Good. That part of my plan worked, at least."

"And just what *is* your plan? Stand motionless in here and pray the creatures think we're made out of rock?" Marcus ignored the prince's mockery.

"You've seen how little space there is in here, right?" Athalir nodded. "Those things may follow us in, but they'll be as restricted as we are. Could you attack a man with your daggers in here?"

Athalir looked affronted.

"Of course! I could attack a man with my daggers anywhere."

Marcus sighed.

"You're missing the point. This *maze* will provide cover, perhaps long enough for those things to get bored and go home – wherever that may be."

"Fair enough. Then let us utilise this place as best we can. I suggest moving further in." With that, Athalir slipped his lithe body between two columns and instantly disappeared from sight. Marcus paused to consider trying to locate the others, but quickly realised the futility of any such task. He'd already 'lost' the prince, even though he'd seen the direction in which he'd left. Thinking of Erryn, he made a silent wish that she'd also escaped inside, before forcing his own wider frame through the rocks.

Within the narrow alleyways of stone, sound felt unnatural; muted, as if a person's ears were full of water. Marcus had seen nothing but dark rock edging even darker passageways for so long, his mind had started hearing things that couldn't possibly be there. The song Julia had sung to him as a child, his father's stern lectures, even the cold, uninterested voice of his mother, with whom he'd spoken little in all of his twenty-six years. But those things were inside his head. When he tried to hear anything real, such sound was conspicuous by its absence.

"If I don't get out of here soon, I'll go mad," he said to himself, aloud, just to make sure he really heard it.

There was one positive – no hollows. He felt sure the fast-moving creatures wouldn't be able to pass unnoticed in that environment. And he was convinced that, if any of his companions had encountered them, their cries would have reached his ears. Still, he'd feel better to be reunited with everyone – if only to hear voices other than those from an unpleasant past.

Pushing his way onward, time slipped by quickly. As what light the cavern provided dimmed more and more, it grew increasingly eerie. Marcus had no sense of direction at the best of times, and it was already more luck than judgement that he'd not found his way back to the path.

Confused and disorientated, he thought he may already have turned back the way he'd come, when a sharp prod in the small of his back startled him. However, he had little time to think much of it as, a split second later, his feet were swiped out from under him, leaving him dazed and sprawled face down on the ground, his body and head bruised as he'd hit columns on the way down. The next he knew, he was being tugged by the legs, but in which direction, he had no hope of knowing. Coming back to his senses, he attempted to kick himself free, but to no avail. Grabbing at the pillars, he cussed as his fingers slipped away from the wet stone. With his nails scraping at the gritty cavern floor, survival instinct making him continue to struggle even though it was achieving nothing, he silently vowed to put up a fight before being eaten from the feet up.

After being dragged a good twenty-five feet, the hold on his ankles gave way. But, before he could do anything, a weight pressed down hard onto his spine, his arms jerked backwards and held tight while something was tied around his wrists.

"Get up!" a raspy, female voice ordered.

Marcus hadn't expected to be spoken to before being consumed, and quickly turned over to see who the voice belonged to. Now, in some sort of clearing amidst the rock maze, more of the odd green glow emanating from the periphery, he craned his neck back enough to see a surprisingly small and delicate-looking woman, leaning on a long staff and scowling down at him, greying, blonde hair churning in tangles around her shoulders.

"I said, *get up*!" The woman jabbed at the mage's foot with her staff.

"Alright, alright! But enough of the prodding." Marcus hauled himself to his feet, wobbling a little as he couldn't use him arms to steady himself.

"Marcus!"

He turned his head abruptly to see Erryn, with what seemed to be relief in her eyes. Alongside her were Vess, Athalir, and Hessan. All four were bloodied, with their hands bound similarly to his own, and lined up against what appeared to be a cave within the cavern. Seeing their faces more clearly than he'd done elsewhere, he realised they were almost directly beneath the source of the light they'd used as a compass. Just off to the side, opposite his friends, he could follow the beam upwards until he was just able to make out a large hole in the cavern ceiling. The daylight was fading, but what was left lit up the immediate area. Water trickled down from various ledges high up near the opening, adding to a small pool that had formed in a shallow dip. But something else caught Marcus' eye; spreading its way across the glistening rock and boulders around the pool was some kind of lichen. Its luminous green glow radiated upwards, revealing hundreds of moths flying to and from the plant. Marcus watched as they flitted about, and, with a small smile, understood it was the insects that had been providing the green glow all over the cavern, glowing even brighter than the lichen itself. He'd been so caught up in his discovery, enthralled by the genius of nature, that he'd almost forgotten his predicament. He went to tell Sathom about the moths, but suddenly remembered he wasn't there. *Always mysteriously absent when things look bleak,* Marcus thought to himself. Returning his attention to the matter at hand, he looked at his captor and wondered how such a woman had managed to best three capable fighters. Taking down Vess alone would have been an extraordinary feet – not even a band of rebel elves had succeeded in doing that.

And what was she doing in the cavern, anyway? With the discovery of not one, but two lone women wandering within, he might have believed the place's hostility to be a vast exaggeration, had he not experienced some of it himself.

"My lady..." Marcus began, opting for the manners he'd been so well taught.

"I'm no one's 'lady', lordling. Not anymore. Oh no. No ladies here, in the dark place. No, no no no no..." The woman stopped the rambling that had ceased to be addressing Marcus, and stared up through the hole in the ceiling. But, in no time, awareness flashed back into her eyes. She lashed out at Marcus' legs with her staff.

"None of your noble nonsense. I *know* what you are."

"Hey! Leave him alone!" Erryn shouted, the mage having dropped to his knees at the force of the blow.

"Ah, the girl has love for you, mage. I see it. Love, love, love. I would say I remember *love*… had I ever actually had any myself." Again, she drifted momentarily before speaking once more. "But enough! I know… you, *you*, mage of Whitestone. Come to take me back, have you? My sons are dead, then. Yes, that's it. The skaithen killed them anyway. Now you come to take me back to… wait! If they are truly dead, *he* has no heirs, no vessels. He wants… No! I'll not go back to him. Never, never never never never!"

Without warning, the woman lashed out at Marcus, her staff meeting his newly-standing body, raining blows that forced him back down to the ground, cowering to try to protect his head as best he could. Vess, Erryn, Athalir, and Hessan all reacted in kind, frantically yelling at the crazed woman to stop and writhing about trying to loosen their binds on their wrists and ankles.

"Aemilia! That's enough!" A familiar voice broke through the din, loud but inexpressive. The woman ceased her assault mid-flow, a look of confused surprise taking over from wild fury.

"It can't be!" She said, slowly turning around while Marcus took in the sight of Sathom with relief.

"Aemilia, I…"

"You bastard!" Before Sathom could continue he was interrupted. Aemilia wasted no time with further insults. She lunged at the elemental, her sinewy arms outstretched and her filthy, claw-like nails reaching for his face, but he managed to dodge and rushed over to Marcus' side.

"Curse you!" Aemilia shrieked. She paused, and then spoke again. "Wait a moment. I know this. I do. Yes, it makes sense now." Cackling, she stared pointedly at Marcus, taking singular steps forwards, with the ragged grey dress she wore hanging loosely from her thin frame. "He's the one." The tendons corded in her neck as she eyed the mage with visible vitriol. "He's the reason I'm here."

"Looks like the elemental's got some explaining to do," Hessan said, sounding almost pleased.

"Sathom, what's going on? You know this woman?" Vess asked. Erryn and Athalir both looked from one person to another as each spoke.

"Know me? Hahahaha! You could say that, yes."

"Aemilia, wait. I did what–"

"No! You don't get to lie this time, Sathom. The big, shiny boy already doubts your... nature. Allow me to validate his fear."

"To be fair, the vessel doubts a lot of things. But, if you feel the need to go on, then let it be so." Sathom closed his eyes as if bracing himself for what was to come.

"A vessel is it?" Aemilia walked slowly towards Vess, touching his cheek with coarse fingers as she stood before him. "Funny." She said as she stared up at his face. "I'd n'er thought about the others. Not in all the years I knew my own sons were… sleeping, alongside them."

Vess' expression softened and his voice quivered.

"You… you are a mother to… to others like me? Do you know of my own mother? Tell me, does she live?"

"Let me look at you, big, shiny boy." Aemilia's mad eyes seemed calm for the first time since the group had been taken as her captives. She studied his features for mere seconds before looking shocked and roughly yanking his head to one side. Tugging at his ear on the exposed side, she leaned closer, standing up on tip-toes and using the warrior's shoulder to pull herself up to see better. "Yes. It is just as I thought. You carry his mark. You *are* his!" She dropped back down to stand normally, yet her face had paled, and her eyes appeared more crazed than before.

"I am whose? What do you mean? What mark?" Vess pleaded, confused by her odd reaction.

"Tell me, vessel. How are you awake? Where is your brother?"

Vess looked to Marcus, who spoke before he could answer.

"He's 'awake' because his brother… died."

"You killed him, soul-bound mage?"

"Well, not me, personally, no. But –"

"Do you realise what you have done?" Aemilia gestured with her hand at Vess. "This is the second vessel of Alerick – you killed the first. Oh, his wrath will be great! You have brought a vengeance down upon yourselves the like of which I am certain you are not ready for. I'd wager the only reason you are not yet dead, or worse, is this place – he cannot reach you. If you are sane, you'll never leave." She cackled maniacally, then approached Sathom, stopping in front of him and wringing her aged hands together as she glared at his face from close-quarters.

"What's so special about this 'Alerick'? He's just a governor, like the others, right?" Erryn spoke out, having quietly watched until that point.

"Hahahahaha! Oh, my dear girl, he is *so* much more than 'just' a governor. Alerick is the ringleader. His heart is colder than ice, and his soul is jaded by regret he's too proud to acknowledge. He will kill you slowly in an attempt to feel something other than his own empty shadow, believe me."

There was a heavy atmosphere as Aemilia's words brought an air of dread to the gathering. It came to an abrupt end when Hessan spoke.

"So, are you just going to stand there glowering at Sathom, or do we all get to find out what he did?"

"I would gouge out his eyes if I could," the woman said through gritted teeth. "Do you call this creature 'friend'?" Her question was not aimed at anyone of them in particular.

"I call very few people such, woman. Least of all someone I've known less than a day," the dwarven king responded.

"He's *my* friend!" Marcus piped up. "And there's nothing you can say to alter that."

"Really? Then I pity you for your poor choice of allegiance, lordling."

Marcus started to struggle to his feet.

"Stay down!" Aemilia thwacked him with her staff once more.

"Aemilia! It is me against whom you seek vengeance. Leave him out of this." Sathom moved to place himself between the mage and the woman.

"But I cannot claim my vengeance upon you, can I, Sathom? Incorporeal as you are. Your 'companions' wish to know, and I assume you've neglected to mention our shared past. I will tell them of it."

"As you wish."

"As I wish? As I wish? Remember what I *wished* for, do you, elemental? Do you recall how I longed to hold my two sons in my arms? To nurture them as only a mother can? It was such a long time ago, yes. But I could never forget. Oh no! You promised to help me, came to me with your mutually beneficial 'deal'. I agreed – what else could I do? What other option did I have? You came to me with an offer of that which I desired most and I… *trusted* you."

Everyone was now caught up in the woman's revelation, save for Sathom, who simply stared, unflinching, at the rambling woman.

"I was granted just one chance to be with both of my boys. After each birth, my baby would be placed at my breast. There he would stay until he'd had his fill. *Long enough for mother's milk to give them strength*, I was told. Long enough for that bond to be established before it was broken, is how it felt. T'would not surprise me if it had been but a cruel trick, played by monstrous men who had lost all humanity centuries ago. Their skaithen took great pleasure in torturing me and the other wives with our grief, of course. But I was a *strong one* – they told me that once, before I was whipped for my insolence. I would spend my enforced solitude attempting to find a way to free my children. I was a mage. I was able to command magic as any other, but naught I was capable of could compare with the dark magic wielded by my husband and his brethren. I was powerless, and they knew it. The skaithen revelled in it. Taunting me, showing me visions of my two sleeping babes, entombed beyond my reach. The day I finally snapped, you came to me, didn't you, Sathom? Your request was too easy for me not to grant. A simple binding spell was all you asked. How could I refuse when what you offered was so important to me? And so, with your aid, I escaped my locked room, using the key you'd procured from a guard and your ability to walk through solid stone. Little did I know you'd thought of every little detail to cover your own tracks. I wonder – did that guard really believe I'd seduced him just because his body bore the scent of my perfume?"

Sathom remembered passing his hand over the sleeping guard's face, the permanent false memories so easily inserted as he dreamt.

"I… have ways of making memories come to be."

"My, my, Sathom. I don't know why, but such honesty was never part of my vision of the time when you and I would meet once again. It's… *annoying*!"

Sathom shut his eyes, feeling guilty but, of course, unable to show it.

"I'm still not clear what he did that was so terrible." Erryn said, even though she was beginning to think Vess had just cause to be suspicious.

"No, little girl with a curl, you wouldn't just yet, as there is more of my tale to tell. And so I shall." All the while the woman paced around Sathom, around Marcus, up close to those she had tied up near the wall of the smaller cave that appeared to be her home.

"Sathom brought me the babe. Not my babe, oh no, no no no. You must know that. This one was no fruit of my loins. *A mage child*, he said. Newly born and '*borrowed*' in the night as his parents slept. *Of great importance*, he told me, but nothing more. *For my safety and the boy's.* Ha! My safety? That was a good one, creature. Would that you had given one slice of a care for my safety, I would not be here now, would I? So, I cast the spell, the one to block out his soul. It would still be there, within him, shaping him as he grew. In truth, though, I knew not what my magic was doing. I was n'er privy to that information. I was just asked to place a mystical… *shield*, around his soul. To this day, I know not why. Do *you* know why, lordling?"

Marcus looked up from where he sat, bruised and dishevelled on the ground.

"Yes. I know why."

"Ah, good. Yes, I suppose that *is* good. Anyway, moving on. Once I crafted the boy's shield, the elemental provided the details for how I was to receive my boon from our partnership. I was to meet with him at the crypt, the one where the vessels slept. Told me to bring my dagger. I thought it to be an odd necessity at the time – but bring it I did. I would have done anything he said at that point. I could almost feel my children's heartbeats, his promise was *so* sincere. While he returned the babe, I made for the crypt."

"How did you get in? The lock was sealed with dark magic when I went there. I had to clear it," Marcus interrupted.

"There was no such seal back then. Had there been, I'd– did you say… you *cleared* it?"

"I did. Though it took a lot out of me."

"Then I underestimated you, lordling. Few ordinary mages can work against the governors' magic." For a moment, Aemilia smiled, but it didn't last long, and she returned to her story.

"I'd been inside the crypt barely any time at all when Sathom arrived; just time enough to find my sons. Older than I remembered them, yet the little boys' faces still recognisable to me. A mother always knows. I wanted to reach them, to scoop them up into my arms. But they lay beneath a roof of glass, blackness swirling all around them. 'Get off them!' I shouted. 'Leave my babes alone!' You came to me then, didn't you, Sathom? You took me to you and soothed my pain, stroking my hair, wiping away my tears. Whispering, a retelling of the promise you made to set them free, to return them to me. I asked you what I had to do, composing myself and remembering I was strong, so very strong. And that was the last I saw of you… until now."

Athalir spoke softly.

"Where did he go?"

"That moment, I knew not. The next thing I was aware of was my husband and the skaithen, shadowed by the sleeping guard and two others. I was in a daze. Bewitched. Isn't that right, Sathom?"

"I… made you forget, yes."

"But I remembered eventually. Didn't expect *that*, did you?"

"Well actually, yes."

"Sathom, what are you talking about? What did you do?" Marcus looked up at the elemental, seeking answers.

"There are – abilities – possessed by all of my kind. Unlike the elemental magics, which were dampened along with my emotions, passage through solid walls, ethereal travel, and the capacity to alter memory are innate and, thus, have remained available to me. When a person is asleep or unconscious, I can affect a permanent change to their memories. When they are conscious, it is more like a glamour, fading away with time or external influence. I passed my hand across

Aemilia's skull as I held her, presuming she'd forget everything just long enough to..." Sathom's voice trailed off. "I suspect the atmosphere here returned her mind to its original state."

Aemilia nodded.

"Hmm. It did. As they wrestled the blade from my hand that was poised over the glass, I had no recollection of anything that had gone before. Not you, our plan, the spell I'd cast – none of it. As they accused me of attempting to murder my children, there was naught I could do but weep." Aemilia went silent, a steady stream of tears running down her sorrowful, yet still crazed face.

"But that's not the full story, is it? It can't be? How did you come to be here?" Hessan had not succumbed to the pervasive, emotionally-charged atmosphere as the others had, but he was curious.

"Why don't you tell them, creature? I think I'm done talking."

"I have no idea what happened to you, Aemilia. I presumed they would..." Sathom said, his answer trailing off to silence.

"Kill me? Oh, if only they had. governor Ealdwin – my *loving* husband – deemed '*dealing*' with me beneath him, and left my punishment to be meted out by the skaithen. That dark being cared nothing for justice or vengeance. His delight comes from pain – emotional and physical. And so I was exiled here, the sleeping guard who had run to his master with news of my 'treachery' sent as my escort. He didn't survive to return, though. Just as the skaithen desired, I'm sure. I, however, have been here ever since. What would it be now, ten years?"

"Almost twenty-six," Sathom quietly corrected.

"My, how the years can pass by unnoticed when banished to a place of death and darkness."

"Why are you still here, Aemilia? Surely you would try to escape," Vess said.

"Oh, my shiny, *shiny* boy. You are how I like to imagine my sons now. You'd all be of an age, the magic that keeps the vessels asleep halts the ageing process at their twenty-fifth year. The governors believe that age to be the optimum for the 'inhabiting'." She cupped the giant man's face between her palms and smiled up at him. "I may well have attempted to flee this hole, had I not heard the skaithen's final words as he ordered my departure from Vaharia. '*Should you leave your prison and be discovered – and discovered you will be – your sons will be subjected to pain the like of which you can only imagine in your worst nightmares.'* He couldn't kill them, he knew I knew that." Letting go of Vess, she turned her back on the group. "Indeed, they thought I'd been attempting to kill them to prevent their father from using their bodies. No, their death wouldn't have prevented my return, but subjecting my children to a life of pain until such time they were required as vessels… well, the skaithen may not have mothers themselves, but they certainly understand maternal instinct. I had no choice but to stay here."

Erryn lifted her bound hands to wipe a tear from her cheek.

"But how did you survive here for so long?"

"Hahahaha! Did you not hear me say I was '*strong*'?" Aemilia returned to Sathom. "The cavern has provided everything I needed to stay alive. Shelter, food, water, some… friends. Besides, I've had one thing in my mind throughout my time here. One thing above all else that has kept going through the darkest nights and fighting through the longest days – vengeance!"

"Aemilia, I am sorry you have known such suffering, but you have to realise… you cannot harm me."

"I don't even have to touch you, liar! You've unwittingly brought something of importance to you into my domain." Aemilia nodded at Marcus. "I have to admit, I n'er truly believed I'd see *you* again, let alone the babe you so obviously cared about."

"Leave him out of this."

"I think not. He is in possession of something that belongs to me – I think it's time to take it back." Aemilia grinned, the look in her eyes madder than ever.

"You're insane!" Erryn shouted. "You can't take back a spell!"

"Maybe, maybe not. A mad scholar from Whitestone once hypothesised that magic conjurations could be… reabsorbed via the stomach. Perhaps I shall get a chance to test that theory. After all, it's been – what was it – twenty-six years since I last tasted the flesh of anything but rats and beetles. And this boy looks a good deal more appetising than the sleeping guard."

"You *ate* him?" Hessan resisted the urge to vomit, screwing his face up to curb the gagging reflex.

"Well, with a little help from my… pets. They only take the skin, you see? You'd be surprised how delicious raw human flesh looks when you know not where you'll find your next meal. And on that note, I believe I've talked away enough time. Feeding time should be just about–" An odd noise started to come from a wide alley at the back of the cavern. "Now! My pets will be delighted. They usually have to suffice with the rats. You'll forgive me if I don't stay for the feeding. The *process* is a little… *revolting.* Sathom, I wish I could say it was good to see you again. Remember what you did as you watch your boy skinned alive." With that Aemilia moved quickly to her makeshift home, disappearing through a door made up of what looked like bones tied together with the same twine used to bind her captives.

There wasn't long to process her words. Throughout the woman's closing speech, the noise had gradually become louder. It could only be one thing – the pounding of something large moving towards them. Vibrations rippled along the ground as a gigantic bird, over ten-feet tall, emerged from the alley. As the group stared in open-mouthed shock at the wide, yellow eyes and heavy, pointed beak, a scuffle broke out, and two more identical, winged beasts pushed forwards from either side of the first. Three huge bills opened wide and let off deafening squawks as three sets of powerful legs propelled the creatures towards their helplessly-bound prey.

CHAPTER TWENTY-TWO

Athalir finally managed to get his hands loose from the rope. He'd been twisting and turning his wrists the whole time Aemilia had been speaking.

"Time to move!" he said, then bent over to hastily untie his ankles. Able to move freely, he made a dash to Marcus, releasing the mage's wrists before sprinting to the others to assist them.

"It's too late!" said Erryn, eyes widening as the giant birds came into view over Athalir's shoulder. They'd stopped moving, but were now looking curiously at their food, heads cocked to one side. "There's no time to free us all. You and Marcus will have to hold them back while..." She trailed off.

"While what? While we wait for those two to be flayed, and hope elf and mage skin is so filling they have no room for dwarf and human?" Hessan picked up where Erryn left off.

"Hey! I'm human, too!" Marcus called out.

"Really not my point."

Athalir unsheathed his daggers.

"Marcus, get everyone else untied. I'll buy some time." The elf prince didn't look back. As the birds made their first lunge forwards, he drew in a deep breath then sprinted at them, breaking into a leap as he got close. The sight of Athalir flying through the air with his daggers at the end of outstretched arms was enough to draw the attention of the advancing enemy. Elf met fowl in a frenzied clash of beak and blade, blood and feathers scattering, and squawks drowning out Athalir's pained grunts.

Erryn watched on, downturned brows and wide eyes supporting the concern in her voice.

"He's not going to survive long!"

"Marcus, get a move on, before the elf is once again on his back! I happen to like my skin where it is." Hessan was getting agitated while Marcus desperately tried to make his clumsy fingers unscramble tight knots.

Erryn, now able to move her arms, didn't wait for her ankles to be liberated. Taking her bow in hand, she aimed over Marcus' head in an attempt to fire at the creatures, but Athalir kept appearing in her line of sight.

"Ugh! It's no good. I can't get a clear shot!"

"Just fire through him," Vess mumbled.

"I'm going to pretend I didn't hear that."

"Oh, for Morsynia's sake, Marcus! Get me loose. I'll do the rest. You can stand in a corner and look pretty. I hear from a certain larn's daughter you're good at that."

"Hessan!" Erryn tried to forget hearing the dwarf king's remark, but couldn't, so put extra aggression into loosing an arrow. The second she let it go, she regretted the burst of temper. The arrow flew towards Athalir's back. "No!" she cried, expecting the worst.

With a second to spare, a flash of silver armour and blonde hair sped from the stony labyrinth, shield held aloft as Roh skidded between Athalir and Erryn's arrow. It struck the shield and bounced a few feet away.

"Nice shot!" The blonde warrior glanced fleetingly at Erryn before joining the fray. "If you were trying to kill the elf," she called back, slashing at a bird and immediately raising her shield to cover the beak strike that followed.

"Seems she didn't go home after all," Marcus said, finally removing the twine from Erryn's ankles. He went next to the dwarf, fortunately finding his binds much easier to deal with. "I did a whole lot more than '*look pretty*'!"

"Yeah, yeah! Whatever you say. Just get my hands free and go fumble one of the others."

With his hands untied, Hessan made short work of the knots round his boots, before swinging the two axes from his back and rushing into battle. "That's better!"

With everyone mobile again, there was a scramble to assist those already fighting. One bird down, it's head removed by one of Hessan's axes, it looked like they'd be out of trouble before long – until the moment two more birds emerged from the alley, closely followed by several others.

Not for the first time during their time in the cavern, Marcus felt impotent watching everyone else fight, but this time, he was in no mood to act as bystander while others took the risks. Taking the staff from his back, he gripped it around the middle, examining the pointy end and gulping extra air. Taking a step towards the battle, he was held back by Sathom's hand around his arm.

"Marcus, what are you doing?"

"Helping. I can't just stand here and watch."

"That's exactly what you can do. You are too important to risk."

Marcus stared at Sathom, determination evident in his eyes.

"That may be what a man such as *you* would do – but then, you're no *man*, are you, Sathom?" With that he pulled his arm free and ran, holding the staff like a spear.

The birds were powerful and now, numerous. Just one leg was strong enough to break a man's spine with a well-positioned kick. Their beaks were as hard as stone and large enough to fit a skull inside. Roh had never travelled this far into the cavern, and therefore had no wisdom to offer this time. The birds were new to her, and for the first time in her life, she wasn't certain this was a fight she could win. Soon, her shield carried multiple dents from beak strikes, and her sword arm was feeling weaker than she would have liked. Stepping backwards to evade one such lunge, she tripped on misplaced footing and fell. From the ground, she looked up to see herself surrounded, and being slowly advanced upon, by a number of birds that'd noticed her weakened state. As quickly as possible, she got to her feet, keeping her shield before her and biting her lip through the ache in the arm that was wielding her sword. Behind the advancing fowl, everyone else was preoccupied with their own fight and oblivious to her predicament.

"You're going to have to get yourself out of this one, Roh." She shrugged and stiffened up. *Nothing new there*, she thought. "Come and get me!" she yelled.

Vess put another bird down with the edge of his blade as he heard Roh's war cry. He could just make out her silver armour glinting with green light from within a circle of the feathered killers. Without another thought, he ran as fast as his bulk and heavy plate would allow, pushing through the first birds he collided with until he stood in front of the female warrior. Squeezing the grip of his great-sword, he spoke without looking at the woman.

"Get down and stay there!"

"What?"

There was no time to explain. The giant man pushed the woman over, sending her onto her backside.

The birds immediately thrust forwards, while Vess extended the sword with one arm and spun around like a hammer thrower, cutting a swathe through the creatures. Those not wounded were thrown back as they manoeuvred their plump bodies out of the way. With the imminent danger averted, he offered a hand to Roh, who ignored it and jumped up unassisted. She glared at Vess, her dark-blue eyes boring into him.

"I could have handled it!" she said, shoving past the confused warrior and joining the others as they fought.

Eventually, it became clear victory was beyond hope. More and more birds continued to arrive. For every one killed, it seemed four more took its place.

"It's no good. We have to get out of here. Now!" Erryn said, returning an arrow to its quiver.

Hessan was reluctant, his earlier panic having been replaced with bloodthirsty desire, but agreement for escape was otherwise universal.

Quickly sheathing weapons, everyone followed Roh, who'd called out before heading back the way she had come. There was another smaller alley on the opposite side of the clearing, too narrow for their attacker's substantial bodies to pass through, and thus, providing the perfect route through which to flee.

As the last blood-spattered person sprinted down the alley, the birds, furious at the loss of a meal, could be heard screeching collectively, a sound that would stay with them all for a long time to come.

Everyone had run for what seemed like an age. Logically, they all knew the birds were too big to have followed, but no one had been thinking logically as they forced themselves to push their beaten bodies onward.

Huddled around a small camp-fire, all but Sathom tended to wounds and wiped blood from weapons. The elemental stood away from the group, staring out into the half-light, his arms folded across his chest as if keeping himself warm – though he was unable to feel temperature of any kind.

"Should we… talk to him?" Vess asked Marcus, who was sat at his side, rubbing the top of his arm and looking sorry for himself.

"What is there to say? After what he did to that poor woman…"

"I'm not sure 'poor' is how *I'd* describe her," Hessan said, polishing an axe blade with a blood-stained rag.

"I thought you didn't like him, Vess?" Erryn asked

"I said I didn't trust him."

"And now you know why," she persisted.

"Yes, and so there's nothing left to mistrust. I know now what he had to hide."

Hessan stopped polishing and leant forwards to look pointedly at the vessel, resting his elbow on his knee and in turn, his chin on his hand.

"You're a very complicated person, Vess."

"He's an idiot!" Roh spoke without looking up from the process of trying to push out the dents from her shield.

Everyone stopped and stared at the woman.

"Care to elaborate?" Hessan asked, intrigued.

Roh put down the shield and stood up, walking to stand between Vess and the fire.

"You were a fool! You put yourself in unnecessary danger. You left your comrades to do so. As I said, you're an idiot!"

"I saved your life, woman!"

"I didn't ask you to."

"Does that matter? You were surrounded. You couldn't have handled them all."

"And how do *you* know that?" Roh's face was bright pink, and her fists were clenched at her sides. "When I need help from a lumbering simpleton, I'll ask for it – and I'll *never* ask for it." She stormed away from the centre of the group and stood next to Sathom, leaving a state of confusion in her wake.

"Well, that was harsh." Hessan resumed his rigorous polishing, holding up the blade every so often to admire the sheen on the metal.

Vess was embarrassed, confused, and, for reasons he didn't care to admit to, hurt. For just the second time since he'd been woken, someone had managed to cause him to question his own nature, to acknowledge flaws he hadn't yet grown accustomed to having. What irked him more was that, on both occasions, it had been the same someone. At that moment, he made a mental note to stay as far away from Roh as possible. *Hopefully*, he thought, *she'll be on her way home soon – for real this time.*

"Don't worry. I don't think you're an idiot." Erryn shuffled up close to Vess, linking her arm through his and leaning her head against his shoulder.

Vess smiled and said "Thank you," before disappearing into thought, staring off into the distance.

An uncomfortable silence hung over the party while rations were consumed. Nobody cared to allow the night to drag on longer than necessary and so, before too long, with Sathom on a full watch, everyone got as comfortable as the hard ground allowed and went to sleep.

No more than an hour had passed when everyone woke simultaneously at the sound of steel being drawn from scabbards. As each member of the group opened their eyes, they were met with weapons being held just a hair's breadth from their skin. The fact they were weapons was unquestionable, but though the form was clear, there were no details. Every sword, every axe, every arrow-tip was black, and appeared to be nothing more than a well-defined shadow. The strangeness continued as the eye followed on to those that brandished the arms – figures, nothing more. Just as their weapons, those that wielded them were simply black shapes. As sight rushed back to newly awoken eyes, each person realised the same thing. Their assailants weren't just any shadow, they were their *own* shadows. Every figure was the exact same height and build as the one they stood over. Outlines of clothing and hair were precise copies. Even pointed ears were clearly distinguishable on Athalir's shadow, which was crouched and holding two daggers at his throat.

At the advent of scrapes and scuffling, Sathom had turned around to view the scene at the camp. He'd been vigilant, his eyes scanning the perimeter while the others had slept. Nothing had passed his field of vision. How could this be?

"Soul shadows! I wondered if they'd show up," Roh said, her eyes fixed on the black long-sword held to her chest.

"You knew about them – and didn't think to mention it?" Vess had unintentionally fallen into a light sleep. With a large black blade now hovering above him, he vowed that would never happen again.

"Well, I'm not putting up with this!" Hessan began to scramble to his feet, one hand already gripping the haft of an axe. His shadow took a side swipe with the flat of its blade across his counterpart's shoulder, sending the dwarf back to the ground.

"Don't...! Don't make any sudden movements." Roh spoke again, a little too late for Hessan. "They will stay as they are while we do the same. Just… stay still."

What she said seemed to be true. The shadows remained as they were, weapons poised but unmoving, a bizarre stand-off between captive and featureless captor.

"Roh, what are these soul shadows?" Sathom asked

"Currently, they're us."

"Yes, I think we all got that part, but why are they here?" Marcus was getting increasingly uncomfortable with the sharpened tip of a staff resting against his throat.

"And, more importantly, how do we fight them?" Athalir joined in with the line of questioning.

"We don't! We absolutely do *not* fight them. They are manifestations of us, of the dark thoughts we fell asleep with. This place… conjures them. We fight them, they die, or rather vanish… and so do we!"

"You mean, if we kill them, we–"

Roh cut Vess off mid-sentence.

"We kill ourselves, yes. I think I made that point *quite* clear."

"So what *are* we going to do? We can't just stay here, indefinitely." Erryn had had just about enough of things trying to kill her. The idea she may be killed by her own shadow was taking things a little too far.

"Well, we could try thinking happy thoughts," Roh suggested. "That might work. Maybe."

"Maybe? You mean you don't know?" Were it not for the situation, Vess would have revelled in the opportunity to put the woman back in her place.

Marcus ignored the bickering as he tried to think. To destroy the apparitions would be suicide. Presumably that meant to fight them at all would result in pain, or even injury, to the members of the party. With no answer coming to mind, something occurred to him.

"Hold a minute. Roh, how do you know of these things?"

The warrior woman looked sheepish.

"I had my own encounter with one."

"So how did you deal with it?"

Roh paused before answering.

"I… ran away."

"And I was just beginning to like you," Hessan said

"Good! So that *will* work then? They won't follow – hunt us down?" Marcus sounded hopeful. He, more than anyone, understood the merits of 'running away' as a plan.

"Oh yes, they'll follow. They'll even try to attack you as you run."

"Then, how did you escape?" Erryn asked

"I don't know. I just left the cavern as fast as I could. I dealt a few cuts with my sword and my own body bled. Something about being attacked by myself didn't appeal. I sheathed my weapon and ran. When I reached the outside, I looked back and it had gone. I guess they can't pass beyond the mountains."

"How far did you have to run?" Marcus asked.

"Not too far, actually. I was quite close to– wait a second." Roh looked around, slowly, so as not to antagonise her shadow. "It was right here. It must be this part of the cavern that causes them to appear. That means the way out isn't far, it's just…"

"Up that slope. I see it. There's a bit of light coming from up there," Erryn said, pointing to, what appeared to be, the opening to a short tunnel at the top of an ascending pathway. "I'd wager if we run fast, we'll make it out with minimal injury."

"So we flee? I've never run from a foe in my life," Athalir said, his dark eyes still focused on the black blades.

"You ran away from the birds, Athalir," Erryn pointed out.

"That was different. I drew blood before doing so. I am no coward. I'll not scamper away like a frightened rabbit."

"I agree with the elf. I seek out fights, I don't avoid them," Hessan said, adrenaline making his skin tingle.

"Fine. If you're both so keen to end your lives, so be it. I'm no craven, but I happen to enjoy living, and I'm not into self-inflicted pain either. Every swipe of your blade, you will feel – and that's in addition to their attacks on each of us. With the birds, we gave it our all, and realised when we were bested. Trust me. This is one fight we definitely can't win."

Athalir jumped up from the ground, brandishing his daggers in one swift movement.

"I don't believe you!" he shouted, swiping at his soul shadow. The metal met its mark, causing a wispy gash that only stayed present for a few seconds before blending back together. However, at the same time, a sharp pain ripped across Athalir's chest. Looking down, aghast, he saw a gaping tear across his tunic, a line of blood apparent beneath.

All of the other shadows remained where they were, their plain forms eerily still, and seemingly untroubled by the movement nearby.

"Believe me now?" Roh said, as the elf dropped back to the ground, his hand covering the shallow cut.

Marcus had no desire to lend any further supporting evidence to Roh's point, but he'd be damned if he'd come this far to be held hostage by little more than an apparition.

"We're leaving… *now!*" Without hesitating, he stood up. He flinched as his shadow jabbed him with its staff, yet he remained standing.

"Marcus! What are you doing?" Erryn was worried the mage had taken complete leave of what senses he possessed.

"We can't stay here. We've no choice but to go – probably quickly, to avoid as much injury as possible, but–"

"But nothing. It's merely a few bruises for you. Our shadows have bladed weapons, not pointy sticks." Athalir was still nursing his cut, his free hand fumbling around inside the purse tied at his waist. Sathom's eye had been caught by the elf's odd fidgeting as he'd turned to the sound of his voice. The elemental continued to watch the prince with suspicious curiosity as Marcus tried to assuage the doubts of his companions.

"Look, I know I'll fare better, but what else can be done?" The shadow poked him again as if to emphasise pointy sticks could still hurt. "The way I see it, the choices are limited to just two; suffer cuts, gashes, maybe even gaping wounds, or lie here and die from starvation."

"That's not strictly true," Erryn piped up.

"There's another option?" Vess asked.

"Oh no, Marcus is quite right, there *are* only two. I simply meant that we'd die of thirst way before starvation became an issue."

Marcus smiled at Erryn.

"There you go, that's why I like you, Erryniya Constantine – always ready to set me straight."

Why, oh why, did he have to wait until their life was in peril to say something that made her heart pound faster? Erryn wondered, before the memory of seeing him and the larn's daughter together got in the way of the pleasant thought. The hexan jumped up, snatched her pack and weapon, and ran off in the direction of the narrow slope. Her shadow hesitated, as if taken by surprise, then cocked a wispy arrow and shot at Erryn. Her keen hunter's hearing detected the whistling approach and she just managed to dodge in time, the arrow whooshing harmlessly past her before fizzling out into nothing.

The time for postulating done, the others realised they had no choice but to follow Erryn. Noting the manner of her departure had given her shadow pause, everyone else followed suit. Of course, their shadows were bound to remain at close quarters, so out-manoeuvring wasn't likely to work as easily as it had for their companion, but, with packs and weapons hastily picked up, they took off as fast as they were able.

Every step of the way, they had to attempt to keep out of reach of blades and arrows. Injuries were many, but all knew there was no liberty to feel the pain or acknowledge how much blood was being shed. Up and up the group ran for what seemed like an age, getting ever closer to the tunnel that would take them to the exit on the other side of the Dragon Crest Mountains.

"I see daylight!" Erryn called out, then yelped in pain as an arrow lodged itself in her right thigh. Had she looked down at the wound she'd have seen no shaft, but there was no mistaking the pain of an arrowhead piercing her flesh.

"Erryn!" Marcus couldn't see her as she was too far ahead, but her cry was enough to push him on faster than before. Pushing past Athalir, he left his shadow, and the prince, floundering in his wake.

"Hey!" Athalir shouted as he stumbled forwards, almost falling to the ground.

"Get up, elf!" Hessan grabbed the prince's upper arm to steady him as he caught up. Athalir shrugged the dwarf off and shot forwards, a sharp pain in his lower back reminding him of the danger in pursuit.

Sathom had already made it to the cavern exit and stood half in and half out, waiting for the first of his companions to appear. Though emotions were unavailable to him, he knew the tightness in his chest wouldn't subside until every last member of the party had emerged into the land beyond the mountains. He, too, had heard Erryn's pained yell, but as he'd stared into the descending tunnel, there'd still been no sign of anyone coming.

Finally, Marcus' familiar shape appeared in the passageway as he stumbled onward to the outside world. He was carrying Erryn, whose injured leg had buckled beneath her as it had gone numb from blood loss.

"Marcus, are you alright?" The relief at seeing the mage still alive was the strongest thing he'd felt in some time.

Marcus gently set his charge down on a black boulder at the mountainside, and bent over with his hands on his knees to catch his breath. Blood was seeping through his tunic in various places where he'd taken arrows that were meant for Erryn.

"I'm fine – if a little perforated. No sign of our shadowy 'friends', at least," he said, looking back towards the cavern. "That's a good thing." He knelt down to check on Erryn. Her skin had gone pale and beads of sweat were scattered across her forehead and down the bridge of her nose. His concern for the girl evident in his eyes, Marcus took Julia's handkerchief from his pocket and dabbed away the moisture, brushing strands of wet hair out of the way with his other hand.

"I'm okay. Stop fussing!" Erryn pushed him away, grunting as her leg ached from the blood flowing back into it. Marcus looked perplexed for a moment, before standing and turning to stare hopefully at the cavern entrance. Just as he did so, Hessan ran out, closely followed by Athalir, both panting and soaked in a mixture of blood and sweat.

"Did you see Vess, or Roh? Are they far behind?" Marcus asked, looking past the two men into the darkness.

Athalir was using the mountainside to steady himself as he caught his breath, while Hessan was bent over resting his hands on his knees and chuckling.

"They were just behind me, last I knew," the dwarf replied between breathless chortles.

"What's so funny?" Erryn couldn't help but smile as she watched Hessan's strange reaction.

"Ah, nothing, nothing." He laughed a little more. "It's just… phew! What a rush!"

"Are you mocking me, dwarf?" Athalir turned his head to face Hessan, keeping one hand firmly against the black, rock wall.

"Oh, get over yourself, *prince*. Not everything is about you. Well, nothing serious anyway. I have to say your inability to stay upright is a source of amusement for me," Hessan said, a mischievous smile just visible through the mane of damp hair that had fallen about his face.

Marcus noticed Athalir visibly bristling with anger and spoke up before the two came to blows.

"That's enough! Sathom, any sign of movement yet?"

Sathom took a step further into the cavern and strained to see into the gloom as far as he could.

"No. Nothing."

"They should've been here by now. One of us may have to go back in."

"Surely you jest?" The Fell prince moved away from the mountain, a puzzled look on his face.

"Marcus, give it a little longer." Sathom placed a reassuring hand on Marcus' shoulder. "I'm certain Vess and Roh can handle things well enough."

"It's no good. I can't get past." Vess was attempting to follow the path upward, but his shadow had somehow managed to get in front. Now, with his way ahead cut off, Roh also found herself boxed in; Vess in front, her shadow behind.

"For Nexephia's sake, man. Get around it!"

"I can't. The path is too narrow. Do you *want* me to fall to my death?"

"You *really* wish me to answer that?" Roh's frustration was peaking. If the great lummox didn't get out of her way soon, she'd push him over the edge herself.

Both shadows had ceased their attack the moment the humans' progression had been halted. It was as if they knew they'd won, that no more fighting was necessary. However, each time Vess had tried to move past his shadow, he'd been met with the edge of a blade, leaving him in no doubt he'd meet with a sticky end should he try pushing on.

Roh started complaining at him once more, when he remembered something the warrior woman had said earlier.

"Kiss me!" Vess turned away from the shadow and looked intensely into Roh's eyes.

"What?" The woman instinctively stepped back, receiving a short nudge to her spine from a shadowy shield.

"You said something about happy thoughts."

"What *are* you talking about?"

"Before, when we were discussing how to get away from these things. You mentioned thinking happy thoughts."

"Oh, *that*. I was being sarcastic."

"That may be, but it might just work. Kiss me and perhaps we can get rid of the soul shadows once and for all." Vess' look of determination was now replaced by one of sheepishness as Roh's glare made him feel emasculated.

"And just what makes you think kissing *you* will make me happy?"

Vess averted his eyes.

"It was just a thought. Don't make a-"

Before he could continue, Roh lunged forwards, grasped both sides of the armoured man's face, and pressed her lips against his. For a moment, Vess thought about breaking the clinch, but it was only a moment. Instead, he wrapped both arms around her metal-sheathed waist and pulled her closer to him. Her action initially hard and dispassionate, she relaxed more and more, leaning into his embrace and reciprocating the passion with which his lips explored hers. Standing precariously close to the edge of the narrow foot-way in dangerously low light, the pair became lost in the kiss, so much so that neither noticed their respective shadows fizzling out before disappearing completely.

Finally, feeling the need to take a breath, Vess relinquished his hold and they moved apart, awkwardness rushing in to fill the vacant emotional space.

"Well, it seems that little plan of yours worked." Roh could see nothing of Vess' shadow and, turning around, it appeared hers was also gone.

"I thought it might be worth a try," Vess said, his inexperienced emotions tugging in all directions. He knew his confusion was likely to be apparent on his face and so, checking his pack and sword were secure on his back, he took off up the slope without saying anything else. Roh followed, though made sure to keep a comfortable distance behind the warrior. She was as confused about what had just happened as Vess, and there was no way she was going to get close enough that the opportunity for talking might present itself.

"Right, I'm going in." Marcus gripped his staff, as if reaffirming its existence, and started towards the hole in the mountainside. It had been many minutes since everyone had arrived outdoors, and still there was no sign of the missing companions. The mage had rationalised that if anyone should go back it was him. "I only have to worry about a *pointy stick*, after all," he'd said, as Sathom and Erryn had attempted to change his mind.

"Wait! I think I hear something." Sathom once again moved inside, only to be met seconds later by Vess, taking large strides and looking far less exhausted than the last people to escape the soul shadows. Next came Roh, also lacking urgency.

"You made it. Excellent! What went on down there?" The mage's tone was clearly relieved.

Vess brushed past Marcus, positioning himself away from the group with his back turned towards them.

"Nothing 'went on'."

"He kissed me." Roh said as she set foot on the soil of her homeland. "Welcome to Torwick, everyone."

"*I* kissed *you*?" Vess snapped around, flashing a stern look at Roh.

"Ho, ho! It seems some people like a little passion with their 'running for their lives'." Hessan roared with laughter, a devious twinkle in his eyes. "I like it."

"You mean, we were out here worrying about you two, and you were both, what, getting to know one another?" Marcus asked, folding his arms and frowning.

The silver-clad warrior looked pensive before smiling, her cat-like eyes narrowing impishly.

"He *actually* had a good idea. Surprisingly, there seems to be a brain controlling that lump of man-flesh."

"Oh, do go on. I *have* to hear the story behind this one," Hessan prompted, seating himself on a boulder and pretending to get comfortable.

"I'm afraid you're in for a short bedtime tale. There was no passion. We were trapped, when Vess here simply suggested we turn our thoughts in a more... positive direction. We kissed – the shadows disappeared. End of story."

"So, we ran like terrified children when all we had to do was 'think positive'?" Athalir couldn't believe what he was hearing. He'd never have run if he'd known there'd been another way.

"It was a bit more than 'positive thinking', I assure you." Vess returned to his anti-social stance, making sure to hide his face from the group.

"Well, if mass-canoodling was the only other option, I'm happy to have a few wounds and aching legs. There are far too few females in this group, and I don't like stubble rash. If you get my meaning." The dwarf king sniggered at his own remark before turning his attention to a narrow cut on his upper arm.

The elf gave a low humph and returned to leaning against the mountainside. To everyone around him, the prince was simply being 'the prince'; irritable, proud, and unfriendly. However, anxiety about what he had to do weighed on him heavily. Though it was true recent events had left him frustrated, troubling him to a greater extent was the reminder he carried at his waist of the dreadful task awaiting him. He pushed his fingers into his belt-pouch, partly to check the vial of black blood was still there, and intact, but also as a physical aid to his own rumination. His fingertips smoothed across glass as if, somehow, he'd find an alternative to what the skaithen had ordered him to do etched across the surface of the tiny bottle. It was at that point he knew, he couldn't do it – not after Marcus had saved his life. He realised if he didn't do as the skaithen had ordered the deal was off. However, during their time in the cavern, he'd seen a courageous, quick-witted, and honourable man in the mage. *He just might be able to pull this off*, he thought to himself.

"What are you doing?" Lost in his thoughts, Athalir hadn't noticed Sathom's approach. Before he could prevent it, the elemental had ripped the pouch from the elf's waist.

"No! Don't touch that. You can't…" Athalir sprang away from the rock but, even as he spoke, he realised it was too late for protestation.

Predictably, the commotion drew the attention of the rest of the group, who watched on as Sathom proceeded to pull the vial from the leather pouch.

"What's that?" Erryn stood up to get a closer look at the object Sathom was holding up to the light.

"Skaithen 'blood', if I'm not mistaken." Sathom looked at Athalir, seeking a confirmation he didn't truly need.

"Why would you have that, Athalir?" Erryn gave the prince an accusatory look beyond the current capabilities of the emotionally-stunted Sathom. Even before she'd heard an explanation, the sense of betrayal was hard to ignore.

He remained silent, his head hung low with guilt. Sathom answered instead.

"I believe it is a means of summoning."

"Summoning what? A skaithen? Why would you need to…" Marcus cut his own question short. "Oh, I see. And the blood will bring him here, to us."

"Just how does this 'summoning' work exactly?" Hessan's curiosity overrode his urge to cut the elf down.

The Fell prince looked up with shame in his eyes as he answered the question.

"A drop of blood released from the vial will draw him, or part of him at least, to where it lands."

"Summoning? Draw *who* here? What's going on?" Roh was the only one who hadn't been present when the elf had admitted to liaising with a skaithen, and planning to kill Marcus at its behest.

"It's as I thought." Vess marched over towards Athalir, but was stopped in his tracks by Marcus. "You're still defending him? You should have let me kill him back in Geryndor!"

"I simply want to hear him out. Just... hold off on the killing for now, alright?"

Vess paused before stepping aside, a menacing glare remaining fixed on the prince.

"Have it your way… for now."

While the two men had been speaking, Athalir had been staring at Marcus, a questioning gaze that gave away his bewilderment at the human's efforts to protect him. The mage had saved his life before but, to do so at this point – just one moon ago, he'd have scoffed at the notion of entrusting his life to such a man. Yet Marcus had defended him in the face of his treachery, twice.

Before anyone knew what he was doing, the Fell prince had dashed to Sathom, snatched the vial from his hand, and thrown it a few feet into the cavern entrance.

"Athalir, no!" Erryn called out, anticipating the appearance of the starring character in her nightmares.

Inside the darkened mountain opening, the container smashed upon impact, its contents staining the rocky ground and a thin swirl of black rising up from the thick, bubbling liquid. The skaithen appeared fast. *Much faster than he had back in Sa'hahlenfell*, Athalir thought as he watched on, hoping he hadn't made a mistake

Hessan and Vess readied their weapons. Roh instinctively did the same, though she knew nothing of what they were preparing for. Erryn simply stood still, frozen in fear. However, both Sathom and Marcus remained apparently calm. When the black-haired being that resembled a man stood whole within the entrance, the tension in the air at its apex, he looked directly at Athalir and smirked, bearing a blaze of shard-like teeth. But his smugness was short-lived – as was he. With his body fizzling and disintegrating from the edges inward, the skaithen's expression turned to one of shock as he looked to either side, then turned his head a-hundred-and-eighty degrees to see the black rocks at his back. When his face turned around the right way, the horror in his eyes was the last thing to be seen. A terrible shriek echoed into the cavern before trailing off, as the last of his form disappeared completely.

CHAPTER TWENTY-THREE

Governor Alerick sat in the shadows of a room that, despite its vastness, had made him feel increasingly claustrophobic over the ages. He knew his current body would last a few more years, but, as he rubbed one age-spotted hand over the other, he recognised the desire for younger flesh seeping in at the back of his ancient mind. It seemed to present itself earlier with every vessel change. For many decades now, he'd been resisting the urge to switch bodies, knowing, as he always had, that longer-lasting youth may come at too great a price. Two vessels were enough for each governor's period of occupancy. They lived closeted lives, keeping hazards to a minimum, good health sustained by the best apothecaries Whitestone could provide. However, transplanting the soul before it was entirely necessary raised the chances of fate catching up. To run out of bodies – of sons – would see that hard-won immortality expire.

And that, thought Alerick, not for the first time, and with more than a hint of sarcasm, *would be such a waste.*

For now, it mattered not, as the choice was currently beyond his reach. One vessel was dead, the other far away, experiencing a free will that would surely affect its viability for habitation. As the skaithen had suggested, a new wife may need to be taken, new sons produced. But that would take time, and time was not on Alerick's side. Besides, wives were troublesome. He'd endured many over the thousand years he'd lived, and he was definitely not relishing the thought of breaking in a new one.

As shapes flickered across the walls, ambiguous dark patches brought to life by the light of a single candle, the head of the governors missed a breath, his heart forgetting to pump for a split second. He knew what it meant; he'd felt it before, long ago. The skaithen's energy had just been snuffed out, sending it back into the black void from whence it came – albeit temporarily. His thin lips formed a half-hearted smile. *Was it wrong to be pleased?* He asked himself. The skaithen had been brought into existence by nothing more than the governors' use of dark magic and the stain it had left upon their souls. Alerick despised the personification of evil that had attached itself to him. It was like his own shadow had been given form, twisted and soulless, and there to taunt him for the eternity he and the others had subscribed to. In the past, he'd looked into its black eyes and seen a reflection, and so he no longer looked.

Dark magic had taken its toll centuries ago, but he still remembered a time when his spirit was able to enjoy each youthful incarnation. In those days, it had been so much easier to justify what they'd done, to appreciate the benefits and disregard the terrible price. That first generation had felt deserved, even justified. What right did one race have to live without fear of death, while good men and women suffered grief at the loss of those they loved? While mages back in Torwick were dying at the hands of the priests, the Meranells lorded their longevity over others, disguised in the adornments of hospitality and friendship.

They'd not initially set out to harm anyone, to slaughter an entire race. Alerick had attempted to negotiate, sure as he was that the king *had* to know of a way to share the Meranell's fortunate condition. But King Niron had been selfish. Even as Alerick had told him of his people's suffering, of their premature deaths simply for bearing magic in their blood, still the Meranell's ruler refused to share the secret of immortal life. What else could they do after that? The lives of so many innocents could be saved, what the governors had done could not truly be wrong.

Such certainty carried the mages through the first century with relative ease. They enjoyed their advancing years to the full, secure in the knowledge that regrets would not be all they had to look forwards to. Any moments left unclaimed in that lifetime were theirs for the taking in the next, and the next after that.

But, as sons gave way to fathers and the past was eclipsed by the future, time, in its infinite duration, became irrelevant. Levity slipped away beneath a cloud of repetition, the uniqueness of life's ups and downs rendered tedious. The magic they'd borrowed from the darkness slowly leached their humanity, yet, before that, feelings of compassion, friendship, and love had become meaningless in an existence such as that of the governors. The best intentions faded away as the six men revelled in their own success.

Now, once again ready to meet a sixth decade, Alerick couldn't even remember what it was to love, to care. Many, many moons had passed, and countless hours had been lost to a mind that felt stretched too tight. The only people he'd shared those countless lives with were known to him via circumstance, not choice. If choice had been involved, there were only ever two people he'd wish to spend eternity with.

He closed his eyes and winced as the ancient memories rushed to fill the darkness. He'd been middle-aged when last he saw the people in his mind's eye, the only ones he still cared for. His wife, the woman he'd married for love as a man in his twenties, had died just two years before the mage's escape. She'd been his soul mate and his best friend and the months since her death had been the most painful he'd ever endured. But, in a Torwick that was becoming more and more hostile to mages and those that supported them, he'd almost been relieved she'd not lived to have to make a difficult choice. He also had their daughter to think of. Alerick tried to say her name aloud but it was as if his own vocal chords would not allow it. Instead, he remembered the circumstances that led to the last time he'd spoken to her.

It was midnight and the streets of the capital were empty under an enforced curfew. However, a sympathetic guard and his intellectually challenged brother had managed to clear a route through the back alleys, creating a small window of time for those who'd signed up for Alerick's flight to leave their homes and make their way to the rendezvous point. It was dangerous, and the chance of success was slim for each and every person, but they were all too aware of the likely consequence of remaining in Torwick. The priesthood's propaganda machine had been stealthy and concise, turning non-mage against mage, even pitting ordinary family members against their magically imbued kin. If they stayed it was only a matter of time before neighbours, friends, even family turned on them. And though their magic was more than a match for those wielding pitchforks and kitchen knives, no one wanted to harm the victims of the priesthood's manipulation.

As Alerick put the last of his most treasured possessions into his pack, he called to his daughter, urging her to hurry.

"I'm not going, father," she'd told him. "I'm not a mage. I don't see why I have to leave."

It broke his heart to take away everything from the young woman; to force her to leave behind her hopes, her dreams, the man she'd planned to marry. However, the alternative was her death, unless she… He remembered turning to look at her, seeing the guilt in her eyes as the blows came at the door.

"I'm sorry, father. I didn't want to tell, but James said it would be alright, that he'd take care of me. I'm *so* sorry."

The door flew open at the force of a guard's kick and Alerick was cornered like a frightened rabbit. But all that filled his mind was the safety of his child; he'd sacrifice himself if it meant she left unscathed.

The mage held up his hands, a recognised promise not to cast magic. As the guards grabbed his arms, he looked at his daughter's sorrowful face and was about to tell her not to worry, that he forgave her, when another guard caught sight of a pack in which Alerick had begun depositing a few of his daughter's belongings.

"What's this? You part of his plan, missy? This some kind of ruse to get us distracted was it?"

Alerick swore his daughter was not involved, begged the guards to let her go, but his words fell on deaf ears. Before he could free himself from the two guards gripping his arms, his daughter's body fell to the floor, blood gushing from the slash to her gut. At that point, a man that had always been known for honouring his promises hadn't a care for reputation or honour. Alerick had walked from his home that night and never looked back, stepping over the guards' burnt corpses as he shed his last tear.

He opened his eyes, forcing himself to stare into the shadows. Reacquainting himself with the man he'd become, he cut ties with the one he'd left many lifetimes ago. For Alerick *was* worthy of respect for all he'd achieved, he had no choice but to believe that. He had been the one to try, he'd been the one to plan, and he had been the one to lead the other governors throughout the ages. Without him, they were nothing but powerful mages who would have died at the hands of their executioners; too cowardly to fight, too stupid to flee. It was Alerick who'd coordinated their flight from Torwick. Together with the other governors and mage sympathisers, he and countless others of magic blood had left under cover of a moonless night. He'd taken them through the mountain caves when his peers had said it couldn't be done. He'd been the one to discover the ancient texts that would bring the six of them the power of dark magic. He'd carried them all. Now, and for so long, he wished to be rid of the men who'd followed him without question. Ironically, it was their faith in him, the faith that brought them here, he now despised. For what manner of man follows without question, no matter the path? And so, all his many lives he'd known nothing but contempt and mistrust.

Sometimes, when he sat in near-darkness, too afraid to light a candle for fear of seeing his own shadow, he realised he understood the reason the king had denied him and his followers. As years became decades, and decades became centuries, he'd become painfully aware immortality was no gift.

But he would continue to cling on to it no matter how many moments of clarity taunted him throughout his unending life. For it was all he had. He'd long ago chosen eternity over normality and, to that end, he had to have the courage of his convictions, or what was the point?

There in that darkened room, the head of the governors closed his grey eyes, his once-strong body feeling old before its time as if mocking the soul that stole it. Perhaps it would be simpler to allow the events the seer had foretold to come to pass.

"Do I really wish to fight it?" Alerick asked out loud. However, immortality was an addiction; painful, guilt-ridden, but an addiction all the same. He couldn't give it up. He had no will left to even try. A dark soul resided in place of the freedom-seeker who'd fled Torwick over one-thousand years ago, and it would not willingly relinquish its grip on infinity.

CHAPTER TWENTY-FOUR

The land the other side of the Dragon Crest Mountains was far different from anything most of the group had seen before. The visible terrain was a chaotic mix of light grey sand and darker grey rocks, speckled with tall, grassy clumps that swayed in the undemanding wind. The grass's faded-green hue added to the lifeless feeling the desert-like landscape projected. However, on the horizon, the barren vista ended abruptly with towering structures silhouetted against a red-tinged sky. From east to west, there was nothing else to steal attention. The air felt arid in the throats of those not accustomed to it and, though it was seasonably cold, not a drop of moisture appeared to have lingered long enough to freeze.

Torwick welcomed its visitors with nothing more than the sound of small stones rattling across the ground and the distant call of birds of prey.

For just seconds after the disappearance of the skaithen, a stony silence hovered around the highly-charged group of travellers, only ending when Erryn lunged at the elven prince, slamming her fist into his face before anyone could stop her. Athalir staggered backwards. Though taken by surprise – and clearly in pain, as he raised his hand to wipe a trickle of blood seeping from one nostril – he made no move to retaliate.

"What did you think you were doing? How could you?" she shouted, about to strike again with unabated fury, until Marcus dashed towards her from behind.

"Erryn, that'll do!" The mage grabbed her arms, firmly lowering them back down to her sides. But her ire was too great to contain. Snapping free from his hold, she spun around to face the one who restrained her.

"And *you!* How can you be so, so… ugh, annoyingly calm about this? He tricked us, lied to us – *twice!* It's *you* he planned to… to…! Why aren't *you* angry?"

"Well, I'm not exactly full of the joys of spring, but I'm sure Athalir had reason to do what he did. I'd simply prefer to hear his side before pummelling the man."

"But…"

"What good can possibly come from anger, Erryn? Clearly, the prince has regrets. Let's hear them, shall we?" Marcus smiled, attempting to lighten the mood, before setting his companion aside and taking a step towards the elf. In truth, the duplicity of one he'd decided to trust did trouble him. Yet, he'd recognised the prince's purpose when he threw the vial into the cavern entrance. Whatever his initial plan, something had obviously changed.

Hessan and Vess remained visibly furious, hands poised to reach for their weapons, while Marcus offered a lifeline to the prince. Roh simply stared, irritated by the diversion from her introduction to her homeland. She had little interest in the machinations of these strangers, and the least they could do, after she'd so graciously assisted them, was be polite.

"You're a trusting fool!" Erryn retorted, scowling at Marcus before removing herself from the impending discussion. She planted herself well away from the others, folded her arms stubbornly across her chest and glared at the ground, successfully hiding the pain in her now-swollen knuckles.

The air was thick with anticipation and barely restrained anger for the many painful seconds it took Athalir to find the right words. When finally he spoke, something of the Prince of Sa'hahlenfell had returned to the elf's demeanour. It may only have been that he held his head a little higher or pushed his shoulders a little further back than before. However, partnered with his words, those who'd met him in his homeland couldn't help but be reminded of his status.

"I did what I had to do, for my people. As their future king, I am honour bound, but as one of them I would not – could not – let an opportunity to save their lives slip from my grasp." The prince took a step closer to Marcus and addressed him directly, as if no one else were present. "When first we met, I saw you as nothing more than a human mage, kin to those who have indirectly caused the death of so many elves. It was all too easy to see your life as fair exchange for the lives of my friends, of my family. With all your talk of destroying the governors, I thought you to be a fool of the sort even his own people might not miss."

"Well, you got that part right." Marcus said, a small smile illustrating the ease with which he poked fun at himself.

"Yet, I was wrong. A fool you may be, but I know now the only thing that puts you in that category is the trust you placed in me. I've watched you fight, I've seen you try, and I've born witness to the emergence of a better man than I could ever hope to be. With your courage and determination, I think I realised some time ago that you were capable of doing what I alone could not – and you'd do so by fair means, rather than the foul I was too naïve to reject. I was simply too stubborn to accept that and let go of what had once been my only option."

"The 'deal' with the skaithen?"

"And thus, the governors, yes." Athalir went on. "But you have given me your trust freely, so now I return the whole truth in kind. I called the skaithen to me back in my homeland as you and your party slept. It was I who told him of you and Sathom, and your plan to destroy the governors. When he knew, the demand changed. He wanted you alive. Hands severed – but alive. I was to carry out such a heinous task and then summon him again – where you would be his to deal with."

Erryn, who'd listened intently, looked up from the ground and faced the elf.

"So you *did* cast the vial into the cavern entrance deliberately – to *kill* the skaithen? You knew what would happen to it?"

Athalir nodded.

"And how do we know you're not saying this now to save your own neck?" Vess asked, his eyes stern and unconvinced.

"You don't," the prince replied bluntly.

"You're not inspiring a lot of confidence with that answer, elf," Hessan said.

"I can only inspire as much confidence as he who judges me feels I'm worthy. I could make a concerted effort, if I believed Marcus to be easily swayed by a few well-chosen platitudes – but I don't. For once throughout this journey, I've been completely honest. I can do naught but hope the man before me – the *only* man present whose opinion I value – is as wise as I've assumed him to be. It's in his hands I place my life now."

Marcus stared at Athalir. He didn't know if he should feel honoured or concerned that the heir to Sa'hahlenfell's throne valued his opinion. Mostly, he was taken aback by the revelation that someone thought so highly of him – even if that same person had intended to kill him not so long ago. This was not a way of things he'd been used to, in any sense.

"Marcus, this is your decision. No one is more affected by any of this than you… but, for what it's worth, I believe him," Erryn said, as she stood at his side.

"So, one minute you're punching the man, the next he's the elven equivalent of Saint Martin of Lintoft? Hmm." Roh, who'd come to find the whole situation vaguely intriguing, spoke rhetorically, dismissing any response from Erryn with a wave of her hand before seating herself on a boulder to face the distant city.

Everyone was silent as Marcus ruminated. With his brow furrowed but his stance remaining passive, no one could tell in which direction his choice would fall. Everyone waited anxiously until, finally, their leader made his intention known.

"Well, the general consensus of opinion seems to be that I'm a fool, one way or another." Marcus looked down at Erryn and winked. "I can live with that." He clasped Athalir's hand and arm with both hands, smiling as the gesture was reciprocated. "Just promise me one thing."

"Anything." Athalir replied enthusiastically.

"No more deception from now on. I'm not sure I can take any more major revelations in this lifetime."

Marcus' expression was now serious – a rare look for the light-hearted man

"You have my word." The prince made his vow with defined sincerity.

"Good. Come. Time is short and we have many more miles to travel yet – isn't that right, Sathom?"

"Yes." Sathom nodded, and inwardly approved as Marcus chose clemency over any other option.

Much to Roh's apparent disappointment – but furtive relief – those she'd chosen to travel with were keen to leave Torwick as quickly as possible. She had little desire to return to the structured existence she'd grown up with, and this new-found bunch of wanderers seemed to encounter adventure the like of which she'd not experienced before. That in mind, when they asked her to guide them into Maervell, she feigned irritation, before agreeing as if the request were a terrible imposition. In reality, she'd made up her mind as she'd stared towards the city she called home. There was so much she'd never seen, so little she'd been allowed to do. She wasn't ready to return, not yet. If they hadn't asked for her help, she'd have found a way to engineer it so they would.

The exit from the mountains had brought the group to within a couple of hours walk of the next kingdom and, with Roh's direction, they made good time.

It was just past midday when they stepped over the border into Maervell.

"So, this is where we bid you farewell. Thank you for–"

"Oh, I'm not leaving." Roh cut Marcus off.

"You're not?" Vess asked, a little too hopeful-sounding for his liking.

"No. You're going to need me. Not a skilled swordsman among you." The woman made a point of looking Vess up and down with obvious disdain.

"Well, I'm not going to turn down an extra blade. Though, the remainder of this journey won't be easy. The path ahead is fraught with danger, apparently." Marcus looked earnestly at Roh, concerned she didn't quite know what she was letting herself in for.

"Oh, I'm counting on it," she replied, before readjusting her shield and marching off ahead of the others.

Vess grumbled under his breath, prompting a friendly slap on the back from Hessan.

"Never mind, horggen. You're still the one here with the biggest… sword." The dwarf gave a hearty laugh and followed Roh.

Everyone else fell in line and the whole group made their way further into the mysterious, overgrown land that was Maervell.

The further in they went, the more the companions were impeded by thick, twisted vegetation coming at them from all sides. A well-constructed road meandered beneath their feet, but, though it was far from being a dirt track, the rust-coloured cobbles were dappled with moss, and weeds had rooted in the mortar. It was as if no one had walked the road in decades. As they'd reached the top of a rise not far from the border, each could swear they'd spotted tall structures peaking above the trees in the distance. But in the dim light of the overgrown path, none could be certain their eyes hadn't deceived them. Still, the road appeared to be leading them in the direction of whatever they'd seen, and so they followed it, reassuring themselves it was there they'd find a place to rest. Strange screeches from within the eerie thickets removed any notion of spending the night where they were.

Roh had no knowledge of the land that neighboured her own, much to the scepticism of Athalir. He'd questioned her as they walked, his curiosity only intensifying when she'd finally admitted she was '*not permitted*' to venture anywhere outside Torwick, and Maervell was strictly forbidden. When he pointed out they'd met her in the mountain cavern, her icy glare was enough to put off even the persistent prince.

Moments later, Erryn came to an abrupt halt.

"Is that… is that a house?" she asked, squinting into the dark bushes. Sathom stepped off the cobbles, moving in for a closer look.

"It could well be. Perhaps we should aim to reach it."

Roh shoved past Sathom, using her shield to force her way further in.

"There seems to be a whole village in there."

"What? There can't be. Surely no one can get in or out of this mess," Vess said as he arrived at Roh's side.

"They could if this is only on one side. Marcus, can you… light things up a little?" Erryn turned to the mage, who was now looking over her shoulder.

"You want me to set fire to it?" He looked confused.

"Oh come now. You have more control than that. Just, make things glow – *without* the heat."

Marcus wished he had as much faith in his abilities as Erryn did, but he guessed that, if he concentrated on light rather than fire, he might manage to avoid turning the whole kingdom into a blazing inferno. Closing his eyes, he pictured a glowing orb. It took all his concentration to keep it from getting hot but, as he reopened his eyes, he sent the now-manifested ball of light gently through the largest gaps and on towards the supposed village.

There were multiple gasps as Marcus' orb hung over what was obviously a settlement. At least twenty stone cottages lay evenly spaced around a central object; some kind of obelisk, from what could be made out amidst the tangle of branches that spiralled it. Marcus positioned the orb atop the obelisk where it lit up a village abandoned. Doors hung on loose hinges, kept open by a lace-work of creeping plants. Some windows were still whole, but many others were bereft of glass where branches had broken inside. No candlelight shone from the cottages, no sign of sentient life could be seen. Marcus raised the orb higher and sent it floating towards the far side of the village, until it met with a mirror image of the overgrown plant life on the side nearest the cobbled road.

"It's totally surrounded," Erryn whispered.

"And empty." Roh looked away. "I don't wish to see this. Let's go" With that, she walked briskly back to the road, and continued before the others realised she'd gone.

"We're done here. Marcus, withdraw the light." Erryn clasped the mage's arm, and then, with everyone else, returned to the path.

A strange feeling of sadness came over Marcus as he drew the orb slowly back towards his outstretched hand. As it moved closer, a flash in the window of one of the cottages caught his attention. It was as if the trail of the orb's light had glinted off something reflective as it passed. A shiver travelled down his spine as it occurred to him; what he'd seen had been a pair of eyes. Eager to dismiss that notion, he received the orb, and immediately used his will to snuff it out. "Wait for me!" he called as he jogged to catch up with the group.

It was another few hours before the buildings they thought they'd seen in the distance became a reality. Many times along the way, they had noticed signs of a once-civilised community; hidden away, broken, and reclaimed by nature. With each sighting, the mood of the group grew more and more sombre. Many times along the way, Marcus felt they were being watched from the shadows, but said nothing.

CHAPTER TWENTY-FIVE

Maervell was a land whose people had simply vanished; this was the conclusion reached by everyone who now stood gazing up at the elaborate towers that soared into the sky all around them.

The afternoon sun highlighted intricate patterns as the rooftops tapered into twists and turns that should have been beyond the skill of any ordinary stonemason. Not one building was identical to another, even as far as the colour of the stone. From the same burnt orange of the cobbled road, to a grey so pale as to appear almost white, with every conceivable natural shade in between. However, no tower, no wall, no balcony was immune to the invasion of plant life. The entire city had been taken over by vines and tendrils snaking in and out of every opening. As the companions walked slowly down wide streets of mossy paving, it became evident this place was as devoid of civilisation as every other hamlet, village, and town they'd passed along the way. A quick glimpse inside windows had shown nothing but stillness – the kind of stillness that might be visible had the whole world been frozen in time. Furniture lay unmoved, candles still in place but unlit, plates left on tables as if laid out for an evening meal, a child's motionless rocking horse, fireplaces full of half-burnt logs. Shops still offered their wares, the blacksmith still had irons resting in what once would have been the hottest fire, and a magnificent library allowed a view of thousands of dust-covered tomes via two wide-open doors. With every step, any hope of finding a thriving city full of life, any possibility the desertion was simply relegated to the outskirts, evaporated.

"What happened here?" Erryn asked, the emptiness pervading her own emotions.

"It's… it's as if everyone was taken, right in the middle of whatever they were doing. Just gone," Vess replied.

"I'm beginning to think the priests knew about all this," Roh mumbled.

"What was that?" Hessan had arrived behind the warrior without her noticing.

"Oh, nothing, nothing. Where have you been, anyway?"

"Went to take a look in the tavern over there," Hessan said, pointing across the large central square in which they now stood.

Marcus turned to look.

"How did you know that was a tavern? The sign is written in a foreign language."

"Friend, when you spend as much time in taverns as I do, believe me, you know one on sight."

The mage chuckled.

"Did you find any ale?"

"Ha! I wish. Plenty of mugs on tables and barrels behind the bar but all bone dry. Not a drop. You know how long it takes for that much ale to go dry?"

"No. How long?"

Hessan shrugged.

"No idea. Thought *you* might. Thought we'd get an idea of how long the folk here have been gone if we could answer that."

"Why would that be something I'd know? No, wait, I don't think I want the answer to that." Something suddenly occurred to Marcus.

"Where's Athalir… and Sathom?"

Roh, Hessan, and Erryn all looked about for any signs of the missing members of the group, while Vess sat down on a stone bench and folded his arms across his chest.

"Athalir! Sathom! Where are you?" Marcus called out, his voice echoing around the square.

A moment's silence yielded to a shout from inside one of the buildings.

"I'm in the library. You have to see this."

"Well, that's Athalir accounted for. Sathom will be back soon, no doubt," Marcus announced before heading for the library doors.

"Wonderful!" Vess said, frowning

"Come on, Vess. We'd better see what he's found." Erryn attempted to coax her friend into going to meet the prince with her and the others.

"No. I think I'll wait here. Someone needs to keep watch."

"Fair enough." Erryn patted the big man on the arm before running off and disappearing into the weak light of the huge building.

Vess watched the young woman go, then closed his eyes. Shutting out the oppressively empty surroundings, he felt slightly more at ease. He'd kept it to himself, but he'd grown increasingly anxious as they'd progressed further into Maervell. Nothing about this land felt comfortable, least of all the darkened buildings filled with nothing but static shadows and inanimate objects. And it didn't help that the elven prince hadn't gotten lost, never to be seen again.

Inside the library, where a tall tree had rooted and grown beneath a broken skylight, Athalir stood at the back of the anteroom, holding a large leather-bound book in one hand and another smaller one open in the other. The books on the shelf in front of him had had the dust swept from their spines, and some were pulled farther forwards than others, fingerprints marking where they'd been grasped.

"What is it? What have you found?" Marcus asked as he entered the large, open lobby. He walked over to the prince, absent-mindedly glancing around before turning his attention to the open book Athalir was reading.

"These books, they're written in Fellian, elven – all of them." The prince spoke softly, but he sounded confused.

Marcus looked up as he heard the approaching footsteps of Hessan, Erryn, and Roh.

"How many books have you looked at? Perhaps this is the 'elven' section."

"You don't understand. There shouldn't be anything written in our language anywhere outside of Sa'hahlenfell. Not one book, let alone an 'elven section'. Athalir dropped both books to the floor, dashing behind the tree and up the three wide steps that led into the main library hall.

"What's wrong with him now?" Hessan asked as various thuds and thumps, accompanied by elven expletives, drifted out from the larger room.

"Something about all the books being written in elven, but I don't know why that's a problem," Marcus replied.

"Ah, well that explains the sign on the tavern – sort of. Though, it really shouldn't." Hessan was making even less sense than the elf.

"Will somebody please explain what in Nexephia's name is going on?" Roh's patience was wearing thin and her tolerance for the dwarf's ramblings even more so.

"Ugh. Don't any of you know anything? The elves of Sa'hahlenfell are the world's *only* elves. The clue's in the name – *the Fell.* It means true. There really shouldn't be anyone here that even knows of elven culture or language. A library of books written in Fellian – that's impossible. Or it should be. Now I know why that tavern sign looked so familiar. I dismissed the feeling I recognised it because it shouldn't have been there."

"Hold on, you speak elven? But you're a dwarf." Erryn looked puzzled.

"I know a little. A word here, a phrase there. What, I'm a dwarf, so I can't possibly be cultured, is that it?"

"No no no. I didn't mean…"

Hessan laughed.

"Forget it, lass. I know what you meant."

"Ah, there you are." Sathom stood in the doorway, Vess standing just behind him, glowering. "Come. I've found a suitable place to rest."

"Do we have the time?" Marcus asked, remembering the need to arrive at the sanctum ahead of the governors.

"We have made good time thus far. I think we could all benefit from a chance to relax. You all need to eat, and even I am tired of travelling at this point – mentally, at least."

"Good idea. I think I've had my fill of this particular deserted building. I trust the next one is just as pleasantly abandoned?" Hessan asked, sarcastically.

"It is," Sathom replied.

"Excellent," Hessan said, without enthusiasm.

Marcus went to the entrance into the next room and called out.

"Athalir. We're leaving. Come on."

"Should have left him in there – keep him out of trouble," Vess grumbled before following Sathom back into the fading light.

Once outside, everyone waited for Athalir, who soon emerged, clutching a book, and looking to all the world like a lost, confused child. He wouldn't speak when spoken to and offered nothing further on the subject of his native language and its existence in Maervell. The first sound to leave his mouth was an intake of breath when they arrived at the place Sathom had discovered.

After walking through gradually less built-up streets for almost half an hour, the group came to the foot of a gentle incline. A path that bore signs of once being ornately decorated led the eye up and up, finally to rest upon a high wall. However, it was what the wall encircled that prompted Athalir's astonishment.

Sharply-pointed turrets reached so far into the evening sky they seemed to touch the clouds, and supporting them were towers of stone that looked like they'd been plaited by the hands of a giant. Everything beneath the twisting shafts remained hidden until the companions walked through a gigantic set of elaborate silver gates, when the full splendour of the palace became apparent. Before their eyes, a sprawling structure made up of numerous graceful archways, pillars, and buttresses held a central position in an expansive garden. Twin fountains stood on either side of the front courtyard, the water long since evaporated, and ivy climbing its way around in a never-ending loop. But, much to everyone's surprise, the palace itself appeared immune to the invasion of nature that had rampaged through the rest of Maervell. Approaching the front doors, which were tightly closed, glass could be seen in windows and, except for the odd weed rooted here and there, the walls remained intact and free of plant life.

"I thought you said this building was empty?" Hessan couldn't take his eyes off the palace as he addressed Sathom.

"And it is," Sathom replied, pushing on both doors to open them wide enough for all to see inside.

The majestic hall ahead may well have been as untouched as if the occupants of this palace still resided there, but no one stirred within and no candles were lit. Silence prevailed, as it had everywhere else.

"Why?" Erryn whispered, entering the building and slowly wandering about the marble floor.

"Why what?" Roh asked, following the hexan inside.

"Just... why? Why this whole kingdom? Why the lack of people? Why is this... this beautiful place not the same as the villages, the city below? Why?"

Once everyone was within, Sathom pulled the hefty metal doors shut. The fact he'd found no resistance in either opening or closing them simply added to the confusion. With no one to maintain the hinges, they should have seized ages ago.

This fact had not gone unnoticed by Marcus.

"Sathom, are you sure no one's here? It all looks remarkably well-kept, especially compared to everywhere else we've seen."

"I've checked, thoroughly. I am confident not a soul remains here. Though, I will admit, I cannot be certain this palace has been empty as long as the rest of the kingdom, or that somebody will not return here at any time."

"You mean, you've brought us to someone's home while they're out for a stroll? Wonderful!" Hessan rushed to stare out of one of the giant windows that accompanied the double-doors, taking one of his axes in hand.

There are signs it has not been inhabited in at least a week." Sathom attempted reassurance.

"Oh, a week. So they've not just popped out, they've gone to visit their ailing relative in the next town. Well, that's alright then. I'm sure they'll be pleased to see we've come to keep the place warm." Hessan finished up muttering something under his breath while maintaining his watch through the window.

"The dwarf's right. Something about all this is making my skin itch. We shouldn't be here." Roh fidgeted with her gauntlets, glancing quickly about the room as if expecting someone, or something, to attack from the shadows.

"What signs, Sathom?" Marcus thought it was high time someone took the measured, logical stance, instead of resorting to panic.

"Candles have not been lit in some time, the wax has begun to stiffen and crack. There's a fine layer of dust on the surfaces. Spoilt food remains in the kitchens. Need I go on?"

"And there's something else none of you seem to have considered," Erryn chirped up, stepping back from the display cabinet she'd been inspecting. "This isn't any ordinary home. It's a palace, the kind nobility, even royalty would keep. Even if the owners weren't present, the place would be alive with servants at this hour. It wouldn't just be left empty."

Marcus smiled.

"Good point. I knew I brought you along for a reason." He nudged the redhead, playfully. "I think it's safe for you two to relax." Hessan and Roh glanced at each other, an unspoken agreement to reserve judgement, just in case. "Now, let's get some light in here. It's getting darker by the moment." The mage walked to the nearest candelabra and cast the only magic he was confident at. Flicking a flame into life between his thumb and forefinger, he lit each one of the five half-burnt stubs. "Athalir. Everything alright over there?" Marcus called over to the elf who'd been studying something at the far side of the room.

"Light. Excellent. Bring that over here, would you?" the prince said in reply.

Marcus complied, grabbing the candelabra and striding over to the sideboard at which Athalir stood.

"What is it, elf? More books you're able to read?" Vess could find neither interest in Athalir's discoveries, nor sympathy for whatever upset him back at the library.

"More writing in Fellian, yes. But not in a book this time." The elf ignored the warrior's acerbic tone.

With Marcus at his back, holding out the candles so the light was cast downward, Athalir could see what he'd been holding in more detail. Erryn hastened to his side, her curiosity brimming over.

"*Di heth altah, sheath frith tae oth thell. Leth, dieth fe frith.*" Athalir looked up from scrap of parchment from which he'd read the elven words aloud. "That does *not* sound good."

Vess, suddenly interested, rushed over.

"What? What does it say?"

"Di heth…"

"Yes, we heard that bit already. What is it in the common tongue?"

"Exactly? It translates to, '*In the end, death comes for us all. Pray, let it come.*'"

"So, we're now going to spend the night in the dark, empty palace where the final words of the last person here included begging for death. This journey gets better and better." Hessan gave a low, almost humourless laugh.

"You didn't have to accompany us, dwarf. Ah, hold on, you had to come to avoid ruling a kingdom of people who despise you," Athalir said, calmly placing the parchment back onto the sideboard, his back to the dwarven king.

"That's right, they do despise me, but at least I'm honest about my failings. Or is planning to murder your companions your idea of a leadership quality?"

Athalir whipped around to face Hessan, brandishing a dagger before anyone could stop him. Having turned to walk away, proud of his quick-witted retort, the dwarf was knocked to the ground from Athalir's flying assault. Marcus attempted to intervene, but Sathom caught his eye and shook his head.

With Hessan face down on the floor, the prince dug his knees into his foe's back and pinned his arms with one hand. Poking the point of his dagger to Hessan's neck, Athalir leant down to his ear and spoke quietly.

"I could kill you easily, dwarf. Remember that."

"Athalir! That's enough!" Erryn said, forcefully. "You've made your point."

"Aye, that he has," Hessan said, rolling onto his back as Athalir reluctantly released him. After a few moments staring each other down, the elf offered his hand to his grounded companion. Hessan accepted the offer, staggering to his feet. The two men nodded, then clasped each other by the forearm, apparently putting an immediate end to the animosity.

"Ugh, I will never understand men." Erryn sighed, remembering the fights she'd witnessed among her male peers back home, and how quickly all had been forgiven. She'd thought such behaviour had been the domain of the village boys, but clearly not.

"Right, now you two are done with the male bonding, can we find somewhere in this place to eat and sleep?" Roh was not so ignorant of the ways of men, having trained with male soldiers since she was old enough to wield a sword.

The others collectively agreed, none wanting to linger where the ominous note had been left, and all trying to ignore the possibilities awaiting them in other rooms. One thing was certain; none of them intended to let down their guard during their stay.

As they followed Sathom through long corridors and various rooms in the direction of a dining hall, Vess spoke in a low voice as he walked alongside Hessan, well behind everyone else.

"I don't understand. Why did you not fight back? Why'd you let him get away with putting you down like that?"

Hessan gave a knowing smile.

"Respect, horggen, respect." Vess tilted his head to one side. The dwarf chuckled. "The elf and I have been locking horns since we first met, and would have gone on doing so until blood was shed. It was never about the hatred he felt towards my race, nor the contempt I held for his, not really. We're leaders. King or prince, it makes no difference, both of us had something to prove. A man can't respect another who holds back, who takes the blows, who stays down when put down because, if nothing else, he never knows when the worm will turn."

"And… you saw the worm turn?"

"Ha ha! No, I'd never have seen that coming. Had I waited for a *worm* moment, I'd have been slaughtered while I slept. What happened there was Athalir redressing the balance, meeting my test with honest courage – something any warrior can respect."

Vess thought on what his companion had said.

"So, you were… testing him?"

"That's right, horggen." Hessan slapped Vess across the back and laughed once again. "Come on. I'm bloody starving and we're losing sight of the others. I don't know about you, but I just want to eat, sleep, and get out of this place."

Vess nodded in agreement, and the pair picked up the pace until they'd caught up with the group, just in time to enter the largest dining hall any of them had ever seen.

Inside the expansive hall, an elaborate wooden table the length of a small sea-faring vessel provided more than enough seating to accommodate the group at least twenty times over. Marcus wasted no time in bringing to life the numerous candles, both on the table and around the walls, gradually making the room more and more inviting as the light eliminated shadowy corners. Multiple floor-to-ceiling windows lined the external wall but, with daylight fading, more light was required.

While everyone else seated themselves at one end of the table, fishing around in their packs for whatever rations were left, Sathom disappeared through a door. He returned a few minutes later with a small collection of various foods in his arms.

"There is much more where this came from." The elemental said as he arrived at the table to deposit his pickings.

"Food!" Marcus cried out. "Real food!" With that he sprinted off in the direction Sathom pointed.

Erryn laughed.

"I'd better go help him carry… and stop him from eating it all before he gets back." She got up from the table and ran to the door, leaving the others to start picking at the nuts, fruits, breads, berries, and salted, cooked meats laid out before them.

"How has all this remained fresh?" Roh asked as she chewed.

Sathom watched on, content to see his corporeal comrades relish the food.

"There is a larder in the kitchens, cold enough to store ice, I'd wager. The temperature must have kept the food from spoiling in there."

"Mm, well I *really* hope the owners don't arrive back before we've finished all this. That parcel of jerky in my pack just won't taste right now," Hessan said, reaching across the table to grab a handful of berries that had been covered in a fine layer of sugar. "Ah, honey." Cramming the berries into his mouth it became clear the sugar had been glued on by a slick of the amber nectar.

After quite some time of light-hearted conversation, by which time most of the food on the table had gone, Marcus and Erryn's absence became noteworthy.

"They've been gone a while," Vess remarked. "You think we should go help them?"

"What? Interrupt their moment alone? Only if you like singed eyebrows," Hessan joked.

"Are they courting?" Roh asked. "I had no idea."

Athalir smiled.

"That depends on your definition of courting."

"They keep *almost* courting." Vess tried to elaborate, but Roh's puzzled expression made it obvious he'd not assisted much.

"It would help if the idiot didn't go sleeping with dwarven noble lasses," Hessan added.

"He did? The womaniser! How many?" If it were possible Roh looked both shocked and intrigued.

"I do not think we ought to be discussing this," Sathom interjected.

"Just the one… it was just the one, right, Vess?" The dwarf looked to his friend for confirmation.

"I hope so. Yes. Yes, I'm sure it was – and that was only because he was drunk."

Roh leant forwards on her elbows, eager to catch up on the gossip.

"Ah, so he's a *drunken* womaniser, then?"

Sathom sighed.

"Um, no, I wouldn't say that. He's just…" Vess was interrupted by Athalir.

"Desperate?"

"Hey, she's a bonny lass, that larn's daughter – if a bit… eager." Hessan smiled to himself.

"You *didn't*?" Roh grinned at Hessan.

"What can I say? When your wife hates you, you take it when it's offered."

Roh erupted with laughter, her infectious mirth soon having the others, except for Sathom, laughing too.

"Did we miss something funny?" Marcus appeared at the table without anyone noticing. He carried a crate filled with dusty bottles. "I found wine, but it looks like none of you need it."

Erryn was right behind, holding a tarnished silver tray of food which she set on the table. She looked a little flushed and was uncharacteristically quiet.

"I'm not sure we should let you anywhere near the wine, Marcus." Roh winked at Hessan as the mage rested the crate next to the feast and sat down.

"Um, you're not?"

"No, the only 'eager' dwarf here is Hessan, and I really don't see that ending well. Wait, you did say you'd take it when it was offered, right, dwarf?"

Hessan jabbed at the warrior woman in a mock punch, flashing a wicked smile.

"Sorry, Marcus, just ignore her. I think the pressure's finally affected the woman. Come, eat. After all, you must have worked up an appetite. Carrying all those bottles, I mean." Hessan and Roh shared a look and chuckled. Sathom groaned. Athalir smiled, but stopped when he saw an irritated look on Erryn's face.

"Yes, Marcus, Erryn, grab your fill before this greedy pair reach for seconds."

Marcus didn't need telling twice and tucked into a thick slab of bread, adding some meat to his mouth before he'd even started to chew.

Soon, the wine and conversation were flowing fast. For the first time since their journey had begun, it seemed they were finally getting to know one another. Erryn shortly returned to her usual cheerful self, and even Sathom relaxed enough to join in with the banter, though secretly wishing he could still laugh.

With only dried up rations to eat for the last few days, the relatively small meal was akin to a banquet, and the wine was pleasantly aiding the mood.

After a couple of hours, Vess realised tiredness was beginning to set in, but, though he was more at ease than he'd been since waking up in the crypt, the idea of sleep still gave rise to a fear he had no wish to confront. His head was starting to feel foggy, and an urge to be alone and quiet was emerging. He didn't know how much longer he could force his body to reject sleep, but he didn't intend to worry about it this night

"I don't know about anyone else, but I think I've had my fill. If everyone wants to find a bed for the night, I'll stay on watch."

Roh stood up.

"Not on your own, you won't."

Vess frowned.

"It's fine, I don't mind."

"I don't care if you *mind*, you look three sheets to the wind. If you think I'm entrusting my safety to *you*, you're sorely mistaken. We can take it in turns to sleep. If you slip up, I wake easy. Come on, the entrance will be the best place." Roh collected her sword and shield and led a grumbling Vess out of the dining hall.

"Hah! Poor Vess." Hessan said, also picking up his things and rising from his seat. "I'm going to make do in here. Don't fancy traipsing the halls of this place in search of a room. There's a chaise over there. That'll do."

"There are bedrooms just up the first flight of stairs, Hessan. Are you sure you would rather stay in here, alone?" Sathom asked.

"Yep. Never have been one for comfort. Makes a man drop his guard. I'll be just fine here."

"In other words, he's afraid of things lurking in dark corridors," Athalir mocked.

"Damn right I am. Now go, get out of here so I can make myself uncomfortable."

They said their goodnights, then Sathom took Athalir, Marcus, and Erryn out of a door that had gone unnoticed before, a sweeping staircase staring back at them from across a wide corridor.

The stairs were numerous to allow for reaching the level above such grandiose, high ceilings. Once on the next floor, Sathom outstretched his arm to indicate another, slightly narrower corridor, punctuated by many doors.

"There are plenty of rooms. Take your pick."

"Where shall you be, Sathom?" Marcus asked after taking just one step forwards.

"I will be in this first room; awake, obviously, should you need me." He opened the door to the right of the corridor and stepped over the threshold. "Goodnight, and rest well. I shall wake you just before dawn." With that, the elemental went into the bedroom, closing the door behind him.

"I take it you two have no preference?" Erryn looked to Marcus and Athalir, making her way to the next room along from Sathom when the two men shook their heads. With her hand on the doorknob, she turned as if to say something to Marcus, but seemed to change her mind before the words were uttered. Instead, she opened the door and disappeared inside.

Marcus was about to take the first room on the right when Athalir grabbed hold of his arm.

"You know, you'll regret inaction until the day you die."

"What?" Marcus stared at the elf, tiredness diminishing his patience for the abstract.

"A blind idiot could see there's something between you and Erryn. Are you simply going to allow yet another opportunity to tell her how you feel pass you by?"

"I… have no idea what you…"

"Fahldis!"

"Excuse me?"

"It means horseshit."

"Oh, alright then." Marcus tried to walk away but again was held back.

"You know exactly what I speak of. I see it. Vess may be all muscle, but he *definitely* sees it. Even the dwarf knows how you feel about her."

"Well, good to know everyone knows more about my feelings than I do."

"Not everyone. Roh was oblivious, apparently." Athalir smiled, a mischievous glint in his eye. "Look, I have a great amount of respect for you, Marcus, but if you go from this place without at least trying to be honest with her… well, time is a river, my friend. None of us know when it will run dry."

"Is that what you'd do? Be honest?" Marcus asked.

Athalir's eyes took on a faraway stare, his lids became heavy.

"I'm an elf. Matters of the heart are… well, we don't get a choice."

Marcus noted the sudden shift in the man's demeanour and looked at him with concern. Athalir let go of the mage's arm.

"I've said enough. Just… think on it. Arnah-hain, my friend – rest well."

The prince left Marcus standing alone in the corridor, trying very hard not to think; but the more he attempted to avoid thought, the more the memory of the all-too-brief kiss he'd shared with Erryn in the larder earlier that evening revisited him.

Finally, he opened the door to his room and went inside, lighting a single candle on the bedside cabinet before lying on the bed, fully clothed.

Roh paced back and forth across the entrance hall, looking bored, while Vess lay on a chaise, pretending to sleep. They'd each assisted the other in removing their metal plate and a pile of gold- and silver-toned armour now lay in a pile on the floor.

"Why do you do that?" Roh blurted out.

Vess remained silent.

"I know you're awake."

The male warrior inwardly cursed the woman's innate ability to annoy him.

"Why do I do what?"

"Lie about sleeping. You tell them you sleep, yet I know that to be untrue."

Vess opened his eyes and turned his head to watch Roh as she walked from wall to wall.

"I do sleep. Why would you think otherwise?"

"Because I know what sleeplessness looks like." Roh stopped pacing and came to stand closer to where Vess lay. "I've witnessed soldiers who've spent too many nights on the wall. Too proud to tell their superiors they need respite, they pretend. They fear they'll be considered weak and lose face among their comrades. Only, I can see it in their eyes."

Vess sat up, leaning forwards with his arms resting on his thighs.

"What? What do you see in their eyes?"

"I don't know, it's like… like death, marching forwards from a distance, the gap between it and the soldier's soul ever closing. It's like a light dimming with each new day that comes without sleep to greet it." Roh knelt down on one knee in front of Vess, lifting his chin with her hand. "It's a coldness that you should never see in the eyes of the living, and I see it in yours."

"Thank you for your concern, but…"

"Oh, I'm not concerned. I'm curious."

"Right." Vess abruptly rose from the chaise, almost knocking Roh over. "I'll take over now. Get some sleep."

"Oh no, I don't give up that easy. You didn't answer my question."

"Dammit, woman! What question? What do you want from me?" Vess' voice was raised and irritated.

She stood up and blocked his path as he tried to walk to the door.

"Why do you lie? What's wrong with you?"

"Nothing. Nothing's *wrong* with me." He frowned as Roh folded her arms across her chest and fixed him with a determined glower. He attempted to walk around her, but she stepped in front of him each time he moved. He considered throwing her over his shoulder and physically planting her elsewhere, but something occurred to him just in time.

"Hold a moment. You're that curious about why I *lie*, but you don't want to know why I don't *sleep*?"

"I care not why you don't sleep. That's your business. If you were a soldier under my command, I'd insist you tell me, but–"

"You command soldiers? Well, that explains a few things."

"Yes, but that's not the point. You lie to those you fight alongside, the ones you travel with day and night. The ones you've just shared wine and food with. What kind of a person does that?"

"Er, Athalir?"

Roh moved her hands to her hips.

"That was different. He lied to save his family. Besides, you would have had him eviscerated for the lie he told. Is it somehow more acceptable for you to lie?"

Vess made to push her out of the way, failing again as she held out her hand against his chest.

"From what I gather, you've known Marcus longer than most. You call him friend, yet you give him falsehoods every time you offer to take watch. I'd simply prefer to know the man at my back in a fight can be trusted with my life, when it seems he can't be trusted with the truth."

"Aren't you forgetting I saved your life once already? Now let me *pass*, woman." Vess pushed harder this time, causing Roh to stagger sideways.

"You only did that because you had something to prove," she said through gritted teeth.

"Yes, that you needed saving," Vess growled back.

"I did not!"

"Yes, you did!"

"*No!* I didn't!"

"*Yes!* You–!"

Before Vess could finish, he was silenced by Roh's lips firmly pressed against his. He reciprocated without pause, the conflict between them sparking a fire over which both had little control. With her hands either side of his face, the woman pressed her body firmly against his, backing him hard into the wall. With just a tunic and trousers covering her now, Vess could feel every exquisite curve as his hands explored faster than he could think. Knowing he was hers,

Roh's hands left Vess' face and travelled down his torso, finding the bottom of his own tunic and tracing every taught muscle beneath. The two of them swapped position over and over, the embrace barely breaking until, eventually, he hoisted her from the ground, carrying her to the chaise as she wrapped her strong legs tightly around his waist. Laying her down, he stood up to tug off the tunic, casting it aside as Roh hastily did the same with her own clothing. As the giant warrior lowered his body to hers, Roh pulled him in closer.

"I did… *not*… need… saving," she said, her words competing with deep breaths.

"Well, maybe I do," Vess managed to say before their passion took away all chance of talk.

Atop a large wooden bed, still made up with a sumptuous fur blanket, Marcus had spent too long trying to sleep. However, each time he closed his eyes, Erryn's smiling face appeared before him. He could still feel her lips softly brushing against his own, smell the scent of her hair as if it were still touching his cheek. When they'd gone to the larder to fetch the food and wine, they'd talked – really talked, more than they had the entire time they'd known each other. They'd laughed and joked about the others, shared their feelings about the quest, even told a tale or two about their lives before any of this had come to be. It was only as they'd realised they'd been gone a while, and decided to head back, that something had happened; a kiss neither had intended, but that felt as natural as if it had been something they did every day. It was as they talked that Marcus realised he was in love. He'd hoped Erryn felt it, too, but, when she'd pulled back from the kiss and acted as if there'd been nothing between them, his heart sank. Athalir had advised him to go to her, to be honest about his feelings, but, though he was no stranger to rejection, he knew this time was different. He knew he'd never truly loved a woman before Erryn, and that made the stakes so much higher. The thought of her turning him away was painful enough, without actually making it a reality.

Once more, he tried to sleep. He was certainly tired enough.

"Ugh, this is no good," he said to himself, swinging his legs to the floor and sitting up on the edge of the bed. Earlier, the room had grown cold so he'd lit a small fire in the hearth. Now, he was too hot. Taking off his tunic, he relished the feel of a stray draft brushing over his sweat-moistened skin. Shadows seemed to dance around the room, brought to life by flames and candlelight. Marcus looked around, and noticed a bookcase next to a tall arched window. Hoping a book might help, he got up and went to select something to read.

"More elven!" he grumbled, snapping the leather binding shut and returning the book to its shelf.

He stood in front of the fire looking deep into the flames, remembering the fire he'd slept by in Benedict's cottage.

"Ah, Benedict. What would you have said about all this? Probably told me to grow a backbone and cuffed me around the ear." Marcus laughed. "Dammit! You know what? You'd be right, old friend. It's about time I stopped whining and acted like a man. So what if she rejects me? It's not like I haven't been there before. It's not like I'm made of glass." The mage dashed to the bed to grab his tunic, his mind made up. "I'm going to tell her, I'm going to go to her room and…"

A light tap at the bedroom door interrupted his speech.

Great! Probably Vess come to moan about Athalir. Wonderful timing! He thought.

Dropping his tunic back onto the bed, he went to the door and opened it, expecting to see his warrior friend complete with brooding scowl. To his surprise, Erryn stood in front of him, looking up with wide eyes and slightly-parted lips, and fidgeting with her sleeve.

"Marcus, I, er… I…" Erryn stumbled over her words.

"Erryn, I was just, erm, I thought I'd, um, pay you a visit," Marcus said, the confidence of moments ago washing away.

"You did? I mean, you were? I mean… why?"

Marcus wanted the ground to open up and swallow him, but Athalir's words echoed around his mind; *Time is a river, my friend. None of us know when it will run dry.*

"Come in," he said, gently clasping Erryn's hand and leading her inside.

Erryn let herself be led, kicking the door closed behind her. When they were in the middle of the room, Marcus motioned for her to sit in an armchair that sat near to the fireplace, where the orange glow warmed her tingling skin, its light reflecting in her brown eyes.

Standing before her, the nerves began to return. This time, he quashed them and spoke before any more thought got in the way.

"I love you, Erryniya Constantine."

Erryn felt her stomach tighten, twisting into knots. Nothing in her mind felt like the right thing to say. Nothing felt real. Then she remembered the sight that had caused her heart to ache back in Geryndor.

"Is that what you said to her? To that dwarven woman?" she asked, her tone cutting through Marcus' declaration.

"No, of course not. I'm not sure she'd have appreciated being called Erryniya Constantine." Marcus gave a cheeky smile, but stopped when it became instantly obvious Erryn hadn't shared his sense of humour. "Erryn, please forgive me for that… for what I did. You and I weren't, well, I didn't think there was anything between us. You acted coldly towards me. I'm so used to that, I felt sure my chance had gone. You have to believe me – I'd never have… done that, if we'd… if…"

"But we've known each other such a short time. You… you can't love… it's just too soon."

Erryn wanted to stay angry with him, to walk away and never look back – but in truth, when he'd said he loved her, all hope of an exit had begun to dwindle.

"Erryn, we might be short of time. Why would I *wait* to love you? We're here, together, right now. Surely that's all that matters?"

"Oh, so that's all it is. You think we could die, so you're taking your happiness wherever you find it. Great! Thanks for that." She jumped up from the chair, glaring at the man with her arms folded defensively across her chest.

"No… no, that's not what I meant at all."

"No?"

"No!" Marcus did his best to sound definite, inwardly cursing his own inability to make sense when it really mattered.

Erryn turned away, fearing her face may give away the ache in the pit of her stomach.

"Erryn, look at me." He gently turned her around to face him, keeping his hand resting on her shoulder, taking extra care to say what was in his heart this time.

"When I look at you I see a part of me I've always been blind to. I see magic – beautiful, courageous, *stubborn*, magic. You have shown me so much. How not to be afraid, how to feel, how to efficiently set fire to things…" He smiled the smile that Erryn could never be immune to, tilting her chin upwards until he looked straight into her eyes. "How to be the man I was meant to be. You say it's too soon to say I love you – I only wish I'd said it sooner."

A hush settled in the air. Erryn's wide eyes looked intently up at Marcus, a glint of wetness appearing at the bottom of each eye.

"Are you… are you crying?" Marcus asked, looking anxious.

"No, I'm… Well yes, but…"

"Erryn, I'm sorry, I never meant to… Perhaps I shouldn't have said anything, I'm so sorry." Marcus' eyes were downcast and sorrowful as he turned away.

"Marcus?" Erryn put her hand on his forearm and made him face her.

His sad face was just too much for her to bear. This tall man, who should have been everything she despised, had come to mean more to her than she could ever have imagined.

As his broad torso caught her attention, not for the first time, she stepped closer and looked up into his eyes, for once grateful for the binding that held his hidden soul.

"Kiss me." She said, with a small smile.

Marcus leant forwards eagerly, about to wrap his arms around the woman he loved, but stopped without warning.

"Wait – are you sure?"

"Marcus, I love you, too. I'm sure." Erryn said, her certainty clear as she looked into his eyes.

With nothing standing in their way and all doubts removed, they kissed as if for the first time.

When she needed to draw breath, Erryn stepped away, her eyes still firmly fixed on his as she looked up from beneath her lashes. Taking his hand, she walked backwards towards the bed, seating herself on the end and drawing Marcus to join her. Telling her he loved her again, he kissed her tenderly and gently lowered her down onto the furs, snuffing out the candlelight with a click of his fingers leaving the fire to smoulder through the night.

CHAPTER TWENTY-SIX

Roh sat bolt upright on the floor, having been rudely awakened by Vess' shriek. Grabbing her tunic to cover her modesty, she looked around the dimly-lit room for Vess, who was standing naked at the window, staring out into the darkness and clutching his sword.

"What's going on?" she mumbled, wincing from the bruises of the night before as she staggered to her feet.

"I saw eyes, out there!" Vess replied, pointing through the glass.

Roh pulled her tunic over her head and went to the other window, peering into the grounds outside.

"Well, I can't see anything. You slept, you must have dreamt it."

"I know what I saw!"

"Of course you do." Roh slapped his backside. "Put some clothes on, soldier. It's time we were getting ready to leave."

Vess reluctantly moved away from the window and scanned the floor for his trousers.

"How did you know I slept, anyway?" he asked, collecting the remainder of his garments and getting dressed.

"I watched you."

"That's… disturbing."

"Relax. I merely wanted to make sure you did. You needed it – and what happened before, I suspect. How was it?"

"Erm, it was… good, er, nice… and good. Yes, very good, thank you."

Roh laughed.

"No, not that. The sleep, you fool. How was the sleep?"

"Oh." Vess' cheeks flushed with embarrassment. "I slept, yes, though it was full of nightmares. Then, I was awakened by what I thought was a scream, hence why I got up to investigate and saw the eyes. But yes, I suppose I… needed it."

"Good. You owe me. Don't forget that." Roh loosely plaited her long hair as she perched on the edge of the chaise, her belongings gathered at her feet. "Come on, we'll help each other with our armour and go grab something to eat before we set off. Who knows when we'll get good food again?"

The pair of them fully-armoured once more, Vess sheathed his sword at his back and slung his pack over the other shoulder. The warrior woman was about to head off towards the dining hall, when he held her back.

"Wait. What do we tell the others? Are we…"

"We never speak of what happened again, you understand? Not a word."

"But…"

Roh spun around to face him, scowling.

"No buts. It was a release for that pent-up… 'whatever it was' of yours, you hear? Nothing more. I did you a favour, let's just leave it at that."

Vess was confused, and he didn't like it. He felt foolish, but he had too much pride to hang around long enough for confirmation

"Fine." He shoved past the woman and set off briskly towards the dining hall, neither stopping to check nor caring if she followed him.

Roh flung her plait over her shoulder and, just for a moment, looked after him with regret, before following at a slower pace.

Athalir, Hessan, Marcus, and Erryn had been seated at the table for just a few minutes, having some bread and berries for breakfast, when Vess marched in, shortly followed by Roh.

"Ah, there you both are. We thought we'd have to collect you two sleepyheads on the way out," Marcus called out. "Come, have some food before we leave."

Roh seated herself at the table next to Hessan.

"He's cheerful this morning," she whispered to the dwarf as she reached to grab a chunk of bread.

"He's in love. He and Erryn skipped in here this morning holding hands and staring into each other's eyes," Hessan whispered back.

"Really?"

"Well, not quite, but, I know when a man's gotten lucky. It's a sixth sense. That, and the elf told me he heard Erryn go into our leader's room last night. And saw her come out with him this morning."

Roh gave an insincere smile, inwardly hoping the dwarf didn't really have such a sixth sense.

Vess took some food, but stood at the end of the table rather than sitting.

"Where's Sathom?" he asked.

"He left the map in his room – he's gone back to fetch it. He said we should be ready to leave when he returns," Athalir said, getting up from his chair and picking up his pack. "I'm going to the larder to stock up on a few things for the journey. I won't be long"

The others watched as the elf left, then finished their food and washed it down with the water Sathom had procured from a well outside.

By the time Athalir returned with a pack bursting at the seams with food, there was still no sign of Sathom.

"What's keeping him? He can move about in seconds." Marcus wanted to get on with what he had to do – all the more, now he had a reason to get back to the village as soon as possible. Since he'd woken up at Erryn's side that morning, he'd thought of nothing but starting a new life in Eldenvale with her. His imagination was full of an idyllic existence awash with cosy fireside evenings and lazy Sunday mornings. He wanted nothing more than to marry the woman he loved, settle down to a simple life and raise a family – and he couldn't start doing any of that until he'd completed this damned quest.

Just when everyone had started considering sending a search party, the elemental emerged through the far wall, closely followed by a furry creature about the size of a small dog.

"Agh! What in Morsynia's name is that?" Hessan jumped up from his chair, though more startled by Sathom's sudden appearance than the animal at his heels.

"It will not stop following me," Sathom said, walking to the table with his new companion scampering to keep up. When he stopped moving, the animal sprung up to rest on Sathom's shoulder, curling its long, prehensile tail around the man's upper arm. It looked at the gathering with two huge eyes, opened its beak-like mouth and let out a series of chirrups and whistles.

"Oh, he's adorable!" Erryn said, reaching out to touch one of the creature's three-toed feet. As she did so, the two tufts of fur at either side of its head quivered, and it chirruped and whistled again.

Athalir approached from the other side, gently stroking the soft, tan and black-striped fur down its back. It certainly appeared their new guest liked the attention, as each touch elicited more coos of pleasure. That was until Vess also stepped forwards to pet it, at which point its beak opened unnaturally wide and it let out a high-pitched scream.

Startled, everyone instinctively covered their ears.

"That's what I heard this morning! That's what woke me up! And those eyes, I told you I saw eyes!" Vess had his hand to the hilt of his sword.

"Calm down, you idiot." Roh glared at Vess. "I know what it is, and it won't hurt you."

The others all looked to Roh, awaiting the details.

"I call them screamers – which really doesn't seem to fit, now I've actually seen one up close. I used to hear them on my ventures into the wastelands, occasionally get a glimpse of something reflecting the moonlight from within the undergrowth across the border – that must have been their eyes."

"But how do you know it's not dangerous?" Vess asked, lowering his hand, but staying well back.

"Well, I don't know for certain, but I wanted to find out what they were so, one night, I set camp at the border. I must have spent hours just watching, waiting to see if I could catch sight of the thing that made the noise. I never did. I got so tired I couldn't keep my eyes open any longer. When I awoke I found a small pile of nuts and berries – as well as a couple of dead beetles – at my side, between me and the thicket."

"Aw, they tried to feed you. How sweet!" Erryn said, smiling at the screamer.

"Erm, did no one notice the fact it came through the wall? The same way he can?" Hessan pointed at Sathom.

"Yes. I tried many times to lose the creature that way. Each time, it materialised right behind me." Sathom looked sideways at his shoulder passenger. "It is… most disconcerting."

"Well, he… er, she… whatever… seems to like you, Sathom. Looks like you've acquired a new friend." Marcus laughed.

"We're not seriously considering bringing this thing with us?" Hessan eyed the screamer with suspicion. "It's bad enough when Sathom frightens the crap out of me with that parlour trick of his, without 'screachy-what's-his-name' joining in."

Erryn ignored Hessan's objections.

"Of course! We have to give him a name, if he's to be our new companion. How about…" She paused for a few moments, looking thoughtful. "I've got it! Whistler. Because of the noise he makes."

"You call that a whistle? Bloody heffledent! What's wrong with your ears, lass?" Hessan asked.

"What? Oh, no, not *that* noise. The quieter, happier one. The one he made when Vess wasn't trying to touch him." The hexan smiled and winked at Vess, who had resolved not to step foot near the thing again.

"Right. We've tarried too long. Sathom, if you're happy looking after your new friend, it's time we were leaving." Marcus picked up his pack and staff, and, without waiting for replies, left the room. Spurred on by the mage's eagerness, the others wasted no time in following his lead.

"Why's he so keen to finish this journey all of a sudden?" Roh asked as she hung back with Erryn, who took some time to gather her belongings.

"Well, we do have only a short time left to get to the sanctum before the governors. I'm sure he's just realised the urgency, that's all." Erryn straightened her tunic and walked quickly to catch up with everyone else.

Roh matched her pace, staying at her side.

"So, it wouldn't have anything to do with your night together then, would it?"

Erryn laughed nervously.

"My my, I wasn't aware there'd been a announcement. Is the whole group up to date on our relationship now?"

"Ah, so you admit it's a relationship then?"

"Of course it's a relationship. We all have a relationship. Admittedly, some a little more disagreeable than others."

Roh looked straight ahead towards Marcus.

"Yes, but we aren't all intimate with one another. Not as far as I know, anyway."

Erryn remained silent. She had no wish to discuss her private affairs with anyone, least of all someone she found to be a little on the cold side.

"Do you love him?" the woman asked.

"What business is this of yours?" Erryn was growing increasingly irritated with being interrogated.

"Answer the question."

Erryn stopped walking and twisted to face Roh.

"Yes! I love him. Satisfied?"

"No, not really." Roh's stood with her legs planted firmly apart, her arms folded tightly across her chest. "There is no place for love on the field of battle. It could get either of you killed. It could get *any* of us killed. Decisions that ought to be made with the head become matters of the heart, and that puts all of us in danger. You'd do well to think on that, my dear." With that, Roh walked on, disregarding the younger woman's reddened face.

Erryn strode forwards until alongside Roh once more

"Don't concern yourself, *my dear*. It's not you I'm in love with – if it came to a choice, you'd not be around long enough to deliberate on my feelings," she retorted before hurrying to join Marcus.

"That's what worries me," the warrior spoke under her breath as she was left to walk alone.

Leaving the grounds of the palace, just as the sun was rising over the peaks of the Dragon Crest Mountains, the group took a moment to get their bearings before setting off down the hill. Once at the bottom, Marcus led them briskly south-east, back through the city, and treading the first foot-way that appeared to advance in the right direction. The path cut through miles and miles of vegetation and passed by many more abandoned settlements. Thus, it was many hours before the trees, vines, and shrubs began to thin out enough to see they were definitely heading the right way.

The mage had taken up whistling again, his cheery mood infectious as those behind him chatted to pass the time. Erryn had heard the tune he made so many times she found herself singing along, having learnt the words from Marcus back in the village. Hessan spent the journey talking weaponry with Roh. Even Vess and Athalir found civility to share. Sathom was silent but gave the impression of contentment as he listened to Whistler's friendly chatter and offered him nuts from a pouch at regular intervals. Spirits were higher than they'd ever been, perhaps due to a good night's rest and plentiful wine and food, or perhaps simply because the end was in sight. Either way, time seemed to pass swiftly.

Finally, late into the morning, the group came upon a wooden signpost with place names in two opposite directions.

"Maervell," Athalir said, pointing back the way they'd come, then pointing over the border. "And Sah Shaen Fehnehl… Ugh! I've been such a fool. Maervell means 'black water' in Fellian. How did I miss that? I should have known. With that name, this place *had* to have something to do with elves."

"Yes yes, you're a fool. You should have known – but what does the other place name mean? I'd like to know, seeing as that's where we're headed," Hessan asked, staring towards what looked to his good eyesight like a collection of bare trees.

Athalir was still staring at the name 'Maervell' and chuntering to himself, so Sathom spoke up instead.

"I believe I can answer that one. It means 'The Dead Wood'."

Marcus walked a little farther, to where the road started to become less well made and more of a dirt track.

"Athalir, does that sound right to you?"

The prince looked up at the mention of his name, turning to look where everyone else was now looking.

"Yes, though if those who populated this kingdom were anything like the elves of my homeland, I'd be wary of entering any place that included the word shaen – dead – as we name such places by way of a warning. My people know to avoid those locations at all costs."

All remained quiet as an air of foreboding followed Athalir's words. Just for a moment, a little of the old, cautious Marcus became visible in the mage's expression. But it didn't last long.

"Avoiding it is out of the question. The time for the governors' convergence at the sanctum is almost upon us, and it will take too long to take the long route around. We go through The Dead Wood!"

The walk from Maervell into the Dead Wood progressed in complete silence, in stark contrast to the mood of only minutes before. Out from the lush green hue, they emerged into a place of lifeless wooden husks, so dense as to let in scant light despite the lack of a leafy canopy. The empty branches of each tree interlocked with those around it, forming a tightly-woven roof above the group's heads. Thin, spiky shadows stretched frozen ahead, and nothing moved nor made a sound. It was as if all life had been sucked out, leaving naught but time itself.

As the companions walked slowly through the wood, most kept their eyes straight ahead, save for Athalir whose nature compelled him to remain alert. Even Whistler's chirruping had stopped almost the instant they'd set foot beyond the first dead tree.

The farther in they went, the more the atmosphere grew oppressively strange. None could explain what they were feeling but all would agree it was far from pleasant.

Though the air was impossibly still, a shiver of cold ran up Marcus' spine, as if caught in a draft.

"Perhaps we should have gone around," he said, more to himself than anyone else.

"No. It is far too late for that, now. We must continue." Sathom took the lead. Though he could feel what the others felt, as the one among them with no access to emotions, he was able to retain an objective attitude. He knew he'd have to be strong enough for everyone at this point. With a mile or two of the wood ahead, it was to be a long and arduous walk.

Time held little meaning, movement felt like it achieved nothing, yet still the people on the quest to save the ancient souls trudged onward. It took everything they had to carry on. Without the resolve borrowed from Sathom, all would have turned to flee many times. However, in the minds of man, woman, elf and dwarf, a voice urged them to turn back with every step they took. And all heard the same voice; that of a woman, her words of warning punctuated with the sobs of a tortured soul. The voice did not give up in the face of their progression, instead growing ever louder the closer they came to the centre of the wood. Soon, Hessan, Marcus, Athalir, and Roh could take it no longer, slamming their hands to their ears in a vain attempt to block out the sound. Vess, though troubled by the words in his head found he could press on with less distress than the others. He glanced at those who had fallen behind, then back to Erryn, who also appeared to be faring better.

Erryn looked back at Marcus, her heart aching for him as she saw the pain in his eyes. She, too, could hear the voice, but it felt familiar, and, like Vess, she could cope with its intrusion. A vibration at her collarbone caused her to look down. It was the amulet given to her by the dwarf, Erryniya, an almost imperceptible quivering causing it to judder slightly at her chest. She clutched it in an attempt to still the movement, but it vibrated within her hand.

Meanwhile, Sathom was not managing as well as his demeanour suggested. Though he advanced, his head was throbbing, the voice apparently having more of a physical effect on him than it did the others. Like Erryn's amulet, his brain seemed to be pulsating, getting worse until he knew that if he'd been capable of crying, his tears would have become a torrent.

Finally, the voice stopped, a heavy silence filling the void it left – almost the instant the first person arrived in a small clearing in the middle of the woodland.

Sathom had barely a second to set eyes on a figure dressed in white before an almighty bolt of pain slammed into his head. He dropped to his knees, having felt something dislodge between his skull and his skin. There was only one thing it could be – the baranite crystal that held his emotions under lock and key. As memories of the last thousand years flooded his mind, guilt ripped through his senses and, for the first time in centuries, he let out an agonised cry of emotional pain.

As each person succumbed to whatever force was pervading the air around them, those left standing became fewer. Vess turned round in slow circles, staring in horror at his stricken companions, while Erryn rushed to the mage's side.

"Marcus!" she cried out as he fell onto all fours, every muscle in his body convulsing tightly as he writhed with a pain the source of which she couldn't see.

Athalir, Hessan, and Roh were similarly incapacitated, the faces of all of them contorted in agony.

"What is going on?" Vess shouted, causing Whistler to jump farther back behind a tree stump he'd chosen as a place to hide.

"It is too late, too late for you all." The voice from their heads rang out loud with obvious melancholy. "I tried to warn you. I tried."

Erryn jumped up from Marcus' side.

"Vess, did you hear that? Who spoke? Reveal yourself!"

"Erryn, look!" Vess motioned straight ahead at a tall woman standing alone at the centre of the wood, a white, ragged gown hanging from her emaciated frame. Her face was drawn, revealing high cheekbones and eyes surrounded by dark circles, and she looked empty thin, cracked lips opened to speak again.

"I tried, I really tried. Tried to save you, tried to get back to you."

Erryn's eyes widened in shock, her mouth agape as the lady in white looked back at her with a face she'd seen every night in her dreams since she was six years old.

"Mother?"

Vess snapped around to look at his friend.

"I thought your mother was dead?"

"So did I." Erryn couldn't believe what she was seeing, reasoning it must be a trick of this place. And yet, every one of her senses begged her to believe it truly was the mother she thought she'd lost, stood just a few steps away.

"What trickery is this? What kind of magic would do this to me?" Erryn asked the ether with a demanding tone.

The woman spoke, but seemingly not to Erryn.

"'Tis dark magic that dwells here, dark magic that binds me to this place, dark magic that makes me see things that I have no right to see." She turned away, taking herself off to sit on a single wooden chair at the far side of the clearing. "The child isn't her – isn't she. Gone. Dead. My fault, my fault. I did not try hard enough."

Erryn ran towards the seated lady, but halted abruptly when she got close, watching as the woman leant forwards from her chair, reaching out her hand as if to touch someone that wasn't there. Then, she shrank back as if afraid.

Valeria looked at the flickering figure of a six-year-old child with auburn curls and brown eyes. Every waking moment the child was there – her daughter's tear-stained face there to haunt her forever. She reached out again but the second her fingertips reached the form, it would blink out of existence, only to return when she pulled away.

"No no no. I must not look, must not see. 'Tis not right, not right." The woman sobbed, a mournful, wailing cry. She paced around the chair, continuing to talk.

"Oh, why do you torture me so? Why why why? To see, but not to touch. Yes, it's what I deserve – nothing more, nothing less."

"Mother, what's wrong with you? Is that really you?" Erryn once more approached the woman. When she tried to stand in front of her, the lady jumped up, stepping backwards with her arms wrapped defensively around her torso.

"No mother, no daughter. 'Tis not right, 'tis not right. I did not try, did not save. My guilt is all there is, all I deserve."

"Who are you talking to? Mother, please."

"Young one, older one – what cruelty! Years of seeing a child, now you try tricking me with the older one. Both can't be real. No no, not both, not one. Wrong wrong wrong!"

"Mother it is me, it's Erryn. I'm here!"

Erryn could hold back no longer. Closing the gap between them in seconds, she grasped the frail figure by the upper arms.

The elder woman wouldn't look, keeping her face turned away. But the hexan pulled her close, ignoring the lack of reciprocation as her mother's body remained rigid in her arms. As she hugged tighter, Erryn's amulet was caught between the two women.

At first, there was nothing more than a vague crackle, but then it came alive with activity. A flare of light burst from the talisman, gradually enveloping the two women in a soft, orange glow. When the light had cloaked them fully, Valeria, Erryn's mother, relaxed, and embraced her daughter as if she'd never let go. Mother and daughter held each other tight, a bond that had been so cruelly broken, so long ago, becoming whole again in a matter of moments. In that dreadful place, with her friends, her lover, suffering just feet away, the only thought in Erryn's mind was how overjoyed she was to have found Valeria again, that she hadn't really lost her for good. In the magical aura that shielded them from the rest of the world, time seemed to slip away. Warmth spread through Erryn's body and, for the first time in many years, she felt safe – so safe that nothing else mattered. All thoughts of the quest, of the governors, even of Marcus, evaporated as she let herself disappear into the enchantment. As she closed her eyes, she could vaguely hear Vess calling to her, so quiet as if to be coming from a distance. She shut him out, refusing to be dragged away from the only thing she'd ever wanted. Soon, she could see nothing but her home in the village where she pictured herself and her parents reunited, sharing food and laughter by a roaring fire. It felt so real, so right, and somehow she knew, all she had to do to make it last was let go, just… let go.

"Erryn, my darling girl. Be strong. Resist." Valeria's composed voice broke through the magical hypnosis, barely audible at first, but getting louder as she continued to coax her daughter from oblivion.

Erryn slowly opened her eyes and saw her mother's face smiling back at her, the wild look of a madwoman displaced by sanity.

"There's my girl. Oh, my baby. I thought you were dead for so many years. Come back to me, sweetheart. We have little time."

"Mother, I…"

"Hush, my darling. I would wish for nothing more than to hold you forever, but your amulet's enchantment won't last much longer."

The real world came rushing back, jolting her from the dream. Erryn, alert once more, stared into Valeria's eyes, her characteristic determination evident in every pore.

"Mother, it's alright now. I've found you. I can take you home. Father will be so pleased, he'll…"

"I see you've met with Erryniya. She gave you the amulet, did she not?" Valeria smiled, glancing at the talisman.

"Er, yes. She spoke of you. Said you were friends. You must have been close to name me after her. Why did you never mention her?"

A wistful look came over Valeria's face.

"Ah, my bonny girl. You were such a brave child, so strong and courageous – just like your mother. I knew the name would suit you the moment she placed you in my arms – the moment I became your guardian. I vowed to keep you safe as a promise to a dear friend, but you were so easy to love. It was never hard to call you my daughter."

"What… are you saying? I *am* your daughter." Erryn took a step back, confused.

"No, my child. Though I will always love you, it was not I that brought you into this world. I… should have told you, long ago. Erryniya wanted you to be safe, and that meant keeping her from you – though, I think it was easier to believe you were truly mine while the truth remained unspoken."

In the strange, magical haze, Erryn felt the weight of confusion. There, in that awful place, she'd just found her mother after years believing her to be dead – and now she spoke of things that couldn't be true. They couldn't. What she'd just been told was life-changing, but at that moment, all she could think of was that her mother, Valeria, was right there. Then, the guilt came, flooding into her mind. She'd just given up. She'd only been a child but she'd given up, too quick to believe her mother had been killed. How could she do that?

"I'm *so* sorry, mother. I should have done more… I could have…" The words seemed hollow without any idea what she, as a six-year-old child could have done. She looked down, at a loss as to what to say to make things right.

Valeria put one hand on her daughter's shoulder and lifted her downcast chin with the other.

"Erryn, our time is almost spent. I feel the magic waning, and when it fades, I'll not remember any of this. I'll return to how I was when you found me."

"No! We'll get you home – find a way to heal you. Magic! We'll use magic. Come, we must get you away from here. I'm sure that'll help for a start." Erryn gripped her mother's hand, aiming to turn and leave the wood. But Valeria stood firm.

"It won't help, Erryn. I am here at the behest of the governors. Their dark magic binds me to this place. For fifteen years it has been my prison, and it will be thus for so long as a heart still beats within my chest. Trust me."

"Trust you? After what you've just said?" Erryn's thoughts turned to resentment at the deception.

"Sweetheart, there is no time left. Put aside that stubborn streak of yours and listen to me, please. Before it's too late."

Erryn paused, smothering the fire in her soul, then nodded.

"Look around you."

The hexan did as she was told, guiltily remembering Marcus and the others as she saw them suffering in silence beyond the glowing veil.

"My curse is what eats away at them. My guilt in leaving you for dead was used by the governors to make a trap out of this wood. Their own feelings of guilt are being turned in on them like sharpened blades. Right now, your friends have the pain of a thousand regrets boring into their minds. It won't cease until my magic is gone." Valeria pointed to the skeletons of men and women scattered around the clearing. "And it will destroy them."

Erryn paused, still looking at the skeletons, before something occurred to her.

"Wait… why am I not affected by this curse? I have guilt, too – in abundance right now. Surely I should be suffering the same fate?"

"You know Erryniya is a seer, yes? She foresaw this event, crafting the amulet you now wear in order to protect you. Hexans have far greater skill with talismans than us mages."

"Mages? What do you mean? You're not a mage – you hate mages. You always said…"

"I know what I said – and while it's true I detest those I knew as brethren, there is no denying my origin, not anymore. I raised you as hexan, passing on the ways your mother taught to me. That you have learnt her craft is all that matters now. When you leave this place, go to her. She will tell you all you need to know. For now, you must listen to me and do as I say."

Erryn looked defiantly at Valeria.

"I'll get you away from the group. They can continue the quest and I'll take you home. You won't…"

"Until my magic is gone, Erryn. Not simply far away."

The daughter held in a breath, sadly understanding her mother's intent.

"You don't mean… No! I won't do that. You can't ask that of me. I've only just found you." Erryn sobbed, tears streaming down her face.

Her mother held both her hands, a small smile accompanying the certainty in her ageing eyes.

"I'm tired, so very tired, and it will never end for me. There is only one thing you can do for me now, only one thing you can do for him." Valeria nodded her head towards Marcus. "The man you love."

Erryn looked at the mage again, her tears increasing as she saw him twisting in agony.

"How did you know?"

"I'm… connected, to all of them, to him, by the power of the governors' spell. I see what he sees, feel what he feels. It is only the strength of the amulet's spell that stops me experiencing their physical pain at this moment."

"Mother, I can't…"

"Yes, you can – and you must. There is no other way. Be the strong woman I always knew you'd become. I have faith in you."

Erryn looked into the woman's eyes, searching for a sign that it didn't need to end this way. Finding nothing but weary acceptance, she reluctantly nodded once more. Slowly reaching her hand to her belt, she unsheathed her hunting dagger, feeling as if every drop of blood had suddenly been drained from her body.

"That's my girl. I'm so sorry. I never wanted to leave you. I wish I'd been there to watch you grow into the beautiful woman I see before me. I love you, Erryn. You were, and still are, my daughter – my darling girl. Remember that, always."

No sooner had Valeria finished speaking when the magic barrier started to melt away, her companions' cries of pain and the harsh grey light returning with a vengeance.

Valeria was once more a woman with wild eyes, talking incoherently and completely oblivious to reality.

"I love you, too," Erryn whispered before plunging the dagger into her mother's heart with all the force she could muster, a blank, distant look in her eyes. She watched coldly as Valeria's lifeless body slumped to the ground, a scarlet stain spreading across the bodice of her ragged, white gown.

CHAPTER TWENTY-SEVEN

Erryniya Constantine put her wiped-clean dagger back into its sheath and dispassionately stepped over the body at her feet.

"Vess, come on. We should see to the others." Without waiting for a response, she went to tend to Marcus.

"Erryn, are you..."

"I don't want to talk about it!" the young woman snapped.

He stared after the friend who had just taken her own mother's life. The coldness of the usually warm, passionate woman troubled him, but, as he took in the sight of Sathom, Athalir, Hessan, and Roh all staggering to their feet, he resolved to put his concerns aside, for now, as he aided his companions.

Getting over their ordeal, the others were silent and emotionally battle-weary. As Vess joined them, he quietly filled everyone in on what he'd witnessed, in an attempt to make sure they didn't bombard Erryn with questions she wasn't ready to answer. Though Erryn and her mother had been unable to hear the world around them, Vess had heard every word. He knew a time would come when the brave girl would need to open up, but he understood that time wasn't now.

With the warrior's aid, the others managed to compose themselves. However, their leader still lay in a foetal position on the ground. Erryn attempted to get him to sit up, but he kept muttering something she couldn't quite make out, and didn't even appear to acknowledge her presence.

"What's wrong with him?" Roh asked, brushing dust from her armour.

"I'm not sure." Erryn tried to pull him upright but as she took hold of him he tensed up and let out a pained holler, clamping his hands to either side of his head with his eyes tightly shut.

"Dessema, Dessema, Dessema." Again, Marcus mumbled.

"What are you saying? I don't understand." Erryn stroked the man's head in an effort to soothe.

Sathom stepped forwards, his expression solemn as he came to kneel down at the mage's side.

"Dessema. He is saying Dessema."

"But what *is* Dessema? What's it mean?"

"It is a name. The name of the woman he loved, that… Rhyssian loved… No, no, no! This cannot be happening. Not now!"

Erryn was surprised at the outburst from the normally impassive elemental, and ashamedly the tiniest bit jealous at hearing Marcus call out for another woman, yet what was befalling him took precedence in her concerns

"Sathom! Stop talking in riddles. What is *happening* to him? Tell me!"

Sathom stood up, backing away.

"It is the barrier – the barrier is gone!"

"Are you sure? How can you be so certain?"

"We kept everything from him, deliberately. There would be no way of him knowing about her if the barrier remained."

The rest of the group came together, staring down at Marcus as he cried out again, this time his back arching in response to obvious pain.

"What's this mean? Why is he yelling like that?" Hessan asked.

"If the barrier has gone then he's…" A look of horror came over Erryn's face.

"Experiencing the memories of his ancient soul, yes," Sathom said.

"I don't understand. What does this have to do with him being in pain?" Athalir looked at Marcus, a mix of compassion and confusion in his eyes.

"It's the same as what happened with Benedict, yes? His body isn't strong enough to cope with the Meranell soul?" Erryn requested confirmation of what she already knew.

"Yes. But for Marcus, it is a million times worse. Benedict had nigh-on three-hundred years to adapt to his memories. He suffered, of course. Headaches, aching joints, skin that felt as if it had been stretched too thin – but he experienced all of that over centuries. He grew up with it. Marcus has not had that time to adjust. He is feeling the weight of a thousand-year-old soul pressing against his human form – and the force is increasing by the second."

"So put the barrier back! You can't leave him like this!" Athalir demanded.

"Do you not think I would have done so, had I the capability? It was the mage we met in the caves that erected it. Only a mage could do so again."

"Erryn, you have magic. Can you do it?" Vess asked.

"I… wouldn't even know where to begin. I simply don't have that kind of power."

No one spoke as the terrible nature of Marcus' predicament impacted on them all. His agonised cries were coming faster, and there was nothing anyone could do to help him.

Erryn jumped up from the ground.

"Right! We get him out of here. Darkness still lingers within this place, I can feel it. Perhaps if we leave this wood, he'll get even a small amount of relief."

"Erryn, you know that will not resolve this." Sathom spoke, quieter than before.

"I don't care! We have to try. Vess, can you lift him?"

Without speaking, the warrior strode forwards and heaved Marcus up and over his shoulder, the mage hollering the moment his body was touched.

"Good. Now, everyone gather your belongings. We're leaving this place." Erryn took one last brief look at the body of her mother, before setting off in the direction that would lead them to the Sanctum of Souls. Assuming the others would follow, she didn't look back, meaning no one saw the tear that escaped her eye and trickled down her cheek.

"Do you not think you should at least offer your mother rites of some kind?" Roh called out as they walked.

"Leave it, Roh." Vess scowled at the woman who, for once, offered no come back.

"We set camp here." Erryn had steadfastly led the procession forwards until the Dead Wood was a fair distance behind. With Vess tiring and morale dissipating, she'd spied a gathering of rocks and boulders a way ahead, and decided it was as good a place as any to rest. More importantly, it looked to be somewhere they could take some time to find a way to help Marcus; as Sathom had solemnly told her as they walked, the quest was lost without him.

"I'll get a fire started," Athalir offered.

"No, I'll see to that. It's quicker with magic, and we don't have time to waste," Erryn said, glancing at Marcus as Vess laid him down on the ground, placing a rolled pack beneath his head. *Come on, Marcus,* she thought to herself. *We need you – I need you.*

Once a small pile of gathered sticks had been made, Erryn willed a flame to life in the palm of her hand, blowing it gently into the flammable heap. As her eyes were drawn to stare into the low flames, she desired nothing more than a time to grieve, but tore herself away before that longing took hold. She had to be strong for now. There'd be time for reflection when Marcus was back to his normal self, and she had to believe that was possible, despite Sathom's dire warnings to the contrary.

By the time some meagre rations had been consumed by those whose appetites were unnaturally absent, the mage had been quiet for some time, much to the concern of both Erryn and Sathom. His pained cries, though hard for those that cared for him to endure, were somehow more comforting than the hollow silence now emanating from him. His body still flinched and contorted every so often, his skin clammy and glistening with moisture, yet deathly pale, as if gripped by an unholy fever.

The discussion had inevitably turned to what could be done for him, but there was no one present with anything to offer. Once or twice, Sathom had looked as if he had something to say, but he'd stifled it, despite prompts to speak if he had anything useful to add.

Vess watched from a few feet away as Erryn knelt at Marcus' side, holding his hand and mopping his brow with a torn piece of her tunic. He hated seeing both of them so helpless, and realised there and then that he cared for his friends a great deal. He knew little of family or an ordinary life, but he'd had nothing but kindness and friendship from the couple. No matter what happened next, what the future held, he considered Marcus and Erryn the closest thing he'd ever have to family – and he'd do everything in his power to get them through this.

"They'll be fine. We'll find a way." Athalir's voice broke into Vess' thoughts as he approached and sat down next to him.

"I know," Vess replied, picking up a handful of dirt and tossing it aside.

Athalir unsheathed one of his daggers and started turning it over and over in his hand.

"It must have been hard, watching what Erryn had to go through."

"Hard for me? Perhaps. But what about you, and the others? The most I suffered was watching my friend be forced to kill someone she loved. From where I stood, it was worse for you."

"It was… unpleasant." Athalir stopped twisting his dagger and stabbed it hard into the ground.

"And Marcus continues to go through that," Vess said, feeling helpless all over again.

"We don't know what he endures. I, and the others, were torn apart from inside our minds with everything for which we'd ever felt guilt. I don't know about the dwarf, Roh, or Sathom, but I had plenty to fuel that particular curse."

"You're not helping put my mind at rest."

"I wasn't trying to. From what Sathom says, Marcus was and is facing something worse, something none of us can comprehend. It seems the guilt the curse drew out in him was actually that of the soul he is host to. Sathom believes that's what caused the barrier to be dispelled. I simply came to reassure you; no matter how grave this situation appears, we *will* solve it. We have to."

Vess stared into the prince's eyes a moment, then nodded, the two men sitting together in silence as both turned their thoughts to trying to think of something that may bring their friend's pain to an end.

For an hour since they'd eaten, Erryn had not left Marcus' side. She'd disallowed herself any time to reflect on the truths Valeria had revealed, instead concentrating all her mental energy on trying to think of any kind of magic that might restore the mage to health. But, every time, she came up against the same wall – the one made from all the magical ability she didn't possess. Never in her life had her magic left her feeling so useless. If only she'd been a mage. *Damn hexan magic!* She cursed the source of her powers that, until recently, she'd been so proud of.

Wincing as Marcus twisted and made a low moan, she didn't notice Sathom as he approached from behind.

"We are losing him," the elemental said, walking to kneel down the other side of the stricken man.

"Sathom, I didn't… Don't talk like that. We are *not* losing him. Not while I live and breathe."

"I fear the longer he remains locked away, the more Rhyssian's soul will destroy the vessel from within."

"Rhyssian, the Meranell whose soul he carries?"

Sathom nodded.

"But he's still with us right now. I know it." Erryn bent down to kiss Marcus' forehead, feeling heat rising from him the moment she drew close.

"At this moment, I believe he is rendered catatonic by the memories of his life before the spell – and possibly some from his time within the tower. Though he was, at some level, aware of the pain the soul caused before, it is my assumption that, now, his human mind has disconnected itself from his body. A form of self-preservation, I suppose."

Sathom stood up, hoping what he'd said might help the young woman find some respite from her troubled mind. In truth, it had been so long since he'd used emotion to guide his words, he couldn't be sure if he'd helped or simply worsened her despair. Once more, he opened his mouth to say something that had been in his mind since they set camp. Once more, he refrained, hope that the souls would finally be free diminishing yet again.

"Is something wrong, Sathom? There's something… different about you lately. I–"

"Nothing. It is nothing," he said, monotonous. "You should all rest. There is naught to be done for the next few hours that cannot wait."

Erryn stood up, realising the sense in the elemental's suggestion. Brushing the dust from her trousers, she resolved to sound positive, even if it was hard to convince herself.

"You're right. Fresh minds can't hurt, and we still have some time left, right?"

Sathom nodded again. Erryn looked around to locate the rest of the party. Vess and Athalir were close by, but there was no sign of Hessan or Roh.

"Vess, would you find the others? It's time we got some sleep and we should arrange a watch."

Vess acknowledged Erryn's request, got up, and surveyed the surroundings. Large boulders peppered the immediate area, blocking line of sight enough that the two members of the group could have sat down the other side and easily become obscured from view.

The warrior had been gone from the camp-site a fair while when he heard something a little way ahead. Drawing his sword, he followed the sound until he came close to a particularly tall rock. What sounded like the snuffle of some kind of animal reached his ears, loud enough that he readied to defend himself. He half hoped it was just Whistler, who'd disappeared in The Dead Wood and not been seen since.

Taking as delicate a step as his heavy frame would allow, he crept in a wide arch around to the other side of the boulder, brandishing his sword and set to strike.

But when the armoured man sprung upon the other side, his eyes didn't find a dangerous creature. Instead, he found the people he'd been searching for.

Though surprised by Vess' sudden arrival, Hessan and Roh remained intimately entwined, faces flushed and fingers still threaded through each other's hair.

"Vess!" Roh said, visibly shocked.

"Everything alright, my friend?" Hessan asked, slightly breathless, but cheerful.

Vess glowered at Roh as he replied.

"Erryn wants us all back at camp to organise a watch." Before either could respond, Hessan and Roh watched as Vess wasted no time in turning his back on the pair and marching away.

Once the absent duo returned to the camp, a lookout rota was quickly arranged, with Sathom warning that they could not afford to sleep for too long.

As usual, Vess offered to take first watch, though this time he was happy to end his shift after the first hour. He still didn't relish the idea of sleep, but reluctantly accepted the necessity nevertheless.

Just after he began pacing the perimeter, Hessan called his name to get his attention, walking over to meet him.

"All quiet?" the dwarf asked as he got close.

"So it seems," Vess replied, tersely.

"Look, lad, I'm sorry about what you saw. I'd never have touched the woman had I known you two were courting." Sincerity rang through the king's words, his expression earnest. Vess laughed, a happening so rare it took Hessan by surprise. "Well, I have to admit, that's not the response I expected."

"Apologies. Your use of the word 'courting' struck me as amusing. I've not been around long enough to know much about how such things work, but I do believe courting wouldn't be the appropriate word for what we did."

Hessan smiled.

"Ah, I see. Seems our new friend is the sharing sort." The dwarf jovially slapped Vess across the back, a brief glow of relief present in his eyes, before the usual wicked glint took over.

"So long as there's no grievance between us, lad. I respect you too much for a wench – however pleasant on the eye – to come between us."

Hessan was about to leave when Vess caught sight of his finger stump, and remembered he'd wanted to know what had happened.

"Hessan, how did you lose the finger?" he asked.

The dwarf raised his hand and wiggled the stump, grinning widely.

"Herd-gizzler!"

"Excuse me?"

"Herd-gizzler – they eat sheep, the bastards. Have a taste for white ones. Well, the whites were easier for them to hunt in the dark. So we bred all our sheep black. Didn't stop the critters, though. One day, I'd had all I could take of the larns' demands for restitution from the crown, so I decided to deal with the buggers myself. Sat out all night in a field, just me and my axes, waiting. Nothing happened until almost dawn, when one of the scaly rodents managed to make off with a ewe while I nodded off. I just woke up in time to see that damn awful tongue coiling around the old girl and dragging her in."

Vess was enthralled.

"What did you do?"

"What else could I do? Ran over to the beast and punched it on the nose."

"Did that work?"

"No, lad. Bugger just held on tighter. I knew from the farmers' tales that if you kill a herd-gizzler while their tongue is coiled, it causes the muscle to tense and the sheep dies instantly. But if their mouth is open wide enough, they gag, and the tongue gets as slack as a tavern wench's drawers. So, I looked in its beady eyes and stared it down while I prized open its mouth. I swear the damn thing was daring me to keep going. Anyway, I finally managed to get the thing open wide enough that the sheep broke free – didn't think about the teeth, though, did I? I let go, the mouth clamped shut, and there you have it, top half of finger a bite-sized replacement for mutton."

Vess's mouth was hanging open, but he snapped it shut at the mental image the dwarf's tale had conjured. Now, I'd better get some rest, before it's my turn on watch. No telling anyone I fell asleep on a herd-gizzler hunt, you hear? You take that one to the grave, my friend."

With that, Hessan, smiled, and went to return to his bedroll, leaving Vess to resume his pacing. He thought back on things as he walked. He couldn't deny his physical attraction to Roh, but when he'd seen her with Hessan, he'd felt more foolish than cuckolded. Besides, she was right; she had helped him deal with the issue keeping him from sleep. He had a feeling a well-rested body and mind were going to be more needed than ever in the hours to come.

As he walked, Hessan noticed Erryn attempting to get comfortable on her bedroll. Her tossing and turning was accompanied by grumbles and sighs, so after watching from a distance for a moment, the dwarf went to sit with her.

"How you holding up, lass?" he asked, sitting on his haunches.

"Oh, you know. My lover's locked inside a magically-created shell, screaming with agony on the inside, and I just discovered my dead mother was actually alive and insane for the last fifteen years – then I had to kill her. I'm great! Why do you ask?"

Hessan did what came naturally and gave a low laugh. For a moment Erryn wanted to slap him, but something inside her clearly needed the levity. She smiled, seeing the twisted humour in her speech.

With quiet understanding, the dwarf sat down with his legs crossed, and waited patiently until Erryn spoke again.

"Did you know?"

"That Erryniya was your real mother? No, but I knew something was odd when Marcus said you were a hexan." Erryn looked pointedly at Hessan, her face displaying her confusion. "Hexanism is a uniquely dwarven practice. We used to have schools, retreats, tutors. Then, over time, fewer and fewer hexans were born, and it became almost a forgotten craft. When I heard that term coming from the mouth of a human, well, let's just say the wolf in me found his bone." Hessan winked at Erryn.

Silence pervaded once more, Erryn's mind cogitating, then moving on.

"What's she like? My… my mother?"

"You met her."

"Yes but only briefly – and the circumstances weren't ideal for mother-daughter reunions. You really *know* her. She's your friend."

Hessan shifted his weight to one side and stroked his beard, as he pictured the woman who'd been there for him despite his flaws.

"She's the single best person I know. A true good soul. Kind, honest, strong – a lot like someone else I know, actually." He nudged Erryn, whose face lit up for a second before sadness stole the light. "Look, I realise all this is tough, and Morsynia knows I'm not the best person to listen to when it comes to family and feelings – but I can say this; if Erryniya gave you up, she had good cause. There's no doubt in my mind she had your best interest at heart, lass." He patted Erryn on the head and stood up. "Now, I don't know about you, but I could *really* use some sleep. There's nothing we can't deal with in rested minds." With that, the dwarf made for his own bedroll, leaving Erryn alone with her thoughts.

Sathom sat cross-legged beside Marcus; alone, since Erryn had taken herself away for some much needed rest.

"I will stay with him," he'd promised, empathy pinching at his newly-released emotions as he'd observed her distressed face.

Of all the times that would have been convenient for the magical shackles to be broken, now was least among them. Not only was his own heart being weighed heavy upon by Marcus' pain, but it made saying what needed to be said so much harder. It was just this kind of situation that caused him to bury his feelings in the first place. Decisions to be taken, hard truths to present to those around him… *All made tolerable without the hindrance of damned emotions,* he thought to himself. And still, atop it all, now was also not the time to reveal his recently-acquired condition. Thus, he was mentally weary from trying to contain his feelings and maintain his inexpressive tone each time he spoke.

Hovering his hand over the mage's head, Sathom was about to use his ability to look into his unconscious mind, to see if there was any viable way of, if nothing else, lessening Marcus' suffering. Perhaps he could tap into his power to alter memories and place a blank page over the top of Rhyssian's thoughts. It might not be a cure, but it could provide some small relief. However, as the blue light glowed at the edges of his palm, he caught sight of Erryn making her way towards him.

"I can't sleep," she said, retaking her place on the ground. "Any change?"

Sathom shook his head.

She sighed, yawned, and then briefly closed her eyes before reaching out for Marcus' hand.

"You should at least try to sleep, Erryn. There is little you can do here," Sathom urged, silently willing her to leave before he could keep his thoughts to himself no longer.

"I don't think you've ever called me Erryn before," the young woman said, a half-hearted smile crossing her lips.

"I... No, I don't believe I have," Sathom said, barely above a whisper.

Silence lingered between the pair for mere moments.

"I just *wish* there was something I could do for him. I'm not sure I can watch as he suffers for much longer – it's tearing me apart." Two steady trickles of tears formed from the pooled water at the base of Erryn's eyes. She abruptly let go of Marcus' hand and stood up to leave, turning her back on Sathom without a word.

"Erryn, wait!" Sathom said quickly, his mind working fast to get the words out before his heart regained control. "There is a way!"

Erryn swiftly turned around, her eyes still wet, boring into those of the elemental.

"What do you mean? A way to do what?"

"A way to rescue Marcus from the stupor – a way to bring him back, to protect him from Rhyssian's soul."

Erryn dashed to Sathom, grabbing hold of his collar and forcing him to his feet.

"For pity's sake, Sathom! Why didn't you say anything before?"

"Because… because…"

"Because what? Spit it out!"

"Because it is too much to ask – he will never forgive me. I will never forgive myself."

"Damn it, Sathom! If there's something we can do to save him, we have to try, no matter the cost!"

Sathom stared at the hexan, took in the fire in her eyes, and nodded, causing her to let go of him.

"Come. Sit with me and I will explain."

The elemental walked away from Marcus, choosing a rock large enough for two, away from the sleeping party and Vess' watch.

Erryn perched herself next to Sathom and awaited his explanation.

"You are aware the issue is the fact Marcus' body – the vessel – is not strong enough to cope with the Meranell soul within?"

"You know I am. Go on."

"We cannot reinstate the barrier. As I said before, it would take another mage to do that, and I'm not even certain a new barrier would be successful now that he has experienced so much of his past. Thus, he is for evermore to be aware of who he was, of the life he led. However, something – a spell of sorts – may be performed in order to strengthen his body so that it can more comfortably accommodate Rhyssian's soul."

Erryn took a moment to ponder what had been said, before speaking.

"So… he will be conscious of this Rhyssian, of his soul?"

"Yes."

"But, the pain will end, he'll be better?"

"That is correct."

Erryn stood up.

"Then what are we waiting for? Tell me what has to be done – and quickly. He should suffer no more."

Sathom also got to his feet, stepping towards the woman and taking her hands in his.

"There is a price, Erryn, one that has kept me from telling you of this solution. A price so terrible, I fear Marcus would choose to wither away in agony rather than accept the cost. Were it his decision, I doubt this would be the path he'd choose."

"Sathom, he's dying. Experiencing a torture like no other, and dying in the process. Right now, I can't worry about what his choice would be. I must be strong for him. This is my decision. Tell me what is to be done, please. I beg you."

The time for Sathom's emotions to control his mind had passed him by. He'd already said too much. With sadness, he realised he liked Erryniya Constantine very much – and largely due to the strength of character and devotion to those she cared for that she'd exhibited in the last few minutes. He briefly wondered if those traits would withstand the revelation of the price required. With an immense sorrow, he felt certain they would.

"To give Marcus the strength to host the Meranell soul, he would require an injection of energy from another with magic flowing in their blood. No small offering would this be. Such is the enormity of the task, it would take a huge donation of magical essence to adequately strengthen the vessel. It would take all the donor had to give – there would be nothing left to sustain their life."

Erryn's face turned pale.

"You mean… the one to do this would… die?"

Sathom nodded.

The young woman pulled herself from Sathom's hands, turning away from him and staring back towards the camp. For a short while, she stood motionless, her brown eyes fixed on the mage, whose body was once again twisting and turning in pain.

"Erryn, I should not have burdened you with this. I am sorry. We will–"

"I'll do it!" she said, thrusting her shoulders back and holding her head high.

"But…"

She returned to address Sathom, her resolve undeniable.

"My mind is made up. Just… tell me what to do."

"So, you got your emotions back – and you didn't think to tell anyone?" Erryn said to Sathom as they both carried Marcus away from the camp.

"It was never an appropriate time, given the circumstances." The elemental knew his companion was trying to keep things light-hearted with cheerful chatter, but he couldn't find it in himself to act the same.

Erryn drew in a breath, hunching her shoulders to shift Marcus' staff into a better position on her back.

"Right, let me make sure I understand the procedure. Once we are far enough away from camp, we set Marcus down. Then all I have to do is hold the staff in one hand, and hold his hand against it with the other, correct?"

"That is correct, yes."

"Then, you do your lightning – whatever – and my power is drawn through the crystal and into Marcus?"

"Well, that is the basics of it. My electrical charge will begin the process, sparking a cycle that will be impossible to stop until the exchange is complete – until your vitality has… drained. However, the loop cannot begin unless you will it. The choice remains yours until you… turn the tap, I suppose."

"Good." Erryn laughed. "I want to make sure I know what I'm doing. Wouldn't want to do something wrong and turn Marcus' hair pink or something."

Sathom wanted to laugh with her, wanted to help give her the atmosphere she so obviously craved, but it was all he could do not to shout out how wrong the whole thing was, and call an end to it immediately. He had to work so much harder to remain composed since Valeria's curse had dislodged the binding crystal.

"Erryn, remember, you can still change your mind. It will not be too late until you start to let the magic go–"

"What are you two talking about? What won't be too late?" Vess called out from behind them, running to catch up. "What's going on? Where are you taking Marcus?"

"Oh, no! Vess, go back. This has to be done – and there's nothing you can do here." Erryn stooped to lay Marcus down as Sathom did the same.

"*What* has to be done? Tell me!" The warrior stood his ground, clearly not planning on being cowed by dismissal.

Reluctantly, Erryn relayed the plan to Vess, his mouth agape as he realised the inevitable consequence.

"No! I won't allow it!"

Erryn looked obstinately at her friend.

"It's not your choice, Vess."

"Well it could be. I have magic in me, right?"

Sathom stared quizzically at Vess.

"Well, yes – how did you know?"

"I don't know, I just *feel* it now and then. Nothing I can put my finger on, but I know it's there. Plus, my father is a mage, and I know it's hereditary. Whatever, let me do it. I'll pay the price. Rather a man with no loved ones to grieve, no past to cling on to – no future mapped out. It's my father that brought us all here, on this mission. I should be the one to… to…"

Erryn immediately wrapped her arms around the big man.

"Hush. You're a good soul, Vess. One of the most decent I've ever known." She stepped back and held his hands, looking up into his sad eyes. "You're strong, and brave, and I know of no better person to look after Marcus when I'm gone – but the magic in you is born of darkness, and not nearly powerful enough for this spell. It has to be me, my friend."

"Then we'll find another way. This can't be our only option, it can't be."

"I am afraid it is, though I greatly wish it were not so." Sathom spoke, then turned away, fighting the urge to break down.

Vess lowered his head, feeling his first tears welling at the bottom of his eyes.

Erryn lightly brushed her fingers down Vess' cheek, then went to Marcus, taking the staff from her back and planting it firmly into the ground.

"Sathom, are you ready?" she asked.

Sathom choked back his feelings, and looked towards the place where the spell was to be cast.

With Marcus oblivious to what was about to occur, Erryn knelt down so she could reach his hand, wrapping it around the shaft and covering his fingers with her own. She looked down at the mage and then to Vess.

"Tell him... tell him I love him. Tell him I'm sorry and that I haven't abandoned him and that, as long as he continues to believe in – no, to *feel* the magic – I'll be with him. *Always.*"

Vess acknowledged her wishes, wanting to turn away, to not watch. But, as he saw the bravery across the woman's face, he knew he couldn't let Erryn leave without proving her faith in his courage. And so, he stood upright, and stared bravely ahead.

"You can still–" Sathom began, but Erryn interrupted.

"One life to save so many others, right? It's a worthy sacrifice," she said, grasping the wooden stick that her father had so beautifully crafted in a place that felt so very far away. "I'm ready."

Sathom drew upon the elemental power that had been unused for a thousand years, almost hoping it no longer worked. From deep within his being, he felt a still-familiar vibration as the electricity surged up throughout his torso and onward to his hands. He raised both his arms as the power built, thrusting them out and flashing open his palms in one swift motion. A burst of wavy, white light shot forth, crackling with energy and soaring to meet the crystal at the top of Marcus' staff. With the mage's hand touching the shaft, the crystal was glowing softly, but, as the shimmering white light met its surface, a blinding flash lit up the entire area.

Erryn jumped slightly, and then looked down at Marcus' face.

"I will it," she whispered.

The instant the words had been spoken, the light, followed by a humming vibration, shot down the staff, making contact with Erryn's hand. The pulsating glow sped through her body and continued the cycle through Marcus and all the way around again via the crystal. The minutes drifted on, and with each loop she could feel her life-force weakening; yet, it didn't hurt. Her sight blurred as visions of her mother and father appeared in the growing darkness, and, as the sound of electricity grew more and more faint, she thought she could hear her mother calling her to their enchanted place one last time.

Vess and Sathom watched the light travelling around and around until finally, Erryn's body slumped to the ground next to Marcus. Her grip on his hand and the staff gone, both dropped and the magic ended, the night sky seeming darker for the sudden lack of light.

"What in Morsynia's name was that?" Hessan ran to the silent pair, closely followed by Athalir and Roh.

The others had been woken by the bright light and, after a quick check round camp, had sprinted to find its source. Now they walked slowly forwards until they were in line with Vess and Sathom, and stared in disbelief at the sight a few feet ahead.

Athalir dashed to Erryn, lifting her head and shoulders from the ground and cradling her in his arms.

"Erryn! Erryn, wake up! Wake up, girl! Wake up!" He shook her limp body, nearly dropping her as her head fell sideways and her eyes stared vacantly out into the world.

"What have you done?" Hessan asked, transfixed by the scene before him.

Roh said nothing, but just watched as those around her experienced their own private grief. She barely knew any of them, and now she couldn't help but feel like an intruder. She was about to leave, when she noticed a movement on the ground. It was Marcus. Just a slight twitch at first, but soon followed by a low groan, and then the mage slowly tried raising himself up into a sitting position.

Roh felt an odd compulsion to go to him. It filled her with disquiet, but she obeyed it nevertheless. Dropping to her knees, the female warrior supported Marcus' back as he rose. She may not have been blessed with great intelligence, but it didn't take a genius to work out that Erryn had given her life to save his. She had no idea what to say, and so remained silent.

With a return to consciousness slowly drawing him back to the real world, Marcus looked around until his gaze fell upon Erryn.

Athalir gently ran his fingers down over her eyes, drawing her lids shut as Marcus' grief-stricken cry rang out across the night-covered landscape.

CHAPTER TWENTY-EIGHT

As the flames rose higher and higher around Erryn's lifeless body, Marcus stared deep into the pyre. Heat spread out to meet him, and a warm glow caressed the rocks and dusty ground. He felt empty, devoid of anything but the stale memories of a life that didn't feel like his own.

He wanted to be angry with her, longed to tell the stubborn woman it was wrong to make a decision on his behalf, but even anger eluded him.

Sathom appeared at his side and rested his hand on Marcus' shoulder.

"I am *so* sorry, my friend."

Now Marcus could feel the anger he'd been so keen to express – and a better person to direct it at was right next to him.

"You're *sorry*?" The mage turned briskly around, shrugging away Sathom's hand. "It was *you* that told her to take her own life! Tell me, *friend!* Tell me just how *sorry* you are!"

Sathom took a step back.

"Marcus, I know you are hurting, but I did not tell Erryn to do anything. You have to believe me, I agonised over revealing the spell to her. I tried so many times to…"

"You tried to *what*, Sathom? You tried to stop her, to stop yourself from speaking, tried to go back in time and make sure she never met you or started your damned *quest* in the first place? You *agonised* –

please! You know *nothing* of agony. You're a cold, emotionless bastard who thinks of nothing and no one but yourself, and the selfish feelings you locked away because you were too weak to keep them under control. You sicken me, elemental! Now, back away from me before I do something I'll not regret."

Every inch of Marcus bristled with a fury the like of which he'd never experienced before – or had he? Somewhere in his mind it seemed familiar.

"Marcus, I…"

Before Sathom could continue, Marcus had hold of him, his arm pulled back, hand balled into a fist. The fist shot forth – and would have made hard contact with Sathom's face had he not instantly vanished. He reappeared feet away less than a second later, as Marcus fell to the ground, the momentum of his punch too fast to stop himself with nothing to absorb the force.

Vess and Athalir arrived just in time to witness the one-sided brawl. While Vess helped Marcus up, Sathom came close enough for them both to see something in his eyes they'd never seen before – emotion.

"Do not judge me, boy! You know nothing of my pain. I grieve for her. I miss her. But I also miss the thousands of souls taken by the darkness, and if this time could be lived again, and still there were no other options available, there is nothing I would do differently – *nothing*!"

The elemental didn't wait for a reaction, blinking out of existence completely.

"What was that all about?" Vess asked, startled as Marcus snapped free of his helping hand.

"He could have stopped her. He didn't even have to mention the spell. She'd still be here," Marcus said, looking down at his feet to avoid seeing the dying funeral fire.

"And you wouldn't be. Marcus, you know what she was like – she'd never have left you to die. She couldn't, she loved you. She was… a good person." Vess attempted to restore reason and comfort his friend, but Athalir spoke out before he'd succeeded.

"She was stupid!"

Marcus looked up, his wrath now directed at the prince.

"*What* did you say?"

"I said she was *stupid*." The elf's eyes were red from crying, but his face was now stern. "She threw her life away, a life that held such promise. I thought she was the best of us, yet she acted out of nothing more than craven stupidity – terrified of a life without you. She should have been better than that."

Vess couldn't move fast enough to hold Marcus back – and this time, his target couldn't dematerialise out of harm's way.

Marcus' fist slammed into Athalir's nose, with a crunch of cartilage and a burst of blood. From the ground, Athalir saw his attacker coming at him, but had no time to get clear. Dazed as he was from the blow, he could only try to cover his head with his arms as Marcus grabbed his collar with one hand and rained punches with the other.

"Marcus, stop! That's enough!" Vess shouted. He tugged the mage's arms behind his back and heaved him away, giving the bruised and bloody Athalir space to get up as the warrior restrained their grieving leader.

"What's wrong with you? You hate him! You should be *helping* me, not holding me back!" Marcus shouted at Vess, his face red with anger.

"He's not my favourite person, that's true, but *you* are my friend. I hold you back so you don't do something *you* might regret." Vess replied firmly.

With his nose still throbbing and his pride wounded, the elven prince wiped blood from his face and stared at the scarlet stain on his hand. At any other time, with anyone else, it would have been the blood of a deceased man. However, he knew the acidity of what he'd said, and though part of him still meant it, his words came from a grief he'd neither expected nor knew how to handle. He resolved to apologise to Marcus later. For now, he was wise enough to realise it wouldn't help just yet.

"Athalir, I suggest you get back to camp. Tell the others we'll be leaving soon," Vess said, still keeping Marcus subdued.

The elf nodded. Before he left, he turned to look at Erryn's funeral pyre, and spoke the words his people used when saying a final farewell to their loved ones.

"Ahlvaen shael mahn haith. Spirits keep your soul, Erryn."

Once Athalir had gone, Vess released Marcus, watching him closely as he stood motionless, staring at his feet.

"Why did you stop me? I know how you feel about him." Marcus again questioned Vess' motives, this time his voice drained of emotion.

"But you respect him, even regard him as a friend. You'd not thank me for standing by while you killed him. You're better than that. Besides, he's grieving, too. He spoke in pain – any dolt can see that."

The two men stood in silence for many minutes, while Marcus calmed down enough to see things with more rationality.

"What's it like?" Vess asked after a while.

"You mean the soul, I take it?" Marcus spoke quietly without looking up. "Odd. I… have all these memories that aren't my own – sort of like remembering a story you've read, only more… familiar. I remember people and an overwhelming sense of love – and loss. I remember events, moments during a childhood, conversations, sights, even smells. When I first recall those things, they feel like they truly belong to me, and that I'm really Rhyssian, but… the next minute, I'm Marcus and *his* memories feel more… real. It's as if there's no room for both. It's confusing."

"Does it hurt?"

"Hurt? No – well, not now. Not since…" Marcus' voice trailed off.

"Since the spell." Vess quietly confirmed what Marcus had omitted.

"I miss her, Vess. I miss her *so* much."

"I know. I miss her, too." Vess faced Marcus. "I wanted to be the one. I offered as soon as I found out what she and Sathom intended to do but… they said the magic within me wouldn't be enough. Damn, Marcus, I'd never have let her go through with it if it could've been me, I swear."

Marcus offered his friend a reassuring smile, placing his hand on his arm.

"It's alright. I know." He paused and looked out into the sky before facing Vess once more. "I've never felt the need for friends. My whole life I've been content with my own company – no, more than content, I've revelled in it. Except for Julia, I didn't think there was anyone in this world I'd ever class as a true friend. But you, and Erryn, you've both been the best friends a man could wish for. Truly."

Marcus felt the tears welling in his eyes and knew if he started crying he'd never stop. Fortunately, Vess distracted him.

"What about Rhyssian – didn't he have any friends?"

"Hmm, I, er, *he* had a few, yes. But he was so torn apart over the loss of his brother, the closest friend he'd ever had, he became a warrior of the arena, fighting to end his own life – that sort of puts a dampener on most healthy relationships, I'd say."

"And the woman you – *he* – loved? Dessema, was it?" The mage stared into the distance, his eyes then closing briefly as if in pain. Vess spoke again. "I'm sorry. I didn't mean to bring up… I keep forgetting *he* is actually *you*."

"It's strange. When you mentioned her name, I felt a sensation similar to how I feel when we talk about Erryn – but it comes and goes, a bit like a waking dream. I feel great love for Dessema. I remember watching her die, and the pain comes back worse than ever. I think of her in that place, in the darkness; I could hear her voice for most of the time we were trapped there, but I couldn't get to her. I couldn't hold her. I yearn to free her, long to hold her in my arms, and then… then I remember Erryn and it's as if Dessema never existed." Both men stayed silent for a few moments.

"Damn, Marcus. I don't envy you, friend." Vess broke the silence and laughed.

Marcus was grateful for the hint of flippancy.

"Come, we should get back. I… should apologise to Athalir. I believe I may have broken his nose."

"He'll live – unfortunately," Vess said, smirking slightly.

Marcus dealt Vess' arm a playfully feeble punch.

"You go on ahead. There's something I have to do first."

With Vess gone, Marcus waited a little longer for the pyre's flames to die down enough that he could approach safely. By then, there was so little left of the woman, it might have been easy to believe she'd never existed, that she'd been nothing more than a wonderful dream. Now, a dull ache festered in the pit of his stomach, the pain of her absence proof positive she'd been part of his life. Yet he feared even that would diminish in time. The thought of her becoming so insignificant sent an icy shiver up his spine. She was too special to fade into complete nothingness – he wouldn't allow it.

Crouching down to the base of the pyre, he took a small coin purse from his pocket and loosened its ties. Testing the heat with his palm, he reached his hand inside and used his fingers to scrape together a small pile of ash, depositing the fine grey dust into the purse and drawing it closed.

He stood up and bowed his head. Whispering a last farewell, he pictured the memorial garden the elementals had created outside Whitestone's walls, then pocketed the purse and headed back to the others with a fresh determination.

The sanctum could be seen rising up in the distance, as the company progressed along the dirt track to their final destination. Marcus led the way with a new-found confidence, causing the others to wonder if it were still their mage friend in charge or the soul of an ancient warrior. Certainly, something was different about him since he'd come back to them. Whether or not the change was for the better remained to be seen – at least in the eyes of Hessan and Roh, as neither was predisposed towards trust for trust's sake. Marcus was an affable man, likeable if a little scatter-brained, but this Rhyssian was of a race beyond its time and no one knew a thing about him or his people – no one but Sathom, and he was conspicuous by his absence.

That was until they'd travelled to the point in the road where the terrain became a gradual incline. Most of the party had been witness to Sathom's reappearances, so they weren't surprised when a shimmering-blue, magical screen appeared a few feet ahead. However, instead of the recognisable features of Sathom, a man of similar height but burlier build, with blonde hair and blue eyes came into existence as the blue glow vanished. The man began to approach the group until a wary Athalir called out.

"Halt! Who are you, and what is your purpose here? Explain yourself." The elf's hands were poised to reach for his daggers, and he was not the only person ready to take up arms. Hessan, Vess, and Roh were all equally prepared. Marcus, however, nodded at the man.

"Greetings, Sathom."

"Marcus, you recognised me." The man smiled and continued walking to meet them, relief in his eyes.

"Rhyssian recognised you – Marcus is as confused as they are." The mage swept out his hand, drawing his attention to the puzzled looks on the other four faces.

"I should explain." The elemental said, pushing a strand of his cropped ashen hair away from his eyes.

"Yes, because the only explanation I can think of right now is I've had too much to drink – and I know that's not true." Hessan folded his arms across his chest.

"I will be brief. We have little time. We elementals do not possess a physical nature of our own. We… adopted one similar in appearance to the Meranell's vessels back when we first arrived in Gadrionis, to '*fit in*', to make us and them more… compatible, in many ways. Thus, we have the ability to look any way we choose – male, female, young or old. After what happened with… with Erryn, I thought you might not wish to see me as I was. I thought perhaps a change might… make me easier to look upon."

Marcus took a moment to absorb Sathom's words. He had to admit, his ire towards him was still strong – he could never forget – but what was done was done. Nothing he could say, no anger he could direct at Sathom would bring Erryn back.

"Sathom, it's alright. There's no need to change. I think we'd all agree there will be less confusion if you simply returned to the way you were, please."

Sathom smiled, a patent look of relief in his eyes. Before anyone knew what was going on, the old Sathom stood in place of the blond-haired man.

"That's much better," Marcus said, slapping the elemental on the back. "Now, if we're done with this, we should continue. It can't be long before the governors arrive at the sanctum."

All agreed and the journey was resumed. Sathom walked alongside Marcus, taking the opportunity to talk to him alone.

"Marcus, you must know that I attempted to change Erryn's mind, more than once, but…"

"She was stubborn, I know."

"She was strong-willed, determined, courageous, words I feel convey who she was so much more than stubborn. I wish… I wish I had not left it so late to come to know just who she was. I am truly sorry."

Marcus' heart ached as he remembered the woman he'd lost, but he was beyond apportioning blame.

"I know," he whispered.

Part of him, most likely the part that wasn't over a thousand years old, would never totally forgive Sathom for his role in her passing. However, before him, he saw just one way to avenge her death – putting an end to those who had taken the most from both Erryniya Constantine and the kin for whom he now grieved.

Just a couple of hours before sunset, the Sanctum of Souls was finally close enough that its commanding height cast a moonlit shadow, taunting the company's footsteps. Even with the path continuing uphill, the tower rose higher still from a platform of rocky ground, with a surprisingly wide stone footbridge sloping up to meet it. For the group, who were yet some distance away, the terrible nature of the construction was all too clear, and even Marcus gasped at the sight of thick, black tendrils of dark magic snaking over every surface.

The air had become acrid and felt almost scratchy to breathe, the land surrounding the tower mostly bereft of anything but stony ground. As everyone came to a halt, something else drew Vess' eye away from the imposing sanctum.

"What's that over there?" he asked quietly, pointing to a crude circle of large, tree-sized stones enclosed within a low, circular bank.

"It is the henge where the governors perform the ritual that renews their spell of immortality – the ritual they must complete every two-hundred-and-fifty years," Sathom answered in a whisper

Marcus stepped forwards, his eyes remaining fixed on the tower.

"Right. Tell me what to do."

"I will need to scout the area first. The seventh mage, the guardian, should be on that bridge – but I cannot see him."

"Sathom, I can *feel* them in there, now that we're close. I can hear them suffering. I must save them, *now*. I'll deal with this guardian." Marcus made to march up the hill but was held back by Sathom's tight grip on his arm.

"Wait! You will get yourself killed, and the souls will suffer an eternity in that place. Is that what you want?"

Marcus sighed, then shook his head.

"Fair enough, but you've yet to tell me what I must do. What's the plan?"

"It is simple enough. I will lure the guardian away from the doorway at the far end of the bridge, at which point you will have a small measure of time to get to the door and use your magic on that of the governors, breaking the seal and freeing the souls in the process."

Hessan looked incredulous.

"Really? That's all there is to it? No battle, no bloodshed? I was under the impression there'd be blood – don't tell me the blood was a lie."

"I have to say, I'm surprised at such a simple strategy. But, if it means an end to the governors, so be it."

"It will. Once every soul is free of the tower, the spell that prolongs the life of those men will break, causing their bodies to wither and die almost instantaneously." Sathom both looked and sounded confident, and that was enough for Athalir.

"Then, Marcus, you shall have the aid of us all. I presume Sathom didn't factor in our involvement but, now we're here, I think I can safely say we'd all be honoured to assist with the distraction part of this plan."

Sathom turned to face Athalir.

"I am glad of the offer, your highness, but you should know, the guardian is extremely dangerous. Taller than anything you can imagine, and coated in eternal flame, he is a monster beyond your experience. I will fare well enough as he cannot harm me, but…"

"You can count me in." Hessan interrupted.

Vess and Roh added their words of affirmation.

"You have your allies, Sathom. We're ready!" Athalir said, clasping Sathom's forearm.

Marcus took a step forwards and stared at the Sanctum of Souls. Inside him, Rhyssian's soul was restless, rage and sadness boiling over in equal measure as he sensed the anguish of his ancient brethren.

"Now, it's our turn to take, and we don't stop taking until every last governor is dead and every last soul is free."

"Hold a moment!" Roh's eyes were squinting towards the henge. "What's that light coming up from the stone circle?"

Everyone turned to look at the orange halo now surrounding the circle.

"No! How can that be? My calculations cannot be that inaccurate." The elemental's face betrayed intense shock.

"What's wrong?" Marcus asked, feeling his faith in the plan slipping away.

Sathom walked uphill a short way, stopping to stare at the henge with troubled eyes.

"Somehow, we are too late. The governors are already here. Their confluence has begun."

"What does that mean for us?" Vess asked, his positivity replaced by concern.

Sathom remained silently staring.

"Sathom! Answer me. What do we do now?" Marcus prodded.

"The spell is no longer at its weakest. The governors have converged. They are revitalising their life-force as we speak, and that window of opportunity is lost to us. Not only will the lock require more power than you possess, Marcus, but the governors will defend this place with all their might. The guardian is now the least of our concerns."

CHAPTER TWENTY-NINE

The stakes were the same as they had always been. Thousands of souls remained imprisoned within the blackness, desperately clawing at the last vestiges of sanity for far too long already. The voices were speaking madness when Larris had merged with baby Benedict, three-hundred years ago. They were virtually incoherent when Rhyssian's soul had been implanted into the infant that grew to be Marcus Ryan. Now, as the mage stood with his comrades just downhill from the Sanctum of Souls, the Meranell within the man compelled him to continue, no matter how hard things had just become.

"Nothing has changed." Marcus turned around to address his companions. "I still need to get to that door, so a distraction is still key."

"Marcus, we'll take on anyone you throw at us, but can't we just kill the governors? Seems a waste of time distracting them when we can skip to the end goal, now they're right here," Hessan said, the adrenaline building in anticipation of a fight

Marcus looked to Sathom to address the dwarf's point.

"If it were that simple, I'd have found a way to kill them centuries ago. You cannot think men who wished to live forever would risk leaving themselves exposed to attack. They made use of the Meranells' strong bodies and built in a level of invulnerability – and even if they had not, they have their sons' vessels as a fail-safe back in Vaharia."

"Not all of them." Vess spoke up.

Everyone stared at the warrior awaiting elaboration.

"Alerick, my father – his sons are either dead, or not interested in becoming his next soul-suit. Can we use that to our advantage?"

"We know not if he is still able to shift into your body, Vess, You could actually prove to be our undoing," Sathom replied.

"But… he *could* add to the whole distraction thing." Roh's eyes were alive with the beginnings of an idea. She had the group's attention.

"This *Alerick*, he'll recognise his son, yes? From what I know about all this, he'll be keen to reclaim a potential vessel. We also have the guardian to contend with, so splitting our attentions seems to me the practical solution."

"You mean, use me as bait?" Vess glared at Roh.

"Of course!" She smiled at Vess, her azure eyes sparkling.

"Fair enough!" He smiled back.

"Yes, this might just work." Marcus became more animated as the situation seemed to be improving. "The governors will be focused on Vess – who they'll not harm, as they need him – while Hessan, Athalir, and Roh will take on the guardian. Meanwhile, I'll get on to that bridge and head for the door. I've dealt with dark magic before, on Benedict's excursion. I can break through it without too much trouble."

"Marcus, I applaud your positivity, but what you experienced at the crypt was nothing compared to the magic sealing that door. Had we arrived before the governors, while the spell was at its weakest, you could have dealt with it. That is why a mage was needed, after all. However, once that confluence is complete, there is no one person with enough magical energy to break the lock." Sathom was secretly pleased to hear such confidence in the magically cautious mage, but facts were facts. He'd always known the limitations of the quest.

"So we interrupt their little meeting, prevent them from finishing the ritual. All I need is time, Sathom. I *can* do this. Trust me."

The elemental paused for thought. He remained doubtful of Marcus' ability to destroy the dark magic. Nevertheless, he couldn't help but admire his perseverance. If they could prevent the ritual from concluding, perhaps it could still be done.

"I *do* trust you, Marcus. What do you wish me to do?"

"Come, let's make sure we all know what's required. Sathom, I have something fun in mind for you and your newly-available powers."

Hessan, Athalir, and Roh watched as Vess set off towards the stone circle and Marcus made for the bridge. Sathom had already teleported himself to a higher location. From there, he'd be able to carry out Marcus' order without being seen until it was necessary.

The guardian, Sathom insisted, would be close to the tower. The spell that bound him was intrinsically linked to the sanctum itself, and thus, he was unable to stray too far from its walls. With this in mind, once they had run across the preceding wasteland, they crept up the hill via the shadows, heading towards the orange glow on the right side that indicated their target was behind the tower. Sathom's description of the seventh mage had seemed deliberately vague. What met them as they came up over the rise made them understand why.

The guardian dwarfed them all, his huge frame a twisted mess of torn flesh, melting skin, and ripples of fire. A great, horned, skeletal head with a gaping jaw full of jagged teeth sat atop shoulders that measured at least as wide as the hall back in Geryndor. It was crouched and still until it caught sight of the trio. The monster then pulled itself up using limbs with girths the size of ancient oaks and roared, sending a volley of saliva-filled wind straight ahead.

"Attack!" Athalir shouted, standing back while Hessan and Roh held their weapons aloft and charged forwards. Before he'd left, Marcus had given the prince Erryn's bow and quiver, and told him to think of her as he used them. This he did, as he took the bow in hand and deftly began loosening arrows into the legs of the beast. Worryingly, none of the arrows reached their target, sizzling into flames before they could break flesh.

"Sorry, Erryn," Athalir said, casting the bow aside and unsheathing his daggers. "I have to do this my way."

The elf sprinted to join the man and woman now slashing and hacking at anywhere they could reach without being singed, and dodging incoming blows from gigantic fists. The air all around the guardian was hot, making fighting that bit harder, and the smell of burning flesh assaulting their nostrils added the urge to vomit to the trials they would have to endure until Marcus completed his task.

As Vess approached the stone circle, the sound of monotone male voices reciting words in a foreign language reached his ears.

He looked sideways to see the three on guardian detail taking a stealthy route up to the tower. Staring towards the bridge, he could just make out Marcus making his way up the first of many steps, his cloak billowing out behind in the strong wind that had picked up since they had arrived. In his mind, he willed his friend to succeed, before directing attention to his own task. He knew what he had to do, and was even strangely looking forwards to it, but he couldn't deny his nerves were on edge at the prospect of finally meeting Alerick. He had no idea what he'd say to him. All he could do was hope he had a better idea when he reached the circle, and didn't simply stand there, open-mouthed.

"Come on, Vess, time to meet your father." He sucked in a large dose of air, puffed out his chest, and took a stride forwards, before a sharp blow to the back of his head brought him crashing to the ground. The last thing he saw as his vision grew black was the sneering face of the skaithen.

From his vantage point on a platform that circled the uppermost heights of the tower, Sathom could see everything, though with the wind howling around him, he couldn't hear very much. He watched as the guardian rose to meet Athalir, Hessan, and Roh, the group valiantly confronting the creature, but gaining little advantage. The beast loomed over its attackers, adeptly evading their weapons and, many times, swatting them to the ground like insects. The elemental feared for their lives, but told himself they were at least achieving their mission; to keep it occupied.

Turning his gaze towards the bridge, he breathed a sigh of relief as he saw Marcus, alive, and climbing the stone steps that would take him up onto the foot-way. He was in no immediate danger and so, with a silent prayer for the success of the plan, he turned to check on Vess.

"No!" he cried out, his voice dissipating straight into the wind. Even if he'd teleported instantly, he'd not have reached Vess in time to stop the skaithen's assault.

"How could I have been so stupid?" Sathom whispered to himself. He should have known the skaithen couldn't die – being a manifestation of the governors' dark magic. *While it exists, so will he*, he thought, feeling foolish for forgetting. He looked at the henge and saw the governors entranced in the ritual, undisturbed and unfaltering despite the activity all around. Now he knew why they weren't concerning themselves enough to halt the convergence; they didn't need to bother with the skaithen there to take care of things. Another realisation followed which explained why they'd not arrived ahead of the governors. *He has been spying on us. That is why they are here early.*

The skaithen's presence had not been accounted for in Marcus' strategy, so someone needed to deal with him if everything were to go as smoothly as intended. However, Vess had failed to interrupt the governors' spell – if it were allowed to go ahead, they may never be able to release the souls. Sathom prepared to aim his own form of magic at the gathering of mages, hoping to, at the very least, distract them with a localised hail storm, or perhaps enclose the circle within a dome of ice. *Yes*, he thought, *that may even prevent them from casting long enough for Marcus to do what has to be done.* The elemental rubbed his hands together, then raised his arms, but before he could finish, he caught sight of the skaithen's dematerialising body.

"Where is he going?" he said aloud, instinctively turning to check on Marcus. He looked just in time to see the evil being materialise a few feet behind the young mage. Sathom had no choice. Without Marcus, all hope was lost. Even if he kept the governors from their ritual, there'd be no one left to destroy the dark magic seal.

Marcus took the steps two at a time, his long legs making light work of the distance between each stair. Now, just a few remained before he could set foot on the bridge. The wind had grown strong and seemed to be tugging him backwards, yet he pushed on, determined not to waste the efforts of those fighting or hindering.

With one hand, he held the hood of his cloak tight to his face in an attempt to keep the wind from his ache-prone ears. In the other, he carried his staff, certain he'd need its help against whatever kept the sanctum's door shut. He dare not look to the others. Instead, he kept faith their missions would go according to plan. He had to stay positive. Marcus may have been upbeat about life, but Rhyssian's negativity might threaten his resolve if he let it take control. *Balance, it's all about balance*, he thought, ironically stumbling up the last step as he misjudged his stride.

At that exact second, he heard a noise right behind him and spun around to see, with surprise, the skaithen grinning malevolently. There was no time for confusion. The next moment, Sathom appeared, grabbed the skaithen by the throat, and took him with him as he vanished again.

"Whoa! That was close," Marcus said, mentally thanking Sathom and purposely avoiding contemplating the skaithen's return. He had a job to do, and the way ahead was clear, for now.

Sathom and the skaithen whizzed between dimensions, their powers the only weapons required as the skaithen aimed to flee and the elemental aimed to stop him. Faster and faster they dissolved in and out of the ether, ducking and dodging projectiles, and swapping the upper hand over and over again.

Sathom knew he'd not be able to keep the skaithen away indefinitely, but he'd give everything he had to give Marcus the best chance.

Meanwhile, within the stone circle, a dark liquid bubbled along a trench that ran between the stones and the bank. Alerick and his fellows felt a surge of energy vibrate through their bodies as their spell reached its conclusion. Immortality had a distinctive taste, or so the head governor had always thought. He tasted it, like salt and metal, clearer than ever as his longevity was recharged for the next quarter-of-a-century. His limbs felt stronger, his heartbeat faster.

"Ah, I had forgotten how good this feels," he said, licking his lips as magic still crackled at his fingertips.

"Alerick, look to the bridge," Governor Wymond said, causing Alerick and the other four mages to stare that way.

The head governor's refreshed eyesight was nevertheless still that of an old man. He could make out something moving on the bridge, and left the circle to gain a better view. Stepping over the unconscious body of his own son, he barely registered his presence and simply glanced coldly at his body. He was far more interested in the figure of a man heading towards the tower.

"It seems the skaithen failed, again." The head governor sighed "What is the point of having a dark magic familiar? You wish a task to be done, do it yourself, Alerick." The tall, robed man darted his eyes around to see the skirmish in which the guardian was embroiled. *Keep the guardian otherwise engaged, clever… in a rudimentary way.* He thought, a twinge of concern biting at his confidence. Alerick called out to the other governors.

"Brothers, see to it the guardian has a fair fight. I wish to meet the man of whom the seer spoke."

With that, the elder mage enunciated more uncommon language and disappeared, a thin, shimmering mist settling on Vess in his wake.

"I hope the lad gets to that door soon!" Hessan shouted above the din of roaring guardian and clanking steel.

"Why? Are you getting tired, dwarf?" Athalir teased, rolling sideways to avoid the slam of a flaming hand.

"Of course I'm getting tired! We've be swinging at this thing for ages!" As if to illustrate his point, the dwarven king heaved one axe, then the other, serving more to make his muscles ache than to cause the beast any damage.

Roh lunged in with her shield as the guardian aimed to swat Hessan sideways, shoving him out the way and taking the blow herself.

"You can thank me later!" she shouted as she got up, leaving no pause before charging forwards with her sword outstretched.

The noise the beast made as it struck out was deafening; a constant roar combined with the crackle of huge flames.

Attacking and evading, the three continued despite their flagging stamina. The only blood shed was their own as none of their strikes came to fruition. The monster's flaming barrier was impenetrable, and each knew they'd have no choice but to fight on until Marcus broke the spell. All they had to do was keep him away from the bridge. Or so they thought.

With all three distracted by the fray, no one noticed the arrival of the governors until it was too late. With one blast of magic, Hessan, Athalir, and Roh were thrown to the ground by a massive shockwave. As they struggled to get up, the wind knocked out of them, they saw the five robed men chanting, a glistening dome forming around and over them until they were completely shielded.

"Er, I think we're going to need a bigger army!" Hessan quipped as the group stood, arms at the ready, preparing for whatever was about to come.

With the magical shield active, the two mages who weren't predisposed with maintaining it propelled missiles of fire at the group. Each time, they managed to dodge, but it was only a matter of time before their luck ran out.

"I've had enough of this!" Roh shouted, before leaping forwards and ramming her shield into the wall of magic. The barrier responded to the collision as any corporeal object would.

"Hey, it's solid! That means we can break it!" the woman yelled back to the others. She tried again, this time with her sword, and a small crack splintered the surface like broken glass. However, with a surge of magic from the three chanting governors, the crack healed, their defence whole once more.

Athalir leapt to avoid an incoming projectile, landing so that he could see the guardian lumbering towards the bridge.

"Damn!" he said, and then smiled as an idea started to form in his mind.

This might just work, he thought, leaving the others to face the governors' blitz while he sprinted to attract the guardian's attention.

Moments later, he came running backwards, continuously taunting and luring the huge beast closer to the governors.

"What are you doing?" Hessan called out.

"Just keep them throwing magic at you! I have a plan!" Athalir responded, leading the guardian as far as he could, then somersaulting backwards to land on top of the barrier.

Within the shield, the governors realised too late what was about to happen. As the guardian's fist slammed down towards it, Athalir back-flipped to safety and watched from a crouching position as the dome took the beast's blow. Such was the force, the mages powering the shield had the energy knocked from them. All five governors bent over to cover their heads as a sound like breaking glass heralded the shattering of their protection. But the momentum of the guardian's clout was too great, and he couldn't prevent his fist from coming down on the governors.

Hessan and Roh cheered as Athalir returned. They watched as the governors' bodies remained motionless on the ground.

"Do you think they're dead?" Roh asked.

"Going on what Sathom says, I doubt it, but they're not a problem for now," Athalir replied, smiling and obviously pleased with himself.

"Well, I know something that still *is* a problem." Hessan nodded towards the advancing guardian, and sucked in a deep breath.

"Back to work, comrades."

Marcus could see the door clearly as he ran along the bridge. Sathom was right; the tendrils of dark magic were everywhere, constantly undulating across the entire surface, and in far greater abundance than at the crypt. High up on the foot-way, the wind battered him from all sides; he knew his friends were dealing with their own tasks, below but he could hear nothing, and he preferred it that way. He couldn't afford to be diverted from his goal now.

The mage ran on, the door growing closer, the end almost in sight. Then, just as he was nearly within arm's reach, he was staggered by a whoosh of air and the emergence of a dark-robed figure, accompanied by a strange mist.

Quickly reclaiming his stability, Marcus looked up at the face of the man before him. Shadowed as he was by a heavy hood, he could barely make out any features, but the bitter frown of thin lips told him all he needed to know.

"What is your name, boy?" Alerick asked, his voice hoarse and measured.

"Marcus. And you are a governor, I take it?" The mage desperately tried to make his voice sound confident, even as his mind felt failure creeping in.

"I am Alerick, *head* governor. Tell me, who *are* you, exactly? I know you are human, despite the seer's attempt at deception."

Marcus cringed at the mention of Erryniya. Her suffering had felt even more personal since Vess told him of Erryn's encounter with Valeria, and of her true parentage.

"The seer you tortured and left to be raped, you mean?"

Alerick sighed.

"That was the skaithen. He always did have a penchant for acting beyond my orders. But yes, how fares the dwarven seer? I must pay her a visit and… *thank* her for the misinformation."

"You'll get nowhere near her!" Marcus bristled with rage.

"Really? *Interesting.* I ask again, who are you? You seem… familiar." Alerick stepped closer, leaning in as if to get a better sense of who his foe was.

The younger mage stood firm and tightened his grip on the staff. He could almost feel Rhyssian trying to break out as the ancient soul confronted his nemesis for the first time in over a thousand years. Marcus drew on Rhyssian's anger and spoke confidently.

"I am a mage of the city of Whitestone, but I also host the soul of Prince Rhyssian of the Meranells, son to King Niron, heir to the throne of Vaharia. Together, we'll take back that which you stole."

Alerick lifted his hands to bring down his hood, revealing thinning grey hair, but a surprisingly wrinkle-free face. He cocked his head to one side as he stared at Marcus, then laughed.

"*That's* it! The Meranell heir apparent himself. Spoilt brat if I recall. I knew there was something familiar about you. I'll wager it's a whiff of that same royal self-righteousness your father lorded over those of us less fortunate. I will never forget his supercilious answer when I asked for more than he deemed us worthy. '*This gift is not mine to bestow. Only the Meranells can handle the burden of immortality.*' Then we had to watch as cowards like you brawled to give it all up. Sickening! Believe me when I say, I gained more than immortality when I took that royal bastard's head."

Marcus could contain Rhyssian no longer. A fireball formed in his right hand, and in temper, he cast it at the governor, who only had to sidestep to avoid contact.

"You mean to revoke my immortality with power as feeble as that? Surely your elemental friend hasn't led you to believe it would be that easy?" The ancient mage conjured a fireball of his own, thrusting it at Marcus. But dodging magic was something he had managed to master. The fiery orb travelled close enough for him to feel its heat, but it passed by nonetheless.

Marcus looked past his enemy to the door and knew, if he had any hope of freeing the souls, he'd have to incapacitate Alerick. Trying to think fast, he imagined a cage, the first thing that came into his head. He stared at the governor and formed the bars up and around the robed man. However, just as fast as they went up, Alerick disintegrated them with a flick of his hand.

Marcus tried again, this time conjuring a length of rope that he wrapped tightly around the governor, making sure to tie the ends. Again Alerick broke free, burning the rope until it sizzled to nothing but ash. Over and over Marcus' attempts proved ineffective. Never had he regretted his avoidance of magical tutoring more than he did right then. Erryn had taught him the principal, but putting it into practise seemed to be evading him more than ever. The harder he tried, the worse his failure. So great was his frustration at achieving so little, he wasted magical energy casting even the tiniest invocation, until he felt sapped of strength and stumbled backwards as his adversary advanced.

"You think to best me, boy? If so, then you are sorely mistaken, for, in ten centuries, I've not encountered one soul that could offer anything more than a spark to ignite my wrath. It will take more than you possess to incur aught from me but displeased indifference. I'll see you die before I'll bear witness to any further display of your craven magical ineptitude. And people say I know not of compassion! Thank me for this mercy, Marcus. In your death, I offer a kindness." Alerick then spoke in words Marcus had never heard, and raised his right hand, a purple mist quickly forming the shape of a sword.

A sword, why didn't I think of that? Marcus thought. As the son of a magic-imbued, noble family, he'd never even handled a blade; but as the ancient Meranell warrior, swordsmanship was second nature.

It was as if Rhyssian's enthusiasm was separate from his own trepidation. Still stooped beneath Alerick, he put everything he had into forming his sword, rising up, and parrying the governor's blow just in time.

Rhyssian's skill took over, leaving Marcus to uphold the shape of the glowing blue weapon. The two men fought backwards and forwards along the bridge, Marcus mostly retaining the upper hand.

The wind howled as swords clashed, each man sustaining injury, but never enough to break the stalemate. In his head, Marcus surmised that youth was on his side. All he had to do was wear the older man down. And so he fought on.

Vess awoke from his unconsciousness to a shrill, painful shriek. Slowly raising his head, he saw Whistler sat on his chest, staring down at him with his huge, yellow eyes. The creature began jumping up and down and spinning in circles, his long tail brushing over Vess' face on each rotation.

"I'm awake, I'm awake! Enough!" He pushed the animal off and lurched to his feet. As the blood returned to his head, a dull pain spread out across his skull. He raised his hand to feel a sticky patch in his short hair, grunting at the red stain as he inspected his fingertips.

With his memory rapidly returning, he hurried to the circle, only to find it completely empty. Spinning round, he noted the flaming guardian and its three attackers, then immediately turned his attention to the bridge. He expected to see the lone figure of Marcus making his way to the door. However, even from a fair distance away, he could see the sword fight.

With all haste, Vess ran across the wasteland, reaching the stairway and thundering up as fast as he could. But before he could reach the top, he heard Marcus cry out in pain. Picking up speed, he made it to the foot-way just in time to see a robed man pulling his sword from Marcus' torso, blood fizzing on the magical blade.

"No!" Vess shouted, time seeming to stand still as he watched his friend drop to his knees, clutching at his wound. The younger mage's own ethereal blade, loosened from his grip, faded to nothing before it could reach the stone floor.

Vess' cry drew the governor's attention.

"Ah, my son. Just in time to swap bodies as this injured one breathes its last. Be patient while I finish off this pathetic excuse for a mage." Alerick swung his sword outwards, ready to arc across Marcus' neck. In that split second, Vess careered forwards, great-sword ahead, the tip driving through the man's body with only an instant to spare. He thrust the blade deep until it emerged the other side. Still pushing forwards, Vess came face-to-face with his father, staring, emotionless into his eyes, as blood began to spew from his mouth.

"You… cannot… kill… me… boy! I… will… rise… again."

"Not if I have anything to do with it," Marcus said, trying to get up while covering the hole in his side.

"Marcus! You're alive!" Vess felt relief wash over him.

"Only… just," the mage replied. "Get me to that… door, before he makes good on his promise."

"Are you sure? You don't look like you can stand, let alone break that seal!"

"I have… to try. Now… come on, help me… up."

Vess nodded, raising his friend to a standing position and supporting him, with one arm wrapped around his waist.

Together, the pair made it to the door, a steady trail of blood following Marcus' footsteps.

"Right, let's… see to this… wound, first." With effort, Marcus managed to conjure a length of cloth. "Wrap that… around. Should… do the trick."

Vess did as he was asked, all the while trying to avoid looking at the wound.

"Ah, my staff." Vess understood and ran back to collect the staff from where it had been discarded earlier.

With his body no longer feeling like something important was about to fall out, Marcus put his weight on the wooden shaft and concentrated as best he could on channelling his magic through the crystal. He remembered how Sathom had said it would be needed, and felt immediately reassured by its presence.

Vess stared at the winding, twisting tentacles of dark magic, and willed them to surrender to Marcus' power, while the mage used all his strength and focus to break the seal.

But nothing happened. Marcus tried again; the crystal glowed this time, indicating the second attempt was better than the first, but still the dark magic kept hold.

"It's no good, Marcus. You've tried. No one can say you haven't, my friend."

"Just… once… more." Marcus gritted his teeth through his pain, drew in a breath and forced the magic from within. The crystal burst into life, a maelstrom of light and movement at its core and a white halo lighting up the immediate area. The tendrils shrunk back, reacting to the magic surging from the weakened mage.

"It's working. You're doing… something! Keep going!" Vess said, his positivity returned.

"Agh!" Marcus yelled, fresh blood seeping through his bandage. He began to drop, but Vess caught him in time.

"I can't do it, Vess. I don't have enough… energy," Marcus mumbled.

"Then you shall have mine." Sathom spoke from behind. He wasted no time in joining Marcus and Vess at the door. "I really should learn to listen to my own advice," he said, grabbing Marcus' free hand and holding it tightly. "No one person with magical energy… Well, now we have two."

Marcus stared at the elemental, confused.

"Go on, try it again. This time, you will have *my* energy to draw on."

Vess was concerned.

"Will this work? You said back at The Dead Wood that if your energy were drained, you'd cease to exist."

"It is true that my energy is not infinite, but I am sure Marcus will manage before I am depleted. Now, stand back. This could cause a little… heat."

Vess moved away and looked on as Marcus once again closed his eyes and attempted to power up his magic.

Nothing happened for a few moments, but then a low hum began, growing louder and louder until the foot-way itself started to vibrate. The crystal lit up brighter than before, its glow spreading wider. Vess covered his ears as the sound was now deafening.

As the energy peaked, Marcus' eyes flashed open, light pouring from them. The dark magic recoiled again, continuing to shrink back, peeling away further and further from the middle of the door.

Vess noticed Sathom's form was becoming transparent.

"Come on," he said quietly, praying Marcus could destroy the seal before the elemental vanished.

Slowly but surely, the magic was working, but Sathom knew he had little time. He didn't care for himself, but if he died, there'd be no one left to give the souls the last rites. With one final grip of Marcus' hand, he gave the mage the impetus to give one last push.

It worked. As the last vestiges of dark magic slithered back from the door, it burst open. Marcus and Sathom collapsed to the floor as a tremendous surge of sparkling light erupted from within the tower.

CHAPTER THIRTY

Below the bridge, Hessan, Athalir, and Roh were bruised and battered, but still standing as their battle with the guardian continued. The beast was unrelenting, impervious to their blades, and not one of them was confident they could last much longer. Hessan took a blow meant for Athalir and was flung backwards, his head striking the ground with a painful crash.

"Hessan!" the elf called out, before leaping at the guardian, his heart pounding and heat surging through his body. But he was also thrown back. He managed to limit his injury by dropping into a roll, only to feel his shoulder pop out of its socket as he landed wrong. The prince gritted his teeth to curtail the imminent scream of pain.

Roh was now the only one still upright.

"Yargh!" she yelled, her battle cry keeping the monster's attention on her, and giving the others time to get up. But the guardian had seen his chance. Drawing his fist back as far as he could, he punched towards the warrior woman. She braced for the impact, holding her shield over her head and torso.

But the blow never came. After a few moments, she slowly lowered her shield, expecting to see the fiery beast. Instead, as a bright light spilled over the edge of the bridge close to the tower, all that stood before her was the naked form of a young man. He looked confused, as did Roh, but before she could get some answers, the man looked at her mournfully and mouthed "I am sorry." Then he slumped to the ground. The warrior ran to the man that had once been a beast. He was still breathing, but his body was slowly shrivelling up. In that moment, despite her exhaustion and pain, she felt an overwhelming sense of pity for the naked man. As his breath became shallower, she covered his nudity with her shield, offering him some final dignity, then bade him farewell.

Remembering the governors, she called to the others, and together, they made their way to the five mages who were still on the ground where the guardian's fist had left them broken, but alive. They stood motionless, staring at the men as they slowly began to age.

As the dark magic vacated the outside of the sanctum, the inside, too, was rapidly emptying. From his sprawled sitting position on the cold stone of the bridge, Marcus gave a weak smile. He and Sathom looked up, exhausted, but happy, as the souls of their friends and family continued to flow from the open door. The sky above was filling with a pink haze, every sparkling orb within it a Meranell, revelling in the freedom brought to them by one of their own.

"Ugh!" Marcus grunted as he tried to stand, clasping his hands to the bandage.

"You can heal that, you know?" Sathom said.

"I think you're mistaking me for someone with power." Marcus laughed, before wincing in pain again.

"Marcus, you have just defeated the darkest magic this world has ever seen."

"I couldn't have done that without you. On my own, I'm still pretty much useless with magic."

Sathom got up, offering his hand to help the mage do the same.

"I simply provided the energy you had expended. The ability was – and *is* – yours, my friend."

Marcus stood against the wall of the bridge, resting against it for support.

"But you said…"

"I said no *one* person with magical energy had the power. I was wrong. You just needed a boost. Now, I know you are still drained, so take my hand, place it over the wound, and focus on healing. Remember what Erryn said – *feel the magic*."

Marcus hesitated, sadly hearing Erryn's words echo in his mind, but he did as the elemental said, partly because he had no stamina left to argue. With Sathom providing the energy, the mage closed his eyes and pictured the torn skin pulling together. It took minutes, and a huge amount of effort, but, finally, he felt the wound close. It still smarted, but the bleeding stopped, and moving was easier now that he wasn't worried about tearing it further.

"Well done!" Sathom said, a warm smile gracing his face. "Let us check on our friend." He motioned towards Vess, who was stood near Alerick's body a long way down the bridge, and the pair walked slowly away from the tower.

Vess had been filled with awe as the process of breaking the spell took its course. He'd been pleased beyond measure for his friend as his kin had finally been released. However, a coldness now gripped him as he stood staring down at his father, who was still impaled on his sword. The man's skin actively began to age, his voice getting raspier and his eyes clouding over.

"Son… I… have little… time. I wish… ugh… I wish things… had been… different. Perhaps… I could have been… a better man… a real... father. Ugh… I'm… sor… sorry. Th… thank… you."

As the last of the souls fled the sanctum, the governor's body wrinkled so much it became unrecognisable. His flesh fell away like old rags, leaving his skeleton to dry up and finally crumble to nothing more than dust. The heavy robes he'd worn piled on top of the ash just as Sathom and Marcus reached Vess' side.

"Are you alright?" Marcus asked, eyeing his friend's vacant gaze.

Vess reached forwards and dispassionately retrieved his sword from where it rested atop his father's remains.

"I am now," he said, wiping the blade and returning it to his back.

Just then, Roh came running up the steps and along the bridge, followed by Athalir staggering up with the support of Hessan. All three were covered in cuts and blood.

"What happened? Did you do it?" Roh asked Marcus with excitement, the first time anyone had seen her so animated.

"Yes, *we* did it," Marcus replied, smiling at Sathom and Vess, then turning around to look up at the souls hovering in the night sky.

"What happened to your arm?" Vess asked Athalir, noticing the way he cradled the dislocated limb with his other hand.

"His shoulder popped out. You should have heard the crack." Hessan chuckled and nudged the elf, causing him to grimace in pain and scowl at the dwarf.

"Marcus, it is time I sent the souls on their way home. I can… allow you some time to say farewell, if you wish," Sathom said, touching the mage's forearm.

Marcus thought for a moment. Rhyssian's feelings and memories prompted him to accept the offer.

"Will they… know who I am?"

"They will know."

"But how will *I* recognise *them*? They're just… glowy orbs."

"I can give them form. Not solid, but you will see those you loved and cared for. Come, we must do this now."

Sathom led Marcus to the middle of the bridge, right beneath the mist of souls.

He placed his palms flat against each other, bowed his head, and uttered the ancient words last used more than ten centuries ago, only omitting the final phrase that would usher the souls home. In its place, he used the incantation reserved to give an opportunity to loved ones who still had something left to say.

Marcus felt a strange mix of hope and anxiety in the pit of his stomach as the first person took shape on the foot-way and walked towards him. It was bathed in a pink hue, without shade or detail, but was a definite figure nonetheless.

"Benedict?" He gasped at the familiar, yet translucent face of his former mentor, but faltered as he realised the face wasn't familiar as that of the old man. Instead, it was his opponent in the arena. "I mean, Larris." Marcus' face betrayed his bewilderment.

"Ah, Benedict will do. I'll still call you *dandy-headed rich boy*, after all." The man smiled, a characteristic wicked glint in the eyes of a different face.

"What happened to you? How did you end up in the tower?"

"Let's just say an old '*friend*' got his revenge. Got dragged back to this damned place the second my vessel choked."

"Ah, it's so good to see you again, my old friend. Have you... found your son?"

Benedict looked to Sathom, who seemed to understand, and a boy took form and joined them on the bridge. He looked to be about seventeen and had startlingly similar features to Larris.

"Thank you for saving me – and my father," the boy said, looking happily at Rhyssian's ancient arena rival.

Marcus nodded.

"You're welcome. I'm just glad to see you reunited."

"Ugh! Same old noble manners – should have known. You were much the same as Rhyssian, you know," Benedict teased. "Right. We must go. There's a few more folk waiting to speak with you. And… thank you. I knew you could do it. Take care of yourself – dandy-head."

The man and his son drifted back up until they once again became one with the pink mist, their human-like forms melting away.

As soon as they'd gone, another figure emerged, an old childhood friend. They reminisced and then parted, with others patiently waiting to greet and thank the man that had saved their souls. More and more presented themselves before returning, formless, to the pink haze. Then Dessema came into view. Their meeting was painful, Marcus revisiting Rhyssian's memories of that dreadful night clearer than ever. But, though a part of him ached for a love lost, there was still a greater place in his heart for Erryn, and he couldn't help but wish human souls could come back too. Nevertheless, he told Dessema he loved her and whispered farewell, keeping his true feeling to himself to save her from emotional pain he'd not be around to ease.

Finally, one last person from his past arrived before him. The figure was tall and well-built, his demeanour that of a man of high standing and high-born disposition.

"Father!" Of all the people Marcus had conversed with, this was the first time he had felt the least like a mage of Whitestone and more like Prince Rhyssian of the Meranells.

He instinctively bowed before the figure of the imposing royal, but King Niron urged him to rise.

"Son, it is *I* that should bow before *you.* You saved us all. You have made me prouder than any father could ever be."

"Father, I'm sorry I let you down, that I refused the throne. I hated disappointing you that way. I wanted to tell you that night that I'd changed my mind but I… never got the chance."

"Oh, my boy, I wasn't disappointed because I'd lost an heir – I was terrified I was going to lose my son."

"You mean, you aren't ashamed of me?"

"Rhyssian, I could never look at you and feel shame. Not in that lifetime or any other. I love you, my son."

The two men talked for a few minutes, making up in a small way for lost time, before Sathom hesitantly interrupted.

"I am sorry, your majesty, but it is time."

The king nodded and, after a tearful farewell, reluctantly allowed his soul to be drawn back to the others.

"I love you too, father," Marcus called as the image of Niron became nothing more than a circle of light.

Then, with the last person to speak ready to leave, the only elemental left in all of Gadrionis spoke the final words that would allow the souls to depart, and closed his eyes as the mist gradually dissipated, the orbs dimming until nothing was left.

All of a sudden, the entire bridge began to shake, and a rumbling resonated from the base of the tower.

"What's going on?" Marcus shouted as the rumbling got louder.

"It is the sanctum! I think it is breaking apart now the souls have gone!" Sathom shouted back

"Erm, this bridge is connected to that tower that's breaking apart right?" Hessan said above the din. "Think it's time to–"

"Run!" Marcus hollered.

No one needed telling twice. With the tower crumbling down upon itself and the foot-way plummeting metre by metre to the ground far below, the group sprinted across the bridge and down the steps, just making it in time as everything collapsed and a massive plume of dust burst up into the air.

Everyone stared into the rubble below, each breathing a sigh of relief.

"Well, there goes my idea of a luxury tower home, complete with extra-wide bridge entrance, in the southern wastelands," Marcus quipped.

The others laughed, the pressure of everything that had happened finally able to be released.

"Come. Let's leave this place. I'm starving!" the mage said, turning around, only to nearly trip up over Whistler.

"Ah, it is my unnerving, yet strangely endearing, little friend," Sathom said, attempting to coax the animal to his outstretched hand. But it seemed Whistler had other ideas as he ran up to Vess and scrambled onto his shoulder, wrapping his tail around his neck.

Vess look mildly irritated at first, but as the creature cooed in his ear, he smiled.

"So be it, Whistler. Looks like you're coming with us."

The warrior walked past the other members of the party without even a second glance behind him. Stopping briefly at Athalir's side, he used his immense bulk to grab the elf before he could protest, and, in one brutal movement, returned the dislocated shoulder to its socket. Athalir yelled so loud his voice echoed around the wasteland.

"I've waited a long time to cause that sound," Vess mumbled, before walking on.

Marcus chuckled to himself, then followed his friend.

"Alright, everyone. Let's go home."

The return journey seemed to pass faster. It wasn't without its hurdles, but, compared to what they'd already dealt with, nothing was too much to handle. Along the way, they fought, ate, slept, and grew to know each other without the pressure of deceit and quests. But there wasn't one among them that didn't feel the weight of Erryn's absence every step of the way.

Roh agreed to see them safely through the mountain caves. Marcus had been concerned about her returning alone, but she'd reassured him she could look after herself, and no one doubted it – least of all Vess. Not one for long farewells, the woman was gone by the time they'd exited the caves in Geryndor and turned around.

As she started to make her way through the tunnel, she felt an uncomfortable sense of loneliness, something she'd never felt in all her twenty-five years. She'd rarely had a moment to herself growing up and actively sought out solitude as an adult, but now that she was alone, she realised she didn't like it.

Mentally chastising herself for being pathetic and weak, she was stopped in her tracks by a call from behind.

"Thought you might want to say farewell – properly," Vess said, his face stern, but his tone hinting he didn't truly feel that way.

Running to meet him, Roh dropped her sword and shield and leapt into his embrace.

When he finally exited the tunnel, she resumed her journey, determined to make some changes when she arrived home

Meanwhile, outside the cavern entrance, Marcus had invited Hessan to join him in Benedict's cottage for some food and hospitality, but he'd graciously refused, saying it was long past time he acted like a king, and that he had a lot of 'making up' to do – and apparently, that had to start with going home to his queen as soon as possible.

However, he did rally some miners while the others enjoyed some refreshments in the tavern, and brought them along to the blocked steps that led up to the Stone Highway.

"About time this was cleared," he said, ordering the men to remove the barricade.

When it was done, the dwarf bear-hugged Marcus and thanked him for the adventure. Next, he looked earnestly into Athalir's eyes and swore an allegiance that, in his words, "would remain strong through his reign, and for evermore." He then turned to Vess, was shuffling his feet, and looking anywhere but at Marcus.

"You ready, horggen?"

Marcus looked puzzled.

"Ready for what, Vess?"

The warrior lowered his eyes and spoke as if to the floor.

"Hessan has offered me a position within the royal guard – says I'll make a good soldier. I… accepted his offer."

"But I thought… What about returning to the city, you could–"

Vess looked up at his friend.

"I don't want to go back there, Marcus. It's too close, too much of a reminder of what they did to me. Besides, what would I do? I have no home, no skills other than using a sword. No, this will be good for me. A fresh start."

Marcus nodded, reluctant to say goodbye to someone else he'd grown close to, but understanding all the same.

"If that's what you want."

"It is."

Marcus hesitated, laughing as Whistler jumped up to perch on Vess' shoulder, cooing happily.

"Then I wish you luck, my friend. Make sure you visit now and then."

"I will. And thank you, Marcus, for, well, everything."

The two men embraced, then parted company. Marcus stared after them, knowing he'd miss the big man very much, as Vess, Hessan, and the group of mining dwarves walked away.

The route greatly shortened, and made safer in that they could avoid the hazard of travelling through rebel territory in Sa'hahlenfell, Athalir stepped into Vaharia and wasted no time in asking to take his leave. If his parents still lived, they desperately needed the herb, as did many of Athalir's people. With Sathom's instructions on where to find the plant clear in his mind, the elven prince clasped Marcus' arm and bowed his head, explaining that, among the Fell, this gesture was symbolic of great respect.

"I am profoundly sorry I left it so long to trust you, Marcus."

"Well, you had your reasons. The governors didn't exactly help give human mages a good name."

Athalir laughed.

"No, that's true. So, what will you do now? Go back to the city?"

"No, I don't think I'll ever return there – it's still populated by people I dislike. Benedict's cottage is in need of an owner. I've a mind to enjoy a simple life. I *need* it after *this* trip."

"What about magic? Will you still practise?"

"I thought I might use my time to study it, to be honest. Where it comes from, how it works. I think… I think Erryn might have liked that."

"Yes. I think she might." Athalir adjusted his pack and smiled. "Ahlvaen shael mah – spirits keep you, my friend. If you ever need anything of me or my people, you have but to ask."

With that, he sprinted away to collect the life-saving herb.

That left just Marcus and Sathom to return to the village. As they arrived, the sun was almost below the horizon, the familiar torches already lit as they walked the path. The place was quiet, most of the villagers inside having supper, but one man was working late. Catching sight of Haden in his workshop, Marcus' heart sank. A vision of Erryn coming home from an early morning hunt tugged at his buried emotions and brought everything back.

"There's… someone I have to talk to," the mage said. "You go home, I'll be back shortly."

"Are you sure you don't want me to come with you?" Sathom offered.

Marcus shook his head.

"No. This is something I have to do alone."

⁂

It was dark by the time Marcus left Haden's cottage. He'd stayed until Erryn's father had stopped crying, and told him where to find him if there was anything he could do. He'd kept Erryn's bow and quiver safe all the way home, having had them returned by Athalir, and, as he said farewell, he left them there, where they belonged.

The conversation had been the hardest he'd ever had, and he shed many tears of his own as he crossed the green and climbed the small hill up to Benedict's cottage, drying his eyes before going in and closing the door.

Marcus awoke late the next day. For the first few moments, he was confused, recent events coming back to him as if they'd been a dream – *or a nightmare*, he thought, as he swung his legs out of bed.

He rubbed the sleep from his eyes and went to the mirror. Strangely, he half expected to see Rhyssian's face staring back at him. He didn't know if he was pleased or disappointed to still see his own green eyes and messy, brown hair.

Dragging his bare feet to the next room, he saw Sathom sitting at the table, his eyes closed as if meditating.

"Ah, Marcus. You are up. Good," Sathom said, sensing his presence and offering a welcome smile.

"Yes, I know I'm lazy. Should have been up hours ago, but I think I've more than earned a lie-in."

"You most certainly have, but there is somewhere we need to go."

Marcus looked around for some food.

"Can't I eat first?" His stomach growled right on cue.

"Of course. Once you are done, please, get dressed."

Determination was clear in Sathom's voice, though Marcus was still half asleep and paid it little heed.

⁂

Hours later and the two friends arrived at the memorial garden behind Whitestone. The air blew mild through the long grass and leafy trees, and sunlight shimmered on the calm surface of an ornamental pond. Marcus remembered the place from when Benedict had brought him to kill the vessels. However, a new memory also stood out. He recalled sitting in the enchanted warmth, talking to the image of his mother. As a boy, the king had taken Rhyssian there to help him come to terms with her passing. If only the older Rhyssian had done the same when he lost his brother, perhaps he'd not have wasted the time he had left fighting in the arena.

"Do you have the ash?" Sathom asked, as they sat on one of the stone benches that outlined a circular courtyard. Marcus passed Sathom the purse in which he'd deposited the ash from Erryn's pyre. "Now, do you remember what to do?"

"Yes."

The mage closed his eyes and pictured the strongest memory he had of the person he wished to see.

Sathom took the purse and emptied its contents onto a raised platform that stood at the centre of the courtyard. A sound like a tiny bell rang out, followed by a warm breeze that swirled around the circle until all was once again still.

"Open your eyes."

When Marcus did as Sathom said, a crystal clear image of Erryn stood within arm's reach. He got up from the bench and stood with her, sucking in a breath as the projection raised her hand and rested it against his chest. He looked down at her auburn curls and her soulful brown eyes, and he so desperately wished she was there to see the soul in his.

The image was so real, he thought he could smell the tonic she used on her hair, feel the pressure from her hand over the place where his heart beat.

He shed a tear as the image of Erryn opened her lips and uttered the words he'd never forget, so quiet as to be almost a whisper.

"*Feel* the magic."

"I will, Erryn. I *always* will," he whispered back.

EPILOGUE

Three months had passed since the return home. Now, the days were growing longer, and the sun was lending its extra warmth to the emerging flowers and newly-leafed trees. Marcus lay on his back on the grass behind his cottage, his legs resting on the old tree stump. It had been another delightfully ordinary day, and he was rewarding himself for his morning's labour with some relaxation, reading his latest book.

When he wasn't working his small plot of land, or out gathering logs for the fire, he spent his free time pouring over books devoted to magical theory, and had become more than a little obsessed with the subject.

Haden had given him some of Erryn's volumes during one of his visits to see how he was. He'd been grateful, but was clever enough to realise the man had given them to get rid of him when he'd fussed a little too much. The rest of his reading material was provided by Sathom. He didn't know how he acquired them and didn't ask, surmising it was probably better that way. He'd long since accepted the elemental's flaws, and knew he wasn't above a bit of pilfering here and there, for purposes he deemed just.

As far as Sathom was concerned, the ends justified the means; Marcus' study had been so efficient, so thorough that it revealed things about magic that even the most educated mages in Whitestone didn't know. And, as the elemental so often liked to say, *knowledge is power*.

Sathom was a mostly constant companion at the cottage. With his emotions no longer shackled, he was good company for one who remembered living two lives. He'd experienced both, and evenings were often filled with fireside reminiscing. He and Marcus would talk of friends and family who'd returned to Meran. They'd laugh about the good times and share their sorrow for the bad.

As the last of his kind in Vaharia, Sathom harboured a secret hope that Marcus never tired of his presence, never found his misdemeanours too hard to tolerate. Often, he felt his old habits yearning to take hold, but that would take him down a path he swore never to travel again. So he remained on his best behaviour – he, the last elemental, by the side of the last Meranell, hoping that would never change.

And 'never' was more apt than it would at first seem. Sathom had made sure Marcus was aware he was now immortal, Erryn's energy having strengthened his body enough that it would survive hosting his Meranell soul. Living forever was not something Marcus liked to dwell on, however. His zest for life had not completely diminished, but he'd lost too much; naïvety was a luxury that had long since passed him by. Fortunately, his study of magic provided the perfect distraction.

Right now, he was simply happy. Life was modest, but satisfying, and the people in the village regarded him as one of their own, a far cry from his life in Whitestone. His first introduction to a traditional Eldenvale gathering had been a wedding. It had been nothing like the stiff formality of nuptials in the city. The young couple wore hand-crafted wreathes and clothes handed down from generations long passed. The village hall was decked out in anything and everything the villagers could scrape together and the party had lasted until the last reveller had crawled home at dawn. Marcus had, for the first time in his life, felt a true sense of belonging, with none of the expectations of his life in the city.

Whitestone had its own problems, problems he learnt of through Sathom and that he made sure to stay as far away from as possible. As he and the elemental had made their way back from the memorial garden the day after their return home, the city walls had reminded him of his family. After a confrontation with the elemental he'd come to terms with Sathom's deception regarding his father's survival, and he knew he should pay the Ryan household a visit. But, that thought filled him with a dread he'd not experienced for many months.

"Sathom, make them forget me," he'd said to his companion. "Make them *all* forget."

Sathom said nothing about his request until the following day, when he announced, "It is done," and it was never spoken of again.

After that, Marcus felt settled. His soul was at peace and he wanted for nothing.

Lying in the afternoon sun, he began to dose off. His book was just about to fall from his hands when a familiar voice jolted him back to reality. It was Sathom. He'd been gone for nearly a fortnight, much longer than he usually took absence, but now he was eager to get his friend's attention. The mage opened his eyes and squinted up at Sathom's troubled face, the sunlight creating a halo around the figure of his friend. The elemental hesitated as if deciding on the wisdom of saying what he wished to say, before seemingly coming down in favour of necessity.

"Marcus," he said, with a serious expression. "We need to talk."

THE END

ACKNOWLEDGMENTS

To Boo, whose patience seemingly knows no bounds. You've taken the brunt of the demon that resides in your mother these last three years. You've been my editor, my sounding board and my advisor, as well as my teacher and my voice of reason. For being all that and more – thank you.

And huge thanks to my other two children for putting up with my wild and crazy ways, handling my eccentricity and my writing-enforced unconventional hours with more tolerance than most intelligent adults. We're all more than a little crazy in our house, but the last three years have been the height of crazy times.

Mum and dad, thanks for the belief – and the genes. To Kellie, for all the little things you do, that you think go unnoticed – they don't.

To my beta readers, Jim P, Cathy, Mary, and Michelle, for your time, your support, and your invaluable feedback.

To the staff at Lincoln County Hospital's radiotherapy department, and my Oncologist, Dr. Panades, for keeping me alive.

To Skye for the USB stick – the binge-watching was a good reward.

To Bioware, Dragon Age, for inspiration and making me want to create a world and characters where I'd never have to wait for another writer to tell me what happens next.

To Two Steps from Hell for the 'soundtrack'.

To all those people over the years who've left my side; I grew stronger in your absence. Likewise, to all those who attempted to bring me down; I grew stronger in the face of the adversity you threw at me.

And finally, to whatever guardian has watched over me throughout my life, especially in recent years. I know not what you are but, one thing's for sure – *I feel the magic.*

www.ingramcontent.com/pod-product-compliance
Lightning Source LLC
Chambersburg PA
CBHW030821310726
48980CB00006B/582/J

* 9 7 8 0 9 9 2 7 5 1 6 5 4 *